Vault 21-12

By Kendall Smith
© 2015

PERCUSSION PUBLISHING

Percussion Publishing LLC
New York, NY
Copyright © 2015 by Kendall Smith

* Second Edition *

For information about bulk purchases, please contact Percussion Publishing Bulk Sales at: PercPubOrders@percussionpublishing.com

Percussion Publishing can bring authors to your live event. For more information or to book an event, contact the Percussion Publishing Speaker Division at: Authors@PercussionPublishing.com. For all other inquiries, please contact Administration@percussionpublishing.com

Feel free to visit us online and connect socially to find out news about present and future publishing projects, and information about our consultants:

www.PercussionPublishing.com
@PercPublishing

Acknowledgments

There were so many people who offered encouragement, advice and support during the writing of Vault 21-12, I'm sure I will miss a few of you in this acknowledgment section. Trust that I'll try to make it up to those who are owed a debt of gratitude on my part.

The first novel I wrote taught me to not only respect the writing process, but more importantly, to encourage honest feedback. Procuring critiques from friends and professionals helped to dramatically shape the final product that represents Vault 21-12, and the interest my manuscript garnered at Percussion Publishing.

The support and encouragement from my wife, Allison, is something I never take for granted. Your love and friendship represent a cornerstone in my life that I cherish every day. You are, without question, my one true love and soul mate.

A lot of progress was made with help from my Editor, Kathleen Tomlinson. Her initial thoughts on the story helped to sharpen and refine the final manuscript. Katherine not only provided a bird's eye perspective, she deftly handled the line-by-line editing process. I would recommend her to anyone who requires professional editorial services. She is a pleasure to work with.

My graphic designer, Geoffrey Falkner, played a big role in shaping what represents the cover, spine and layout of the book. He was an exceptional listener and spent quality time working with me to craft a vision I had formulated over several years. It's no easy task to create a visual when it exists solely in the mind of an author, but he came through on multiple levels. That takes perseverance, but you can see for yourself the talent he brought to the process. Well done, Geoff!

Brook Ward, one of the most talented photographers I've come across in a long time, captured the perfect visual for the cover of the book. His image of the vault was spot on for the project. I'd recommend him to anyone looking to execute first-class photographic projects.

Some friends, who shared their feedback early in the process, are worth noting as they had a tremendous impact on how I approached subsequent revisions. Doug Moore gave one of my early editions a drop kick when it needed it most, and I'm grateful for it. There is no way this book would have passed muster without an honest (and sometimes brutal) assessment, and Doug helped to move the book forward. That's what real friends do, at least the ones who care about literature. Thanks Doug.

Ziad Darwiche was another voice of reason at a time when I needed it most. Thank you for your input. Other friends who also added their thoughts and encouragement include Andrew Przybyszewski, Christian Francipane, Courtney Pappas, Ken Farber, David Sanderson and Bruce Mello. I also have to call out James Young and Andy Smith, my Social Media Consultants, and Aaron Johnson, my Digital Advertising Consultant for a job well done. You all helped to set a foundation for this book and your optimism kept me going. Thank you all.

As I did in my first novel, I have to thank the author, Stephen King. His book titled, *On Writing*, provided worthy advice to a first-time writer when he needed it most. If you ever read this, Stephen, trust that I try to keep that, 'Tool Box' by my desk whenever I write.

I also have to tip my hat to the author Terry Hayes and his thriller, *I Am Pilgrim*. It is by far the best thriller written since the turn of the century and I encourage anyone who loves the genre to add *I Am Pilgrim* to his/her reading list.

I would be a fool not to exude my gratitude to my fellow author, Presley Acuna. He not only has a fantastic novel in the works, he is a genuine person and wise friend. I wish you profound success with your forthcoming debut novel.

Something that may represent a first in literary history: I have to give a shout-out to my mother in-law, Eileen. You are the saint of the family, selfless and always positive. We are all lucky to have you in our lives, especially your grandson, Connor, and granddaughter, Brooke.

Of course, I have to acknowledge the other love in my life, someone I cherish and love more with each passing day. To my son... my giant baby boy... Connor. Alias Connor The Barbarian, Bam-Bam, C-Dog, Thunder Thighs: Every day with you is a gift.

Dedication

This novel is dedicated to my grandmother, Charlotte, who passed away after living a long and wonderful life. Your memories continue to remind me of the true meaning of family and I will always love you.

Prologue

Outside of Bern, Switzerland, October 21st, 1983

The headlights in the rear view mirror continued to follow him. Snow covered the top portion of each light, making it look like the car was staring at him with a heavy-lidded gaze. Their pursuit was relentless, unwavering and after several hours, Jack Devenger felt like a hunted animal. He could think of nothing to improve the situation. He had to escape the men who followed him: somehow, some way.

That vault... That goddamn vault, he thought. He admitted that it had been his decisions and actions that had led to this moment of crisis. It seemed like a situation that would never end. He checked the fuel gauge and saw the tank was half empty before he made the final turn that led to the first switchbacks of the Swiss Alps.

He was out of options. His adversaries were armed, trained and determined to take what was rightfully his. Refusing to bow to those who confronted him, he promised himself wouldn't let the damn krauts get their dirty hands on the vault's contents.

His mind replayed the scene at the hotel where two German men had confronted him. They spoke about history, about how his grandfather, Everett, had killed their fathers. They argued the contents of the vault rightfully belonged to their families, and they offered to spare Jack's life if he provided the account number and passcode. When one produced a pistol, Jack instinctively battered the man's skull with his briefcase, immobilizing him. The fight lasted another half a minute before he ran for his life.

The gift from his father remained intact deep inside the Swiss bank. Jack saw it for himself, for the first time, earlier that morning. He felt it in his hands and pondered what it could do for him and his family. Nothing in life could have ever prepared him for the experience; it was an awe-inspiring moment.

It had happened at a time his father had chosen and not Jack, and now he realized why Everett told him to exude caution and watch his back. He knew the choices he made were not wise ones, and he was reminded of them every time he looked in the rearview mirror.

He didn't notice the men waiting in the BMW across the alley. When he jumped in his Peugeot, they followed through the streets of Bern, across the bridge and no more than fifty feet away at any given moment.

For three hours, the drive had continued as the two cars made their way to the Italian Tunnelbagen, the international border between Switzerland and Italy. It was the only option available to Jack, but his rented car did not have the horsepower to get away.

He fled for his life, and in doing so he left behind in Vault 21-12 the most important item his father had given him, the post-war journal that contained the account number and passcode he used to access it. These provided him access to his grandfather's legacy. It was now locked in the very same place that Jack was supposed to liberate. Jack thought the situation was purely ironic. The vault that was supposed to open so many doors had turned out to be a Pandora's box that unleashed so many problems.

How did they know I was coming? Who tipped them off?

He turned onto Highway 7R. It was a windy road that ascended to fifteen hundred meters before leveling off to connect with the Italian border. His plan was simple: keep moving, cross the border, and pray the two German men behind him were delayed long enough to facilitate his escape.

His rented Peugeot 205 coupe had but 130 ponies under the hood, far less that the BMW 528 following him. He had tried a few times to outrun them to no avail.

The road beyond started to weave and his car reciprocated with each turn of the wheel.

He noticed a second pair of lights behind him and lower in altitude from his position on the road. He checked his watch in nervous anticipation: 11:45 p.m. He dialed down the heat gauge and unknotted his tie.

Jack waited for the last car to pass the BMW, which never happened. Jack saw the two men in the car behind him silhouetted in the rear car's headlights. When the driver of the BMW gestured for the other driver to pull alongside, Jack felt the lump in his throat double in size. "This is not fucking happening."

Jack's lips pressed together with enough pressure to crack a shell. He witnessed the two drivers communicating with one another.

He pumped the gas pedal and gave the four-cylinder engine a shot of fuel. He hit 140 kilometers per hour and felt his steering wheel quiver. Curves in the road came and went as he rushed towards the tunnel. He searched the sides of the road for an alternate route. There was no escape.

His tires skidded around two more turns before the new car, a Mercedes, came screaming up his backside.

Jack saw the sign ahead:

Tunnel/Bana, International Border, 20 Kilometers

He needed space and options. The Benz was less than ten yards behind him.

Suddenly, he slammed on the brakes. The Mercedes plowed straight into Jack's rear bumper with a bone-rattling jolt. He heard the distinctive sounds of grinding metal and breaking glass, but as the Mercedes backed up to ram him again, that the only damage that Jack saw to the large luxury car was a large dent in its front bumper.

"Shit."

He peeled away and saw the BMW headlights illuminate the cabin before they moved adjacent to one another. He recognized the profile of the fat kraut following him. He noticed his left hand gesture towards the driver's side door.

To his left was the side of a hill, on the right was a slight incline. He floored the engine, and the Mercedes sped forward. He cut the wheel and hit the brakes to attempt to wedge his car between the Mercedes and the incline. The Mercedes turned in the nick of time. The collision lit up his rearview mirror with a flash of light. He regained control of the car and lurched forward with timid speed.

He ducked as the sound of two gunshots rang out in the air. Jack clawed the wheel and steered to make evasive turns: to the oncoming lane, then back, then a quick turn before hitting the brakes.

Pop. Pop.

The turns kept coming. The tires clawed the ground for more speed.

Pop.

Jack jerked the wheel while slamming the gas pedal in complete frustration. *That fucking journal,* he thought.

Pop.

An explosion of sound rattled the BMW's interior as the back window shattered into a million fragments. Air from the side window howled as it blew through the car.

He screamed, "You god damn Nazis!" as he banged the steering wheel.

He floored it through a turn, going into a severe slide before he caught the Peugeot from fishtailing out of control.

Then he heard one last discharge.

The left rear tire hissed. The car skidded sideways. Jack felt his head slam into glass as his car flipped on its side. The roof greeted his shoulder by dislocating it. The arm he raised quickly went past his face then back before shattering on the dashboard. Removed from his seat, the car took two more turns as it stumbled down an incline, throwing his torso around in ways not suitable for survival. With his spleen ruptured and his screams diminished, silence prevailed as the Peugeot coughed out its last breath of life.

***

Jack returned to a state of consciousness and heard men speaking to each other. Twisted and broken, he pieced together the setting: Gas, car lights, stony earth immediately in front of him. *Germans...yelling Germans.* He felt someone toss his arm to the side. The motion prompted a cough as blood trickled down his neck. The actions sparked pains within his chest cavity. It alerted the rest of his senses as to what had physically happened to him.

He felt hands searching his jacket pockets and taking something they found there. After another minute of hearing men scream, he heard the sound of his wallet land with a thud beside him. *Why would anyone do that?* He thought. Sounds of footsteps faded away in the distance. *The journal... they searched me for Everett's journal.*

Pop.

He heard the sound of metal ricochet behind him. *Why—*

Pop. Pop.

Next came the whoosh of the sound of something ignite.

"No… No!"

A bright light illuminated the rear of the vehicle. "NO!"

Pop.

White light enveloped Jack before he could tell himself it was all over.

Chapter 1

New York City, Times Square, February, Present Day

Alan Devenger's thumbs stopped dancing over the keyboard of his iPhone when the town car hit the pothole. He noticed a typo but meticulously corrected it before sending his reply to his Los Angeles sales representative. He'd get the point in a New York second.

Alan then checked his inbox, his packed calendar for the day, and then the power left on his phone: fully charged and as ready to go as he was. The car continued to cruise through a grey landscape, complete with New York slush and heaps of road-stained snow. He looked down at his shoes - polished, black and of Italian make.

When he saw his office building, he packed his bag and did a double take on his shoes. "To the curb please."

"I'll try," said the driver.

Alan opened the door a moment later. Before he exited he said, "We've got a 10:00 downtown, a lunch and then a 3:00."

"Great day for driving. Trying to get us killed?" the driver quipped.

Alan laughed. "Get a Grande at Starbucks, Walter, my treat."

It took a moment for him to navigate the icy slush on the sidewalk. He sidestepped one mess, just managed to catch himself before stepping into a puddle and then hopped a one-foot wide mound of snow. When he was standing on a cleared space, he looked up to see a six-foot blonde woman grinning at him. He smiled and then took the slightest of bows before the gorgeous vixen shook her head in amusement. She moved on, leaving behind a trail of pheromones.

Alan walked towards the entrance of Condé Nast Publishing, his employer.

He entered through swinging glass doors and a cold breeze followed him. He paused to look at the grand lobby and soaked in the view. Daylight radiated from the opposite side of the building through a magnificent three-story glass facade. Marble floors, wood accents and original artwork provided a sophisticated and contemporary feel to the space. He felt right at home.

The employees, most of whom were women in designer clothing, made their way through the lobby. The sound of their click-clacking high heels echoed off the walls. Despite the company's shark-tank reputation, Alan had noticed the camaraderie that existed among the junior-level employees. At the publisher level, where he operated, that did not exist in any capacity.

Alan had spent seventeen years working his way up the ranks to his current position as Publisher at *GQ*, and he knew he had a short window of time to secure his place in the annals of Condé Nast publishing power. He did not intend to squander the opportunity. His first year had provided enough growth to sustain his existence at the company; this year, he planned to make his mark as a true leader in the advertising field.

His long stride carried him up the steps and through the security entrance mechanism after he placed his pass on top of it.

He entered the elevator and recognized *Self* Magazine's Editor in Chief. "Good morning, Jessica."

"Hey there Alan, how was your weekend?" He paused before answering to make room for ten more employees to join them before the doors closed.

"Excellent, thank you. I was at a charity event in the Hamptons."

"The Hamptons? It's quite lovely this time of year." Her words dripped with sarcasm, given the month and weather. "Clients?"

"Why else?"

"Your reputation precedes you."

"I'll take that as a compliment." He refrained from mentioning the second home he owned in East Hampton. He'd learned early in his career that it wasn't appropriate to remind others of the financial rewards he enjoyed. "See you at the Newhouse party this weekend?"

"Of course." The doors opened to the fourth floor, which led to Condé Nast's cafeteria. "We'll catch up Saturday night."

"See you then." He smiled and left the marble-clad elevator.

He turned to enter the Frank Gehry-designed portion of the building. It only added to the panache of Condé Nast. Curved glass stretched from one side of the room to the other, providing a touch of elegance to what would normally be a bland-cafeteria experience. He procured coffee and a protein-laden omelet and was headed for the cashier when he heard his name called. He turned to see the salesperson on his team who managed the timepiece business. She'd been his first hire at the company. "Good morning, Clarice. How are things?"

"Great, wanted you to know I got a meeting with Breitling's top marketing director.

"Great, I haven't seen Thomas in months. When?"

"Next Thursday."

"Get marketing on it today. Let's come up with a custom-publishing concept. They have a soft spot for those types of executions."

"Did you work with the brand at *InStyle* Magazine?"

"Yup, in my previous job. We got to know Thomas very well. He just got his private pilot's license. Ask him about the little Piper Cherokee he keeps at Teterboro. Loves to fly," he paused for a minute and then asked, "Why did it take so long to get in there?"

She exhaled, nervous at being put on the spot. "They are doing more on the digital side. I—"

"Enough said, no worries. Loop me in after you get the process going." Out of the corner of his eye, he spotted the C.E.O. of the company. He furrowed his brow when he saw who he was with, three other men, including his corporate nemesis, the Publisher of *Vanity Fair*. "I have to go."

"Will do." She noticed Alan looking behind her and she turned. When she saw *Vanity Fair*'s top boss stroll through the lobby, she looked back. "And we're going right after those guys."

Alan shot her a look. "Who?"

"*Vanity Fair*, of course. I know what you're looking at." She referred to the inevitable competition Condé Nast titles faced in the market with one another. There were more than a few magazines competing to win Breitling ad pages. Both Alan and Clarice knew every title was after the luxury brand's business.

Alan grinned. Knowing that she understood and thrived on the competitive spirit affirmed his belief that hiring her had been a savvy move. "Go get 'em, tiger."

He lingered and waited for the four executives to pay and move into the seating area. He got in the longest checkout line, paid with his expense account, and walked into the main room. It was organized in curved booths and rectangular dining tables from front to back. One table was always reserved for the C.E.O., Charles, and those he dined with. Seated with him were Grayson Cumberland and two of his top lieutenants. He knew them and their reputations intimately.

Alan's eyes lingered on the publisher. He wore a white dress shirt, a Brioni blazer, pressed charcoal pants and Cole Haan loafers. *Too casual,* he thought. He seemed at ease and laughed while a copy of *Vanity Fair* rested on the table before all four of them. It was a solid inch thick: Their March issue was fashion-themed and chock full of ad pages. He knew the healthy ad revenue stemmed from *Vanity Fair's* reputation, *not from the efforts made by the son of a bitch running their ad business*, thought Alan. On more than one occasion, Alan had been upstaged by the man in several corporate meetings and he looked forward to exposing Grayson's come-hither approach to business.

He had a plan, a smart one based on years of experience and relationships. One by one, he'd chip away at *Vanity Fair's* market lead, and he expected to gain serious traction by 2016. He hoped to survive long enough in Condé Nast's cutthroat environment to deliver the fatal blow to Grayson's uninspired and withering career.

Alan knew enough not to interrupt a C.E.O.-level meeting, so he chose to leave the cafeteria. Moments later he was in the elevator and rising to *GQ's* floor. This time he had the elevator all to himself.

When the doors opened, it revealed a magazine logo on the opposite wall. It was seven feet tall and five feet wide, a reminder on some level that the magazine was bigger in all respects compared to the person viewing it. He turned right and saw the floor receptionist standing. She smiled when she saw him. "Good morning, Alan. There's a package from Chanel that's waiting on your desk."

"Fantastic." Alan noticed her fine-tuned make up and that the dress she wore hugged her curves. *An angel from heaven*, Alan thought, *and dressing for the job she wants, not the one she has. Nice touch.*

"Doing well I hope?"

"Great." Her eyes followed him as he passed. He smiled back and opened the floor-to-ceiling glass doors.

Alan saw his assistant, Bernadette, waiting for him outside his office door. "Morning," he said.

"Hi, Alan. Oh, I see you got coffee. There's another cup waiting in there for you. The candidate from the west coast is interviewing with Georgette right now, and all meetings are on. No cancellations."

"Excellent," said Alan, but what he wanted to say was it's going to be a hell of a day. He thanked her and walked into his office. It was dark as the window blinds were closed. He took off his silk-lined Hugo Boss overcoat, hung it with his suit jacket on the coat rack and closed the door behind him. Near the light switch was another pair of buttons. He pressed the top one and watched as the blinds mechanically opened before him.

As the blinds pulled back, all of New York came into view. Floor-to-ceiling glass windows revealed skyscrapers and an unimpeded view of midtown Manhattan. It took a full thirty seconds to reveal the whole of the city, but the view was one of Alan's favorite perks. The world he knew and loved fit within the windows that framed his view. Light illuminated the interior of the room: a seating area with designer couches to the left, an Eames chair, his glass-top desk, and the entrance to his own personal bathroom. It was twenty-by-thirty feet, but the view outside continued to awe him. He thought of a word to describe it, spectacular, but even that sounded like an understatement.

He sat down and noticed the FedEx package from Chanel headquarters in front of him. He put it aside to focus on his appointments for the day.

American Express, Audi and *GQ*'s largest cologne advertiser were on the docket. He had a lot to cover, not to mention the interview he had to conduct in ten minutes. He was halfway through his fourth email when he heard his office door open and hit the back wall with a thud.

"Alan," said Bernadette.

He did not make eye contact. "Another minute please."

"Stop. Your Aunt Jenny is on the phone."

"Oh... okay." It took a moment to process the look on her face.

"Something wrong?"

"Her voice sounds… off. I think you need to take this."

He sat up in his chair and turned to see one of the phone extensions blinking red. His aunt rarely called him at work. He'd last seen her at a family holiday gathering several months prior.

He picked up the phone. "Jenny, this is a surprise, how are you?"

He heard her exhale. "Not well I'm afraid. Alan, I'm calling with some unfortunate news." Her voice was on edge. "Everett, he had a heart attack this morning."

"Dear God." Alan placed his elbows on the desk. "How bad?"

"It was devastating. Those are the doctor's words. I'm at the hospital now, he's asking to see everyone."

"Really. Now… right now?" He folded the open laptop in front of him and rubbed his forehead.

"I think it's best you get out here. He's calling for you, and everyone else."

"I'm so sorry, Jenny."

"I'm sorry too Alan, I know how close you two are."

"Yeah." Alan bit his lip and made a decision. "Yeah. I'm coming."

He placed the phone back in its cradle without a sound. His shoulders bent forward as he recalled the last exchange he had with his grandpa. He said he was proud of him, but somehow Alan could not paint a picture of the man's face in his mind. He did, however, remember his laugh, which prompted him to rise from his chair.

"Bernadette," He said in a steady voice. "Tell Walter to be out front in five minutes. Cancel everything on my schedule for the rest of the day."

She had not left the room during the call. "I'm so sorry, Alan."

He felt a wave of emotion hit him from all sides, and it all happened in a New York second. He shook his head at the thought.

Parsippany, New Jersey

John Devenger closed his eyes and drew fresh air into his lungs. He exhaled slowly, paused and then repeated the process. His windows were down as he sat in his Subaru. The fresh air was so wonderful, and taking a few minutes to appreciate it helped to put his day in perspective. He'd be inside until late in the evening, in a cube or windowless conference room.

John Devenger enjoyed his moment of Zen, and then put it aside. He told himself he was starting something that should have commenced fifteen years earlier. Namely, making a career and name for himself. It killed him every time he looked at the two-story building in front of him. He said to himself, does a white-collar career always have to take place between four big slabs of concrete?

He looked beyond the parking lot and saw small hills caressed in fresh snow. If it were the weekend, he'd be outside with snowshoes in Bear Mountain State Park. He rolled up the windows of his car, stepped outside and continued to take deep breaths into his lungs.

A moment later he heard a woman's voice say, "Hey there, Johnny,"

He turned to see Rashawna, one of the subordinates who reported to him. She was the only one who ever called him Johnny.

"Hey there, how was your evening?'

"Oh you know, the kids were acting up, but they're alright. You?"

"Hit the gym."

"When are you gonna meet a lady?"

John kept pace and provided a shy grin. "When the right one shows up."

"Well they ain't gonna show up at your door," said Rashawna. "How about I introduce you to a friend of mine?"

"You know, I'm your boss now, what if it goes sour?"

She took a moment to respond. "What if it goes well? Come on, you could use a little more spice in your life," she grinned wickedly, "Besides me, of course."

He sighed. "I broke up with someone a few months ago, so I'm taking it easy."

"Oh. I get it." She was quiet for a moment. "But you know I've got someone in mind. You think about that Johnny, she's a catch." He just shook his head but didn't reply. "You're so stubborn," she said as they approached the building's security guard. "Hey Freddy, do you think Johnny would do well if I introduced him to my cousin?" Rashawna smiled.

———

"Your cousin and John? Him? Damn, now that would be a sight." The two African-Americans shared a laugh. "He'd never know what hit him."

"That's what Johnny here needs."

"Okay, that's enough out of the two of you," John said. He'd grown close to both of them over the past year and a half and was happy they liked him enough to tease him.

Their laughter continued as they walked past the security turnstiles. John walked towards the cafeteria as Rashawna took to the elevators. "She's just what you need, Johnny. She'll treat you right."

John didn't respond when he made his way to the counter. With fresh fruit, coffee and a yogurt in hand, he returned to the elevator bank. The security guard caught his eye. "Like she said, that cousin of hers will treat you right." He waved his finger at him and nodded.

John laughed. "But I've got you. That's all I need." Fred's laughter faded as the elevator rose.

When the doors opened on the second floor he turned to see a fifty-yard stretch of cubicles. He sighed and started to trot down to his cube. To his right were interior offices and conference rooms. As a supervisor to five people, he qualified for office space but John had turned it down to remain close to the window with a view.

It was a bland setting. The four-foot high cube walls were grey with plastic windows, allowing John to see the faces of his coworkers. Fluorescent bulbs glowed overhead and heating vents pumped out what smelled like cardboard-scented air. John was convinced if he spent twenty-four straight hours at work he'd die from exposure to artificial elements.

Tacked to the walls of his cube were pictures he had taken while traveling throughout Southeast Asia. There were six in all, including a panoramic shot of Angkor Wat, the beaches of Koh Tao and a sunset on the Malaysian island of Palau Besar. They were his window to the world, and reminded him of all the places his travels had taken him. In his heart he knew he belonged out there, but his mind remained focused on keeping his feet on the ground, and accomplishing something with his life.

He turned on his monitor and the logo of his employer appeared: Tiffany & Company. He noticed a package in the mailbox beside his desk and turned it over in both hands. He opened it and found paperwork relating to a criminal investigation that required his attention.

His department represented the fraud-prevention division of Tiffany. He supervised a team that checked the financial backgrounds of individuals who planned to make expensive purchases. He also kept tabs on credit balances and was tasked to make sure those who paid on credit were capable of actually paying for Tiffany's product.

John stood up to see who was in the office. Four of his people were at their desks. His team represented a mixed bag of ethnicities and economic backgrounds. One recent college graduate was white and from an affluent household. Rashawna was an African-American from Patterson. She possessed the best street smarts in the group. Juan was an immigrant from Nicaragua and worked two jobs to get by: Tiffany's during the day and as a bouncer at night. An older gentleman, Ryan, was a longtime Tiffany employee who bounced from group to group. He never received a promotion in the ten years he worked at the company and he was now assigned to John's team. He was a devoted father of two, a family man who'd lost his wife to cancer several years before. John was working to help him get his career on solid footing, which John thought to be rather ironic given how far back he was himself in the scope of his professional life.

The missing link was Padinni, a recent immigrant from India and the hardest worker in the group. She had three kids at home so John decided to let her tardiness slide.

He turned back to his computer and heard his phone ring. Before he answered it he grabbed his coffee. "John Devenger."

"John dear, it's Jenny."

The tone of her voice prompted him to put the coffee down. He was already in the elevator by the time the liquid in the cup came to a rest.

Chapter 2

Ridgewood, New Jersey

The Lincoln town car pulled up to the entrance of Valley Hospital. Alan's eyes focused on the doors and his fingers tapped the door panel. He was ready to jump.

"Alan?" his driver asked tentatively.

"Yes?"

"I hope he's alright, I met him a year ago when I dropped you off in Upper Saddle River."

Alan nodded. "Thanks, I appreciate that."

"He seemed like a pretty strong guy. He'll get through this."

Alan nodded and exhaled slowly before he grabbed the door handle. He was outside a moment later. A cold breeze caught his attention before he heard the automated doors swoosh open before him. He checked his watch: it was 10:15 a.m. *Damn tunnel traffic.*

He stepped inside and made eye contact with the receptionist.

The woman smiled before she noticed the look on Alan's face. "Everett Devenger, where is he?"

She looked down at her computer. "Intensive care, room 210-B. Down the hall there." She pointed.

"Thank you." Alan's shoes squeaked against the linoleum floor. A hundred yards down from reception were two swinging doors. He ignored a sign that read 'Passes required,' and walked by air respirators and what looked like a dialysis machine.

He turned a corner to see a waiting room and four relatives looking back at him. The look on their faces did nothing to lift Alan's spirits. The pace of his steps shortened as Jenny stepped forward to embrace him.

"Jenny, what happened?" He bear-hugged her and reached up to feel her shoulders. She slouched into his chest. She looked up and shook her head, not knowing what to say or how to respond.

He felt another relative pat him on the back. "He's not doing well my dear," said Jenny. "I'm sure he'll be happy to see you but I think this is it Alan."

"Jesus." He stepped back and sighed. His uncle moved to embrace him. Alan felt comforted by the strong hug. "What did the doctors say?"

His cousin stepped forward. "I'm glad you made it, Alan. He's holding on, as long as he can."

"The doctors, what's the word please?"

Alan saw the sad look on their faces but no one responded.

The nonverbal answers did not sit well with him. "Okay then, I have to see him."

"He's at the end of the hall to the right," said Jenny. She reached out and put her hand on his arm. "Alan," she said, "he's fragile, do you understand?"

Alan stopped and turned to look at her. "Okay, just please find me the doctor will you?" He turned to walk down the hall.

He noticed he had twenty yards to walk. His pace slowed when he thought about what Everett meant to him. Every time he took one step forward his mind replayed the role his grandfather played in his life. He was his father figure, his role model and the dad he never had. The few faint memories he had of his father, before he passed away, were trivial when compared to the influence his grandfather played in his life.

He thought about his career, his success and the wealth that afforded Alan's education as well as half a dozen other siblings and cousins. He owed everything to Everett.

Halfway down the hallway, he felt pangs of frustration slow him down. *This is not happening, not now.* He pondered Jenny's reaction on the phone. Perhaps she was overreacting. Maybe Everett still had a chance… It could be another false alarm.

He noticed beams of sunlight extending from the room where Everett was located and took a deep breath. He paused and took comfort in the moment and saw it as a sign of hope.

The optimism he felt evaporated when he saw the silhouette of the man appear in the doorway. The man wore glasses, a black jacket and a short white collar.

"Are you here to see Everett?"

"I am."

The priest held a bible in one hand, and the other came to a rest on Alan's shoulder. "He has made his peace with God. Try to make him as comfortable as possible my son."

Alan froze and listened to the priest's steps fade away behind him.

He could not produce words or thoughts. Alan forced a step forward and turned around the corner of the doorframe.

He stopped in mid stride when he saw his grandfather lying in the bed. Before he heard the heart monitor register a second heartbeat, he knew it was the end.

The once-strong man was already pale as death. The color of his skin seemed lighter, almost yellowish in nature and thin. His grey mane of hair was tossed about and his hands just sat there, without a trace of strength or life. Tubes extended from his arms, chest and nose in a variety of directions and he heard the man's heart beep echo from the sound of a machine.

It was the first time in Alan's life he saw his grandfather possess so little of it.

He stepped forward to the side of the bed. Alan's eyes moistened but he fought the urge to cry and leaned forward. "Grandpa."

His blood-shot eyes opened and turned to see his grandson. They lingered there for what seemed like an eternity to Alan. He tried to catch his breath and sputtered a word before waving him closer.

"Al... Alan my boy. I'm sorry you have to see me…" His words faded.

Alan stepped closer and grabbed his grandfather's lukewarm hand. "I'm so sorry this happened. I—." Alan told himself to remain positive. "Did the doctors say when they think you'll get out of here? Back home?"

His grandfather shook his head. "I'm afraid… that's not going to happen son. But I'm so happy you are here."

Alan's chest went numb when he heard the words. "Everett, you had one of these before, you were strong then and you're strong now." He looked down and noticed the barrel chest of Everett Devenger lift slowly in a cumbersome fashion.

His grandfather's grip tightened, surprising Alan for a moment. "You…you've been good to me." His eyes glazed over for a moment.

Alan bit his lip and used his hand to rub the side of his grandfather's face. He was still conscious and he heard him let out a sigh.

"I cherish the moment we came down that hill together in Austria. I'll never forget it."

Alan furrowed his brow. "Everett, try to rest. We've never been to Austria together, it's okay."

"You know, outside of Feldkirch. We were there."

Alan shook his head but didn't want to upset the man. "Oh. Okay."

"Your father. He would have been proud of you. I'm proud of you. You've made a good life for yourself." He saw him smile for a brief second. "Now just get a gal, won't you?"

Alan smiled and thought about the last few girlfriends in his life. They were special in their own unique ways, but none stood out as his soul mate. "I'll keep looking, you know I will."

Alan's mind filled with the memories of his deceased father, and the role Everett had played when things took a turn for the worse during his childhood. He missed those moments, as if they were long lost friends, and turned his attention back to his grandfather. "You were there for me Everett. You were great." The emotion he felt came to the surface and materialized when tears fell from his eyes. Alan pursed his lips together to hide the emotion.

Everett tilted his head to get a good look at his grandson. "I'm sorry."

"You have nothing to be—"

"I'm sorry about your father. I'm sorry I got him involved. It was my fault."

"It was an accident, my father and the car. Don't say that."

"He didn't die the way I told you, he was in Switzerland. He—" Everett tried to sit up but could not muster the strength. Alan heard the heart monitor quicken in pace. "Listen. Your father was getting something for me... for him... in Switzerland." He coughed, and wheezed before saying, "They killed him. It was no accident. I know it for a fact. You have to be careful. I left you the details. I should have talked to you and John.

It's in your hands now."

The heart monitor raced as Alan processed the information. *Murder...
his half-brother... Switzerland.* When he stopped shaking his head he looked
down at the man before him and realized how fragile Everett was. He
refused to let the words get to him.

Everett stared at him with intensity. "Be good to your brother, Alan,
be good to him."

The pace of the heart monitor slowed but it did not stop. "Everett,
talk to me. Did something really happen over there?" There was no
response. He just sat there, seeming to struggle with each breath.

The guilt Alan felt was of his own making. He wanted to shake the
man awake. *Tell me about my father, what happened, why John of all people, how do
you know it was not a car accident?*

Alan took a seat beside the bed. The minutes passed by and still there
was no sign of consciousness from Everett.

He could not help but wrap his head around what Everett told him.
He thought about his father, and the fact he died when he was eight years
old. From what he was told, there was no mystery. It was a car accident,
pure and simple.

He turned when he heard the squeak of someone's shoes outside in
the hallway.

A moment later he made eye contact with a relative he had not
spoken to in several years. Standing before him was his estranged half-
brother, John. He watched his response to the sight of Everett in the bed.
Any flutter of hope his half-brother harbored evaporated when he saw the
man. It looked like a mirror image of what Alan felt ten minutes prior.

His cynical nature thought the moment was ironic. His grandfather's
fate represented the only thing he had in common with his half-brother.

"Is he conscious?" John whispered.

Alan rose from the chair and crossed his arms. "I'd think about what
you want to tell him, but most of all, listen. He mentioned—"

John walked past his half-brother and went to the bed. His scarf
draped across the handrail and he placed his hand to his grandfather's
forehead. Pursing his lips, he reached out to touch the man's cheek. His
other hand gripped Everett's wrist, as if he were feeling for a pulse.

"Hey... grandpa. It's John. Can you hear me?"

Alan walked beside him. John provided Alan with a scowl and then turned back to the bed. "Can you give me a moment with him?"

Alan paused and turned to look at John. "Come again? I thought—."

"Please, Alan." John's pleading tone expressed more than the words ever could.

Alan stepped away and exited the room.

At that moment, Everett drew a deep breath through wheezing lungs, and looked up to see John.

"Hey, grandpa."

"John?"

"It's me. What happened?"

"It doesn't matter." There was a long pause before he said. "You're here... you're here."

"Are you in pain? What can I do to help?"

His grandfather smirked for a moment, seeming to laugh. "Listen to me, John." His head rolled back on the pillow, and John moved closer. "You and your brother, you're the only men left in this family. I mean, real men, who've achieved something. You have each other. You have that. Don't let it slip away."

John shook his head. "Did we fail you on some level?"

He shook his head. "You've failed at nothing. Just... just please, hear this. Go with him. Be what I always wanted the two of you to be. You're brothers. I know you can do it together."

John leaned forward. With a shocked expression, he asked, "Do what together?"

His grandfather opened and shut his eyes. "Just do me the honor of going. You and Alan. I should have talked to both of you years ago. The two of you will find each other, I promise. A lot of men died to get it, John, a lot. Do that for me, won't you son?" His head turned upwards to stare at the ceiling. His grip on the handrail loosened.

The rhythm of the heart monitor slowed while John waited to continue his conversation.

***

Later that morning at 11:05 A.M., Everett Devenger Senior, father of one deceased child and grandfather to three, passed from this life to the next.

Chapter 3

Upper Saddle River, New Jersey

He parked his black BMW 7-Series on the side of the long and winding driveway that led to Everett's home. Leafless trees caressed the landscape and they led up to a small clearing in front of the house where others had parked. He heard another car park behind his vehicle but he could not identify the driver. Altogether, there were twenty cars within his immediate view.

Alan wore a dark suit for the occasion. Two weeks past the funeral, he recalled the emotions he and others expressed. Deep sorrow lead to remorse, which was then followed by acceptance and memories. He knew the final stage, in circumstances where significant wealth was at stake, was about to unfold. The last stage of grief would center itself on greed.

In ten minutes' time, Everett Devenger's last will and testament would be read. Given some of the comments he overheard, he knew the vultures would be out in their full glory. An aura of entitlement had cast itself across a wide swath of the family. Alan reflected on how sad it was to hear others make plans with a deceased man's wealth and property. He knew in his heart the will reading would leave his family more divided than ever.

He chose to wait in the car until the last possible moment. It was 9:20 a.m., and in ten minutes, he'd make his way to the front entrance. He turned his attention to his most trusted escape when it came to the passing of his grandfather: work. It bridged the time between remembrances, focused his energy on something meaningful and on some level it offered him the escape he was looking for.

The smartphone in his hand highlighted four pending deals for the upcoming May edition of *GQ* magazine. Even if all four deals happened, he would be under budget for the issue. Focused on the need to make personnel changes, he sighed and put the phone down. Thoughts about firing employees did not help matters in the least bit.

He looked at the grounds of the estate. Nestled in the center of four lush acres was Everett's home: a testament to the success he achieved in life. There was a pleasant little koi pond to the right side of the driveway, complete with a flat grassy area and benches. Surrounding it were tall trees: oaks, maples, pine trees and a row of hemlocks that marked the far side of the property. The left side of the driveway featured a stretch of rose, azalea and hydrangea bushes. When in bloom, they were a spectacular sight. Everett had had a green thumb and Alan remembered helping him when he was a child. He wondered how the grounds would fair with a new owner.

The home itself was an eight-bedroom colonial, a structure Everett completely refurbished when he bought it in the seventies. Alan spent many evenings at the estate over the years. It represented the heart and soul of the family. The home, in contrast to the man's humble beginnings, was the centerpiece of his life. Now it would fall into the hands of someone else in his family. A few waved to him but others provided concerned looks as they made their way to what would inevitably represent an orgy of wealth.

Alan wished he had never been named in the will. He had no interest in the spoils of wealth and made efforts to avoid conversations relating to it. He sat in a $70,000 car, owned a two-bedroom condo in Manhattan and a small home on half an acre in East Hampton. He was content, and given his salary and title as publisher, he felt confident he would earn a tidy living for the next several years. Even if the floor gave out on him, he'd find work at another publishing house, given his experience and track record.

He was startled when he heard three quick taps on his window. He turned to see his sister, Charlotte, smiling at him. He looked at her and opened the door. "Hey, Charlotte."

They hugged for a moment. "I'm happy to see you." Said Charlotte before she tried to smile. "How are you holding up?"

Alan sighed as he locked the door. "I'm not looking forward to this

Charlotte, not at all. It's going to get ugly in there."

The two started to walk. "I really miss him, Alan. I really don't care what happens here today." She grabbed his hand and stopped them from walking further. "I miss his voice."

Alan turned and gave his sister a kiss on the cheek. "I hear you." She took a deep breath. "Let's just try to get through this."

"I don't want anything, I don't want to be here, in this house, when this happens."

"Same here. Why don't we grab a bite this weekend? I'll come out to Hoboken."

She raised an eyebrow. "You'll come out to see me, on a weekend no less? That's a first."

Alan grinned. "It's not a first, but I admit it's been awhile."

"I'd really like that, Alan." They turned to look at the house in the distance. "I can't find any closure in all of this."

They turned and walked up the final incline to the circular parking area outside the front door. Alan turned to look at the koi pond but it was out of view. He frowned when he realized that by the end of the day, the grounds would be in someone else's hands.

He turned back to see Charlotte waiving to their half-brother, John. Alan waved, provided a fake smile and released Charlotte's hand. She walked over to talk to him while Alan retrieved his phone.

"Alan?" she said. He turned away and tried to ignore the knot in his stomach. He thumbed through email messages. He knew he'd get an earful from his sister later that day, but the history he shared with his half-brother left him without a trace of guilt.

Hoping the encounter would not take place, he lingered for a minute, then turned back to face the front entrance. John stood there waiting to greet Alan. For a second he thought about going through the back door but chose to take the stairs in front of him.

"Hi, John."

"Hi, Alan." He moved to shake his hand. "I'm sure you miss him as much as I do."

Alan nodded. He did his best to keep a neutral expression during the moment. "I'm sorry he's gone, we're all going through a lot." He swallowed.

John released and let his hands hit his sides. "Hopefully today will remind everyone how successful he was, and there are no hard feelings."

"Indeed."

Alan watched John walk into the house. He was relieved the moment had passed. John's presence meant he would receive some form of inheritance. Alan could think of no one in the family who achieved so little in life. Whatever Everett left him, he assumed it would represent the only thing of real value John ever possessed.

He shook off the thought and made his way into the interior.

Alan surveyed the room and noticed twenty relatives in total. They were all seated in the great room, an open area that stretched forty feet in each direction. Several rows of seats faced two rectangular tables that were placed on the left side of the room. On the table were stacks of documents, which sat on top of a black tablecloth. Opposite the main entrance was the staircase to the second floor.

He considered the relatives in the room and what was at stake. There was no question that those cited in Everett's last will and testament would stand to gain from the man's death. There were tracts of land in wine country out in the Russian River Valley in California. There was property in Mattituck, Long Island, which was valued over two million dollars and the home he stood in could easily sell for a price north of that figure.

Alan perused the room and looked at the faces of his relatives. From what he overheard at the wake and after speaking to his sister, expectations ran the gambit. There was an uncle who had an interest in the Upper Saddle River estate, which he claimed was promised to him. Another close friend of Everett, seated two rows away, shared Everett's passion for art, and thus he felt entitled to Everett's art collection.

With the exception of a few trinkets in his grandfather's study, Alan could think of nothing that would help diminish the pain of losing such an important role model in his life. A doorway led to the study and he thought it coincidental to see it open at that particular moment.

A short man with salt and pepper hair and wearing a charcoal-grey suit exited the room. Behind him were two young associates. *Lawyers*, Alan thought. The three of them exchanged words before the young men left to climb the staircase.

A hush settled over the crowd. The older lawyer, a man Alan

recognized from one of his grandfather's dinner parties took a seat at the front of the room and unfolded a document. He remained silent, which seemed odd given twenty people were waiting for him to speak.

Alan took out his phone and thumbed through his calendar. It was clear for the remainder of the day. His eye caught one of the young lawyers walking down the staircase to his right. He noticed the veins bulging from the man's neck, the result of carrying a dated and heavy television set. A moment later he crossed the room.

Voices picked up around him as the older man seated in front of the folding tables continued thumbing through documents. Alan witnessed the second young associate walk down the steps. What he carried stopped Alan's thumbs in mid-motion.

The man carried a small table, one sturdy enough to hold the weight of the TV. On top of it was a cardboard box. Within the box were a multitude of extension cords, a VHS tape and what appeared to be a can of lighter fluid. He squinted to see a red flame beneath the brand label when he passed Alan's chair.

He turned to see if anyone recognized what was going on and asked a distant cousin behind him, "Did you see that?"

"What?"

"There was a can of lighter fluid in the cardboard box." Alan watched his dim-witted cousin shrug his shoulders. "Doesn't that... never mind."

"May I have everyone's attention please? Thank you." The older lawyer stood up and moved in front of the table, and clasped his hands. "My name is Larry Goldstein, and I want to start by expressing my condolences to everyone. Everett was a close friend of mine and I managed his legal affairs for twenty years. We met in the eighties and I, like all of you, had a deep respect for the man. I'm sorry for your loss."

Alan gave a slight nod and did not question the man's sincerity. He remembered the conversation he shared with Larry Goldstein and recalled the man's sense of humor.

"We have a lot to cover this morning, we'll need signatures and I have two associates who will assist with questions afterwards. I kindly ask each of you to withhold questions to the end. That's not for my benefit, it's for all of you. In matters such as this, where a rather large estate is being divided, I've witnessed proceedings like this go sour. Can we all agree to that now? Any objections?"

No one spoke. Alan turned to see several anxious relatives look around the room.

"Good then. Oh, and two of you have been named within this will through other means. I will ask that those not mentioned to remain behind until everyone leaves."

A slight murmur ran through the crowd upon hearing this fact but Alan thought nothing of it.

Larry Goldstein moved behind the desk as the two associates returned to the room. "We have twenty different divestments of property and we will start with matters pertaining to the California wine estates in the Russian River Valley. From there we will move to matters relating to properties out here on the east coast, the bequeathing of finances and finally single items of entitlement, cars and such. I have a statement to read as they relate to my counsel that I am required to provide all of you."

When he cleared his throat Alan once again turned his attention to email. Having been named in his mother's will and testament, he saw no reason to pay attention to the boilerplate statements. It lasted five minutes, and in that time, he had sent three emails to work colleagues. He was irritated while responding to a fourth email when he heard the lawyer say, "To my nephew Thomas, I bequeath rights to the Iron Horse estate in the Russian River Valley of California."

Alan's eyes shot wide open and he snapped his head to look forward. The most profitable acreage of land had just been left to someone with the most questionable reputation. Alan knew for a fact the man had a cocaine dependency in the past.

A murmur rushed through the crowd. "What was he thinking," said a relative across the room, loud enough for Thomas to hear. Goldstein stopped speaking and provided a scowl upon hearing the comment. The woman who said it promptly shut her mouth.

The proceedings went on for an hour, and over that time, Alan witnessed two major trends. No one was satisfied with what they received, but the logic of Everett's dissemination of wealth was well conceived from start to finish. The land in California was carved into fifteen allotments. Those who had good hearts and zero business experience received the smallest and more profitable tracts of land. They received little to no money. Those who were educated, successful, and motivated received financial support and larger tracts of land. The logic was obvious: those who had made something of their lives were now well financed and challenged to turn around less-profitable wineries. Those without business experience took ownership of established and profitable acreage. In essence, it was up to them to maintain the winery's success. They were not given any money, so it was up to them to maintain their own income.

Alan ran through the numbers he jotted down. Close to ten million dollars and several thousand acres of pristine wine country were handed down to fifteen relatives. One person, Alan's uncle, received three million dollars and the largest piece of property. He believed it was well deserved, despite the man's health.

Several articles of artwork and cars were then dispersed. The proceedings were winding down to the two remaining properties. Alan could not keep track of who hadn't been named yet in the will beside himself.

"To my niece, Charlotte Devenger, I hereby bequeath my Mattituck estate and all the contents held within, sans the previously cited Mercedes."

Alan grinned and nodded. He would have one of his most loved and trusted relatives over for summer barbeques. He turned to look at her. She appeared torn between the guilt of her grandfather's passing and the property she just inherited.

"Lastly, the home we are in here today. To my sister, Jacqueline Francis Devenger, I hereby bequeath my Upper Saddle River estate."

Alan once again grinned. Jackie was second to Everett in terms of being a patriarch of the family, and deserved every square inch of the property. He was unsure if she could afford to keep it, which saddened him. He would hate to see the home sold off to someone outside the family.

"That my friends brings us to the end, and as I mentioned, I ask that the two of you not cited yet remain behind. My associates and I are open to taking questions."

As good as Alan felt, he turned to see pointed fingers and frustrated voices echo across the room. Pent up anger was released as several family members stormed towards the front desk.

Jackals, Alan thought, *all of them*. He was disgusted by what he was witnessing. The comfort he felt about the proceedings, and the sight of objectionable greed replaced the joy he felt for his sister and aunt.

"He promised me that particular estate. There must be a mistake."

"When did he revise this document? And Fred got all the cars? Something's wrong."

"You've got some nerve, Jackie, I thought more highly of you."

He had concerns about certain relatives: their motives and their insincere condolences. When he saw them barking at the lawyers at the front of the room, Alan went right to his phone and ignored his family.

It took fifteen minutes for everyone to settle down. From the corner of his eye, he could see relatives start to filter outside the room. One asked to speak to him and Alan shook his head and waved him away.

When he turned to see the one remaining soul in the room, a wave of dismay washed over him. The only person left was John Devenger.

He remembered the lawyers asking that the two people not cited remain behind, and with significant concern, he realized it was he and his estranged half-brother.

He approached the table.

"Excuse me," said Alan, "What does this mean for... us?" He pointed to John.

The older lawyer looked up, eyeballing Alan from top to bottom. "Ah yes, you're Alan. I believe we met several years ago." He extended his hand.

"What is going on, why are we, the two of us..."

"Alan, settle down," John rose to his feet. "Don't kill the messenger."

Alan dropped his hands. "Were you privy to this?"

"No."

"I certainly hope not."

"Christ, here we go."

"Gentlemen, enough. Everyone take a deep breath." Larry Goldstein stepped around the desk.

Alan swore he heard Larry say, "Talk about *meshuga*."

"Follow me, gentlemen." The lawyer pointed towards the dining room.

"I'm terribly sorry for your loss. Both of you lost someone special.

Both of you." Larry's eyes lingered on Alan's to make the point. He chose not to respond.

John stepped closer to his brother. "Can you take it easy? We've been through enough. Now, what is this all about?"

Alan waved his hand. "Pardon my reaction gentlemen, this just seems a bit odd."

"It's odd indeed, but this represents Everett's wishes." He clasped his hands together. "This is how it's going to work. A video has been made for both of you to watch. I, along with my other associates have not viewed the contents. After we showed him how to use the video camera, he ordered us out of the room and locked the door. He made this recording nine months ago, after a visit to the hospital. You remember the incident, yes?"

"Of course."

"I was there."

"Good. Needless to say, he was a bit rattled after making this video. He refused to use digital technology. Why he chose to make a recording, for both of you exclusively, I have no idea."

"Why us?" said Alan.

John folded his arms and tapped his chin with his forefinger. "Video. I hope to God this is not about some journey."

Alan's looked at John. "Come again?" John just shook his head. "So how does this relate to the can of lighter fluid?"

"What the fuck are you talking about, Alan?" said John.

The lawyer held out his hands. "That's enough. Gentlemen, we have a television, chairs and a table waiting outside for you. My associate here will get everything set up. You'll sign several documents, and you can take as much time as you need to absorb the message on the tape. Feel free to rewind and play back at your leisure. We have some pens and pads of paper if you'd like to take them with you."

Larry reached back and tapped several notepads.

Alan sighed in frustration. "Can we watch it separately?"

John shook his head in disgust.

"No, Alan, you can't. What's the harm in watching it with your brother?" quipped Larry.

"Half-brother," said John.

"Oy vey. You two are quite a pair."

"And the lighter fluid. You never answered my question."

"I advise you to listen closely, replay it if need be. Take notes." Larry smiled.

Alan shook his head, "Why?"

"After you view it, we have been instructed to incinerate the tape."

Chapter 4

<u>**Upper Saddle River, New Jersey**</u>

John opened the back door and tried to shut it behind him. Wires prevented a tight close. Alan's voice carried into the courtyard. *There's no escape from him.*

Having something Everett bequeathed to him, an element not shared with others, should have brought a smile to his face. Knowing he'd share the experience with the biggest snob in the family sent a shiver straight down his spine.

He looked out to see a young lawyer checking power cords and the cable that connected the VCR to the TV. The screen remained blue. Two chairs rested four feet away from an old TV.

He shook his head. "Hey, what's your name?"

"Geoffrey. I'm sorry for your loss."

"Is there any way around this? An out clause in the will, anything?"

"You can refuse to sign the documents until your lawyer looks at the details and such." He looked up at John. "He's your brother, no?"

"Half-brother." He rubbed the sides of his arms. "And why are we doing this outside?"

"Those were Mr. Devenger's instructions. We'll torch the tape as soon as the viewing is complete."

"Jesus Christ." John stepped towards the center of the courtyard.

He turned when he heard the sound of Alan's and Larry Goldstein's voices grow louder. He felt his heart start to pound in his chest when the back door opened.

"I'm not arguing with you, Larry."

"Yeah, you are. I do not disagree it's unusual."

John watched as Alan's polished shoes come to rest ten feet away from him. He shook his head before he said, "I assume this bothers you as well?"

"Let's just get this over with, shall we?"

Larry Goldstein stepped between the two and gestured with his hands towards the chair. "Gentlemen, take a seat. Geoff, grab their jackets please."

John moved closer to Alan. "I asked Geoff if we should have another lawyer look at the documents."

Alan remained still. "You want your lawyer involved in this? Interesting, I had the same thought."

Larry looked back and forth between John and Alan. "Hold on a moment. You want your personal attorneys to review the will and testament?"

The brothers turned to look at Larry. He provided a startled look for a moment. "It's no skin off my nose, we can reconvene and I'll charge both of you our firm's hourly rate for the three of us. Do you want a quote for our fees or do you want to view the tape?"

They each paused. Alan sighed while John mumbled something under his breath before they took their seats.

"Okay then. A touching moment of progress."

"Get on with it, wise ass," quipped John.

Geoff returned with their coats. When they were done putting them on John and Alan looked towards the lawyer.

"We have documents for both of you to sign. You agree to view the tape, and thereafter, you will be handed an envelope addressed to each of you, sealed and witnessed by Everett himself. Agreed?"

"Yes."

"Fine."

Larry handed a clipboard and document for each brother to sign. They did so quickly after each shared the pen with one another.

"Okay. Everett made this tape behind closed doors. I'll state for the record, witnessed by my associate here, that we have no knowledge of what is contained within the tape or envelopes. He wanted to convey discretion, we honored that request of course. We are required to incinerate the tape when you have completed viewing it. Rewind and replay it as many times as you want. Understood?"

"Okay," said Alan.

"Let's get on with it."

"Very well. Geoff, grab the envelope with the tape in it please." The attorney returned a moment later and they saw a large manila envelope with a wax seal covering the lip of it. "You can see it has been sealed, I'll open it now." He cracked the envelope, removed the tape and handed it to Geoff.

The associate placed it in the VCR and then turned to nod to Larry. "I assume you know how to work the machine?"

John exhaled a slight laugh and shook his head. "I think we can manage."

Alan provided a fake grin, raised his eyebrows and said, "Thanks." The chill in his words prompted the lawyers to leave the courtyard.

John watched the lawyers close the door behind them as best they could. "Fucking lawyers. Wise-ass lawyers to boot."

Alan turned to look at John and cocked his jaw. "Ready to see Everett?"

John remained silent for a moment and sat back in his chair without looking at him. Alan saw the color in John's cheeks fade and he regretted making the comment. "I mean—"

"Hit play, Alan."

Alan took a deep breath and stepped forward to hit the play button.

The image of a conference room table and chair appeared before them on the video. Seconds later, their ailing grandfather took the seat with the help of a cane. His white mane of hair, thick and combed, came into view before he looked at the camera.

John leaned forward. His heart warmed for a moment before he saw Everett Devenger's expression, which radiated serious concern.

"John... Alan." his grandfather smiled. "If you are both watching this, it means I have died and you have agreed to the terms the lawyers set out for you. I know you are not keen on secrets, so I appreciate the fact you are watching this tape." His grandfather clasped his hands together and it reminded John of Andy Rooney on the television program, *Sixty Minutes*. He felt his heart well up and turned to see Alan using the arm of the chair to lean against. His head rested in his raised hand.

"You also know this tape will be destroyed once you view it. That, I am sure, is not sitting well with either of you. Son, both of you, there is some unfinished business I am leaving behind, a project that requires the two of you to tackle together. I want you to listen carefully because I thought a lot about this… a lot more thought than I anticipated." Everett turned away from the screen, took a deep breath, and exhaled.

"I have to pass along this information to you discreetly because I don't want anyone else to know about it. I chose both of you for one reason. You both represent the men in this family, the last remaining real men who've accomplished something with their lives outside of distant cousins, uncles, and what not. You are both, in your own ways, more qualified than anyone else I can think of to pass this information along to."

Everett paused for a moment and raised his hands to his face before putting them back on the desk. "It is my last dying wish for both of you to take this next step together. Neither of you formed the bond of brotherhood that I hoped would happen over the years, not even after your father passed away. This saddens me, more than words can express. I cherish both of you, with equal pride and love. It is time for the two of you to find that love I shared with each of you."

John's heart pounded while his head tried to make sense of the words.

"In the final days of World War Two, my unit was on the outskirts of Feldkirch, Austria. I never spoke at length with either of you about this particular part of the war. This is only the second time I've ever brought it up with anyone. The other time was with your father. There was an incident, one that resulted in the death of three of my fellow soldiers, one that…" their grandfather turned his eyes away from the camera. "It's hard to speak about my friends who lost their lives, just know that good men died for what I'm about to give you."

Alan leaned forward and rested his arms on his knees.

"The incident involves what I found and retrieved for myself, left behind after a run-in with Nazi officers. It happened near the border of Switzerland where my unit was temporarily stationed. I was a military police officer, as you know. My cohorts were as well, and we were ordered to guard roads that lead to the Swiss border. What I found is waiting for you in a bank in Switzerland. I deposited it there at the end of May in 1945. The war was over in Europe then, most of the cities lay in ruin,

Switzerland was spared. I crossed the border with what I found and deposited it in what is called vault twenty-one dash twelve. You're not going to be chasing down shadows, guys." Everett shook his head, "This is my last possession, and I am leaving it to you and your brother."

John's eyes were glued to the screen.

"This is a journey I want both of you to take. You have to do it together. The only other person with knowledge of this deposit was your father. I regret to tell you that the car accident that killed your father was by no means an accident." His grandfather appeared to fight back the tears in the video. "I... I could never prove it at the time, and I couldn't share this with anyone. Your grandmother, your mothers, your sister, I never had the courage to tell them I put my only son into harm's way. I'm sorry I didn't have the courage to speak to you about this. I hope you will forgive me." Everett's eyes returned to the camera. "When I returned to Switzerland in 1947, what I brought back with me, it raised some eyebrows in the Swiss banking community. I could not return. You have to be extremely careful, you have to watch each other's backs. Together, I know the two of you can do it, but God forgive me for not doing what I could to protect your father. The bastards outwitted me and him as well."

His grandfather composed himself and turned his dark eyes to the screen, seeming to move through the tape, the glass, and time itself to stare through John's soul.

"I'm leaving an envelope that contains the name of the bank to you, John, and the other envelope contains the account number, which will be given to Alan. Unless you work together, and agree to do so, you will not be able to access the vault on your own. It is too dangerous, so I'm trusting both of you to work out your differences. To bring the two of you together, and to successfully pull this off, I have no other choice but to force collaboration. You'll see why I'm being so secret when you get to the vault. It's not a security deposit box, that I can assure you. And I'd be a fool to leave it behind without giving you the option to take ownership of it."

John watched Everett raise his eyebrows and sigh. "Two last remaining items. I left ten thousand dollars aside to finance your trip and what not. And, you'll be asked to provide a passcode at the bank. I changed it recently, so remember the word." Everett looked directly at the camera. "The word is brotherhood." He smiled for a faint second and then nodded. "I pray both of you find the means to get there. Watch your back and provide yourself with the means to get in and out quickly. I love you both, more than you will ever know. I wish you both God's blessing and God's speed."

A moment later Everett used the desk to help him stand up, walked around the desk in front of the camera and reach up towards it. The screen went black.

John leaned back and felt his torso hit the back side of the chair. His head felt unattached to his body and he slowly turned to see Alan. He watched him take a deep breath and exhale, seeming lost in a haze of shock and dismay. Without looking at John he said, "I need a moment. Watch it again if you like."

John opened his mouth to say something but Alan just got up and left. John stood up to replay the video but his body felt like it weighed four hundred pounds.

Sao Paulo, Brazil

Karla Vargas listened intently to her subordinate's explanation. It was the third conversation she had shared with the man in the past week, and the Vice President of Vivo Telecom was unimpressed.

"The organization chart is inadequate. We went over this the last time we discussed the matter. Was I not clear?"

She could practically feel the machismo coming over the cellular connection, one her company managed for several hundred thousand Brazilians across the country. Karla wondered if her youth hindered her colleague's ability to understand her senior role in the company.

"I understand you are pressed for time. This is the board's wish but we have infrastructure needs that cannot go unmet. I'll ask again, is the extension of headcount going to deliver the necessary software upgrades by the middle of next month or not?"

She stood up from her desk and stepped around it. She looked beyond the glass panels that separated her office from the main work floor. The subordinate tasked with company-wide software implementations provided one excuse after another. She saw a dozen employees milling about but most were at their desks. She turned to look out her office windows and the view from 40 stories high was spectacular.

She heard her smartphone chime, letting her know she'd received a message. She disregarded it and listened to the young man make his excuses yet again.

"We will not be able to serve Vivo Telecom's data sharing needs within a few months, get back to me by end of day about the headcount you require to meet the deadline. Otherwise, you're welcome to join me for the board meeting to explain the situation. Understood?"

She got the response she expected. "Good then. Good bye." She pulled the phone away from her ear, moved to sit down, and rubbed her temples.

"Machismo. God help me." She put the phone down but recalled the text message. She sighed and picked it up to read it. She paused when she noticed it was from the private eye in Jersey City, New Jersey:

>>> PER OUR AGREEMENT, THIS TEXT IS TO INFORM YOU EVERETT DEVENGER DIED ON FEBRUARY 19TH OF THIS MONTH. IF YOU WANT MORE DETAILS, FAMILY-RELATED BACKGROUNDS, CALL ME TO DISCUSS THE TERMS OF OUR CONTRACT. - GUS <<<

She froze when she re-read the name, 'Devenger.' She noticed a link embedded below the message. Karla immediately clicked on it and a moment later an obituary posting appeared on a local news-related website. She zoomed in to read it.

When she was done she placed the phone on her desk. It took her a moment to process the development and what it meant. Karla looked up and glanced at the office workspace in front of her, thought about her career, and the pending board meeting.

Thoughts of her deceased father ran through her mind: The arrangements he made prior to his death, the history he shared and the introductions he made for her back in his home country, Germany. She thought about the ongoing communication she shared with the private investigator and how it may finally pay off for her.

She looked back at the office workspace and thought how wonderful it would be to walk away from it all. There was only one thing standing in her way, and with help from several cohorts back in Germany, she could take possession of her grandfather's share.

It was waiting for her in Vault 21-12, and she had the financial means and motivation to take possession of it.

Chapter 5

Hoboken, New Jersey

He could not say no to her. Charlotte was his half-sister, and the only relative outside of Everett he was close to. The cousins, and Alan for that matter, represented distant relationships, but when his half-sister asked him to join her for dinner, he could not decline.

She asked him right after he left Everett's house, and Alan was standing there when it happened. The fact that Alan would be there did not sit well with him, but Charlotte espoused a maternal instinct and they both succumbed to her wishes. She knew about the video, but not the content. She wanted to see her brothers break bread and she thought it best to host a dinner.

John felt the anxiety well up in his chest as he strolled down Washington Street in Hoboken. He was ten blocks away from his sister's condo, which was located in a building perched at the edge of the Hudson River. He remembered the view from her windows revealed the length of Manhattan's skyline in all its glory. The night was crisp but his pace was slow to give him time to think about the delicate situation that now existed between him and his half-brother. On top of it all was the knowledge they shared about their father, which was a tragedy unto itself.

He wore gap jeans, a button-down shirt, and a casual pair of lace up shoes. He also wore a thin insulated jacket, one he often wore when he was outdoors on the weekends.

He was coming up on thirty-seven years, older than his half-brother and sister, and he represented the first child of their mutual father, Jack Devenger. The path he chose in life was an entirely different one than the two relatives he would be dining with tonight. They had condos, the city, and careers. Although he had a job, he always felt he was on the outside, separated from others in the family. In many ways he was.

He recalled his childhood, and the anguish he and his mother went through when his parents divorced. They lived outside of Philadelphia and his father commuted to the city for a short time before the relationship started to crumble. John remembered the fights, the bickering, and finally hugging his dad's leg on the day he left, imploring him not to leave when the end finally came. But end it did, and Jack Devenger moved back to Upper Saddle River in 1977 and started a new life in the family business under Everett Devenger's wing.

His mother did not struggle as child support paid the rent, but his father's abandonment took its toll on him. He fought his way through grammar school and the experience toughened him as the years went by. He turned out to be a bully to those younger than him and a target for those who were older and bigger. He sought an escape from the humiliation. The Boy Scouts, with their outdoor excursions and structure, provided him with confidence and strength. The Scouts, in many respects, helped make a man out of him.

The connection he shared with his father's side of the family thinned as time wore on until his untimely death outside of Bern, Switzerland. The subject was now an open-ended discussion given the videotape and the insights his grandfather shared. He knew they would all be speaking about their father tonight, but his mind kept coming back to the visual of Everett on the screen.

He thought about the role the man played in his life. After his father died, Everett stepped in and played a significant part in his upbringing. He provided a healthy perspective on family, work and what it all meant.

He provided financial support as well to his mother, which helped them to keep the house in which John was raised. His grandfather essentially saved them from a much more difficult life, and for that he was grateful.

His half-brother and sister, the children from his father's second marriage, lived on the grounds of Everett's estate in Upper Saddle River. He recalled during visits how Alan treated him, referring to John as "the rotten kid from Philly." He turned out to be his nemesis and rival, a kid born with a silver spoon in his mouth who felt entitled to everything and anything. For all the time he knew him, he wanted to firmly shove that spoon straight up Alan's pompous ass. At one point, he even tried to do so, albeit with a steel-matchbox Camaro. That did not go over so well with the adults, but it prompted a grin that stretched from ear to ear when the disciplining subsided.

He had a stronger bond with his youngest sibling, Charlotte. She was always sweet, kind and loving. His half-sister made efforts to keep John connected with others, despite the fact he spent several years in his twenties backpacking around the world. While Charlotte and Alan were busy making names for themselves, John was visiting places like Angkor Wat in Cambodia, Europe, and scuba diving off the coast of Thailand on razor thin budgets. He befriended dozens around the world from all walks of life. Beside Everett, Charlotte was the only real connection he had with any of the Devenger clan and she deserved all the details shared with them in the video.

He wondered why Everett left her out of the process. He remembered that she now owned an estate out in Mattituck, New York. Perhaps that's why Everett believed it was best to leave the matter of the vault to the men in his family. He came from a generation where men were men, and women were the family gatekeepers.

He thought about Alan, and the possibility of going to Europe with him to retrieve what Everett had left for them. The idea stopped John in his tracks two blocks from Charlotte's building.

He was standing on 10th Street and Hudson, looking straight up towards the condominium. It was immaculate: glass windows, red walls, and an impressive view of the Hudson River and New York City. The building was known as the Tea Factory, a brand new luxury condo unit complete with all the amenities. John had been here several times since she bought it a year ago.

He felt completely out of place: Noise, congestion and car fumes permeated the surroundings. A car honked behind him for no apparent reason other than to move more quickly from one area of town to the next. *An endless cycle,* he thought, *no balance, no rest.* He pulled the lapels of his jacket closer. He failed to put his thoughts together amid the distractions before he entered the building.

He walked in to the grand entrance. A receptionist took his name and called Charlotte's apartment. A moment later he was on the elevator going to the 15th floor.

He walked down the pristine hallway, complete with flower vases and decorations. He found the door numbered 1512. Before knocking, he could hear their voices inside. He paused and felt the emotion he often experienced as a child. He was on the outside looking in, trying to find his place in a structured and wealthy New Jersey family. There he stood, on the outside of a condo door hearing faint words from a family he never truly connected with. The exception was Charlotte, and if it were not for her, he would never share a meal with Alan.

John checked his shirt to make sure it was tucked into his jeans and knocked.

Charlotte opened the door and tried to smile. Without words the two embraced and shared a kiss on the cheek. "Thanks for coming," she said.

"No problem." John rubbed the sides of her arms.

She dipped her eyes for a moment and then met his gaze. "Come on in."

He surveyed the surroundings. It was an open floor plan with a dining area to his immediate left and a modern kitchen behind it. He noticed the cherry cabinets and black marble, complete with stainless steel appliances. Water boiled on the stove, and whiffs of steam rose in the air towards the vent above. Before him was a spacious and well-decorated living room. New and modern paintings hung from the walls.

"Wow, you've decorated nicely Charlotte. New paintings?"

"Yup, they're prints to be honest. Taxes here are a bitch."

The couches looked comfy, and in the corner he noticed a new and massive flat panel TV. Parallel to the entrance were floor to ceiling glass windows, overlooking Manhattan. At night the city looked spectacular.

Alan was nowhere in sight. "Where is he?"

"In the bathroom." A moment later, they both heard the toilet flush.

"Is that him, trying to escape? Through the plumbing work?"

She provided a stern look. "I think we're all going to need a drink tonight. What's your poison?"

"Jameson if you have it, on the rocks please." John moved closer to the windows.

Charlotte walked towards the kitchen and paused. She turned and said, "John, he lost a grandfather too. Okay?" Her eyes lingered before she left for the kitchen.

John tilted his head. She always had a way of getting through to him. He heard what sounded like high heels walking into the room.

Alan stopped when he entered the room. John turned to see him. The two men froze after they made eye contact. John nodded. Alan walked over and grabbed John's hand to shake it, catching him off guard for a moment. "I'm sure you miss him as much as I do."

John's mouth opened for a moment. To him it felt like the first sincere gesture Alan ever expressed to him. He nodded and gripped Alan's hand tighter. "Yeah, I've been a little overwhelmed."

Alan grinned for a second. The moment lingered as the two looked at each other before turning awkward from the gap in time. Alan reached for his glass of wine on the nearby table. "We should sit."

"Yeah." John didn't know how to size up the moment in his thoughts. Outside the forced encounter at the will reading, he had not spoken to Alan in several years. "How have you been?"

Charlotte entered the room with two glasses. "No one's yelled yet, that's progress. Sorry, no Jameson, but try this Scotch on for size. I think you'll like it."

John was thankful for the drink. To take the edge off, he was ready to drink anything she put in front of him. He took a long and deep pull on the contents and was caught off guard by the wonderful and smoky taste. "Damn Charlotte, good stuff, what is this?"

"That is a new friend of mine, Macallan's, the twelve-year variety. I love it."

"Be nice to her and you might get the eighteen-year variety."

John nodded. "Well, I'm not the host, but let's toast our granddad."

"Here here," said Alan. The three glasses clinked as they shared a smile.

For the next hour, they went back and forth taking turns to share stories of the old man: Childhood memories, trips to the hospital and visits to Upper Saddle River. In many cases they shared a laugh, or a fond piece of advice Everett shared. Memories of the man's grounds, his passion for artwork and gardening skills prompted more than a few smiles. John was on his second glass when a timer went off in the kitchen.

Alan turned on the TV after Charlotte mentioned she cooked gnocchi pasta with fresh Bolognese sauce. They were too consumed with fifty inches of ESPN in HD quality to hear her mention how she had purchased fresh rolls.

"Wow, look at that picture."

"This technology is awesome. This has a 1080 resolution, 240 megahertz processing. Top of the line."

"I'm not familiar with it. Thought about it a few years ago, going with an LCD TV and all."

"It's actually an LED TV." Alan corrected him.

"Pardon me." John withheld the wisecrack he wanted to make. He tapped his leg. "So how's work Alan?"

Alan leaned back away from the glow of the TV and turned to John. "I was promoted about a year ago."

"Good for you." John pursed his lips. "What's your title?"

Alan hesitated for a moment. "I'm the publisher of *GQ* magazine." Alan looked up after saying this to see John nodding distractedly, still staring at the screen.

"Congratulations." John took a long pull on his drink. "Still getting a wardrobe allowance? Hugo Boss suits on the company dime? That cracked me up when Charlotte shared that with me."

Alan cocked his jaw. "You want the truth or the whole truth?"

John looked at him. "Let's leave it at the truth."

"Good, it's a fine job. A demanding one but I enjoy it." Alan noticed the look on John's face. Either his scotch or envy was getting the best of him. "Remember what gramps used to say? Love what you do and you'll never work a day in your life?"

John did not respond.

The awkward silence remained as John shuffled his feet. "I was promoted as well, you know."

"Really?" Alan said with surprise. "Good for you. What's your role now?"

"Same thing. I'm managing several folks who monitor Northeast retail locations." John nodded. "Ten Tiffany retail locations."

"I bet you're multi-tasking all day. Still checking credit scores?" He regretted saying it the moment the words came out of his mouth. "I mean—"

"Yeah Alan, we check everything. We get into everyone's business if they decide to buy a $20,000 necklace." John exhaled with slight disgust. "I was wondering when you were going to take a fucking jab."

Alan put his glass down. "I didn't mean to, it was the only thing about your job I remembered. Sorry."

"You know what's funny Alan?"

"What?"

"We're both in the luxury business."

Alan bristled. "How is that exactly?"

John stood up. "Your advertisers spend millions every year in an effort to get people to their stores, and ultimately, my department has the final say on any purchase. So your efforts, in essence, boil down to whether or not people like me approve the final transaction." John grinned and rattled the ice cubes in his drink. "Kind of ironic, don't you think?" He took a pull on his scotch.

Part of Alan wanted to see John grab his coat and leave, but felt some level of relief when he saw the man stand up to walk into the kitchen. He knew that ultimately, he needed his brother as much as John needed him. He gulped the remnants of his wine and clenched his teeth.

***

Alan smiled with content when he finished the meal Charlotte had prepared for them. He wiped up the last remnants of sauce with the bread. "That was spectacular Charlotte. Thank you."

"Same here," said John.

She shrugged. "You're both easily impressed. It was fresh gnocchi from one of those refrigerated packs, and I bought some local sauce at an Italian store in town." Charlotte noticed John's smile. "Do you want me to get you a jar?"

John held his hands up. "Nah, I want to remember this as it is. Thanks though."

Alan rolled his eyes. "If you enjoyed it, let her get it for you."

John shook his finger. "That's not it, it will just be a warm memory. That in itself is a gift." He rubbed his hands and turned to Charlotte. "So we've been yapping about ourselves, how's your job going at the U.N.?"

Charlotte finished her third glass of red wine and refilled her glass. "I was promoted, I'm overseeing some Middle East projects."

John clapped his hands. "So you got promoted too, excellent. A toast to all our promotions."

She shook her head. "It's a bitch. On some level it was a demotion. There's no end to the festering. And the Egyptians, Christ have mercy." She took a long sip. "They have a new ambassador every few months, and the communication changes with every new contact I make."

"So what exactly is it you do?" said John.

"I essentially represent the United Nations efforts to monitor peace and promote stability in very unstable parts of the world. Egypt qualifies by any measure you use, and I sincerely don't know if there's anything we can do."

She spent the next ten minutes sharing her assessment of the region; its divisions and the toll it was taking on the youth of the country. She concluded by saying that it would not surprise her if civil war represented the ultimate conclusion.

John giggled for a moment and laughed. "You make my job look easy."

"I think we need to find you a new career."

"Thanks Alan, but on some level I feel like I'm doing some good in the world. So I'll stick it out for a while." She looked at her brothers' plates. "I'm going to clean up. You boys talk."

Alan knocked on the table with his fingers. The sound of jazz lingered in the background. He didn't know what to say other than to address the elephant in the room.

John spoke first. "I'm assuming you don't want to let sleeping dogs lie tonight?"

"I was just thinking it was the elephant in the room, funny. I don't know, maybe another night?"

"What's in the vault, Alan?" John waited for Alan to look at him. "What's in that damn vault?"

"Your guess is as good as mine."

"You seriously have no idea? Not a clue?"

"Nope."

"Charlotte! What's in the vault dear sister?"

"Hitler's head on a silver platter! How the hell would I know?"

John grinned and shook his head. "He's a clever son of a bitch. I'll give him that."

Alan furrowed his brow and cleared his throat. "By son of a bitch, are you referring to our grandfather?"

John smiled. "I am indeed. He knew exactly what he was doing when he set this whole thing up. The whole god damn thing."

"Please don't refer to our grandfather that way again, or we will never know what's in that vault."

John sat up in his chair and crossed his arms. "You know what Alan? I think you're afraid of what's over there. Maybe it would show you how much more of a man Everett was compared to the two of us."

"Speak for yourself."

"Oh I will. I think if we pried open that vault, there may be something in it that rips apart—" He stopped and took a deep breath. "I don't know if we can do this." He shook his head.

"Together… That's what this whole thing is about. That was Everett's wish."

"Do you really think you can do this, Alan?" John leaned back. "Do you really want to go over there with me? Can you stomach it?"

"I can, I'm more concerned about you."

"And how is that?"

"Your temper, John." Alan looked him straight in the eye. "It's always been the same. When you're backed in a corner, you come out with fists blazing."

"And sometimes that's what the situation calls for."

"It's your default reaction to everything."

"You're exaggerating. Our father died going back there to get it, that warrants a little preparation, and protection."

Charlotte stepped back in the room. "I'm gone one minute, and—"

Alan held up his hand to stop her. "I don't know what kind of preparation or protection you're talking about. Maybe you should stop resenting me first, then we can have a discussion of what we need to do."

John smacked the table and stood up from his seat. "There it is! I was waiting for that." He walked away from the table and turned back to his brother. "Let me ask you something, Alan, have you even held a gun in your life?"

"What the hell does that have to do with anything?"

"That's what I thought. A family member is murdered and you plan to saunter around Switzerland like you own it." He waited for an answer but Alan did not respond. "What... haven't thought that far ahead?"

Charlotte stepped between them. "John, settle down, Alan, stop provoking him."

"There's only one thing I need."

"Lay it on me," said John.

Alan leaned forward. "The name of the bank. I have the account number. I can talk my way in there, and I can talk my way out, without the need for a gun."

John shook his head. "You're so fucking naïve. Our father died—"

Alan shot up from the chair. "Just give me the bank name! I'll do this quickly, over a long weekend for God's sake."

"Your mouth won't work so well if there's a gun in it!"

"That's enough!" Charlotte stood there dumbfounded. Moments ago they were enjoying themselves. "Jesus Christ, the two of you sit down. Sit."

John and Alan squared off on opposite sides of the table. Charlotte walked into the living room and dialed down the volume on the stereo system. She turned to face both of them.

"Both of you are either too stubborn or too blind to realize that there's another person affected by all of this, and that's me. There's something I want to share with both of you." She stepped towards them. "Our father." She put her hands on the back of a dining room chair. "I have two memories of my father from when I was a little girl, and only two. One was of him holding me in his arms at grandpa's house. Just holding me, rocking me back and forth. I was probably three or four years old."

She paused to give her brothers time to let her words resonate.

"I can't tell you how many times I've thought of that moment. I shared this with Everett years ago. We guessed it was right around the time he left for Bern, to go to the vault. Do either of you know the last living memory I have of the man? Do you?" Both men shook their heads. She took a deep breath. "His funeral."

She gripped the chair and fought the urge the cry. She paused for what seemed like a minute before she looked up to see her brothers lost in their thoughts. "My mother held me as I grabbed her leg and cried that day. I... I never got the chance to get to know him. Ever."

Alan moved to stand up but she gestured for him to stop. "Listen, I want you to go over there, together, I want answers about why he died, and I think what's inside the vault will tell us. This talk of, I don't know, not working together, not being prepared, I've heard enough. It's complete bullshit."

She looked at both men. "You have to do this, and Everett wanted you to do it together. If this was his last dying wish, then you owe it to him, and you owe it to me as well."

John's mouth was agape as he turned to look at Alan. "Charlotte, I don't think—"

"You're not going to say another word. Find a way, both of you, to make this work. Put your god damn differences aside for once."

"Now wait—"

"Alan, shut up. Wait here."

She left the room. Both reflected on what she had told them but neither spoke. John looked to Alan and shrugged his shoulders. Alan sighed.

They both turned when they heard the sound of a cork being removed from a bottle. They saw Charlotte holding three glasses and a bottle of what looked like white wine.

John provided a puzzled look. "Charlotte, I have to drive. I should probably take a break."

"Just a taste then. Do you know this brand of wine? Iron Stallion?" Both men expressed puzzled looks. "This is wine from the first vineyard Everett purchased, from the land he bought out in California. I think it was in 1948. It's a Chardonnay."

"And?"

"Well, we know the land he bought represented a new start for him, I think we should toast a new start for the two of you."

"Charlotte. This is very sweet but—"

"Shush." She handed one glass to Alan and another to John. "You're brothers, act accordingly. Are you going to do this for Everett or not?"

Her eyes turned from one man to the next. Neither appeared ready to refuse the toast. "Good, then to our father and to Everett, may your journey be safe and sound." She held the glass at the center of the table and waited. She looked forward, patiently waiting for a final response.

She did not remember who clinked glasses first. It did not matter. She recalled, to her satisfaction, how both men made the toast to a new beginning.

Chapter 6

<u>Upper West Side, Manhattan</u>

He opened his eyes and saw the alarm clock read 6:30 a.m. Alan closed his eyes to no avail. Instinct or anxiety had set the alarm in his head after years of work, waking him at 6:30 even on Saturdays.

He rolled onto his back and stretched. He exhaled slowly and turned to see the blond hair on the bed's other pillow, opposite his. He smiled for a second, put his hand on the warm body and noticed she was under the sheets. He gave her a shove, "Time to go? Hmm?"

Alan heard a slight moan and when she turned to look at him, Alan was staring at a drop-dead gorgeous and purebred blond Labrador named Vix, short for Vixen. "Hey Vix." His dog's three-inch long tongue gave him a kiss square on the mouth and he put both arms under the sheet to rub her tummy.

Alan tried to spoon her and she wanted nothing to do with it. She hopped out of the bed and sauntered towards the bedroom door. She stopped for second to see if Alan would follow and he did. Her pace was slower now that she was ten years old. Vix was the closest thing to a soul mate he had ever come across. Despite a respectable number of dates, girlfriends and near-fiancées who had come and gone through his bedroom door, Vix was the constant in his life.

The pat on the head he gave her prompted the dog to follow him. He figured he had thirty minutes before he'd have to walk her and went straight for the coffee grinder. The half-pound of Papua New Guinea coffee that rested in the device was ground to a fine consistency, and moments later the machine was percolating.

Alan turned to look at the open floor plan of his two-bedroom condo. He had bought it shortly after earning an Associate Publisher title at another publishing company. Despite his financial advisor's advice to take out a bigger mortgage, Alan thought it was best to tamp down the debt and monthly mortgage payments. Since then, his bank accounts had recuperated to the point where he was able to afford a small cottage out in the Hamptons, which he had purchased two years ago. He took pleasure in reminding his financial advisor that the lower mortgage on his condo provided the means to take on a second mortgage out on the island.

He turned to look at the alcove office across from the living room that housed his technology and computer. The top of it held his iPad Air, iPhone 5S, work laptop and a 27-inch iMac, complete with a razor-thin screen. Alan paused before he clicked on the laptop's mailbox icon. He heard the processor go into overdrive as one email after another in bold filled the screen from top to bottom. He sighed and stopped himself from taking a seat. It took a minute for him to receive over one hundred emails, which stemmed from after-hours activity. Fifteen different subordinates and four senior executives had emailed him after 6:30 p.m. East Coast time, which seemed to be the new normal in his and everyone's work life. He next opened his tablet and tapped it to life and saw a few dozen emails and texts from friends but one was sent after midnight. One message was from a woman he had taken on a date several nights prior. The brunette was very young, beautiful and forthcoming in all manners, so he decided to wait before reading or replying to her message. He grinned and wondered when he'd be waking up beside her.

Alan picked up his phone to check his calendar and he saw a reminder pop up for eleven a.m. He stopped in mid-stride when he read the details, having forgotten what was on his agenda. In a few hours' time he'd be visiting Everett's home with John to look for clues that might explain what was in Vault 21-12. The relative who inherited the house said they were welcome at any time to visit for the next few months.

He turned back to look at his open laptop and thought about how much more he would enjoy reading work-related emails compared to spending time with his half-brother. The moments and life he had shared with Everett and other relatives at the house, were too good and too many to count. He knew in his heart that the time he planned to spend with John at Everett's home would not be one of them. The anxiety within him grew when he thought about John and the scheme Everett came up with to bring them closer together.

He believed the old man's naïveté might ultimately result in moving them further apart.

Upper Saddle River, New Jersey

He parked the Subaru in the driveway and exited the vehicle. Moving to the right side of the house, he turned to see the old Weber grill resting beside the side yard deck. It was concealed with a fabric cover and he lifted it to open the front compartment. He noticed the coffee can on the bottom shelf and within it was the house key.

He stepped back to the front door, opened it, and then noticed the home security system to his immediate left. He entered the digits and it beeped, confirming it was safe to enter the home without alerting the authorities. The house was now his to enjoy alone until Alan got there. He felt a slight pang of satisfaction.

He walked into the dining room and kitchen and noticed nothing had changed since his last visit. On many levels it was a relief. He did not want anything to change and he wanted it to stay the same in honor of Everett. When he spoke to his aunt, they never talked about what her plans were for the house. For all he knew, the house could be emptied and sold before summertime.

He opened up a cabinet in the kitchen that contained dry goods and beneath it was a drawer of knives. Nothing was out of place, which on some level was a relief but on another saddened him. Everett was gone and there was no one left in the house to disrupt the order.

He paused to think about where it would be best to start looking for clues about the vault. One place came to mind: the study.

He walked through the great room and moved into the study, a room on the left side of the house. He turned the doorknob and entered the room.

It was a grand presentation and continued to be so when he looked around. Dark wood shelves housed what looked like a thousand books, stretching from one side of the room to the other. A Persian carpet greeted him as his eyes canvassed the thirty-by-twenty-foot room. He

62

turned on the lights and saw the lawyer's desk before him. The window drapes were closed and John widened them to reveal daylight.

He'd spent quality time in this room with Everett and many stories passed between the two of them. The trips he took overseas resulted in long conversations with his grandpa at the seating area to his immediate left. He'd come back to find him there working on a writing project or reading one of his many books. Everett always enjoyed listening to his tales about trips to Asia, Africa and Europe. John realized that one of the best memories he had of his traveling days was the time he spent sharing stories with Everett here in this very room.

He looked at his grandfather's desk. He remembered going through the drawers as a child, but not since then. It would be a good place to start looking for clues about what could be in the vault.

He stepped around the desk and saw seven drawers in total. He tried to open the long drawer above the kneehole but it was locked. After trying several others, he realized all of them were secure. The contents on top of the desk were nothing out of the ordinary: several bills, pens, a stapler, desk lamp and writing pads. A small tray housed a staple remover, letter opener and erasers.

He sat back in the leather chair. He had to find out what was in the drawers. He thought about calling his aunt to see if she knew where the desk key was and decided against it. After trying to force the drawers open, he shrugged off any guilt and decided to jimmy the locks. It didn't take long for the letter opener to pop open the first one, and after a few minutes, they were all unlocked.

He turned on the desk lamp and opened the long drawer that ran across the desk's front. There were several nondescript papers, some holiday cards and a five-by-seven photograph. He lifted it and saw a black and white image of Everett and his grandmother when they were very young. He was wearing his Army uniform and his grandma was wearing a lovely dress with polka dots. They were smiling. John loved the photograph. He planned to ask his aunt if he could have a copy of it.

The next drawer he opened looked like a tornado hit it. It was what Everett called his shit drawer, and it was filled to the brim with paper, an unsigned baseball, an empty coffee mug, and dog-eared paperback books. He looked over to the rows of books on the walls beside him and realized these were the only paperbacks Everett seemed to own.

The next few drawers didn't reveal anything that contained what he hoped to find. No papers mentioned secret Nazi vaults in Switzerland, no maps with X's, and no deposit documents. There was one drawer left.

He sighed and moved to open the long and deep drawer to his right. He saw what looked like fifteen years of tax returns stacked high within it. He decided to look further and moved the documents to the top of the desk.

What he saw at the bottom of the drawer made him freeze. It was in immaculate condition. "Wow."

John picked it up and held a German-made World War Two Luger pistol. He felt the weight of it, noticed the magazine was still inside it and aimed it at the wall. Rather than pull the trigger, he toyed with the weapon to release the magazine and it popped out a moment later. It was a remarkable find.

Aunt Jackie would have no idea what to do with it, but John did. He hoped she would let him add it to his collection. He placed it on the desk and smiled. He turned his attention back to the drawer and saw something else that caught his eye.

Shoved in the back was what looked like a leather-bound journal. He lifted it up and saw it was yellowed, worn and scuffed with marks on the outside. It was held together with a leather cord and he unfastened it.

He paused when he saw the date on the first page and Everett's name, rank and unit number. The last page was dated: May 27th, 1945.

"Finally," he said out loud. He skimmed several pages but did not see serial numbers, the name of the bank or a comment about what was in the vault itself.

He heard the front door open in the distance. John knew it could only be Alan given the time. He put the journal down and waited to see what happened.

He heard Alan call out, "Hello? John?"

"In here."

Alan walked in the room and he seemed displeased by the sight of John sitting behind the desk. John picked up on it and leaned back and clasped his hands in front of him.

"Good morning," John said.

"It's all there," John tossed the journal to the opposite side of the desk. "Pull up a chair, Everett left us two million dollars in foreign currency and a trove of diamonds found after the war."

Alan walked over warily while John tried to maintain his poker face. He watched his half-brother pick up the weathered journal and turn back to look at him. "You know, I would advise against trying to bullshit a bullshit artist." John did not blink. "Come on, you're completely full of it."

"Your methods of deduction are quite astute, Watson," John leaned forward, "I am completely bullshitting you." He smiled but Alan did not return even a hint of warmth. "Come on, just trying to lighten things up."

Alan took a seat and flipped through the pages.

"Oh, I did find a German Luger pistol."

"Okay there, Sherlock."

Alan flinched when John pulled out the weapon and placed it on the desk with force. "Jesus! Be careful."

"I took the magazine out, no rounds, and the safety is on Alan." He shook his head. "Do you think I'd put us in danger? I've handled weapons like this since I was ten."

"Still the Boy Scout?"

"It beats the fucking choir, pussy."

Alan turned and gave John a cynical look.

"I assume you did the same, you got Aunt Jackie's permission—"

"Yes. Check out the gun." Alan hesitated before he moved his chair closer. "Go ahead, hold it."

Alan picked the pistol up and held it like a delicate object. It seemed completely out of place in his grip. "If you think you're taking this to Switzerland you can forget it."

"Nah, that's a collectible. Hopefully our aunt will let me have it."

"Not my business, or cup of tea." He put the pistol back on the desk.

"The journal itself is the real find. From the date of it, I think he started using this at the conclusion of the war."

Alan's eyes lit up. "Really?" He saw the leather-bound book, opened it and leaned back in the chair. He thumbed through the pages and said, "This is awesome."

"I skimmed it." He watched Alan's eyes pore over the pages. "Take a look to see if you find anything. I'll read it this week and let you borrow it when I'm done."

Alan's eyes turned to one of the last written pages in the journal and read:

May 5th, 1945

> *"Same shit, different day. On the outskirts of Nenzing, Austria. Germans are surrendering en masse, they are all over the roads. Mitchell, Walter and Freddy are stationed with me, we're watching the grass grow out here, in the middle of nowhere. Nothing going on. Some brass drove through at first light, a major and some other asshole, asking about the investigations. We didn't have much to share. We told them our unit is further ahead, climbing mountains, hunting krauts. Word is they have some kind of mountain hold out, Hitler's bunker or something. It's all bullshit, let's end this, get on a boat and go home. I'm sick of this army crap."*

Alan frowned. "And why do you get to keep it?"

"Because I found it." John leaned forward. "You know, this is not going work if we keep secrets from each other. I'm willing to be open-minded if you will."

"Agreed, no bullshit, no guns, no secrets."

John withheld his response to the issue of having a weapon. He figured it was not a good time to start a debate. He watched Alan thumb through more journal entries and with each turn of the page his brother glowed with excitement. "It's kind of nice to hold that in your hands, isn't it?"

"Yeah, this is special." Alan put the book down and tapped it. "It would be nice to know what's over there, if it's worth the trip."

John started closing the drawers. "Beats me, have a look around. Check out the rest of the house?" He didn't look up when Alan stood up from the chair and crossed the room.

Standing before the bookcase, Alan pulled out a few books, thumbed through them and replaced them. He leaned down and saw a tall shelf at the bottom that housed large books of artwork. "Maybe the answer isn't in a drawer, maybe it's right in front of us."

"What do you mean?"

"You know as well as I do Everett loved art. Check out his collection." He pointed out inch-thick books on Cezanne, Monet and van Gogh. "There are ten pieces in this house alone, probably worth half a million dollars, not of this caliber of course."

"Yeah. So?"

Alan stood up. "Have you ever seen a movie called *The Train*?"

"Never heard of it."

"Maybe you heard of that *Monuments Men* movie?"

"Oh yeah, saw the trailer somewhere. What about it?"

"You should watch them." Alan's eyes canvassed the collection. "It's about how the Nazi's plundered Europe. I saw *The Train* when I was a kid. More importantly, it's about stolen art."

John froze when he heard the words. "Well, he did say he found something over in Austria."

"What if there's artwork in the vault? What if it's just sitting there, a masterpiece or something?" Alan put his hands on his hips. "Do you have any idea what it would be worth?"

John furrowed his brow. "Well, I wouldn't be too keen on possessing a piece of stolen art, that seems asinine."

"I'm not saying we do anything with it, but what if it's there, just waiting inside a decrepit vault?" Alan returned to the chair seated before the desk. He tapped his fingers on the table.

"What are you thinking, Alan?"

"We're going to need some contingency plans. If we find something large or small, expensive or fragile. We've got to think this through."

"And we've got to be prepared." John picked up the gun and grinned.

Alan did not return the smile. The thought of a long drawn-out process with John frightened him. "More importantly, let's make it quick."

Potsdam, Germany

He checked the tracking number on the large cardboard box. It matched the document on his clipboard. He walked down the long aisle and checked another container and found it matched his documents. Satisfied with his process, Henrick chose to finish the job on Monday after he heard the evening bell echo throughout the storage facility.

The old man walked the one hundred yard stretch back to his desk and placed the clipboard in the top drawer. His feet ached when he turned to lift his jacket from the chair and felt a twitch of pain in his shoulder. Younger men walked past him and got in line to stamp their time cards in a machine. He was by far the oldest man at the warehouse facility. When he checked out, he waved to a fat Bavarian woman and said, *"Guten nacht,"* but she ignored him.

A cold breeze smacked him square in the face when he stepped outside. He pulled his lapels close and watched those with cars pull out of the long parking lot. Unable to afford one, he had no choice other than to walk home.

When he was half way there, he could only hear the sound of his sore feet hit the narrow sidewalk.

The first building he passed looked identical to several other five-story buildings. It was an old development built during East Germany's communist days and the residents were either very old or poor. He looked down one alley between the buildings to see a feral cat. He stopped and grinned for a moment and thought about calling out to the animal. When the cat noticed him she hissed and scurried away. "Little shit."

He walked the remaining hundred yards to the front entrance of his building and was relieved to get inside. Henrick took a deep breath and looked towards the elevator. He cursed when he saw it was still out of service. Turning his attention to the staircase, he was required to climb three flights to get to his apartment.

By the time he was at his door, he was panting and fumbling with his keys. His knees, and the elevator situation, would require him to stay home and consume whatever food he had on hand. He felt no urge, nor did he have the strength, to walk down and back up the stairs to retrieve a hot meal.

He stepped inside the small apartment and turned on the lights. The coat rack beside the door was next to a framed picture of his parents. His father was in uniform and his lapels indicated he was once an officer of the Grenadier 41st army during World War Two. He barely remembered him, but his mother looked both proud and affectionate in the picture. It was one of his favorites.

When he turned he noticed the answering machine beside the telephone indicated there was a message waiting for him. Hoping it was a distant relative who had finally returned his call, he stepped forward. He sat beside the small end table and hit the play button.

When he heard a young fraulein's voice he immediately rewound the old answering machine's tape. He hit play and listened.

"Henrick, this is Karla Vargas, you likely remember my voice, or I hope so. There's been a development in New Jersey, and the Devengers," Henrick's hand gripped the arm's chair and he leaned towards the machine. "The old man is dead, there have been some developments and it's time to regroup. Get in touch with the others and call me back."

Henrick replayed it and his eyes opened wide when it concluded. "Oh my god. Could this be it? After all these years?"

He could not contain the smile that stretched across his wrinkled face from ear to ear. He gripped his fists before him and considered Everett Devenger's death, and what it meant. It was nothing short of great news, and he hoped one day to spit on the man's grave, and take vengeance on anyone who tried to access Vault 21-12.

He had to contact the others, but before he did, he walked back to the picture of his parents. When he took it off the wall, Henrick held it in his hands. He thought about his father, his death and three other German soldiers who were murdered. More importantly, he recalled the information passed down to him.

He said to himself, *after all these years, I may yet still have a chance to secure what our fathers left us. For all of us.*

He knew it was waiting for him in Vault 21-12.

Chapter 7

It was 10:00 a.m. and the start of another boring day of work. John finished his coffee and checked his email again for the fifth time in as many minutes.

The downtime between holidays did not prompt many credit security checks. When the holidays did arrive, his team would be overwhelmed with calls from retail locations and overtime. Until then, he'd have to appear busy and professional, two things he was not very good at.

His mind focused on something that had consumed him over the past week. He started reading Everett's journal and he could not stop thinking about the bank vault. It was exciting to read about Everett's experience in World War Two, but there was not a word about the contents inside the bank.

John opened his computer browser and typed in the bank's name, which according to Google he had spelled incorrectly. He ran through a few web pages that explained the bank's functions and services.

He paused and considered the consequences of inquiring with the bank itself. When he opened the sealed envelope given to him at the Will reading, it was a simple document signed by Everett Devenger. He cocked his head and thought whom he could trust to lend some advice. The answer came within seconds, an old cohort and friend he made when he was studying criminal justice during his undergraduate days.

He retrieved his company-issued Blackberry, scrolled through the contact database, which included friends and coworkers, and found Jimmy DeAngelo's cell number. He dialed.

"Jimmy," he answered.

"That's it? No last name?"

"Who's this?"

"Devenger. How goes it?"

"Dude, holy shit, where have you been?"

"Working, still at Tiff's. It's been a while. What's new with you?"

The two caught up for five minutes. John explained his promotion months ago and the intense holiday season, which seemed to impress his friend from Staten Island. "Still with the Police Department out there?"

"Yep, ten years to go and then I can retire. Full pay and benefits after twenty years of service, can you believe that shit?"

"Then what, move to Miami and hit the strip clubs?"

"With a wife and two kids? Please, you'll never forget that bachelor party for Tommy, won't you."

"You were the guy that…" John remembered his coworkers could hear every word he was saying, "You're lucky I'm at work. Never mind."

"Pussy."

John paused for a second. "Look, I'm calling because I need some advice. It's a bit sensitive, but I need perspective."

"Hit me, I'm all ears."

***

John thanked him and ended the call. John sighed as the advice his friend provided did not result in any substantive advice. There was only one thing he could do.

He scrolled his computer browser back to the home page of the bank. A moment later, he heard the distinctive sound of a European ring tone.

Scheibzerische Bank, Bern Switzerland

"Private banking, may I help you?"

"Yes, hello, do you speak English?

"Of course."

"Good, I hope this is the right department, I've talked to several people. I'm inquiring about a private deposit made in 1945."

"How may I assist?"

"I don't have the account number to the vault, but—"

"I can assure you we don't have vaults sir."

There was a long pause. "I see. Do you refer to deposits in some other manner?"

"Perhaps, but if you don't have the account number I cannot provide assistance." He heard the man mumble under his breath.

"If I provided a name associated with the deposit, would that suffice?"

"I can check our name registry but you will still need proper authentication, if there are any deposits under your name."

"Yeah, I get that. The name is Devenger. John Devenger." He spelled out the last name for him.

Carl Heinzen opened his computer and typed in the last name. The name did in fact correspond to an account. "Please hold."

He stood up walked over to the armchair that held his briefcase. Within it was a small laptop. He retrieved it, turned it on and waited for the welcome screen to dissipate. He checked to see if the call was still on hold. "Another moment, sir, please hold."

Carl Heinzen's personal computer was operational and he clicked on the Microsoft Excel icon. From there he scrolled down to a non-descript file name and opened it. He hit the search function and typed in DEVENGER.

He saw the name appear, but more importantly, he saw the red asterisk beside it. This prompted the bank official to grin.

He went back to the call. "Mr. John Devenger, yes?"

"Yup."

"We do have a record of your name in our files. It appears you have an account with us."

"Thank God. Beside the account number, what else do you require?"

"The password of course and proper identification, a passport is recommended. May I have your phone number?" The client complied. "And your address please, for our records?" Carl jotted down the information on his personal computer in a column marked, CONTACT INFORMATION. "Is there anything else I can assist you with?"

"I also want to verify what was deposited years ago."

"That is not possible sir. We keep no formal records nor do we share confidential information about private deposits made at the bank."

"That's an issue, is there someone else—"

"I manage all private accounts, Mr. Devenger, and have been doing so for over twenty years. I cannot legally comply with your request, based on Swiss banking laws. Is there anything else I can do to be of service?"

"Nope, you've been helpful, thank you." The call terminated.

Carl Heinzen scrolled to the right side within the excel document. One column housed the name of another contact associated with the vault. The last column provided a number, which read 5,000 Euros.

He retrieved his personal cell phone and called the other phone number associated with Vault 21-12. The phone went to voicemail.

"Miss Vargas, this is Carl Heinzen of the Scheibzerische Bank in Bern, Switzerland. The owner of Vault 21-12 has contacted us. Based on our agreement, let me know if you are interested in further details. My personal cell phone number is 02-34-54-92-23. Please call after business hours."

Chapter 8

Rio de Janeiro, Brazil

The elevator doors opened and Karla stepped out of it. She used her hands to primp her auburn hair and turned to look down the long hallway. Her high heels accentuated the lines of her long legs and the dress she wore was a blue and white patterned material made of fine satin. She dressed for the occasion, and when she recognized the direction of the penthouse, Karla turned to walk down the hall.

She walked with confidence as her shoulder strapped purse dangled by her side. The door to the penthouse was open and she pushed it wide to see a dozen others chatting inside. The sound of calypso music filled the room.

"Karla, my love!" She recognized Raphael and stepped toward him. Her high heels echoed on the polished floors. "So good of you to come."

"Hi, Raphael, thanks for having me. I love your new condo."

"Thanks. It took six months to furnish. Let me introduce you to my friends."

Her eyes were glued to the surroundings when he spoke. The condo had an enormous open floor plan, high ceilings and a devastating view from what appeared to be a glass-panel sliding wall parallel to the entrance. "My God, look at that view."

When she turned to look at the others waiting to meet her, she noticed three men and four women. One man surveyed Karla's figure and seemed more interested with every second that passed. She could practically feel the man's testosterone increase the more he glared. The women seemed off-put by her presence, which was the usual response Karla encountered in social situations.

After introductions were made, Raphael swept his arm around her thin waist and escorted her towards the terrace. "Now I want to show you a new view of Rio." The glass panel doors were already open and a mix of cool air mixed with the warm Atlantic sea-scented breezes.

She immediately thanked herself for making the trip from Sao Paulo. She had met Raphael at a telecommunication conference a year prior, and their friendship had blossomed during that time. She knew he came from money and was a successful entrepreneur, but the view captured her heart the moment she stepped outside.

"Incredible." The terrace seemed to stretch from one horizon to another. She could see the hills across the bay, Christ the Redeemer overlooking the city and the golden sunlight caressed nearby buildings. Before her was an infinity pool that was centered on the terrace and appeared to spill over the edge of the building itself. "I cannot believe… just how many women have you seduced with this view Raphael?"

He just smiled and kissed her on the cheek. "A gentleman never tells. But if you spend the night we can enjoy the sunrise together."

She looked at her host, or rather down, as she was three inches taller. She grabbed his chin and smirked, "You couldn't handle a woman like me, and you know it."

"I know. That's why I bought the penthouse. You'll eventually fall in love with the view and throw yourself at me."

"That's a lovely fantasy." She stepped back and placed her hand squarely on his chest. Her hand lingered there as she provided him with a devilish smile. She softened the look in her eyes and made a kissing gesture as she pushed him back one step at a time. His eyes remained fixed on her. He backed up within a foot of the pool and she stopped him by hooking her fingers in his silk shirt. "Right there. That's where I'll leave you."

He looked down to see his left foot was two inches from the edge of the pool. He laughed and stepped towards her but she was already six feet away after two long strides. "I need to make a call."

She looked over her shoulder and made her way to the opposite side of the terrace. Every man at the party followed her with his eyes.

She put her arms on the railing and soaked in the most stunning view of Rio she had ever seen. Her business mind started to turn over the numbers in her head, trying to pin a number on the cost of the penthouse.

She knew Sao Paulo real estate better than Rio's, but the penthouse must have cost several million *real*.

She turned back and saw two men were ready to approach her so she delayed them by retrieving her smartphone. She needed a moment before acquainting herself with other guests and she noticed a voicemail icon on her phone. She hit play and put the phone to her ear.

She did not recognize the man's voice right away, but she was well aware of the arrangement made with a man named Karl Heinzen in Bern, Switzerland. She listened to the message and realized the Devenger situation had just escalated. She had the name of the relative who possessed the rights to Vault 21-12, which until that very moment could have been one of thirty different people related to Everett Devenger.

She looked up once again to see the night sky descend across the scenery. It would take another ten minutes before the city lights consumed the view. She pondered what her first move would be if she took possession of her share of Vault 21-12. She herself could own a slice of heaven, and dozens of views equal in caliber anywhere in the world.

She had calls to make and arrangements to put into place. Karla would have to wire the equivalent of five thousand Euros to a man in Potsdam, Germany, a person she had never met in person. He would then hand deliver it to the Private Banking Manager at *Scheibzerische* bank in Bern.

Times Square, New York

Alan realized he had not touched his coffee. Three internal meetings had transpired before 10:00 a.m. and he did not have the time to blink, let alone caffeinate himself. He had a lunch meeting with clients, a 4:00 sales call downtown and in the evening he had a promotional event at the Ralph Lauren showroom.

Later in the evening he planned to work on his senior management budget presentation. His business manager was preparing it, but Alan was responsible to present revenue forecasts to the board.

He stepped towards his office door. "Clarice, hold my calls for ten minutes." He closed the door and sipped his coffee. Outside the sun reflected against the skyscrapers and he sighed. Alan sat down in one of the armchairs and reviewed recent developments in his work life.

He felt he had slipped in the past few weeks. Sales were down, his subordinates did not exhibit the urgency he felt and he was playing catch up on multiple fronts. He had negative numbers to share with the board, which meant he would need to show how he planned to turn things around before the end of the year. Anything less and he would have a gun to his head. It would only take one bad stretch of time, equal to several quarters of negative results before he'd be tossed out of the job. He'd seen it happen dozens of times across the publishing industry.

Alan turned his mind to other matters outside of work and realized he planned to get together with his half-brother on Saturday. The plan was to meet at his house and they never confirmed the time.

He took his phone out of his pocket and scrolled down to John's office number.

"John Devenger."

"It's me."

"Hey there, how goes it?"

"Extraordinarily busy."

"No rest for the wicked, dear brother?"

"Yes actually." There was a pause on the line. "What time works for you on Saturday?"

"Say... 11:00?"

"That works. Everything okay by you?"

"I just denied a celebrity in our New York retail location the approval to buy a twenty thousand-dollar necklace."

Alan chuckled. "Really? Who?"

"Can't say, he has a horrible credit history. Screw him."

"So you were serious. Credit histories can kill a sale."

"That's why we check before we approve a sale like that to someone we don't know."

"Okay big brother, tell George Orwell I said hello."

"He sends hugs and kisses. See you at eleven. Take it easy." John ended the call.

Before Alan rose to his feet, he realized it was the first civilized conversation they had ever had with each other.

Dresden, Germany

Henrick left the train station and walked down the pedestrian thoroughfare, *Prager Strasse*. There was light foot traffic given it was the middle of the afternoon. He assumed at rush hour the bourgeoisie elite would turn out en masse to catch trains at the station behind him.

His hips ached while he walked and he retrieved a cigarette. Before he lit it he noticed the cafe where he was supposed to meet his old cohort. He slipped the cigarette back in the packet and walked into the small coffee house.

He asked for a table for two, sat down and looked at his watch. He was five minutes late and there was no sign of the man.

"May I take your order sir?"

"*Ja*. Turkish coffee, black."

"A pastry perhaps?"

"*Nein*." He waved him off and kept his eyes on the front door. He retrieved his cigarette and lit it. The nicotine felt wonderful as it passed over his wrinkled lips and coursed through his lungs.

A few minutes later he stubbed out his smoke, saw the waiter serve the coffee and turned to see Otto standing in the doorframe. He rose to his feet.

Otto provided a concerned look before the man reached to shake Henrick's hand. "Henrick. Hello there."

"Good to see you my old friend."

"Same here." Otto continued to stare before realizing he had yet to take a seat. "It's been years... a decade since we met. You've lost a lot of weight, are you well?"

"I have been better, then again, now I have something to look forward to."

Otto looked down to see the cigarette butt in the ashtray. "Is that yours?"

"Never mind the tobacco."

Otto hesitated when he took a close look at Henrick. He had aged well beyond his years since their last rendezvous. Deep wrinkles stretched across his forehead, his hair was thin and he was ghostly pale. The man he once knew was vibrant, full of energy and strong. He looked now like a cancer patient in the middle of chemotherapy treatments. "I'm concerned Henrick, you have not been taking care of yourself."

A scowl crossed Henrick's face. "Okay, I will take better care of myself, you on the other hand are as wide now as you are tall." He watched Otto look down at his belly. "We have more important matters to talk about."

Just then the waiter stepped over to take Otto's order. He took his leave and Henrick leaned forward. "They are coming back."

"The Devengers."

"The old man died, one of his grandsons, John Devenger, it appears he's entitled to it, so he thinks. Karla got word from our contact at the bank."

Otto shook his head. "I don't know about this, Henrick. I'm worried about you, and the others."

"Do you still have the weapons?"

"Of course I do. I take them to my gun club occasionally."

"We only need to threaten him, get the information we need to access the vault. You know how this works."

Otto sighed. "We tried that once. It did not turn out so well."

"We will do things differently this time."

Henrick spent the next ten minutes reviewing his plan with Otto. What it would entail, the money they would need and the bribe they had in place with the *Scheibzerische* bank official. He was thorough, but with so much at stake, it was no surprise to see Otto warming up to his ideas.

"I have reservations about our younger cohorts. Remember Josef?"

Henrick paused to think about their friend who died at the hands of Jack Devenger in 1983. "How can I forget?"

"The hotel hallway, by the elevators. He did not see it coming. His son, Fritz, he is now in his early thirties I think. When did you last see him?"

"When we all met, before Karla's father passed away."

"He called me five years ago. Do you know why?"

Henrick shook his head.

"He was incarcerated. He needed money for bail. He had no one to turn to, so he called me."

"You? Not a family member?"

"His mother died years ago, no one in his family complied." Otto placed his strong arms on the table. "He's got no one, I represented his last-ditch effort. He got caught up in the drug trade."

Henrick pursed his lips. "Should we cut him out?"

"That's my concern. A young man like that, we will likely need his help, given our age."

"I don't see why. We never made—"

"We are not young men, that's why. And I made a promise to his father. So did you."

Henrick watched Otto sit back in his chair.

He thought about the picture of his parents, and more importantly, his Father. His deceased relative was an army comrade with Otto's father in World War Two. They fought together in the Reich's army and survived the battles. They and two other comrades died near Feldkirch, Austria while trying to deliver a deposit to a vault in Switzerland. That possession represented their escape from desperation and poverty. The man who took what was theirs, and murdered their fathers, was named after inquiries were made with the bank: Everett Devenger.

Henrick nodded in agreement. They needed Fritz. He was a risk, but they needed the young man involved with their plans.

"What about the girl, Karla?" said Otto.

"Who is still very involved, how could she not be? She plans to wire the funds we need and then some. She passed along John Devenger's name to me two nights ago."

"Interesting. And the plans you have devised, the cost?"

Henrick tapped the table while his eyes turned to the window. "I conservatively estimate we'll need eighty thousand Euros."

"Dear God, rethink your plan then. She'll never agree to that figure."

"She has no choice, and that doesn't even cover the costs of her connections in the states."

Otto furrowed his brow. "How did you come up with that number?"

"A detached house in a quiet neighborhood, the van, private eyes in Europe. This will escalate quickly."

"You are going senile Henrick."

80

"Contact the private eyes I've reached out to, do some research, I have." Henrick waited before he lifted his hand. "Do you have the funds? I have no concern eliminating her from the process."

"Of course I do not!" Otto lowered his voice. "Scheisse."

"She has the means, you and I do not." Henrick retrieved a cigarette from his jacket and lit it. "We need her money, she needs our muscle."

Otto nodded. "There will be more than enough to go around if we're successful."

"*Ja.*" Henrick exhaled. "I will contact Fritz. Tell him what has transpired, remind the young man what it as stake." He exhaled a plume of smoke. "We will meet in Potsdam, and soon. When Devenger's grandson shows up, we will be ready."

Kiev, Ukraine

"They will be here any moment, Fritz."

He checked his watch. They were twenty minutes late. "Where are these bitches?"

"Things happen, I can't control them."

"You sure they got through airport security?"

"Yes, they called me."

"Good." He walked over to the window. The dimly lit street and grey slush made for an ugly setting. There were no signs of trouble and his car was parked thirty yards down the block.

"How much for the hotel room."

"Fifty rubles."

He opened his wallet and tossed several folded bills on the bed. "Rubles, not Hryvnia, figures. We'll be wiping our asses with one thousand dollar notes if they ever get here." He crossed the room and slowly opened the door. He peered down a long, dank and empty hallway.

He closed the door, leaned against the wall and retrieved a cigarette. He took a long drag and looked at the man he put in charge of the operation. "When is the other pair coming to town?"

"Two weeks."

"Straight from Pakistan this time?"

"Yes. We're planning to bring in three kilos."

Fritz nodded. He did the math in his head and figured if all went well, he'd make 20,000 rubles over the course of two trades.

The phone in the room rang and his young associate answered. "Send them up." He turned to look at the tall blond German. "Here we go."

Fritz crossed the floor to look out the window and check the front entrance to the hotel. An old man sauntered about and a Soviet-era car drove by. There was nothing else there to raise his suspicions.

A few minutes passed before they heard a knock at the door. Fritz watched as the young Russian man hurried two women of Indian descent into the room.

Fritz looked at the two women. They were short, ugly and fat around the waist: A perfect cover in the heroine trade.

"Okay, let's have it."

The women objected and asked for privacy in broken English. "Shut up and get in the bathroom then." Fritz pointed towards a door in the corner of the room.

When they closed the door behind them he turned to his associate. "Like I care if I see their fat little tits."

He laughed. "They are flat-chested you know. That's our product they are carrying, in their bras."

Fritz nodded in agreement. He lit another cigarette. He put his pack in his inner jacket pocket and nestled it beside a deadly piece of steel. Being reminded of the weapon comforted him.

When the women exited the bathroom, they were clothed and carried what looked like several brown disks covered in plastic. "Good then, put them on the bed." Fritz moved beside his cohort. They lifted the packages, squeezed them, felt the weight of it their hands.

Fritz tossed them back on the bed. "Good then." He retrieved two wads of cash from the side pockets of his jacket. He counted off a thousand U.S. dollars and gave them to one girl, then repeated the process. "You're going back in a few weeks' time?"

"Yes."

"No."

Fritz looked at the girl who refused. "Why no?"

"No go. Finished."

"Whatever. You," he pointed to the other girl. "Got another friend?"

"I... maybe, I don't know."

Fritz took out two hundred more dollars. "Find a friend. If you do, I'll give you five hundred more." He turned to his associate. "Let's get going."

He packed half the heroin within the left-inside sleeve of his jacket. Checking to make sure the button snaps were secure, Fritz whipped his arm downwards; the drugs were secure down length of his arm. His cohort did the same and he watched him gesture to the girls to stay. He pointed to his watch and held up ten fingers, and said, "Ten minutes, wait here," then followed Fritz.

The tall German opened the door, stepped out and turned to see two men start to walk towards his position. He immediately recognized the fat one. Shit.

"Fritz. Funny running into you here." The obese man grinned.

Fritz turned to face the men. "I'm not laughing. Stay there, Ivan."

He snapped his fingers and gestured with them to come closer. "Hand it over."

Fritz sensed his cohort moving to his left. He turned his head to say, "Stay put," then stepped towards his adversaries. "Time to chat? Okay, what the fuck do you want?"

"Product, hand it over. You picked the wrong side of town."

Fritz was five feet away. "Coming here is going to cost you." The German watched Ivan's companion put his hand in his pocket.

"Let's not escalate this, our bosses would not—"

Fritz's right fist landed square on Ivan's mouth. When he recoiled, the blond stepped towards the shorter one. He slammed his right boot into his left knee. He hit the wall and collapsed with a scream. A second later he launched over him and planted three hard jabs in the side of the man's skull. He patted his pockets but felt no weapon.

"Fritz! No!"

He jumped up, pivoted to face Ivan and used all his force to tilt the fat man further off center. They both crashed to the carpet. The floor shook when they landed.

Ivan turned to look at him and saw a pistol staring back. "Wrong fucking move, fat man."

"You are going to pay for this."

Fritz slammed the butt end of his weapon into Ivan's skull. His head flopped to the right but he was not out cold.

Fritz was on his feet a moment later. "Run!"

He stood up and turned to take flight. He saw the short man reach inside his inner jacket. Fritz neared the entrance to the staircase right before the first shot rang out. He didn't return fire.

He saw the stairs and double-timed them to climb down three flights. At the bottom and before the lobby door his partner waited for him. "That was stupid! They will kill us!"

"Shut up, catch your breath. Follow me."

Fritz shoved the lobby door open but saw no one. He heard someone yell behind a closed door. He gestured to move quickly.

They walked through the lobby and saw the front doors. They were closed.

"When we get outside, run to the car. Get it going."

"Okay."

"Let's go." Fritz kept the gun at his side. His partner exited first. When Fritz got outside the cold air hit him like a splash of ice-cold water.

He turned to see panic in the eyes of his comrade. "There!" He pointed to a black sedan outside the hotel.

Fritz turned to see a car with a man inside retrieving something from the glove compartment.

"Fuck." He pointed his gun but the man was not looking at him. He aimed the barrel at the front left tire and squeezed off two rounds. The man inside froze when he saw the gun directed towards him.

He yelled to his partner, "Go! Go! Go!"

They raced across the road. The car doors squeaked when they tossed them open.

"Drive!" screamed Fritz.

He rotated in the seat but the force of the car moving prevented him from sitting upright for a moment. He used his arms to keep from shifting when the car turned.

He looked back but no one else followed. He made eye contact with the man driving. "Holy shit!"

"What were you thinking? We're dead men now. They were Mafia!"

Fritz stopped to think about what transpired. "How did they find out about this?"

"I do not know."

"That's bullshit! Who did you talk to?" He felt satisfied when his young partner's look of horror told him what he had done. His head hit the seat's headrest and he exhaled. "Well, we got it."

"Where now?"

"Anywhere outside the city."

"We are going to face hell when they get word of this."

"That's not your problem, so shut the fuck up."

They drove for ten more minutes in silence to the outskirts of Kiev. By the time Fritz's cell phone rang, he felt weak as the adrenaline started to subside. He didn't recognize the number so he chose not to answer it.

"Is that Tomas? Shouldn't you take it?"

"No, it's not him." Fritz tapped his leg. "Wait, pull over." His cohort complied. "Let me check voicemail."

He did so and listened to the message. When he looked at his partner, he exuded a completely different expression. "Stay here, I have to make a call."

"Was it Tomas or not?"

"No. It was someone else." He stepped out of the vehicle and hit redial on his mobile phone. He closed the door behind him.

The young man sat in the car and observed Fritz's hyper gestures slow throughout the phone call. After several minutes, he was just standing on the corner of the street, frozen in time for a moment, before the arm that held the phone to his ear dropped to his side. He didn't know what to make of it.

Fritz stepped back to the car. "We have to go."

"Who was that?"

"A friend from Potsdam. A very old friend. I'll drop you off at home."

"Not... our other friends?"

"No."

They drove for twenty more minutes down decrepit streets. When they arrived at a lower-income housing complex, they both exited the vehicle.

Fritz stepped beside his partner. "I'll be gone for a while."

"Potsdam? Now, of all times."

"Something's come up."

"You're putting me in a serious situation."

Fritz nodded. "Yeah, I am. The timing fucking sucks." He checked the perimeter but there was no one in sight. "Here, take this." He handed over the drugs he carried and five hundred dollars in cash. "Do the trade, keep the money. It's yours. Keep the operation going."

"All of it?"

"It's yours. I'll be back in a few days. Don't fuck it up."

He hesitated before saying, "Okay. That helps, but what do I do if—"

"They won't. We sent them a message. We have others watching our back. I'll call the boss, they'll work it out." He gestured with his chin. "Go."

Fritz got back in his car and tore off down the street. He had flight and hotel reservations to make, and he'd have to make them under an assumed identity back in his home country of Germany.

Chapter 9

Pompton Plains, NJ

Alan's navigation system directed him to turn onto West End Avenue. The playlist on his iPhone, synced with Bluetooth technology to his car, featured Dave Brubeck on the eight-speaker sound system. The music did not match the scenery, which from the appearance looked like a working class neighborhood. The homes represented two-family row houses built side by side with little to no space between them. Rusty iron fences extended to the sidewalk and separated the buildings and driveways. With little to no landscaping, the area looked like a scene out of a black and white 1940's photograph taken on a cloudy day.

Alan read the home numbers and pulled up to the one where John lived. He parked the car, got out, and did a double take of the neighborhood. The sound of his car alarm rang out when he locked it. His casual loafers took him to a front door that was in serious need of a paint job.

He rang the bell but a moment later John opened the door and smiled. "That was quick," said Alan.

"I heard the car alarm and figured it was you. Come in."

Alan shrugged his shoulders and stepped into John's world. His steps echoed on the bare wood floor before they came to rest on a tan carpet. What looked like the living room was a cramped space sandwiched between a staircase and an entrance to another room on the right side of the house. It was decorated with the bachelor in mind and featured used couches, an old cathode-ray television and a half-eaten bowl of cereal on the coffee table.

"How long have you lived here?"

"Let me take your coat." John took it from him and hung it up on the coat rack beside the front door. "I've been here two years, after I got the job at Tiffany's. Have a seat." Alan complied. "It's bigger, nice to have a house, and the rent is reasonable."

"I see." Alan looked at him. "Work's going okay with you?"

"Yeah, the promotion helped." John watched Alan purse his lips and nod. His eyes canvassed the room. The expression on his face radiated with a look of judgment and one that seemed to disapprove of the surroundings. "Like it?"

"Like what?"

"The house."

"Oh, yes, very nice. Do you... own it?"

"No." He watched Alan sit down and open the issue of *National Geographic* before him. John withheld a snide comment as he watched Alan slowly turn from one page to the next.

"Great magazine. We compete with these guys occasionally."

"*GQ* competes with *National Geographic*?"

"For certain accounts, yes." He closed it and saw the image of Angkor Wat on its cover. He pointed to it. "Your travels took you here, yes?"

"They did. I spent six months in Southeast Asia."

"After college, that long vacation, I remember."

John chuckled. "Vacations are for fat old ladies. I did a walk about."

He held up his hands. "Pardon me."

John just shook his head. "Do you want to see something pretty cool, from that trip?"

"Sure."

"Follow me." John walked beneath the framed entrance beside the living room. Alan followed.

They were standing in the dining room and behind them was the entrance to the kitchen. John pointed to a beautiful wood cabinet on the far wall beyond a small table.

Alan stopped when he saw it. "Well that's a nice piece." It stood six feet tall. French glass doors enclosed the top half of it and several drawers housed the bottom portion. The hand-carved chestnut wood outlined glass panels and it curved with gentle lines from one side to the other. It was handsome from top to bottom, and compared to other pieces of furniture, it was the nicest piece in the house.

"Where did you get this?"

"It was handed down to me a few years ago. I restored it last year."

"Well done."

He watched his host open the glass-cabinet doors. "This is what I wanted to show you." John retrieved a black spherical-sized object that was the size of salad bowl. The sides of the object curved from the bottom to a six-inch diameter opening at the top.

John handed it to Alan and it weighed close to five pounds.

"This is a handful."

"That sir is an alms bowl. It is part of a ritual in the Buddhist faith, and it's important to the religion in many ways. Every day at sunrise, in villages across Southeast Asia, Buddhist monks make their way from home to home in the community and the people provide them with food. Rice, in particular. They receive their sustenance every day, week in and week out, from villagers. Their entire existence relies on the community, which provides for them while they are studying at the Wat, or their temple. I got up a few mornings, watched them trail around the neighborhood and witnessed dozens of people giving them food."

"Amazing."

He took the bowl back from Alan. "They rely on one another. The monks supply spiritual guidance, and the community provides sustenance and support. It's a beautiful relationship."

Alan didn't know what to say. He nodded and provided John with a genuine smile. It was an expression John had rarely ever witnessed.

"Not what you expected, Alan?"

"Not at all. Impressive. Where else have you traveled of late?"

"Nowhere in the past few years. I have to put some roots down. I've got something for you."

John walked back into the living room and opened the drawer in the coffee table. He picked up Everett's journal and handed it to Alan. "It's all yours to read."

Alan's eyes grew wide. "You read the whole thing?"

"It didn't take long. Pretty wild stuff. Wait until you read about the boat back home from Europe. Some bad news I'm afraid. No insight into

Switzerland, not a word, just a note at the end about switching to another journal."

"Locations? Nothing?"

"Nothing." John watched while Alan flipped through the pages. "I checked it thoroughly."

"I heard you the first time."

John gestured to Alan to take a seat. Alan's eyes barely left the pages he held in his hands. "Have you figured out those contingency plans you mentioned at Everett's house, Alan?"

"Work kept me from it, unfortunately." He kept turning page after page. "This... this is truly remarkable. This journal I mean, the fact we have it."

"Can you put the book down for a minute?" Alan complied. "Look, I have to insist on one element of this trip, and I know you're not in favor of it."

Alan exhaled and sat down on the couch. "What?"

"If we get into any trouble over there, I want to be armed. It's not worth the risk."

"Jesus Christ."

"Just hear me out." John sat forward in the chair beside the couch. "What happens if we run into the same people our father ran into?" Alan stared forward without saying a word. "Doesn't that bother you?"

Alan exhaled. "If you share the name of the bank with me, I can manage this myself."

"That's not going to happen. Look, why don't—"

"I can go," his voice trailed off, "I can call you when I get there."

John paused and sat back in the chair. "I've got a friend over there who can lend me a handgun, otherwise I'm not going." He watched Alan turn to look at him. "No bank, no vault and no deal."

Alan cocked his head. "No deal. Really."

"Sorry, those are my terms."

Alan stood up and stepped away from the couch. He put his hands on his hips. "This is outrageous." John remained silent. "I'm taking orders from credit checker."

"What was that?"

"So if I do not comply, we'll never find out what's in the vault."

"That pretty much sums it up, yes."

Alan dropped his arms and tapped the side of his leg. "Okay then, if we're negotiating, I'll put my cards on the table." He retrieved his iPhone from his pocket. He thumbed through a few pages, nodded, and then turned to face John. "It's April 6th. We're leaving in three weeks. We will fly out on Wednesday the 24th and fly home on Saturday the 27th."

John placed his elbows on his legs and leaned forward. "Three weeks from now?"

"Yes."

"So... It's actually less than three weeks away. I don't know if I can get time off from work that quickly."

"That's what I can do scheduling wise. I've got three business trips in May coming up."

"Why not, I don't know... plan it for June?"

"Because I want this to be over and done with as soon as possible." Alan stepped forward. "I don't like the fact I have a distant relative forcing demands on me."

"Come on."

"I don't like the fact we're going to be at greater risk with a gun than without. And for the record, if you're thinking of bringing it to the bank with us, you can forget it."

John nodded. "Yeah, I know, but other times we'll have it."

"Who's lending you the weapon?"

"A buddy from France I met while backpacking overseas. His name is Francois."

"Francois." Alan crossed his arms. "Really, a guy named... Francois."

"Yes, is that a problem?"

A slow chuckle emanated from Alan. "This is going to be riot." Alan rubbed the sides of his head. "Okay, onwards. We need contingency plans."

"Any ideas?"

"Yeah. I'm going to take a day off from work this week to figure it out. All we really need is to have shipping options on hand when we find out what's in the vault."

"Do you want me to look into it too?"

"That's okay, I'll manage." Alan had no desire to involve John any more than he had to. "One thing that came to mind is what happens if we bring it home immediately. There could be tax implications, we may need an attorney, or an accountant, depending on what we find."

"Okay, I'm following."

Alan nodded. "I think we should ship whatever we find to England. We can store it there, find a secure location. And flying it out, if we find something that's rather large, I can see this escalating significantly from a cost perspective."

"Why not Ireland, or we cross the border to Spain or something?"

"Honestly, I'm concerned about language barriers and the business culture on mainland Europe. I think we'll have better security options in London."

"Seems like a smart option."

"Good." Alan paused for a moment and wondered if it was the first thing they had ever agreed to since becoming adults. "I'll call in sick one day, I could use the break."

John nodded. "Good then. I'll check flights as well, and call my friend."

The two shared a compliant look. Alan returned to the couch and settled into the deep and broken-in cushions.

"Oh, and by the way, I called the bank. Just to double check if we needed anything else."

Alan's leaned forward and turned to look at John. "Come again?"

"I called the bank. It would suck to get over and find out we're missing something." John didn't understand his brother's puzzled expression. "Identification or what not. Right?"

His brother shook his head and said, "I have to go."

"What's the fucking problem now?"

Potsdam, Germany

He held his hands behind his back and walked towards the wall near the apartment's front door. The floorboards creaked beneath his feet. He stopped when he was a few feet away from the picture frames.

Henrick sighed and picked up the black and white picture of his father in uniform. He ran his arthritic finger down the glass and across his face. He wished he had survived the war to raise him, given his reputation for being strong and authoritative. He knew for certain his situation in life would have improved had he lived.

His eyes turned to another picture of his deceased father and mother. He was in uniform and their eyes were both warm and inviting. She was a proud officer's wife, and given his senior rank, he would have retired in comfortable fashion.

But that retirement never happened, and the wealth his father was entitled to fell into the hands of an American G.I.

He thought about what his mother had told him when he was a teenager, and what transpired in the months leading up to the war's end. There was no doubt the Reich was going to fall, despite Hitler's wishes. Russians were pouring through the flat lands of Poland and the Americans had crossed the Rhine. It was only a matter of time, and those in authority knew they had to set themselves up for lives after the war. That involved the procurement of wealth and options before the Americans and Russians converged on Berlin.

His mother, at the time, spoke about the conversations she shared with Henrick's father, what they planned to do and what was necessary. German officers were starting to make arrangements for lives outside of uniform and Henrick's parents did the same. Many Nazi officials were opening private Swiss bank accounts, and three of his father's cohorts agreed to a plan during the winter of 1945.

Unbeknownst to the allies, resources and treasure were streaming into the mountains of Austria in what was billed as the last Nazi holdout. The plan, had it transpired, was to use the mountains as a last stand against the Allied drive. SS officers like his father had a role to play in those plans, with one divergence: A jaunt to Switzerland would be made with the holdings procured by four German SS officers. That plan ended in disaster, but the knowledge of what they planned to deposit, and the vault details, were shared with the wives in each family.

The families made attempts to access the vault after the war, but Everett Devenger had changed the passcode and signed over access to the vault to himself, and no one else. The families did not have the means to take legal action, but given their newfound poverty, they made sure to pass along details of Vault 21-12 to future generations. That, in turn, led to Henrick and Otto's involvement, along with two other cohorts who had since passed. The children of the deceased, Karla and Fritz, were now entitled to their family's portion, and Henrick knew he needed their help.

He turned to walk back into the living room when he heard his home phone ring. "*Ja*," he said.

"Did you receive the wire transfer?"

He recognized the young woman's voice. "Karla, my dear, I did indeed." He grinned. "I pray it will not be the last."

"And I received your text, why are you requesting another twenty thousand Euros?"

He crossed his legs. "It is time to provide you with the details. We have many things to put in place. I will be in Bern this weekend. I have an appointment with a real estate agent."

"Considering the fact you're spending my money, and not yours... yes, perhaps you should give me the update."

He picked up a pack of cigarettes and lit one with a silver lighter. "Just remember, dear Karla," he exhaled a plume of smoke, "You do not have the means or the stomach to manage this, which is why you will get nothing without my help." She started to speak but he cut her off. "Silence... now listen."

He spent the next twenty minutes explaining what they would need, the costs of each element, and he asked about the private eye in New Jersey. He remained focused on the end result when Karla expressed discomfort, which in his words, 'would justified the means.' Henrick had no doubt the information he was passing along to her made her uncomfortable, which he used to his advantage throughout the conversation. It helped to position him as the man in authority, despite the fact the young *fraulein* was financing the entire operation.

The alternative scenario, which was to cut her out of her share, would require every last penny he owned and it would leave holes in the plan. He kept that to himself when he approached the final financial figure he was ready to share with her. "So we will need eighty thousand total, not including the five thousand Euros I plan to give Heinzen."

"That is outrageous!"

"Do you have any suggestions then?"

"Have you shared this with Otto?"

"Indeed, I will bring Fritz up to speed when he arrives. Perhaps he has cash, I do not know."

He listened to her speak at length in Portuguese, which he could not understand. "Karla, settle down... Karla!"

"You have to work with less."

"If I leave out our Spanish private eye, that saves twenty thousand, but I would seriously advise against it."

"How do you know we even need him?"

"I won't until we do, and then it will be too late. You understand we need eyes and ears on this side of the world, yes?" Henrick heard her sigh. "And they will be able to monitor their movements, their transactions and such."

"Are they competent?"

He retrieved another cigarette. "Very. We used them back in the day when I was a Stasi officer. I can assure you they won't let me down."

"I will wire you thirty thousand then, the rest will come at a time of my choosing."

He nodded. "This plan covers every angle. We will secure Vault 21-12 for ourselves." Henrick felt the chill in his chest dissipate when he gave thought to what was waiting for them inside the bank. "Wire me the money when the banks open on Monday in Brazil. I'll find an appropriate dwelling and it will be in my name by week's end."

Chapter 10

<u>Upper West Side, Manhattan</u>

Alan looked at the clock after the buzzer sounded. It read 7:20 a.m. He rubbed his face and sat up in his bed. He grabbed his smartphone on the bedside table and turned to his calendar. The only meetings he had for the day represented a budget meeting, two candidate interviews and low-priority internal meetings.

He texted the following to his assistant:

UNFORTUNATE NEWS, DOWN SICK WITH A STOMACH BUG, WILL BE WORKING FROM HOME. PLEASE RESCHEDULE MY APPOINTMENTS.

That was all that was required for him to take a sick day. He turned off the device, put on his bathrobe and walked into the kitchen to start the coffee machine.

When he stepped out of the bedroom, Vix was by his side and crying. "I know girl, I know." He looked at the coffee pot but knew what his first priority would be for the day.

He threw on some clothes and grabbed the dog leash.

***

He concluded the call on cell phone and put it down on his desk. He exhaled and rubbed his face with both hands.

His day started with the urge for a tall cup of coffee, and it ended with an even stronger desire for a tall glass of single-malt scotch. Alan turned to look at the notes he took while preparing for the trip and each contingency.

Flights – Lufthansa, direct to Geneva, 4/24 – 4/28, $2,700
Car – Avis, BMW 1-Series - $101 per day
Hotel – Bellevue, $1,600 per night, two rooms

Contingencies
DHL – Retail location in Bern. Weight max – 80 lbs.
Curator – May need… two days. $3,000 per day, packaging not
           Included. Pay on arrival
Security transport/truck to Neuchatel, $5,000, paid, refundable

Air Transport – Recommended, Neuchatel airport to London
           $15,000 nonrefundable deposit paid, $50,000 total
    NOTE – Need storage in London – FOUND, Chelsea Storage,
           $400 per month, refundable.
    NEED – Secure transport from airport and storage –
           Whitingham Security - Paid $3,000, refundable.

    REVISED – Flights, fly out Tuesday for extra time. Same rate,
           Lufthansa 4/23 – 4/28 – 3 business days in Bern.

    Costs paid: Flights -$2,700
                  Car, 5 days – $505
                  Hotel, 4 nights – $6,400
                  Secure transport, Bern - $5,000 (refundable)
                  Air Transport deposit - $15,000 (non-refundable)
                  Secure transport, London - $3,000 (refundable)
                  Storage, London - $400 1st month (refundable)

TOTAL PAID, NON REFUNDABLE - $24,605
REFUNDABLE - $8,400
W/ AIR FREIGHT, TOTAL - $68,005

He sat back in his chair and exhaled. He felt a tremendous sense of relief and smiled: there was no question as to whether or not they would be prepared.

The relief he felt dissipated when he tallied the total cost of the trip, not including the Curator or DHL shipment options. The total figure could exceed $68,000 when all was said and done. Alan did not believe John would feel as comforted as he did.

He picked up his phone, dialed John's work number and waited for him to answer. "It's Alan."

"Hey there."

"It's done. Everything is booked."

"You booked my ticket? Shit, I have miles and—"

"No. Everything is booked. All of the contingency plans we spoke about."

There was a long pause on the phone. "You planned everything? When?"

"Today, I've been going non-stop since 7:30 this morning."

"Wow, that's great."

Alan cleared his throat. "You'll need to take Wednesday the 24th off as well."

"Oh, okay. So what's the damage?"

Here we go, Alan said to himself. A review of the plans and costs left John speechless. "John? Are you there?"

"Are you fucking serious! You spent twenty... twenty four thousand dollars?"

"That's what all the contingency plans required."

"You have got to be shitting me!"

Alan listened to John spew epithets with reckless abandon. At one point he pulled the phone away from his ear and sighed. When the man ceased to speak he placed the phone back against his ear. "Are you done?"

"What happened to the ten thousand dollar budget, asshole?"

"Gone. Look, I made the best decisions possible for the contingencies we agreed to. Back off."

"I don't have that much money on hand. It's... tied up in retirement funds."

"You know what John? Tough shit! Get over it. Pack up and be at Newark Airport by 5:00 p.m. on the 23rd. I'll talk to you later." He ended

---

the call.

He stood up from the desk. "Imbecile!" he yelled. Vix snapped her head up out of concern and Alan turned to look the other way.

He stepped away to walk towards the kitchen but then stopped dead in his tracks. He turned to look at the computer screen and saw Google's home page in the browser. He stared at it for a long time before he sat down before it.

He typed into the search bar, BANKS IN BERN SWITZERLAND, then clicked on MAPS.

Thirty-five banks were highlighted on the map of the city. He spent twenty minutes reviewing them. He picked up his phone but paused when he thought through the scenario in his head. He held the phone for a minute, looking at it.

He had two options: Call his boss, take an emergency leave the following week for what he could call family-related matters, or go through with the original plan.

One person, who was no longer a part of his life, haunted him every time the phone inched closer to his ear. His love for Everett stopped him from going through with the idea, but in his heart he knew he'd never share the same relationship with his half-brother.

Chapter 11

"Do you find these accommodations adequate, Herr Henrick?"

The old man turned to look at the real estate agent and smiled. "I appreciate your patience. It has been a long day. How far did you say we were from downtown Bern?"

"Ten kilometers at best. It is an older home, but well maintained and affordable. Does this provide the privacy you desire?"

"It is indeed private." He looked out the window and trees blocked the view to a nearby home. "The cellular reception. I have business clients whom I work with on a daily basis."

"What about it?"

"Is there reception?"

"I have no idea sir, check your phone." The realtor appeared weary after spending the entire day with the old man. The home they were in was the eighth one they had visited.

Henrick retrieved the new cell phone he had leased from a German mobile company. He did in fact have reception. "Very good." He then clasped his hands together behind his back and walked to look out another window.

It was a simple structure that met all the necessary requirements. Privacy was an imperative and the closest house was an acre away. The two-car garage was attached to the house itself, which would play a critical role in the process. The first floor consisted of bedrooms and the second floor represented the living space.

He turned, wheezed out a cough, and then looked at the agent. "This will do fine."

"Excellent. It is unoccupied at the moment and furnished as you can see. When would you like to commit?"

Henrick was not about to take any chances. "Immediately."

"You want to occupy this today?"

"By tomorrow's time, can that be arranged?"

"I am unsure, I did not know you needed it so quickly."

"I can pay the entire six months in advance. What else is required?"

"The security deposit of course." He used his mobile phone to tally up the total cost. "Fourteen thousand, five hundred Euros."

"Fine. Please see to it that the paperwork is ready to sign. I can stop by your office tomorrow morning."

"Wonderful. Staying in town tonight then?"

"Indeed. I have an old acquaintance to catch up with." Henrick provided his host with a wrinkled grin.

Parsippany, New Jersey

He wrote down the name of the town after Francois repeated it and spelled it for him. "Okay, we'll grab a bite when we meet. I really appreciate what you're doing for me."

"No problem, I'm excited for you, John. Looking forward to meeting your stuck-up brother."

"Ha, yeah, I think you may fall in love with him. I'll email you the night prior."

"Okay. *Au revoir* my friend!"

He put the phone back in the cradle and felt relieved about what his friend would supply him after they landed in Switzerland. He could not wait to see the look on Alan's face.

He took out the paper that noted Larry Goldstein's phone number. He dialed and spoke to a receptionist for a moment before his call was transferred.

"Hello, this is Larry."

"Hi, Larry, this is John Devenger, we met at Everett's funeral."

"How can I forget? How are you?"

"Good thanks. Hey, I was speaking with Charlotte the other day. I believe you worked with her on Everett's Mattituck estate?"

"I did indeed, she was very nice to work with. Your grandfather as well, he was a great guy."

"Thanks. I wanted to connect with you on something."

"What can I do you for?"

John lowered his voice and leaned forward on his desk. "I... well, Alan and I actually, we wanted to see if it made sense to have legal representation here in the states."

"What's this all about?"

John paused and gave thought about what the lawyer did and did not know. "I'm not sure how to ask this. Do you have experience with, or rather, have you worked with clients who have inherited items overseas?"

"Yes. What is it?"

"I can't share that at this time, but we think it would be wise to have legal counsel on hand."

"My God, you Devengers and your secrets! Sealed videotapes and now this? So you want to hire me to represent both of you?"

"If you're experienced in these matters, yes."

"And you'll call me after you know what this is all about?"

"In a few weeks. We'll know more."

"Okay, I'll send you and Alan some documents to sign. I charge two hundred and fifty an hour."

"Come again?"

"My fee. Is that an issue?"

It took a moment for John to answer. "Seems... reasonable. I'll speak to you soon."

"Very well then, goodbye."

John put the phone down and decided to email Alan later. It was a warm day outside and he decided some fresh air would do him good. He stood up and caught Padinni's eye. "Back in a minute." She nodded.

***

He put the doughnut down on the passenger seat of his car when he saw the bald man exit the building. His right hand grabbed the Canon EOS 5D, complete with an EF 400mm lens, and trained his sights on him.

It took a third of a second for the lens to focus and two seconds later, he had 15 high-res pictures of John Devenger. He checked the LCD screen and smirked.

He watched the man walk in the opposite direction of the Subaru he owned. Gus Sluberski zoomed in but he could only see his back.

It was the second full day he had observed his subject. He had to place listening devices into the walls of his home, and he knew he would have to orchestrate a break in to tap his computer. Having visited the row house the day prior, he wondered if the man had the means to afford a personal computer. He knew it would be nearly impossible to hack a Tiffany-supplied laptop, and one assigned to a fraud manager.

John Devenger continued to walk away from his position on the road adjacent to the office building. He put down his camera and tapped his steering wheel. He didn't know why the young and affluent Brazilian had such a keen interest on this particular Devenger, but given all the jobs he'd taken over the years, he knew something was coming to a head.

He had a week to arrange everything, and if all went according to plan, he'd receive the final installment of fifteen thousand dollars. It was a lucrative proposition, to say the least.

Bern, Switzerland

Henrick finished his meal, left a paltry tip and retrieved his cell phone from his pocket before he left. He opened and found the email message with the address he was looking for and turned to the Maître d'. "Where is *Schanzistrasse?*" He received instructions and walked out of the restaurant.

He spent ten minutes walking down the long and empty street before he turned left at a road called *Moserstrasse*. He walked to the number of the building, climbed the stoop's stairs and pressed the buzzer next to the name he was looking for: HEINZEN.

"Who is this?" said the man.

"It is Henrick Kohl. I need to see you."

"It's 10:00 o'clock at night."

"Your clock works, congratulations. Get down here."

Henrick waited patiently on the building's stoop for several minutes.

When he turned to press the buzzer again he saw a figure of a man walk down the steps. His expression was not pleasant when he opened the door wide enough to speak.

"What the hell are you doing here?"

"Do you want to get paid or not?"

"Now? How in God's name did you get my home address?"

"Does it really matter?" Henrick retrieved an envelope from his pocket. "Here is the money we agreed to pay you, plus two thousand additional Euros."

"Seven thousand then."

"Correct."

The short man with a skinny mustache paused. "Why would you pay me a higher fee?"

Henrick handed him the envelope. "You are going to delay John Devenger if and when he gets to the bank."

"I will not. I gave you the information, that's all that was required. We're finished."

"I don't think so."

"This is ridiculous." He took the envelope, opened it and thumbed through the cash. "Here, take two thousand back."

Henrick took a step back. "Delay him for one day, then we're done."

"I told you it's over."

"One day, or there's going to be trouble. Enjoy the money, Heinzen." He turned and walked down the stoop.

"I cannot do that!"

"Shut up. We'll be in touch."

Henrick walked down the block as quickly as he could. When he was a block away, he opened his phone and forwarded the email from the private investigator to Otto, then dialed his mobile number.

Dresden, Germany

He saw the name 'HENRICK' on his cell phone after he heard it buzz. He opened the phone to answer the expected call. "Yes Henrick."

"Our friend may need encouragement, but he took the money."

"All of it?"

"Yes. I forwarded the email from the private investigator to you. Call him tonight."

"Very well then." He ended the call and accessed his email account on the phone itself. He saw Henrick's recent email, opened it and found Heinzen's phone numbers, home address and miscellaneous facts about the man.

He scrolled over the bank director's home number and clicked to call him. He answered it on the third ring. "Yes, may I please speak to Herr Heinzen?"

"Who is calling me at this hour?"

"I am calling to see if this friend of mine is still in critical condition, at the hospital. I assume it is not you of course."

"You must have the wrong—"

"Heinzen. I heard he had a terrible spill." Otto paused before continuing. "Perhaps you know him? The doctors say he has excellent insurance, thankfully."

"You have some nerve."

"If you have the chance, tell our mutual friend to take his medicine. Otherwise, God knows what will happen. Perhaps you can tell him yourself, does he still live at 723 *Schanzistrasse*?"

The line went dead a moment later.

Otto looked at his watch and decided it was time to go to bed. He polished off the last sip of schnapps in his glass and set his phone alarm to 7:00 am. This would give him enough time to pack his car in the morning and make it to the location of his rifle club. Fritz would be there at 10:00 a.m. to receive a refresher course in how to use the firearms Otto possessed and planned to have on hand in Bern.

Chapter 12

Dresden, Germany

Otto paced beside his car in the parking lot and checked his watch. The man he waited for was twenty minutes late, and he felt more and more apprehension as the time passed. He was not worried about the contents in the trunk of his car, which would concern most people. Otto concerned himself with the young man himself, Fritz. His young cohort had one hell of a reputation.

Back in 1945, Otto's mother, as well as three other wives, received the postal note weeks after their father's bodies were found. Their corpses had apparently been dragged and tossed off the side of a hill. Otto was old enough to remember his father in uniform, and the fact he was killed prompted him to sigh.

Fritz Senior, Otto, Henrick and Gustav represented the children of the officers killed near the border. Fritz Senior, Otto's friend since childhood, died in 1983 when the four of them confronted Jack Devenger. Tipped off on his arrival, their first attempt to obtain what was hidden in the vault failed when they confronted the man in the hallway of a hotel in Bern.

Otto recalled the scuffle, the pistol flying out of his hand and then the briefcase slamming against the face. He fell to the ground, and from a sideways vantage point, he watched Jack Devenger pummel Fritz Senior. He impaled him with kicks and slammed his briefcase on the base of the man's skull. By the time Otto got to his feet, Devenger had escaped and Fritz Senior was dead. They hunted the bastard down, who refused to give up the vault, and later that evening Jack Devenger was nothing more than a highway-death statistic. The incident left Fritz's wife, now widowed, and her only son to make it on their own in the world.

He promised himself that would never happen again, which explained his visit to the gun range, and the contents in the trunk of his car. Otto would not rely solely on one weapon.

Fritz Senior's demise prompted the question about what to do if they were able to secure the contents of Vault 21-12. Fritz Senior's widow screamed for answers: Why did her husband die, what would happen to her family and what was in the vault. They had no choice but to tell her, and it was Otto who swore to avenge the man's death, and made assurances that his deceased friend's wife would receive his family's fair share.

By 1995, things had changed. Fritz Junior was raised in absence of a strong German father and evolved into a disillusioned young man. Bearing the same first name of his father, it was the only thing he had in common with the deceased. Drug use, disobedience, a connection to skinheads and gang crime—the time he spent in jail only exacerbated his bad behavior. Fritz Junior was a morally and ethically bankrupt young man.

Otto thought about his childhood during those horrible post-war years in East Germany. His history was not as pure as the driven snow, but he had never been associated with skinheads, drugs or incarceration. The man he waited for was bringing that baggage with him. He assumed Fritz's involvement with drugs did not abate after his release from prison, and there were rumors he was involved with the Russian Mafia. He knew Fritz spent significant time in Kiev, but other than that, he knew little about the man.

When Fritz's mother passed away, and Gustav died from cancer a year later, the three men got together to discuss the vault. With Gustav out of the picture, his daughter Karla inquired about her father's share. She reminded them of the financial assistance he had provided over the years, and the relationship she had become privy to. It was her father who managed the relationship with the Private Banking Manager, Heinzen. She agreed to keep up the relationship and maintain the ongoing bribe her family paid in exchange for one fourth of the vault's contents. The men had limited financial means and no connection to Heinzen, so they agreed to let Karla in on the action.

Until they received a tip on the vault, they were forced to wait it out until Henrick received word from Karla. When the opportunity presented itself, the four of them agreed to do what was required to secure what their fathers had taken for themselves at the war's end.

Otto's plan for the day was to introduce Fritz to the weapons, ensure the man's shortcomings would not interfere with the plan and if necessary, eliminate him from the process. They needed the muscle and energy of a young man, however they would not involve themselves with a psychopath.

Otto noticed a handful of other cars, which provided him with some level of relief. He took comfort knowing other members would be present. An Audi turned into the entrance. He watched as the car drove past, circled around him like a shark, and came to rest one parking spot away from Otto's Mercedes.

He watched the young man exit the vehicle. His eyes searched the perimeter for someone or something. Finally he turned and smirked. "I didn't realize how much weight you'd gained."

"And unfortunately you're not any smarter." The two walked towards each other without sharing a smile. The young man wore designer jeans, a black leather jacket, and calf-high black boots.

"Is this legit?"

"Pardon?"

"This Devenger guy. The whole thing, are you confident Henrick didn't screw up?"

"I'm confident this is going to happen. Otherwise I wouldn't be here."

"This better not be a fucking waste of my time."

"Calm down." Otto sensed things were already going south. "Henrick and I, we've been waiting decades for this to happen. We have to be ready to go at a moment's notice. You know the drill."

Fritz waved him off with his hand and stepped away. "What do we know about John Devenger?"

"We discovered that his grandfather passed away three weeks ago, and based on a call he made to the bank recently, John Devenger is the obvious beneficiary."

"So Johnny boy is coming back for the goods his grandfather left behind. Sounds too easy."

"You can either get with the program or get back in your car and leave. We'll cut you out of your share." Otto said this before realizing the guns he had brought were stowed in the trunk of his car. He worried Fritz, who was several inches taller, might physically confront him.

"Whatever. So we're here, let's see what you have."

Otto turned and opened the trunk. Before him was a dark green crate, minus the lock he used to keep it safe in the basement of his home. "When was the last time we saw one another, ten years ago?" Shots rang out from afar. Fritz jerked his head to the location from whence it came.

"Yeah man, maybe eight."

"Before your time in prison then." Fritz turned and sneered at the fat man. "Just putting the pieces together, Fritzy."

"Don't call me Fritzy." Fritz groaned from the weight of the trunk. "Jesus."

Otto chuckled for a moment. "Use two hands." Fritz did as he was told. The two struggled for a moment to free the one hundred-pound container from the trunk of the car. "Are you still running around with skinheads?"

"What the fuck's in here man? A tank?"

The two lumbered as they carried the tank. "Skinheads, yes or no."

"What? No, that was years ago. They don't do shit anyway. Boring."

"No chums with swastikas on their foreheads? How about heroin addicts?"

"You don't know me old man, a lot's happened since those days, so back off."

Otto let go of the handle of the trunk and it slammed on the ground. Fritz stumbled as he moved out of the way, trying not to trip over it. "Watch it!"

"No, you watch it." Otto stepped closer to the man. "We've waited a long time for this. I don't need a little drug-peddling shithead to screw everything up. Henrick and I wondered if we should involve you, now I'm second guessing myself." Otto stepped closer to Fritz. "You know what is behind that vault door. We will not take unnecessary risks, and right now, you are one."

Fritz put his hands on his hips. His expression was one of annoyance mixed with acceptance.

"We need someone who can use their head and a gun. If I can't count on you for this, then I have to know right now."

"Okay." Fritz put his hands up.

"Are you certain?"

"Yes, alright already. You have my word."

Otto gave a quick nod before they made their way into the one-story structure. Otto greeted the manager, signed some papers and motioned for Fritz to continue walking towards an exit across the room.

They stepped outside to see a row of parallel firing positions stretching fifty yards in the distance. Several people were reviewing their firearms.

Otto kept an eye on him. He seemed clear-headed, alert and not intimidated by members firing weapons. On some level it provided Otto with confidence that Fritz was not a lunatic. They continued to walk down the path in silence to the last firing station.

The station was not large but was covered by a small roof to protect them from the elements. To their immediate left was an area of ground covered with what looked like a green artificial turf.

"Over there." Otto directed Fritz to the area where he wanted to put the crate. His young cohort grunted a few more times before the crate came to a rest. "Good." He tapped the top of it and stepped in front of the three by four-foot wide container.

"That's some heavy shit."

"Open it."

"I'll let you manage. These are not my weapons."

Otto sighed and walked around the crate and opened the hinged top. It squeaked when opened. Fritz looked in and saw a tan blanket covering the top surface on the contents. Otto removed it and tossed it on the far side of the artificial turf.

Fritz noticed the contents were neat, well organized and appeared to be in exceptional condition. Two pistols were nestled inside foam, cut to the exact dimensions of the guns themselves. Tiny grey nodes of foam extended upwards and away from the base. There were two ammunition boxes placed in the foam as well. One was red with white trimming and the other one looked older, yellow and made of plastic.

"Two Walther PP pistols. Their range is 20 yards at most, the magazine holds 10 rounds. These provide basic protection, good of course to use as a threat, and concealable." Otto handed one to Fritz and placed the other on the AstroTurf.

Fritz felt the weight of the two-pound weapon. He removed the magazine, checked the barrel, and snapped it all together again before taking aim with it towards the target range beyond.

"You have experience with this kind of weapon?"

Fritz turned to Otto. "I own a Glock nine millimeter."

"A requirement for... your line of work?"

Fritz answered the question with an unpleasant look.

"These are the not the only weapons we will use today. Place it down."

Otto reached behind the foam at each corner where it intersected with the crate. He untethered four snaps that were attached to the wooden shelf that held the soft material. He fumbled around to get a grip on the wood, lifted it, and removed what turned out to be the first layer of storage. Fritz walked behind Otto to see what was beneath it.

Otto grabbed a larger pistol from the crate.

"The Beretta nine millimeter, complete with a silencer. This one takes a bit of handling." He handed the weapon to Fritz. The silencer resulted in a far heavier handgun. The barrel was nine inches in length.

"A silencer, impressive. I could use this back home."

"Without the silencer, the range is close to thirty. Keep that in mind. With it, one can direct fire from fifteen feet at best. This is our most discreet weapon."

Fritz rotated the gun in his hand. "This is some serious shit. Where did you get these?"

"That is not your concern. I have another weapon to show you."

The third layer contained a significantly larger and more deadly weapon. "Holy fucking shit." Fritz was staring at a submachine gun.

"The MP40, also referred to as the *Schmeisser*."

"This cannot be legal. What the hell are you doing with it?"

"I told you not to concern yourself with these things."

"You brought me out here man, I'm not getting arrested again, not over this." Fritz started to back away from the crate.

"Silence." Otto stepped closed to the young man. "You don't

understand. I'm a member at this gun club, I've shot all of these here before. There's nothing illegal taking place. You have my word."

"Tell me where you got the machine gun then."

Otto turned his head, looked back and sighed. "They were my father's. The *Schmeisser*. The Walther PP's. He knew he needed them to protect his family after the war."

"You're going to bring those to Switzerland?"

"Yes."

"We need a submachine gun?"

"You were not there in eighty three, you didn't see what happened."

Fritz shook his head. "This is some fucked up shit."

Otto turned to face down range. "If we all had weapons with us originally, your father would likely have survived the encounter with Jack Devenger. I'm sorry about that, we were naive and foolish."

Fritz nodded. "I see." He stepped over and took a close look at the weapon.

"It was an accident. That I can assure you. And when we caught up with Jack Devenger, we finished him. That's why we need you to understand how to use these weapons. To protect each other," Otto removed the submachine gun from the crate. He held it waist high and gripped the magazine that extended down from the front half of the heavy weapon. "These weapons, my membership here, it is safe." He reached down and exchanged the empty magazine in the weapon for one that held thirty rounds. He snapped it in place and confirmed the safety switch was latched. "We will fire these today, you will be prepared when the time comes."

Fritz looked at the fat man holding the machine gun and started to chuckle.

"Is something funny?"

"You are one crazy fucker, Otto."

Otto proceeded to show Fritz how to properly handle each of the four weapons. Targets were arranged at varying distances to test range and accuracy. Otto went further and explained how to correct each weapon in the event it misfired. He illustrated how the submachine gun, in particular, could be tricky to operate and was sensitive to dirt and dust.

During the process, Fritz expressed surprise at how quiet the Beretta was when used with the silencer. The short and brief 'quip' of sound impressed him. He found himself smiling throughout the process.

Otto lifted the *Schmeisser* off the AstroTurf. "I will show you how to properly discharge the weapon." He aimed the submachine gun downrange. "Short bursts only. Watch." When the gun fired, the bullets hurtled themselves down range. The valley echoed from the rattling sound. Each time he fired, he limited the rounds to three or four bursts at a time.

"That was incredible!"

Otto grinned. "Yes. That it is. It is your turn to handle the weapon."

Otto placed his ear protection squarely against his ears. Fritz fixed his eye on the bull's eye thirty yards away and pulled the trigger for half a second.

That half-second of time thundered as ten rounds exploded from the barrel, short white flames illuminated from the far end of the weapon. It sounded like a massive chainsaw churning into the trunk of a tree. He tapped it again and the recoil shuffled him back several inches. Beyond in the distance, a haze of dirt and dust peppered the ground behind the target, but nowhere near the bull's eye.

"Holy shit!"

"*Nein*! You have no aim. Short bursts." Otto reached down and retrieved another magazine. "These are my last rounds for this weapon."

"Out of ammo?"

"I ordered more. They are coming next week." Otto showed him how to quickly remove the magazine and replace it with a fresh one.

"Now, short bursts this time. And try to aim."

Fritz furrowed his brow and turned to face the target. He pulled the trigger and he lurched backwards with the weapon. He had fired five rounds. The scent of gunpowder and smoke filled the air.

"Again! Short burst! Fire!"

Fritz corrected his balance and aimed.

"Fire now! *Achtung*!"

Fritz tried as best he could to control the weapon. He was soon down to his last six rounds. In two bursts, he noticed he skimmed the top portion of the target. The last click of the trigger indicated the ammunition was spent.

Fritz exhaled and turned to Otto. "Jesus Christ that was intense!"

"Your aim, Fritz... not so good."

Otto grinned and motioned Fritz to put the weapon down.

"I was not expecting automatic weapons this morning. *Danka shen*, Otto."

"You're welcome. Now come help me load up the crate."

Fritz knelt beside Otto. They inspected each weapon to insure they were unloaded, free of debris and placed snugly in their respective compartments. Otto noticed a difference in Fritz's composure. He realized what had been missing all along: respect. He shared a compliment with the young man and in return he smiled.

Otto realized something else. Despite his past, Fritz seemed energetic, clear-eyed and sober. His felt more confident about working with him. As long as there was someone there to keep him in line, Fritz could end up playing a critical role in the process, if not the most important.

When they reached Otto's car with the trunk, the older man patted Fritz on the back. "You are flying back to Kiev tomorrow? After our get-together with Henrick?"

"Yes. An evening flight. You?"

"I am taking tomorrow off. We will meet at Henrick's place at ten in the morning."

"I will be there." The two shook hands. "What about Karla, is she coming?"

"She will not be making an appearance unfortunately."

"What's her problem?"

Otto gave him a reassuring nod of the head. "*Ja*, she should be there, however it is a long-haul flight." Otto closed the trunk of his car. "You should know she has agreed to finance the entire operation."

"What are we talking about?"

"Roughly eighty thousand euros."

Fritz froze for a moment. "Holy shit, I didn't know she had that kind of money."

"We need it. I do not have that money on hand, and Henrick is all but destitute." Otto extended his hand and Fritz shook hit. "We can count on you to move when the time is right?"

"I know what's at stake."

"Very well then. We will see each other tomorrow in the morning."

Fritz nodded and stepped forward to his rented Audi. It unlocked when he was ten feet away.

Otto watched his car take off down the road. He knew he'd have to keep an eye on him, but otherwise he felt relieved. Henrick no longer possessed the physical means to intimidate anyone, but weapons, and Fritz's temperament represented exactly what they needed.

Chapter 13

Pompton Plains, New Jersey

Gus checked his watch and saw it was 8:00 p.m. The van he had driven from Hoboken was now decorated with a magnetic decal that read, "Sluberski Pest Control," on both sides of the vehicle. It was Friday night and the drive from Hoboken took forty-five minutes to complete. He had followed John Devenger from work, and after confirming the suspect was sharing beers with a friend, he felt confident he would have enough time to complete the task at hand.

He checked his iPad to confirm the apartment unit. Attached to the topside of his vehicle was a ladder but he was glad the job did not require the use of it. He zipped up his green jacket, which featured the same Sluberski logo and placed a green baseball cap on his head.

The street was calm and the ten minutes he waited paid dividends. There was not a car or person in sight. He exited the vehicle and checked the home in front of him. He noticed lights illuminating the windows above John Devenger's apartment so he reminded himself to be quick. He took a small duffle bag with him when he crossed the street.

He opened the rusty front gate and walked to the right side of the row house. The next building was no less than fifteen feet away and he noticed a car parked at the end of the alley. He peeked inside both windows; he saw a dining room and the other was the kitchen.

He double-checked the perimeter before he surveyed the building structure itself. It represented a shingle-sided structure made of wood and he had the right tool for the job. He retrieved a foot-long metal object with a spherical and sharpened edge. The back end of the device was made of rubber, complete with a few indentations.

He then retrieved a hammer from the bag. Taking the circular end of the rod, Gus placed it five feet high against the planks before he slammed the hammer against the rubber end of the rod. A few swift hits later, he removed the rod and saw a two-inch wide indentation on the structure of the home. He removed the material from the rod and took hold of the circular piece of wood that was once part of the shingle.

He turned to look around but no one had witnessed him, or likely heard the sounds of the rod hitting the house. If the residents upstairs took notice and inquired what he was doing, all he'd have to do is point to the pest control logo on his jacket. If it ended up being the landlord, he'd apologize for being at the wrong address.

He removed a one-inch wide and three-inch long cylinder from the bag. He moved a switch at the end and noticed a green L.E.D. light illuminate and blink for a moment before going dark. He then slipped it into the structure of the building and checked to make sure it would remain imbedded in the wall. When he was satisfied, he took the circular piece of shingle and placed it back in place. He stepped back, and with the exception of a small dark circular shadow, there was no trace of the WiFi-enabled listening device.

He walked back towards the front of the home and crossed what appeared to be a lawn in desperate need of water and fertilizer. He crossed to the left side of the building and looked inside to saw the living room. He repeated the process and lodged another metallic cylinder into the wall. When he was finished, two identical devices, worth ten thousand dollars apiece, were placed on the opposite sides of John Devenger's apartment.

He stowed the additional material taken from the wall, which consisted of stucco and insulation, and placed it in the bag he carried. He walked towards his van. He looked at the pest control logo, complete with a website address, and anyone who checked it would find a friendly small-business web page. He even paid to make sure there was a "Contact Owner" tab for web visitors to send inquiries. No one would ever guess on the surface it was a complete facade for Gus's other business.

He opened the back doors of the van, put the bag in the rear of the vehicle and closed them before he moved to the driver's seat.

When he closed the door he immediately retrieved his laptop. After it booted up he checked the reading from the devices to test for WiFi signals.

Nothing came back, which prompted him to sigh. He'd be required to use cellular service to eavesdrop on John Devenger. If any WiFi came into service, he'd utilize software to hack into it from afar and then monitor Devenger's web browsing.

He dialed into the service that triggered cellular communication but heard nothing on the receiving end. He would learn soon enough if he could hear any sounds and conversations taking place within John Devenger's home. Given he could do it in a place of his choosing, he turned on the engine and headed back home.

While he drove the van onto the onramp of Route 80, he dialed the international phone number given to him by the Brazilian. A moment later she answered.

"His home has been bugged. I'll know tomorrow what I can and cannot hear."

"When will the report be ready?"

He sighed. "I'm waiting on some colleagues to get me his credit records. I said I'd get it to you next week."

"I need them by Tuesday, latest. That was the date we agreed on."

"Look, sometimes this process takes a while, it's nearly finished."

"Then send me what you have tomorrow."

"Fine, good night Karla." Gus would be happy when the job was done. He was not enthused to be working with someone so naive about the process, but he did appreciate the premium she was paying for his services.

Potsdam, Germany

Henrick unlatched the door and watched Otto step into his apartment. The two did not share pleasantries. Henrick watched Otto remove his cap before he walked into the living room.

"I see you're living in the same dwelling."

"*Ja.*"

Otto nodded. "Twenty years?"

"Fifteen, maybe seventeen. How did—"

"Your parents... here?" Otto pointed to the black and white

photograph on the wall to his left. Henrick stepped into the room and turned to look.

"Yes, those are my parents. Why do you ask?"

Otto nodded. "We would have had much different lives, had our fathers succeeded."

Henrick looked back forth from the picture to Otto. "Is this supposed to be some kind of tender moment? Otto, meet my dead parents, mom and dad, here's Otto." He held up his hands and dropped them to his side in utter confusion.

"We went through the same thing, you and I. Our fathers' lives taken, their war treasure lost. I have to remind myself of that, and what's at stake."

"What other use would I have for you otherwise?" Henrick waved him off and took a seat in a wooden armchair. It creaked from his weight. "Fritz will be here shortly."

Otto turned and faced a man who looked twenty years older. He took a deep breath and wondered how Fritz would react when he saw him. "You last met Fritz, when... eight, ten years ago?"

"Yes, when the three of us met to discuss Karla, our friend's demise and her involvement."

"We spent time together yesterday as you know." Otto saw Henrick gesture to continue speaking with his hand. "I have to say, he's an asset."

"How so?"

"He was clear-eyed, sober, edgy and somewhat short-tempered. But for our purposes," he nodded, "We need him."

"You are absolutely certain?"

Otto took a seat. "We have no choice I'm afraid. I will have to keep my eye on him."

"As I have to keep my eye on you. I'll let you know whether or not I want him involved in this plan."

Otto shook his head. "You don't get it Henrick." The old man in the chair furrowed his wrinkled brow. "You and I, we are not young men. You are pale and weak. You've aged considerably."

"Not this again. You're twice the size you were ten years ago."

"But I have the strength to pick you up over my head."

Henrick turned to find a pack of cigarettes but he forgot they were in the kitchen. "So what are you implying, I have to agree to work with Fritz?"

"I'd rather not, with his criminal record. You do not possess the physical means to intimidate anyone."

Henrick nodded. "I'll remind you that I'm a former Stasi officer and—"

They heard the lobby buzzer echo in the apartment. "There he is." Henrick scowled at Otto as he crossed the room to the intercom. "I was so enjoying your assessment of the situation." He pressed a button and said, "Four zero eight." He left the door ajar and returned to his seat.

They both heard the sounds of heavy foot falls grow louder. Henrick turned to see Otto staring at him. "You'll agree to work with him Henrick. If you screw this up, you'll put the entire operation in jeopardy."

"I'll let you know my decision when he takes his leave."

They heard boots approach the door and come to a stop. The older men shared a look when the pause lingered for ten seconds. A moment later the door swung open to hit the backside wall. Fritz appeared ten feet away from where they sat. "How goes it?" He stepped inside the cramped room and Otto and Henrick stood up from their seats.

Otto extended his hand. "Fritz, you remember Henrick of course?"

Henrick provided Fritz with a strained smile and shook his hand. The young man gripped it with force. "Young Fritz, come in, take a seat."

"Henrick," Fritz took notice of his physical composure and decided not to make a comment. "This is your flat?"

"Ja. Please, take a seat, we have a lot to discuss."

Fritz's eyes canvassed the room. "Looks like you have all the motivation you need to get the job done."

"Sit down, Fritz... please."

"Yeah, sure." The young man returned his gaze to Henrick and he grabbed a cheap wooden seat from across the room. "You two, cooking up ideas? Is our connection at the bank still intact?"

"We will explain everything, but first you need to answer some questions."

"Whatever man, I've got a flight in four hours. What's the plan?"

Henrick gestured with his hand to pause the discussion when he got up to go to the kitchen. He returned with a pack of cigarettes and a silver lighter. "So... Fritz." He lit up a cigarette and exhaled a plume of smoke. "I need to know if we can rely on you, if we can trust your judgment. Can you tell me please what you've been doing these past eight years?"

Fritz nodded, rubbed his hands and turned to look at Otto. "Is he serious?"

"Pardon?" said Otto.

"You think I flew back from Kiev on short notice, went to a gun club and drove here to be interrogated, old man?"

"I—"

"I'm not the fucking toddler you met years ago. I was twenty two when we talked about Karla and her dead dad, I'm thirty two now. What are you, ninety?"

"I don't think you understand the circumstances."

"Henrick is right, your insolence is unnecessary."

Fritz pointed towards Henrick while he looked at Otto, "You didn't mention this the other day, did you?" Otto looked puzzled. "You should have mentioned his condition."

"That's enough! I'm not a feeble old man." Henrick jumped out of his chair. "You listen you little shit, if you keep it up, you're out. You'll be left with nothing."

"Is that a threat?"

"That's enough." Otto stood up, "We have no choice in the matter. May I remind you what is in the vault? That should remain the focus." Otto looked to both men and waited to make eye contact. "We can go our separate ways when the job is completed, yes?" Fritz nodded. "We're not planning to share a Greek villa and sip ouzo during sunsets. We do the job, and then we're done."

Henrick pointed towards Fritz, "I need to know if you're a liability."

"You are the liability, Henrick. So you better explain your plan in detail with Fritz and persuade him to remain involved, or you lose both of us."

"Henrick, what's the fucking plan?" Fritz sat back, crossed his legs and clasped his hands in a gesture to convey impatience.

Henrick took a long drag on his cigarette and stubbed out the remains. "Herr Fritz, do you remember my history at all? My days in the Stasi?"

"Yes."

"Very well then."

Henrick spent the next twenty minutes discussing every minor step and detail of the plan he was putting into operation. It included private investigators financed by Karla, a safe house out the outskirts of Bern, and black market connections in Eastern Europe when they procured the vault's contents. Throughout the conversation, Fritz remained alert, intrigued and more interested in the final result and financial figures at the end of the process. By the time Henrick completed his overview, Fritz's eyes were glued to the floor, appearing deep in thought.

"What say you, Herr Fritz?"

He nodded. "I don't know if you missed anything, but I have to admit, you are nothing less than thorough, old man."

"Can you just call him Henrick?" said Otto.

"*Ja*, sure. So John Devenger, will we know when he is coming?"

"Karla has arrangements in the states. We're keeping a close eye on him."

"When we get the word, we rendezvous in Bern the next day, or as soon as possible." Otto pointed towards Fritz. "He may be weak, but he does have a plan and connections that we need, especially on the back end."

Fritz nodded. "That part is more than appealing. I apologize if I was rude before, I was taken aback when I saw you, Henrick."

"Such a heartfelt apology, I'm touched." Henrick stood up to imply the meeting was finished. "We can trust you will be there?"

"Absolutely. What about the Brazilian?"

"Karla," Henrick grinned, "She will be there." The three expressed nonverbal cues that they were done with the meeting. "Very well then. The next time we meet, it will be in Bern, and Devenger will be on location."

The three exchanged handshakes.

Chapter 14

<u>Sao Paulo, Brazil: Tuesday, April 15th</u>

It was thorough, from start to finish. Karla didn't expect a forty-page document, complete with scanned visuals and an outline of John Devenger's travels. She was shocked at the extent of his world trips, but then again, he was a trust-fund baby. If Karla and the others secured what was rightfully theirs, the man profiled in the report would be left with nothing, from what she read.

She sifted through several more pages on her laptop screen and looked at the pictures of John Devenger. She found him surprisingly attractive. He did not dress well, but in every shot, his face radiated confidence. Perhaps his world travels had provided him with some sense of self-worth. God knows he had nothing else going for him that anyone, least of all a successful woman, would find appealing.

She hit reply to the private investigator's email and sent the following message:

KEEP TABS ON HIM AND CONTINUE TO MONITOR HIS MOVEMENTS AND COMMUNICATION. I WILL WIRE SEVEN THOUSAND DOLLARS INTO AN ESCROWED ACCOUNT IN ADVANCE OF ACCESSING DEVENGER'S HOME LINE AND COMPUTER. I'LL RELEASE THE MONEY WHEN I RECEIVE PROOF THE JOB IS DONE.

- K.

She picked up the phone on the side of her desk and dialed Henrick's new mobile number, which she had programmed into her iPhone.

Parsippany, New Jersey

John Devenger completed the monthly report for his management team and sent it via email. He looked up to see the picture of Angkor Wat tacked to his office cube. The panoramic, taken at sunrise, was the best picture he'd ever taken during his travels. It reminded him he would be traveling soon enough with his half-brother to find out what Everett bequeathed to them.

He rubbed his chin and gave thought to what Jimmy had told him during their get together in Hoboken. John picked up the phone and dialed Alan's number. He answered on the third ring and said, "What's up?"

"Hi, Alan, wanted to see if you had a minute."

"Now? Can't, I'm traveling on business in Los Angeles."

"Didn't know you were, bad time?"

"Yeah, driving to a client meeting. Or crawling, the traffic is nuts out here."

John almost asked, are the seats in the Bentley not to your liking? Can you ask you chauffer to turn down the heat? He chose instead to say, "So, when can we talk?"

"Back Friday evening, have a few things going on this weekend, maybe Sunday evening?"

"Can't. Hey, can I swing by your place Monday night?"

"Ah… give me a second. Let me check my schedule." John waited before he heard him say, "I can meet around eight. Want me to text you my address?"

"Sure, that would be good. Nothing urgent, but—"

"See you Monday night."

"Okay then." Alan said goodbye and the call ended.

John put the phone back in the cradle and sighed while he rubbed his hands. He kept reminding himself to take the high road, but on some level the tone in Alan's voice put him off: He felt like Alan had managed the request like any other appointment. It gave him a chill for some reason.

He put aside his other feelings and got back to work.

Potsdam, Germany

"Very well then, dear Karla, I look forward to reading it. Let me know when we get word from the private eye about accessing Devenger's home." He concluded the call and planned to check his email at the Internet cafe in town the next morning.

He stepped towards the chair by the window in his small apartment. He looked outside to see leafless trees bend ever so slightly from the wind. He took a seat.

His cold hands embraced a glass of schnapps that rested on a nearby end table. Nothing was helping to warm his bones, which ached from the trip back home from Bern. When he put it down he exhaled with pain.

He heard his new phone buzz and lifted it to see Karla's email had arrived. Henrick put it down a moment later as he could not read the contents in the attachment.

"It's coming together," he said aloud. "A lifetime of waiting, and finally..." His eyes closed when he thought about what success would bring. The dreams of his youth flashed across his mind: Palm trees, a terrace overlooking the Mediterranean, a vista with views that stretched for miles. It was right there, waiting for him, and all he needed was fraudulent identification, an account number and the passcode. He had spent so many years, and tried so many ways to access what was rightfully his. They had all failed.

That could all change, and more importantly, he could avenge his father's demise and the death of his friend, Gustav.

He looked forward to the day he could put a bullet in the head of the American, John Devenger.

Chapter 15

Upper West Side, Manhattan

"Eighth floor, unit 3." The doorman pointed towards an elevator bank on the right side of the lobby.

"Thanks," said John.

He turned and noticed a woman exit one of the elevators as he approached them. She was caked in makeup and held a small dog under her arm, which growled at John the moment their eyes met. To complement the view, she wore a leopard-patterned jacket. "Marty, did that package come yet?" John noticed her accent was as thick as her waistline. He promised himself to make a joke of the incident. Alan, I met your lover in the lobby.... She seems like quite a handful.

He chuckled before a tall and slender woman got into the elevator with him. He froze when she turned and gave him the quickest of grins. She was stunning and wore an athletic outfit suited for running in cold temperatures. The elevator doors closed and he tapped his leg.

"Cold for a run."

"Yup." She did not turn and put her hands on her hips and drew in deep breaths. John felt somewhat aroused from the scent of her hair and sweat. He couldn't help but feel she was giving him the cold shoulder as they rode silently in elevation. He didn't blame the woman for ignoring the bald stranger wearing a crappy dress shirt and unpolished shoes. He felt completely out of place.

"Bye." He got out of the elevator but she did not respond. He turned to see a pristine hallway that extended in both directions. A vase of orchids rested on a rectangular coffee table and he noticed soft up lighting illuminate tan walls and carpet. It was a charming. He realized it was his first visit to Alan's condo. It reminded him of the sophisticated luxury he found in Charlotte's building in Hoboken.

He walked past a few units before he found unit number three. The door was slightly ajar and he gave it a quick knock. "Come in, John."

When he pushed the door open he heard the pitter-patter of a dog's footsteps approach him. When he looked down he saw a golden Labrador greet him with a bark. "Hey, girl." He entered an entrance hallway and rubbed the dog's head and neck. "You're gorgeous, look at you." He kept rubbing the dog, felt a quick lick on his cheek and loved it.

"That's Vix."

John looked up to see Alan wearing an ensemble of clothing fit for a cover shoot. "Hey there, I didn't know you had a dog."

"I guess it never came up, had her for a few years now. Come on in."

"Thanks. She's awesome." He stepped forward and looked at Alan's living room. There was a sixty-inch TV above a fireplace mantel, handsome couches and a recliner of sorts with black cushions and curved wood. "Nice pad."

"Thanks, find it okay?"

"Sure." He felt the dog by his side and gave her another quick rub. "When did you buy this place?"

"Couple of years ago, four actually. Can I take your coat?"

"Sure." John gave it to him while he turned his attention to Alan's desk. Resting on it was a razor-thin iMac computer screen, iPad and what looked like two iPhones. He looked behind him and noticed the kitchen, which was not surprisingly fit for a king. The refrigerator had see-through doors. Dear God, he said to himself. "Well, you'll always know when you need milk."

"Huh?"

"The fridge."

"Oh, that. My designer got a deal on it. When we redid the place, she went a little crazy." He smiled but John just nodded.

"Must be nice."

"Thanks, it is." Alan put the jacket in the hallway closet and returned to the room. "Can I offer you a drink?"

"Actually, allow me." John opened the shoulder satchel he brought with him and revealed a bottle of wine. "From one of Everett's first vineyards."

"Awesome, where did you find it?"

"Had to call one of the distributors, a liquor store in Ramsey sold it."

Alan nodded. "I could use another glass. I had one with dinner. That was thoughtful, but did you drive all the way to Ramsey to pick it up?"

John nodded. "No problem. I thought it would be nice to enjoy a glass before our trip."

Alan pressed his lips together and nodded. He paused before he turned to walk into the kitchen. "I thought you wanted to get together tonight to rip me a new one."

"Come again?"

"The money and all, what I spent on the contingency plans."

John heard Alan remove the cork and he rubbed his chin. "Well, I do want to talk about that, but there's something else."

"Great."

He watched him pour the wine and return to the room. The white dress shirt he wore did not have a single wrinkle on it. "Wait, I have a question." Alan froze as he stood there, seeming to anticipate a nasty comment. "Your shirt."

"What about it?"

"How do you go through a day at the office and there's not one wrinkle?"

"Why do you ask?"

"I'm just curious. I assume it's not one of those wrinkle free rayon ones."

Alan blurted out a laugh. "Rayon? Seriously?"

"Well, I don't know. What the hell's the trick?"

"Jesus Christ, take a seat. No, the good chair." John complied and he sat in what looked like a designer seat. He noticed John's demeanor change, seeming to relax. "Nice, isn't it?"

"Man, this is comfy."

"That's an Eames chair, here." Alan gave John his glass of wine. "*Salude.*" Their glasses clinked and Alan moved to take a seat on the couch.

"An Eames chair. So... how much do one of these go for?"

"Five thousand dollars."

"Whoa, okay." John leaned forward to stand up.

"Sit back! Enjoy it."

He reclined back in the chair. "That's insane, does that include the cost of the ottoman?"

Alan nodded. "To answer your question, two shirts. I keep several shirts at work. When I have an evening appointment, a date or an event, I change into a fresh shirt."

"Huh." John nodded and he crossed his legs. "Clever son of a bitch, aren't you."

Alan took a long pull on his wine. "So tomorrow, all set with work and what not?"

"Yeah, leaving at five sharp, I'm packed, and I'm bringing a few things we may need."

"I'm sorry to say you can't bring a gun on the plane." Alan grinned. "What are you bringing?"

"I picked up some maps, a phone that works overseas."

"Good."

"And I confirmed our get together with Francois in a town north of Geneva." John grinned and took a long pull on his drink. "So thankfully I can leave my Glock nine millimeter at home."

Alan cocked his jaw. "So what else did you want to discuss?"

John clasped his glass with both hands. "I think we need to make assurances with the vault."

"What kind?"

"We should pass along the details in case something happens to us. And I think that person should be Charlotte."

Alan sat back and crossed his legs. "So what do you propose?"

"I think we jot down the account number, the name of the bank on paper, and simply mail it to her." John shrugged his shoulders. "If we don't make it back, whatever's in the vault will be gone forever."

"A little dramatic, don't you think?" Alan shook his head. "I've got a board meeting on Monday the 28th, I'll have bigger problems if I miss that meeting."

"Not if you're lying dead in a morgue."

"Such drama—"

"Stop, our father died shortly after he went over there. Let's just make sure Charlotte gets the details before we leave, okay?"

He watched his half-brother nod in agreement. "Okay, point taken. I'll get some paper, a pen and an envelope." He stood up and used the remote to turn on the TV in front of them before he handed it to John. "Here you go." The TV powered up and all sixty inches of it came to life. The sound turned on a few seconds later. John was in awe of the screen's clarity. He sipped his grandfather's wine and looked down to watch the contents in the glass stir in his hand. *A vineyard instead of a vault*, he said to himself. He had run that phrase through his head a thousand times.

He wondered what he would be doing right now if he had taken ownership of a vineyard out west. His boss would have received his two-week notice by now, and he'd likely be searching for a residence out in California. He'd be strolling down a barren vineyard, perhaps one that stretched for a hundred acres in neat and organized rows. He'd be checking the books and speaking to employees who managed the property. He figured his immediate net worth would be half a million at minimum, and if he chose to sell the vineyard, he could retire by year's end and travel the world. When he looked up, he saw LeBron James slam-dunking a basketball on a huge TV. He was sitting in a five-thousand-dollar chair purchased by a designer that his half-brother hired when they remodeled his million-dollar condo.

Fortunately, all Alan had to do was look into his glass-paneled fridge to see if he needed milk. *Son of a bitch.*

When he put his drink to his lips, he placed the glass between his teeth and felt the urge to bite through it.

Alan placed an envelope, pen and a sheet of paper before him on a nearby glass coffee table. "There you go, write it up, and I'll mail it."

"Would you rather have had a vineyard?"

"Come again?"

"Instead a vault. I mean, did we get stiffed?"

Alan moved before him to look him in the eye. "Why would you think he'd do such a thing?"

"Who fucking knows," He finished the last third of his glass in two long gulps. "A vault instead of a vineyard. I'd rather have the grapes." He shook his head. "Thanks for doing this."

"Sure." Alan heard one of his mobile phones ring. "Pardon me."

"Two cell phones, dear brother?"

"Can you just zip it for once?"

John rubbed his hands and tried to lean forward in the chair. It was hard to position himself to write so he stood up to move to the couch. He took the pen, paper and envelope and noticed Alan had left his folded paper on the table. He moved it directly in front of him. If Alan had complied, the account number was written on it.

John froze for a moment. In the background, he heard Alan speaking to a work colleague about a business deal that needed his immediate approval. John realized that before him was the missing piece of information required to access the vault. He had the name of the bank, and with the account number and passcode he could access the vault himself.

An evil thought crossed his mind: Blow off the flight... email Alan to tell him he's sick... leave the following Monday and take everything in the vault. He wondered what would happen, but the option was right there in front of him. He could jot down the digits on something else and just get up and to take his leave.

The person whom the envelope was addressed to stopped his thought process. Charlotte's name and address were written down, and a stamp rested in the top right corner of the envelope. He knew if he went through with it and cut Alan out of the process she'd never speak to him again, as it would represent a cruel and unusual decision. His fingers moved to pry open the folded paper Alan had used but he stopped short and sighed. He knew he'd be on a flight with him tomorrow night, but he felt relieved he'd have a weapon on hand if things took a turn for the worse in Switzerland.

In a flash, he wrote, *Scheibzerische Bank*, folded the paper and placed both of them in the envelope. He sealed it with a lick when Alan concluded the call.

"It's done."

"Okay. Good." Alan took a seat across from him on the opposite couch.

"Business deal?"

"Yeah, or lack thereof." Alan shook his head. "Ray-Ban is going to run more pages in *Men's Health* and *Details* magazine."

"Not *GQ*?"

"Three pages of business. Only three."

"So what does that net out to be?"

Alan jostled his head around for a moment. "Roughly two hundred and thirty thousand dollars."

"Sounds great."

Alan provided him with a condescending look. "You're a bit naive there John. It's all about market share."

"A penance for *GQ*, forgive me, I forgot about the trials and tribulations of high society." John tapped the top of his legs. "Well, I have to get going."

"Not another glass?"

"I have to drive. My driver took the night off."

"Come on, give me a break."

John held up his hands. "I'm just joking. But I do have to go." He picked up the envelope. "I'll mail this tomorrow."

"Hold on there, give me a moment." John watched Alan retrieve two jackets and a dog leash from the hallway closet. "There's a mailbox down the street."

"Oh? You don't want me—"

"Nah, I should take Vix out for a quick walk anyway." Alan turned as Vix was already by his side. The sight and sound of the leash must have caught her attention.

"Huh, I get it."

"What?"

"Let's just go."

Alan gave him a perplexed look. "What do you mean?" John ignored him and headed for the front door.

***

"Well, here it is." Alan pointed to the mailbox and watched John drop the envelope to the bottom of it. A second later, he watched him check to make sure it had fallen. "Double-checking to see if you can grab it?"

"No, just a habit I guess."

"Okay."

John turned to face Alan and Vix. "So tomorrow night, I'll see you at Newark."

"Yup." Alan nodded and rubbed the top of Vix's head. "I think we'll find something very special over there, John."

"What makes you say that?"

"The vault, as opposed to the vineyard. You asked before what I'd rather have."

"Oh... yeah, I forgot."

"Everett was one of the most decent men I've ever known. He wouldn't wrong us, there's something over there."

"That reminds me, I never got the chance to rip you a new one. For spending so much money." He watched Alan provide a stern look. "I'll cover my half, somehow, even if that means I have to sell my portion of the vault's contents."

"Don't worry about it."

"I will." He extended his hand and Alan shook it. "I'll see you tomorrow night. I'll bring a box cutter on the plane, a big one in case we run into trouble." Alan's eyes grew wide for a moment. "Only kidding."

"Jesus."

"I'm just fucking with you."

"You always are, that's the problem."

He watched Alan cross the street with Vix. He looked at the mailbox for a moment and wondered if there was any way to procure the envelope he had just mailed. When he looked back at Alan, he realized that he wouldn't just be fucking with him, he'd be fucking him over if he could get it. He turned to walk down the street towards his car.

Chapter 16

Parsippany New Jersey, April 22nd

Gus bit into the last bite of his Butterfinger and used the side of his hand to wipe his mouth. He'd purchased the candy bar at the Exxon QuickMart when he filled up the van with gas an hour prior. He needed a boost of energy and he knew the candy bar would hold him over for a while.

He saw the exit for Route 10 in Parsippany and steered toward it. When he looked down, he saw his iPad screen indicated the location bug he planted on John Devenger's car remained stationary as the map centered itself on his location. Everything was working properly, and by tomorrow night, if everything went according to plan, he'd be seven thousand dollars richer.

The bitch from Rio had wired the funds into the escrow account they had used over the past month. It was just waiting there, and when it was released, he'd use the money to book a trip to the Caribbean.

He ran the figures through his head and he could not believe the money he was making. Every year, for seven years, he was paid a thousand dollars to keep tabs on Everett Devenger. The mission was simple: keep an eye on the old man, and when he passes away, call the provided mobile number. He was told, and occasionally had to report, on other Devenger family members, which brought in a few more payments.

He had complied, and when he received word from Karla to profile everyone in the family who was present at the funeral, he received ten thousand dollars in compensation. When he was given John Devenger's name, she ordered a full-on surveillance. A detailed report was given, complete with the man's financial details, photography and audio clips from the man's home. A profile of his daily life painted a more refined picture, which resulted in another eight thousand dollars. He placed a tracking device on Devenger's car when he made a trip to the gym last week and he was now able to monitor his movements on his iPad.

He used his turn signal to embark onto Route 10, a road he was now familiar with. He looked down and noticed the map indicated John Devenger's car remained parked outside of Tiffany's New Jersey headquarters. It was too easy: Devenger was not a criminal or a wanted fugitive. Those jobs paid less and were significantly more difficult. The irony prompted him to grin as he belched from the candy bar he had consumed.

He parked his van, complete with the Sluberski pest control logo, on the side of road. Fifty yards ahead of him he saw the turn to Tiffany's office park. Devenger's car was no more than 30 yards away but it was out of view.

He knew his routine and planned to follow him to the man's gym five miles away. He checked his watch and set the timer on his Casio Ironman watch to fifty minutes. The moment after Devenger entered the gym, he knew he had fifty minutes at most to drive to his home in Pompton Plains. He had the equipment to tap his phone, which he would tether to the phone's wall socket. If that failed, his backup plan was to plant another type of device within the phone receiver itself. It was less reliable and not Wi-Fi enabled, which would complicate matters, so he hoped he didn't have to use it. Last but not least was the USB drive in his pocket, complete with piracy software. If he could access his computer, and get around the password issues, he'd simply plug in the USB device and the software would upload in three minutes. If he succeeded, he'd see everything on Devenger's monitor, know his browsing history and with keyboard recognition, every key he used. It all depended of course if he owned a personal computer, which he could not verify from afar.

His other pocket contained a set of devices he would use to pick the front lock. If by chance anyone took issue with him on site, he had doctored up a work order with Devenger's name in order to provide the appearance of legitimacy. He was simply checking on a job he had done a week prior, and John Devenger wanted to rid his apartment of bed bugs. If there was one particular bug that warranted a follow up visit, bed bugs more than qualified. He also planned to carry an extermination container, complete with tubing and a spraying nozzle. He doubted anyone would question him, however, *Sluberski pest control was prepared for anything*, he said to himself.

He pulled out an old Blackberry to check email before something caught his eye on the iPad screen: Devenger's car was in motion. "Oh shit." He turned on the engine and waited for him to leave the parking lot. "Leaving early today, are you?"

When he saw his crappy Subaru turn on to Route 10, Gus's Pest Control van was fifty yards behind him.

He turned on the radio and checked his rearview mirror. Everything was clear, and he had no reason to worry. There were jobs that required him to pack heat, but a civilized Tiffany employee did not represent a life-threatening situation. The gun remained stowed in the glove compartment.

The radio was tuned to an oldies station and the DJ played "Superstitious" by Stevie Wonder. Gus tapped the top of the steering wheel and kept fifty yards behind Devenger's car. He was out of sight, but never out of the picture, thanks to the iPad map and tracking device. Route 202 would be coming up in a minute or two, and Devenger would take it north in order to connect on Route 46.

It was during the second chorus of the song when Gus looked down to see Devenger's car pass the turn for Route 202. That wiped the smile right off his face. "Fuckin' A." He gave the engine some gas and caught the light before it turned red.

He furrowed his brow a few minutes later when he spotted the Subaru turn onto Route 287 south, which was not part of John Devenger's routine.

Gus sighed and tossed his cap onto the passenger seat as he knew his plan was shot. Without knowing where he was going or how long Devenger would be, he would not risk penetrating the man's home. The worst-case scenario was Devenger showing up in the middle of the operation. Jail time and another stint in the clink represented a likely outcome if things went sour. He also discovered that John Devenger possessed a New Jersey gun license.

He looked down and saw the man driving at a steady clip. Devenger was thirty yards ahead in the middle lane. It did not take long for the man to change roads, and both he and Devenger slowed down on Route 24, eastbound. After the traffic snaked through Madison and past the Short Hills mall, Gus followed Devenger onto Route 78, eastbound.

Gus opened a bottle of water and took a long pull. The drive Devenger was taking represented something entirely new. He had tracked him from afar when he went into New York City the night prior, but he had another job to tend to, so he did not follow him.

He was very curious. He wondered if this was a girlfriend he had not identified. Maybe he was going back to Hoboken to meet with his cop friend from Staten Island, whose license plate Gus had procured later that evening.

The traffic picked up and he started passing signs for Newark airport. When Devenger's car turned on the embankment, Gus gripped the steering wheel. What... the fuck... is going on?

He looked up to see a large sign illuminated above the road, and his eyes were glued to the words:

NEWARK INTERNATIONAL AIRPORT
ALL TERMINALS STRAIGHT AHEAD

"Holy shit."

He recalled his conversations with the bitch from Rio. We need to know his travel plans... when and where. There was no indication from his credit card transactions he had booked a trip.

He weaved the van around the turns but kept his distance. A friend? Is he picking up a friend at the airport?

His concern magnified when he saw Devenger pull into long-term parking. It represented an outdoor parking facility. Gus passed him and pulled the van over to the side of the road. He grabbed his iPad and put on his reading glasses. It took five seconds to open the documents he had emailed to Karla and put in a search query for 'Newark.' The word did not appear within the document.

"Long-term parking, what the fuck is going on?" He kept the engine running while he jumped into the back of his van to grab his camera. He checked the lens and returned to the driver's seat. He put the camera on the passenger seat.

He surveyed the area and saw a bus pass by. It turned into the long-term parking area and drove back towards his position. He turned the van around and drove in the same direction on the outside service road.

When he looked he saw a bus come and go past a waiting area. A minute later, John Devenger showed up carrying a suitcase, which prompted Gus to swallow hard. He had a clear sight of the man and there was enough daylight to capture his image. He rolled down his window and snapped twenty pictures. He noticed Devenger check his watch.

"Where are you going baldy?" The next bus came and Devenger got on it. Gus took note of the driver: an Asian man with chin hair several inches long.

He wondered if he'd get to the Caribbean if Devenger left, and Karla stopped paying him his fee.

The bus motioned out of view and Gus opened the driver's side door to try to see it. It crawled passed a hundred cars, turned left and came around to pass by Gus's van. It looked like Confucius was driving the bus and Gus stormed off in pursuit.

He banged the steering wheel in frustration for not having known Devenger was traveling. He watched the bus pull up to Terminal A, but he did not see a bald man exit the bus. The same thing happened at Terminal B. "Where to dude, where the fuck are you going?"

It was at Terminal C when he saw John Devenger exit with his luggage. He looked up and saw signs for Air India, Emirates and Lufthansa.

Gus put the van in park and turned on the emergency lights. He hopped out and saw a security official thirty yards in the distance. He watched Devenger stroll towards a baggage area and turn into the doors below the Lufthansa sign. "Son of a bitch."

He moved to the closest entrance before the security official yelled, "Hey!" and caught his eye. He ignored him and stepped inside, and figured he had five minutes before his van was towed.

His steps took him past several entrances and he stepped beside a support beam near the Lufthansa check in area. Devenger was at the counter and Gus cursed he did not have his camera. The area was not as crowded at night compared to the day. Observing the man from afar was not an issue.

He looked up to see the flight board on an LCD screen and noticed a half dozen Lufthansa flights. He checked his watch. He'd be taking a taxi back to the Bronx if he remained much longer. He looked back at the screen and saw gate numbers beside each flight.

He saw Devenger hand his bag to an official at an X-ray station. A moment later he walked away with a shoulder bag. He took the escalator down to the floor below.

Gus sauntered over to the terrace wall and watched Devenger stroll straight towards the security gate. He tapped the top rail before he returned to the flight board. He reviewed the departure flights, takeoff times, and one was leaving at 8:15 p.m., direct to Geneva. There were others leaving before and after that time.

He walked towards the security area to see if he could identify John Devenger's black suitcase from afar. He was fifteen feet away but he could not tell which one belonged to him.

"Shit." He knew what he had to do.

Gus sighed and turned to walk back to his van. When he checked his watch he double-timed it across the floor.

He noticed the security official pointing at him when he exited the building.

"Yo, is this your van?"

"Fuck off."

"I'm talkin' to you."

He ignored him, retrieved the ticket from the front windshield, and put the van in drive. He retrieved his mobile phone and dialed the international number associated with Karla.

"Yes?"

"Karla, it's Gus."

"Bad timing, can—"

"Listen up. Your boy, he's traveling." Gus did not hear a response. "Are you there?"

"Yes, give me a minute." He heard a commotion in the background. "What did you say?"

"Devenger, he just checked in for a Lufthansa flight."

"Where?"

"Newark. I'm pretty sure Switzerland is the destination."

"How is that possible?"

"We didn't see this—"

"You imbecile. When?"

"Tonight."

"You were paid handsomely. We needed one piece of information... one!"

"Karla—"

"You incompetent little maggot."

"You are way out of line, lady."

"If you ruined this, trust me, we will find you."

Chapter 17

<u>Lufthansa Flight 716, 5:50 a.m.</u>

He returned to a state of consciousness. The air was filled with delicious aromas: eggs, ham, and the scent of fresh-ground coffee. He listened to himself breath, which in itself was relaxing and therapeutic. It reminded him of the sound of waves hitting the beach when he exhaled. He remembered where the sounds came from; it was the earplugs he was wearing. When he removed them he heard what sounded like two small corks pop out of his ears.

He fumbled around, groggy from the Ambien, and reached up to his face. He removed the eye patch that kept the light out of his eyes. He squinted to see a stewardess several rows ahead of him serving food. A few moments later she was standing before him. "Morning," he mumbled. His eyes adjusted as he reached for the buttons on his armrest. The distinct sound of whirring lowered his legs and raised the back side of his first-class seat. He looked up to see a fair maiden holding his breakfast. She smiled.

"Good morning Herr Devenger, I have your breakfast here, would you like it now?"

He cleared his throat. "Sounds wonderful, thank you so much." He untethered the metal silverware from the plastic sleeve and grinned from ear to ear. After a comfortable night's sleep, he took his first bite of fresh eggs, served at 30,000 feet.

Alan thought they were quite scrumptious and the accompanying ham and toasted French bread rounded out the meal. The guilt he felt about first-class seating started to settle in at the end of his meal, knowing John was seated in coach. He turned to look in the back of the plane but saw a blue curtain drawn to a close. John was back there somewhere, but he could not recall where his half-brother was seated. He offered to pay for his upgrade, but John refused the offer. Two thousand dollars, that's outrageous! A quick sip of freshly squeezed orange juice alleviated him of any guilt. He offered, John declined, and if he was gnawing away on a half-ripe apple, so be it.

Alan's mind started to hit on all cylinders before he was finished. He was pleased with his decision. Knowing he'd spend twelve hours jammed in the back of the plane, in a middle seat, prompted him to upgrade to first class.

He used the second hot towel provided to him to cleanse his hands and face and then went to use the bathroom. He brushed his teeth, coiffed his hair and splashed himself with a dab of cologne. His eyes looked tired, but otherwise he looked and felt refreshed.

The orange he left on his tray was now placed in a white ceramic bowl. He nodded to the stewardess, grabbed the orange and pulled back the curtain to coach seating.

He walked halfway down the plane and noticed John seated in a middle seat.

Alan grinned when John looked up from his magazine. He was seated between a young man and a heavy middle-aged woman. "How goes it?"

"Fine, thank you very much. How's the royal treatment going?"

Alan's grin did not diminish. "Fine thanks, did you sleep?"

"Not much." He tilted his head to the napping young man and whispered, "Snoring."

Alan responded with an unpleasant expression. "I offered to pay."

"Two thousand—" John lowered his voice. "Two grand? That's outrageous. You should be more thrifty."

Alan calculated his income in his mind. His salary and bonus totaled $860,000 dollars. By his calculations, he was being thrifty. "Let me treat you on the flight home then. I'm trying to do right by you." John shook his head. "Hungry? Want my orange?"

"No thanks."

"Just asking. Get some caffeine in you, we've got a long day ahead of us."

"Okay there, Alan." He watched his brother turn to walk away. "Try not to stub your toes on the foot cushion, your majesty."

Alan thought it best to ignore the comment. He returned to his spacious and comfortable seat and took a sip of the fresh coffee waiting for him.

Berlin International Airport

"You must get me on that next flight. I implore you, check again!" Henrick tapped the counter in rapid succession.

The agent and manager returned their attention to the screen in front of them. "Sir, I told you, we're booked. Our next available flight is at 1:30 this afternoon."

"Is there a stand-by available?"

"Unless you want to pay for first class, no. I would recommend taking a seat for the early afternoon flight. That is all we can do.

Henrick rubbed his forehead. "Book it... book it now."

The ticket agent worked quickly to expedite the transaction with the angry old man. Fifteen others passengers looked on with concerned stares.

He grabbed his ticket and stormed away from the counter. He bumped shoulders with a traveler behind him. "Look out," Henrick warned.

His legs ached after the long walk from the train to the terminal and his head throbbed. The bag he packed the night prior weighed thirty pounds. Each step he took brought with it a shot of pain down the right side of his body. Before he made it to the security gate, he was forced to take a seat. He retrieved his cell phone to call Otto and dialed.

Irbersdorf, Germany

When he heard his cell phone ring, Otto slowed down to 120 kilometers per hour, and answered. "*Ja.*"

"Where are you?"

"On Highway 4 outside Irbersdorf." Otto decelerated further when a car crossed his lane. "I'm in transit."

"How far?"

"I have roughly six or seven hours left to drive."

"My flight, I won't be there until the afternoon."

"Fine, goodbye then, I'm driving." Otto tossed the phone onto the passenger seat and throttled back up to speed. Fields of wheat flew by when his car accelerated from 120 to 180 kilometers per hour. His car careened down the autobahn and the motor hummed at a heightened pace.

The car leaned and twisted to the left as both hands gripped the wheel. Given the heavy contents in his trunk, the weight provided extra stability from the high speed and acceleration.

He anticipated that he would cross the border sometime around noon, and from there, he would drive to Bern. If necessary, he'd drive straight to the bank itself.

Kiev, Russia

At 11:35 a.m., he heard his cell phone ring for the third time in as many hours. Someone was desperately trying to get in touch with him. When his wobbling hand retrieved it, he saw it was Henrick. He pushed back the arm that lay across his chest and belonged to a very attractive and expensive prostitute. He sat up in bed. Fritz rubbed his face and shook off the hangover. "Yes, Henrick?"

"I've called you four times since last night! Where were you?"

"Out. Home. Whatever man, what do you want?"

"It's happening now. He is coming, we have to move."

"Devenger? How do you know?"

"Karla confirmed it. We need you in Bern immediately."

Fritz repositioned himself on the bed. "You mean today. As in stop everything I'm doing, and catch a flight."

"Yes."

"Are you absolutely sure? If I get there and it's a false alarm, you and I are going to have a big problem."

"Just get yourself to the airport and get on the next flight."

He sighed. "I'll call you in an hour. I expect details when I call."

He tossed his phone on the nightstand and turned to look at the brunette beside him. He roused her from sleep. When she barely moved, he lifted the sheet and gave her a good smack square on the ass.

"You have to go."

"Huh?" she mumbled.

"Now."

Sao Paulo, Brazil

Karla looked at her mobile phone in disbelief when it began to ring. The clock on the face indicated Henrick was calling her at 3:05 a.m. She had yet to fall asleep after several failed attempts so she took the call. "It's the middle of the night, Henrick."

"When do you arrive?"

"I booked the flight yesterday. It departs at 4:45 p.m. today, I connect in Munich, and I'll be in Bern Thursday evening."

"Why did you not fly out last night?"

"There were no flights. Stop over-reacting."

"Your arrangements in the states failed us."

"You think I'm pleased with this process? Deal with it, Devenger isn't going anywhere in twenty-four hours' time." She heard him sigh.

"I should trim back your cut of the take."

She stared at the phone for a second, processed the threat, and then said, "Go ahead, I'd be happy to tell Heinzen to deny you and the others entry to the vault. One call and I can cut you out entirely."

"Just get your ass to Bern."

She heard him hang up. She smirked at Henrick's feeble threat and turned back to the laptop beside her. She reread the email she drafted to her boss, whom she had alerted last night about not feeling well.

>> THE DOCTOR CONFIRMED I HAVE THE FLU, UNFORTUNATELY. MY TEMPERATURE IS FORTY DEGREES, CELSIUS. I'LL LIKELY BE OUT THROUGH THE WEEKEND. KARLA <<

It did not matter whether or not her employers questioned her honesty. If all went according to plan, she'd never have to work another day in her life. She planned to send the email at noon.

Unable to sleep, she decided to accomplish something, so she stood up to start packing.

Berlin International Airport

Henrick thought about the timing of John Devenger's trip. Was he planning to do this over a long weekend somehow? What could he accomplish in five days' time? Impossible. Perhaps the man was staying longer.

He looked at his watch and it read 11:00 a.m. He knew Otto would arrive in Bern around the same time his plane would land and there was no word from Fritz. Karla would not arrive until Thursday evening.

His mind focused on what he could do to prevent Devenger from accessing the vault. He knew he had to do something immediately. If he did nothing, there was a risk they'd lose everything. His mind flashed with memories from the debacle in 1983 when they had confronted Jack Devenger. He turned his thoughts to the process of going to the vault with identification, an account number and passcode. He could be in the vault itself right now.

He thought about Karla's response, but it was he who handed Heinzen the money. Karla was not the only person who could influence the banker.

He opened his suitcase, retrieved a pad of paper with information written on it, and found the phone number he was looking for. He dialed.

A woman answered the phone and said in German, "Bank Scheibzerische, how may I assist?"

"Place me through to Herr Heinzen please."

"One moment."

Henrick heard the man answer the phone. "Heinzen, this is Henrick."

"Pardon?"

"We met outside the front door of your building two weeks ago."

"I have no idea what you are referring to—"

"Shut up. John Devenger, he may pay you a visit today."

He heard the man sigh. "That does not concern me. Goodbye—"

"You took the money. We expect you to delay him."

"That's not going to happen. I'm not getting involved."

"My associates and I will be happy to pay you a visit then. You get off work, at what, five… six o'clock?"

"Then I'll notify the bank's security department and the authorities. Please old man, this is pathetic."

"Maybe your wife will serve us tea while we wait for you to return home. We are outside Bern, not fifteen minutes from your flat. I'm not sure she'll be up to the task though, broken arms and all." Henrick waited for a response but jumped on the delay. "Delay Devenger."

"I do not have the authority to—"

Henrick ended the call.

He placed the notepad back in his suitcase and thumbed through the leather bag. When he found what he was looking for, he took it out.

He looked at the blue cover and saw it read the following: The United States of America. He opened it and saw a picture of himself laminated on the first page. Alongside the falsified information was the name, John Devenger. He obtained it the week prior from someone who was well compensated and wanted by the authorities.

Besides the fake identification, all he needed was the account number and passcode. The person named in the fake passport would be persuaded, by any means necessary, to give him the information.

Chapter 18

Karlsruhe, Germany

The sign read: Basel/Karlsruhe (5). The road was a straight shot to the Swiss border, and from there it would take two hours to get to Bern. Otto veered right at the sign and connected to Route 5, a road that represented an extension to the autobahn.

With his coffee consumed, his mind focused at the task at hand. He thought about the last time he confronted one of the Devengers who entered the vault. His hands knotted themselves against the steering wheel and venom coursed through his veins. Everett Devenger had killed his father. Jack Devenger had beaten his comrade from Argentina, Gustav, to death. He did not feel a trace of remorse when he pulled alongside the car wreck back in 1983 and saw Jack Devenger bleeding within it. He did not have the vault's information on him, nor was it in his briefcase. This prompted the question of what to do with Jack Devenger and Henrick answered the question with several gunshots and a lighter. It took seconds for the leaking gasoline to ignite the car and inflict revenge.

The contents in the trunk of his car represented the insurance they needed to maintain the upper hand when they confronted the dead man's son. Given what was waiting for all of them in the vault, he felt reassured to have the weapons on hand.

He looked at his watch and realized his wife would be waking up soon. It would not take her long to find the note he left her. Henrick's call came late in the evening and he packed what he needed after his wife fell to sleep. She knew about the vault, as did his children. Leaving the note was cowardly, but not unwise. She would have implored him not to go, citing the risk and the dangers. Otto knew it was a risk worth taking.

Given the years they had waited for this very moment, he had no interest in passing down the opportunity, or the risk, to one of his children.

It was time to settle the score.

He floored the accelerator and thanked the Fatherland for never having posted speed limits on the autobahn.

Saint Prex, Switzerland

John caught a glimpse of the lake from the passenger seat as they passed one home after another. He saw brilliant, translucent blue water lapping on the shore.

"The lake. Is it... glacial water?"

"Yes, you should see it at dusk. It is magnificent."

"You've been here?"

"Several times. There's a huge trade show once a year in Basel, for timepieces."

"You mean, watches?"

"That's not the term they use, but yes."

"Hmm." John watched as they passed neat and well-maintained homes. The roads, scenery and rolling hills provided what looked like an extremely affluent setting. "This really is a rich country, isn't it?"

Alan nodded as his hands worked the steering wheel. "There's a lot of money in Switzerland, very affluent people. Some are nice, some not so nice. They can be rather snippy."

"This is unlike any place I've been to. Maybe I'm a glutton for punishment and poverty."

"What do you mean?"

"Go to Cambodia, go overland from the Thai border. It could not be a broader contrast when you compare it to this."

"Yes, but Cambodian companies don't buy ad pages, so I'll take your word for it."

"Look, there's the turn we are looking for." John pointed to the sign: Route D'Aubonne.

Alan sighed and turned the vehicle and the road narrowed to two lanes. After several more turns and directions, they found themselves in the heart of Saint Prex. "Is this really necessary?"

"I don't want to hear it."

"Who exactly is this guy Francois?"

"An old traveling buddy, met him overseas years ago. Fortunately, we share an interest in rifles and what not."

Alan decelerated the car. "I don't like this one bit."

"He's doing me a big favor, to say the least. He had to take a day off from work, and his drive is a long one."

"Francois," Alan lifted his hand and waved it gently in the air, "The French assassin. *Tres' bon*!"

"You'll thank me later."

Alan parked the car and looked up to see a vulgar and modern sculpture in the town square. It consisted of cylinders that arched up from the earth on white pedestals. It contrasted with the historical setting of the town and looked out of place. "Ghastly."

"What was that?"

"Never mind."

"He may already be here, we're a bit late." John opened his cellphone and scrolled down to 'FRANCOIS - CELL' and dialed.

Alan turned his head when he heard his brother speaking a language other than his own. He switched to English a moment later. When John concluded the call, Alan asked, "When did you learn French?"

"I barely speak it, Francois taught me some phrases when we backpacked." John's eyes darted around. "He's looking for us."

"He's here?"

"Yea, I don't see him though." John's eyes searched around the perimeter. "He knows we're in a Beemer."

A moment later they both heard a loud thump from the roof of the car. "Jesus!"

Alan flinched. "Hey!"

They turned to see a man with long black and curly hair smiling in the passenger window. They heard him say, "*Bonjour*, John!"

John opened the door and embraced his friend with a bear hug.

Francois grabbed John's shoulders. "You're skinny, my friend!"

"You look the same as always."

Alan stepped out of the car and approached the two men. "Francois…

I would like to introduce you to my half-brother, Alan."

"So this is your brother, eh?" Francois extended his hand. "Nice to meet you."

"Hello there." Alan smiled thinly and gripped his hand.

"I've heard more about you in the past two weeks than I have in the past ten years. John tells me you're quite a character."

"Okay Francois," said John, "that's nice, but—"

"Pardon me." He raised and lowered his hands. "I'm a bit outspoken."

Alan nodded. "I see."

"Let's grab a bite guys, there's a cafe across the street."

"Actually, we have to be moving along," said Alan.

"Oh. I was unaware... John?" Francois shared a concerned glance with his friend.

"Alan, come on."

"Yes, we have business to tend to in Bern."

"Really? So I drive four hours to see an old friend, and I can't share a baguette with him?"

"Of course we can, Alan, just—"

"The bank, John, they close at four. We have a schedule." Alan tapped his Rolex watch.

"That's the bank of course that's holding your grandfather's gift or something, right?"

"I didn't know you were aware of—"

"A friend calls and asks to borrow a deadly weapon. Yeah, he shared some details with me."

"Alan, what the fuck?" His half-brother turned to walk back towards the driver's seat. "Francois, I apologize. You have to forgive—"

Alan closed the driver side door and missed the rest of the conversation. John returned to the vehicle a minute later. He slammed the door shut.

"What was that all about?"

"Let's get this over with."

"You embarrassed me, asshole! We could have shared a cup of coffee with him."

"Fine. Go ahead, have a picnic with Rambo. Give me the bank name, I'll check things out, then I'll drive back and pick you up."

John pursed his lips before he spoke. "Drive."

"What?"

"Follow him, he's right there."

Alan looked up to see an old Peugeot sedan pulling out of a parking spot.

"You're unbelievable," said John.

***

The drive lasted five minutes, and the landscape turned from a small coastal lake town to expansive green farmlands. In every direction there was nothing to see except for an occasional tree and rows of green and amber colored earth.

When the Peugeot stopped, Alan did the same. "Wait here in the car."

Alan watched John exit the vehicle, slam the door and saunter up to the trunk of the Peugeot. Francois got out, looked around and smiled when he spoke to John. Alan considered what to do next. He decided he was not going to sit there like a chauffeur. He turned off the engine and opened the door.

Alan kept his distance and could hear the men speaking in hushed tones. He closed his eyes, stretched his back and breathed in the fresh air. The greenery and rolling hills made for a picturesque moment. The setting was spectacular, but his mind turned to what brought him here. He frowned at the thought.

He turned to see Francois pointing to something in his trunk. He decided to walk over and have a look.

Francois heard the steps and brushed his long dark hair back. "Oh, nice of you to join us," he said sarcastically.

"I'm sorry to rush things along. I... I don't like guns, that's all."

"What?" Francois said. "I thought everyone in America liked guns. Lawyers, guns and money, isn't that right?"

Alan felt like smacking the condescending smile right off the man's face. Given his height, he'd have to stretch to hit him.

He looked down to see a leather satchel, and cradled in the center of the felt lining was a rifle, complete with a telescope sighting.

"Deer hunting?" said Alan.

"Zip it. No more wisecracks." John unfolded his arms and lifted the rifle. "You brought the big one."

"The best I own." Francois grinned. "Ammo is in the front pocket, do you remember the recoil of this gun?"

"And how."

"Careful with it. Now, that pistol I mentioned." Francois reached further into the trunk of his car.

"What else do you have in there, a flame thrower?" Alan shook his head.

"Alan, Enough!"

"Boy oh boy. This guy, how do you say it, he's a real winner." Francois removed a covered holster. "My snub nose forty four." He handed it to John.

"That's awesome, Francois, you shouldn't have." John unsnapped the bronze clasps and revealed the handgun. He felt the weight, which was minimal. It fit comfortably into his hand, and the color of the weapon was black steel. "Is is loaded?"

"Of course not. The ammo is in the box."

"I gave this model a test drive years ago. Love them."

"A magazine you say? I've got a magazine too." John and Francois turned to look at Alan. "One with lots of ad pages, and there are a hundred subordinates who report to me who are working on it right now." Alan smiled. "Pardon the rush. John, we have to be moving along."

"You can shove that *GQ* magazine straight up your—"

"No, no take them, please John, it's okay." John retrieved the weapons and Francois turned to look at Alan. "It's a good thing you've got John for a brother. Every pussy needs a good man in her life."

Alan smirked before he leaned against the passenger door and retrieved his smartphone.

John turned to Francois. "I can't apologize enough. The snubnose was over the top Francois, thank you."

"It's very lightweight and concealable, do you really think you will need these weapons?"

"I doubt it, but I'm not going to risk not having them. I owe you one. Wait here." John walked behind the BMW and placed the weapons within it. He returned and hugged his friend goodbye.

"Oh wait! I forgot." He reached back into the trunk of the Peugeot and untethered a plastic button. He fumbled before he found what he was looking for. He turned and handed John the handle of a knife, whose blade was cradled in brown leather. Straps dangled underneath it. "My buck knife. Take it."

"Thanks, Francois."

"No problem my friend! Give me a call when you wrap things up, and we'll figure out how to exchange the weapons. Maybe share a café." He tilted his head towards Alan.

"I promise."

John walked back to the trunk and placed the blade within it. He turned to see Alan thumbing away on his phone. "I'm driving?"

Alan waved his hand. "Sure, I don't care. Feel any safer?" He listened to the Peugeot drive away. They were left on the side of the road with no one in sight.

Alan was consumed with an email he was reading and heard the faint sound of sliding metal. He heard the sound of something snap which reminded him of a deadbolt lock. The email from a senior executive at Condé Nast kept him focused when he heard John walk away from the car.

The air cracked with a high decibel gun shot.

Startled by the gunfire, Alan dropped his phone. He turned to see John aiming the pistol at a tree.

"Hey!"

John turned his head. "Yes?"

"What the fuck are you doing?"

"Your question. Yes, now I feel safer. So should you."

Alan's eyes darted across the landscape. No one was around. "That was the dumbest thing… we have to get out of here."

"Get in the car, shut up and drive." He walked over, removed the magazine and placed it and the trunk in the car. He moved and sat down in the passenger seat. He watched Alan retrieve his cell phone and then moved to the driver's side of the car. "If we run into trouble, you'll thank me." Alan turned on the engine. "That way you won't be stuck holding your dick in your hand."

Alan slammed on the gas and dirt flew up from the road. "That was so

154

uncalled for."

"Shut the fuck up."

Chapter 19

The BMW pulled to a stop in the parking space on a road called *Speichergasse*. John parked the car and turned off the engine. John took over driving duties after a brief stop at a gas station. He turned to see Alan typing incessantly on his iPhone. The clock in the car read 12:45 p.m. "A nice car to drive, I'll say that. Hey, are you done with that thing yet?"

"Halfway through emails."

"That many?" His brother nodded. "Okay then. Well, this is it."

"Okay."

John turned off the engine. "Have you calmed down?"

"Let's not get into it." Alan turned to look at his half-brother. "I apologize if I was rude to your friend."

"If?"

"Okay, I was rude." Alan shrugged his shoulders. "Sorry about that."

John stepped out of the car, locked it, and Alan followed. The weather was pleasant and sunny as they looked down the street. The buildings were four stories high and their exteriors were trimmed with concrete that ran lengthwise, parallel to the street.

"Do you know where to go?"

"I got it right here." John held up the folded laminated map.

Alan grinned and started to walk down the street.

"Wait," said John. "How do you know which way to go?"

"I'm guessing."

"Give me a minute." He unfolded the laminated map and used his finger to trace their location. He looked at a street sign, then back down at the map. He pointed towards the direction to take but stopped short.

Alan noticed a peculiar look on John's face. "What is it?"

"You know, after we get there, you could access the vault by yourself."

"Oh."

"Think about it. Two pieces of information, my half will be shared, yours will not."

"Do you trust me, John?"

John paused. "Yes."

"But you had to think for a second, didn't you?" He pointed at his brother. "Show me the way, John."

John walked down the street and passed well-dressed professionals and a few mothers with baby carriages in tow. Five blocks away the road opened up to a square. The center of it was painted off-white with square dimensions running on the ground horizontally and vertically. It was sealed off from car traffic.

"The Swiss, go figure."

"What do you mean, Alan?"

"They have a penchant for being organized, and being very unimaginative. See the squares?"

"Yes."

"I bet you every single one is the exact same size, and perfectly separated. They need more Italians in this country."

"How so?"

"They make everything beautiful. They'd use this space for something more artistic than a simple geometric pattern. Everything here has to be organized to a fault."

"I see. Well, let's get on with it." John walked across the square, which was flanked by two parallel streets. He crossed it, made two left turns after he checked his map. At that moment he froze and put his hands on his knees.

"You okay?"

"Yes, I'm just... thinking about Everett and our father."

"Oh." Alan nodded. "Yeah... It's a bit much."

"That's it? A bit much?" He watched his brother put his hands on his hips and shake his head slowly, confirming for John he felt something too. He stood upright and turned to look at Alan. "They could have stood in this very spot. Everett said a lot of men died for this, during the war I mean."

Alan nodded. "Hard to forget that video."

The two shared a long look at one another; neither seemed sure what to say next. Finally John pointed to the building perpendicular to where they were standing. "There." Alan turned to look. "Scheibzerische National Bank. That's it."

The building was, as the others around it, four stories tall and the color of light tan. Iron bars covered the windows and the building anchored a public square that opened in front of it. They walked around to the front entrance and trees flanked it. To their right was a more grandiose building with a dome and the entire area remained closed to car traffic. Dozens of pedestrians crisscrossed the area in random directions.

Alan looked up and felt a lump in his throat. He remained there for a minute, deep in thought. "Shall we go see what this is about?"

John turned to see his brother looking at him. "Let's go." They stepped forward together.

They found themselves standing on plush carpet with several teller stations on the right side of the entrance. The red carpet continued down a pathway towards the rear end of a large room. Two pairs of elevators flanked the far side and in between were rows of handsome wood desks. Behind them were two uniformed officers who possessed side arms. It was not an unusual setting, but it was rich in design and wealth. Multiple chandeliers illuminated the room from the ceiling.

They looked around for someone to speak to but no one individual looked like an obvious person to speak with about a private vault. Alan walked up to one of the tellers seated behind fine-polished brass bars. "Excuse me."

"May I help you?"

The process of finding the right person took fifteen minutes, given the explanation of what John and Alan were trying to accomplish. In two incidents, they were asked for identification and the same questions were repeated. Alan maintained his composure and did most of the talking, but it was apparent that their request to access a vault was uncommon.

After Alan spoke to a senior officer, he shared Everett's name and the year when the vault and account were opened by their grandfather. The director walked away and said he'd be back momentarily.

"What's taking so long?"

"It's annoying, I agree," said Alan.

John sat down on a nearby bench and Alan joined him. "You hungry?"

"Starving."

Five minutes passed before the director walked over to them from a nearby office. "Gentlemen, I spoke to our director in charge of these matters, Herr Heinzen. He has an appointment outside the office and asks that you call back to make an appointment for tomorrow morning."

"Unfortunately, that's not going to work with our schedule. Perhaps this afternoon?"

"Excuse me," John interjected. "We'd like to see it now please."

"We cannot accommodate you at this time, but if you return, say at 3:00, I can personally assist with your request."

Alan put his hand on John's shoulder. "That will suffice, we appreciate your efforts."

"Of course." The officer stepped away.

Alan motioned for John to leave the building without making eye contact with him.

***

John pushed away the empty plate after consuming a ham and Swiss cheese sandwich. He sipped his coffee and shook his head. "They better have someone there to open the vault. Otherwise this is not going to be pleasant." Alan was working on email. "Aren't you pissed?"

Alan put down the phone. "Yes, but we did not have an appointment. A few hours delay won't kill us. We have all day tomorrow and Friday to wrap things up."

John looked down and his watch read 2:45 p.m. "We should go." He removed his wallet and retrieved his credit card.

"I'll get it."

"Nope, I insist." John handed his Visa along with the bill to the waitress. "*Danke schoen.*"

Alan went back to his inbox. He read the email from his west coast representative and it mentioned they had acquired five pages of Apple Computer business. Alan said aloud, "That's it?"

"What's it?"

"What? Oh, sorry, some bad news at work."

"Spill."

Alan looked at the man who possessed no advertising experience. "We got five pages today of Apple business."

"So, isn't that good news?"

"Remember our chat about market share? We're getting shortchanged, again." Alan dropped the phone on the table. "And now I have to fire someone."

"Come on."

"Yup, we're getting killed in the L.A. market. I have to make a move."

John raised and lowered his eyebrows while he stirred the remnants of his coffee. "Is that to save your own skin?"

"It's business, John."

"Did you hire him?"

"What does that have to do with anything?"

John smirked, signed the bill and stood up from the table. "I guess it's easier to let someone go than to actually manage them. Nice touch."

"Who the—" Alan got up to follow him out of the restaurant.

They were walking down *Kramgasse* Street when Alan caught up to John. "You know, I don't critique how you do your job."

"I just don't get it. Firing someone for winning business."

"Hey." He put his arm on his shoulder. "This is how the best publishers operate, and I'm trying to be one of those."

"You live in a different world than the rest of us, Alan. Even the people who report to you. That's what you don't understand." John turned and saw the bank in the distance. "Look."

Alan sighed and said, "Let's get this over with."

John walked ten more paces and opened the door to the bank. They went back to the same window and waited for someone to help them.

John looked to either side as his hand tapped the counter.

"Take a deep breath."

"I should have brought the gun."

"Ha."

The teller they met before moved to greet them.

"Yes, we are looking for the manager please."

After several minutes, Alan turned around and saw a very concerned look on the face of the bank director as he walked towards them.

"Gentlemen, some unfortunate news I'm afraid." He cleared his throat. "The manager responsible for our private security vaults, he has left for the day."

"That's not our problem." John crossed his arms. "I thought you offered to assist us."

"That is not possible, I'm afraid."

Alan shook his head. "Pardon?"

"The keys to access the vault chambers, as well as Herr Heinzen's set. They are both missing."

Chapter 20

Charlotte muted the TV after she saw the name, 'ALAN-CELL' pop up on her phone's LCD screen.

"Hey there. How's the trip going?"

"We're fine."

She thought he sounded disappointed. "What's wrong?"

"The bank. We can't see what's inside the vault, not until tomorrow."

"You've got to be kidding me. What's the problem?"

"They are missing some keys, misplaced or something."

"Come on."

"No joke."

"What a cliché. All this time and energy. How can that possibly happen?" She leaned back and listened while Alan walked her through it. "So, tomorrow then."

"If not, I think John is going to lose it. He's furious, and armed."

"He has every right to be." She waited but heard a faint laugh over the phone. "Alan, what's funny?"

"Wait a minute, this should be fun."

"Alan?" She waited for him to speak.

"John, come here, your sister wants to know more about the buck knife, handgun and rifle your friend Francois lent you."

"Jesus! What's up with the arsenal?" said Charlotte.

She heard John curse before he spoke into Alan's phone. "Hey Charlotte, how are—"

"What the hell is going on over there? You have multiple weapons?"

"Listen, I—"

"A buck knife? What's next, a set of nunchucks?"

Scheibzerische Bank Square, Bern, Switzerland

The cab pulled up to the curb. "Here." Henrick paid the driver and exited the Mercedes.

He stood twenty feet from the entrance and looked up at the building. He removed his cell phone and dialed the main number of the bank before him. "Yes, I want to speak to Herr Heinzen."

"One moment," the receptionist said. He heard the phone ring several times before it went to voicemail. He ended the call and then walked up to the front door of the bank. He saw employees milling about inside, but when he tried to open the doors they were all locked.

He stepped back, furrowed his brow and made another phone call. A moment later, Otto answered. "Where are you?"

"Crossing the square right now. I see you."

Henrick turned to see Otto walking towards his position. "Did you see Devenger?"

"No, I got here ten minutes ago, the bank was closed."

Henrick looked at his watch, which read 4:15 p.m. "We need to find Heinzen. Where is Fritz, he should be here with the van."

"I told you he's getting in tonight." Otto motioned for Henrick to step away from the entrance. They walked into the middle of the square. "Are you absolutely certain Karla was right about John Devenger's trip, and that he's in Switzerland?"

"Everything she explained made sense. He could be walking around here right now."

Otto watched Henrick turn in various directions to look. "Henrick, what would we do, right now, if we found him?" Henrick squinted his eyes and ignored the question. "Henrick."

"We would get him of course. You have the weapons, we—"

"We could do nothing. Look at all these people. We don't have the van. This area is closed off to traffic."

Henrick dropped his shoulders and his face exuded futility. "We have to get him."

"And we will, but we're not ready yet." The two started walking to Otto's car. "The house you rented, you have directions?"

"Of course."

Henrick stopped walking at that moment and put his suitcase on the ground. "Wait a minute." He opened it and retrieved the notepad within it. He found Heinzen's cell phone number. He entered the digits into the phone and hit send.

"What are you doing?"

"Our little friend inside the bank, he needs to get the message."

Bundegasse Street, Bern

John handed the phone back to Alan when they were seated in the BMW. "Why in God's name did you tell her?"

"Why not? You made your bed, now sleep in it." Alan watched John unfold the map. "Besides, I want her to know what's going on."

"It was a douche move."

He took his phone and scrolled down to the name of the woman he was looking for. "I'm going to update the curator."

Before he did, John asked, "Where's the hotel?"

Alan stopped before he called and found the email with the hotel's address. "Forwarding this to you." Then he called the curator.

He called and explained to the curator they were delayed and would not know if they required her assistance and employment until the next day. She mentioned that it would complicate the process and perhaps delay shipment. Alan told her he'd get in touch with her tomorrow and thanked her for being flexible.

"That sucks. We may not get the artwork ready to ship in time."

"If... there is art to be found."

Alan put the phone down. "Okay, let's write this day off. I need a drink. Where's the hotel on the map?"

"Drive down the street parallel to this one. Make a left there." He pointed down the street.

Alan turned on the engine and followed John's directions. "I stayed at this hotel once before."

"You don't know where it is then?"

"I had a driver. I'm not acquainted with these roads."

John directed Alan through several more turns and the car came to a stop outside an enormous hotel.

John saw the bellhop move to open his door. "*Guten tag*. May I take your bags?"

John thought about the contents within the trunk. "I got it, thanks." John walked to the trunk and saw the leather satchels and his luggage bag. He squirmed when he noticed the bellhop walking towards him. He jammed the handgun and knife into exterior luggage pockets, left the rifle and grabbed Alan's bag before he closed the trunk.

The valet manager walked up to Alan. "Are you staying with us?"

"Yes."

He held out his hand and gestured for the keys.

"John, give the man our bags, won't you?"

"I've got them, thanks."

When he climbed the stairs and entered the building, he took ten paces, looked up, and then his bags immediately hit the floor. His mouth parted as his eyes canvassed the surroundings.

The opulent and plush interior of the hotel was like nothing he ever experienced before. His head could not stop turning. The marble floors stretched from end to end and red carpet outlined several seating areas. Columns of Romanesque design stretched from floor to ceiling while sunlight extended through long and tall windows. He looked up to see a massive chandelier glisten with soft yellow lights, which reflected off polished brass. He turned to see Alan grinning from ear to ear.

"You should see the look on your face."

"This is unbelievable." His smile evaporated when he turned to see half-brother. "Alan, how much is this going to cost us?"

"Try to enjoy it, John, my treat." Alan padded him on his back and handed him the set of keys to his room. "Go enjoy yourself, take a long bath, let's grab a drink and dinner later tonight. Sound good?"

John handed Alan his bag. "Okay... yeah... sure." He walked across the floor, appearing memorized by the scenery. Alan followed.

John turned to see a well-dressed employee smile as they approached the elevators. "Gentlemen, welcome to the Bellevue Palace."

Englische Anlagen Boulevard, Bern

He fiddled with one set of keys in his hand while the other set remained motionless in the passenger seat. His car was parked on a small turnout from the road, which overlooked the glacial river. There was a river beyond the incline from the road. He looked beyond to see the spire of the Berner Munster gothic cathedral.

He looked down at the four keys attached to a circular and worn piece of metal. Two of them were modern in design and finish and they extended three inches in length. The other two were older and provided access to the vault chambers on the third and fourth-floor levels beneath the building. He rarely accessed the deeper chambers and debated whether his life, or his wife's, was worth the risk.

His spouse of twenty years had no idea the trouble he was in, and if he did not comply, he feared for both of them.

Heinzen rubbed both cheeks with one hand and thought about his choices. There was no way to access the vaults, given he had both sets of keys: One pair was trusted to him, the other was taken from his director's office.

He had complied with Henrick's wishes. That provided him with some level of comfort and he sat back in the driver's seat.

Several minutes passed before he decided to pick up his phone and explain his absence from the office. He would arrive early in the morning, place his supervisor's keys in the back of one of his desk drawers before he got there, and apologize for not leaving his keys behind. He knew he would be reprimanded but he didn't believe his actions would cost him his job.

He also decided to cut off all communication with Henrick. Even if they were veiled threats, there was greater risk in telling him that two men, not one, had shown up to access Vault 21-12.

When he opened his phone, he noticed several voicemails from both the bank and Henrick. He deleted them all, emailed his boss he had a stomach bug and decided to text Henrick to let him know he had complied with his request. He then turned off his phone and started his car. He would be home before his wife and planned to unplug the home phone.

Gumligen, Switzerland, Outside of Bern

"He will be here any moment," said Otto.

"Good, then we will return to the city." Henrick paced across the living room. He noticed a musty smell in the air but it was too cold outside to open the windows.

"When did you rent this?"

"I signed the papers two weeks ago."

"What if the landlord stops by? Have you thought that through?"

Henrick turned to face him. "We just tell him we have business in Bern, is that a problem?"

"And if we have... company?" Otto raised his eyebrows.

"We introduce him to one of the weapons." Henrick pointed to the pistols and machine gun resting on the coffee table.

"We will do nothing of the sort."

Henrick nodded. "*Ja*, I know. Let's hope we get what we need from John Devenger quickly." He waved him off and continued pacing. "He'll talk, one way or another. But we don't know where he is staying in the city."

"If we did, we would not dare attempt to get him in the hotel."

"Why not?"

"Remember 1983, dear Henrick?" He watched Henrick furrow his brow and then nod in agreement. "That is what the van is for."

Otto stood up when they heard the sound of a vehicle pull alongside the front of the house. Henrick was closest to the window and stepped towards it to look outside. He saw a white van and then noticed Fritz bounce out of the driver's seat and head to the front door. They both heard him knock.

"It's Fritz," said Henrick, "Get him, won't you?"

Otto complied and a minute later both men were standing in the living room with Henrick.

Fritz leaned over the two men and tossed his bag on the couch. A wave of dust rose from the furniture. "Henrick, you better be right about Devenger. That flight cost me a lot of money."

"He is."

"Did you see him?" Henrick did not answer Fritz's question. He moved closer to him. "Yes or no?"

Otto stepped between Henrick and Fritz. Then he turned to look at the angry young man. "We did not see him. We're quite certain he is here though."

"Sounds like bullshit, I want answers. Where did we get the tip, from the private eye in Jersey?"

"Late last night."

"So help me God, if you fucked this up I'll—"

"Fritz, back down. Now!" Otto used his hands to move him away from Henrick.

Henrick snarled and retrieved his mobile phone. He noticed Heinzen texted him hours ago. "*Scheisse.*" He opened the message and read its contents. He looked up to see Fritz and Otto arguing with one another.

"Both of you, shut up. The banker, he mentions here that he has complied. Devenger was there, he did not access the vault." He pointed towards Fritz. "There Fritz, the proof you were looking for."

Otto stepped back and placed himself between Fritz and the guns lying on the coffee table.

Fritz noticed the movement. "Yeah, I see the guns fat man."

"Listen," said Henrick, "Tonight, we settle in. Tomorrow, we have no choice but to wait outside the bank. When we see him, we grab him and then get him back here."

The men standing before him nodded in compliance.

"He'll never see it coming."

Chapter 21

Bellevue Hotel, Bern

The last sip of coffee hit his palate and John admitted to himself it was wonderful. The breakfast he ordered was delivered on a wheeled-in service tray and placed in front of the television half an hour ago. The scrambled eggs came with fruit, crisp bacon and fresh squeezed orange juice. The waiter also delivered an English language newspaper, to his surprise.

John Devenger felt refreshed, excited and well fed. The bed was comfortable and the windows radiated with sunlight. He exhaled and checked himself in the full-length mirror.

He quickly scanned his clothes, fresh shave and then looked at the room within the reflection. It was spacious, well decorated and he could see the glacial waters of the River Aare flowing in the distance through the window.

He turned back to look at his face and saw himself grinning. For a split second he didn't recognize the man looking back at him. He struggled with the emotion of a self-consciousness moment, which prompted him to turn away from the mirror. He didn't understand what set it off, but it did not sit well with him.

He thought about all his travels, the experiences he had and wondered why he never once chose to stay at a five-star hotel. His mind reflected on all the hostels and guesthouses he frequented: the bunk beds and shared bathrooms, the tight budgets he stretched over two, four and six months when he traveled. The sight of the room contrasted to other accommodations he stayed at, but he would not have traded one day, or one week of his travels to afford a night in a place like the Bellevue.

He answered his own question and looked once again in the full-length mirror. The blue color of his dress shirt peaked out from the maroon sweater he was wearing. His gut told him to give in and enjoy the experience, but he just couldn't let go. He turned to retrieve his jacket, room key, wallet and passport.

When he left the room his mind turned to the task at hand and his heart started to pound in his chest. After two months of mystery, they would see for themselves what was waiting for them inside Vault 21-12.

He pressed the elevator button and a moment later he was downstairs in the lobby searching for his half-brother.

John turned when he heard his name called. Alan crossed the room to stand beside his brother. "Well, shall we try again?" said John.

He smiled. "Yes, we shall indeed. How did you sleep?"

"Very well, actually."

"Did the Ambien help?"

"I didn't need it, thankfully. I was wiped out. I ordered room service this morning."

Alan smiled. "Good for you. Getting accustomed to five-star room service?" He turned to the west to walk down the street. John followed.

"Let's just say it was good coffee."

They walked beside one another down *Marktgasse* Boulevard towards *Scheibzerische* Bank.

Bern, Switzerland

He dialed Otto's phone. He answered, "Where are you parked?"

"On *Bundegasse*. It is a one way street, two blocks west of from *Scheibzerische* Bank."

"Keep the engine on, no matter how long it takes."

"Yes."

Henrick reached down and felt the concealed handgun in his pocket. He dialed Fritz who was also on the street looking for John Devenger. He answered on the second ring. "Where are you situated?"

"I'm three blocks to the east of the square, on *Marktgasse*."

"Good. Remain there. Keep your eyes open and don't expose your weapon. If you see him, call Otto immediately and follow Devenger."

"Got it."

Henrick stood two blocks to the east on *Kochergasse* and his eyes drew themselves to every man who passed in the hope of finding the bald man. Had Karla been there, he'd feel more confident they would have every approach covered. The moment Devenger appeared, the van would swoop down and either Fritz or Henrick would escort John Devenger into the rear of the vehicle. Henrick knew he could not manage a physical confrontation, but his weapon would be persuasive nonetheless.

He leaned himself against a leafless tree and watched a trolley roll by with commuters inside of it. He looked at his watch: 9:10 a.m. Further ahead of him were rows of motorcycles. They did not impede his view of pedestrians. He also had a clear line of sight across the street when trolleys were not present. Further beyond was the river itself.

He felt the urge to pace after several minutes of waiting but he chose to remain still. One hand was on his mobile phone; the other remained on the handgun. He tapped the trigger with his finger inside his pocket.

When he felt his phone vibrate he retrieved it quickly and answered.

"I don't fucking believe it. There are two of them, right here!" yelled Fritz.

"Two?"

"That's his brother. I recognize him from the old pictures."

"That cannot be."

"What should I do? They are twenty paces ahead of me."

"Call Otto! Follow them, no wait, I'll call Otto—"

"How do I manage this?"

Henrick ran with a limp down *Bundesgasse*. He ended the call and dialed Otto who did not answer. He was one block away from the square when he redialed Fritz and tried to catch his breath. "Where... where are they!"

"I am walking towards the bank entrance. I don't see Otto, they are turning the corner."

"Dammit!"

"What should I—"

Henrick pulled the phone away from his ear. He turned towards Southwestern side of the building. Across the way he saw the entrance to the bank. He dialed Otto.

"You see him?" said Otto.

"The Devengers! There are two of them!"

"I'm driving, one block south of the bank on *Kochergasse.*"

Henrick double-timed it across the square. He froze when he saw the bald man, and his half-brother, walk in tow with one another. They turned the corner. He did not see Fritz. The two men were thirty yards, then twenty, then ten yards from the entrance.

He looked back and saw his blond counterpart walk around the side of the building. He lifted his arms in a gesture of disbelief. When he looked back he saw John and Alan Devenger open the doors to the *Scheibzerische* Bank. When they were out of sight Henrick placed his hands on his knees, shook his head and tried to catch his breath.

***

"Gentlemen, this is Herr Heinzen, our director of private deposits."

"Greetings."

John looked at the frail man and shook his soft white hand. His short mustache was a hairline or two away from looking like Hitler's. "Hello." Alan did likewise.

"I apologize for my absence yesterday, I ate something that did not agree."

Alan sighed upon hearing the man's excuse. "I was surprised to find out you were the only man with access to the vault."

The bank director in charge spoke, "There was an unfortunate complication on our end. We are now able to service your needs and the bank has corrected some internal procedures."

Alan watched the small man provide a quick nod. He did not, by any means, appear comfortable. "Well, gentlemen, if you will follow me this way." He gestured with his hand to follow him down the red carpet towards the elevators at the far end of the room.

They left the other man behind as the three men walked between rows of desks, many of which were unoccupied. John caught his half-brother's attention and smirked. "Banker's hours."

The man called Heinzen remained silent as he punched the second floor button in the elevator's console. He clasped his hands in front of him. "So the two of you are from the States, yes?"

"Yup."

"What part if I may ask?"

"New York."

"New Jersey."

The banker seemed uncomfortable from the brother's terse replies. "Very well then. This way please."

The second floor was similar to the first with a large area of open seating in front of them. There were offices on both sides of the room and fogged glass hid the interiors. "How old is this bank?"

"We were founded in 1823, but we took residence of this location in 1905. Please," He pointed to the open door and within the room were two chairs and a large wooden desk. Heinzen took the leather-bound seat behind it. John and Alan sat down in the guest chairs. Behind the banker was a curtain-drawn window and a small green lamp illuminated the desk.

"Again, gentlemen, I apologize for yesterday, but I have all the paperwork prepared." He opened a drawer and placed a set of keys to his right. He then retrieved a folder that appeared dated and aged. The sides were worn and a musty smell wafted into the air when the banker turned the front cover.

"We have some paperwork here to administer. Please look."

John looked down to see a yellowed and thin paper with dates, names and times entered in black ink. It was hard to read and he squinted. Both men read the following:

VAULT 21-12 XXXX XXXXX XXXX XXXXXX
ESTABLISHED: 30th OF MAY, 1945
DEPOSITOR: EVERETT DEVENGER
CONTENTS: FULL

DEPOSITOUR DATE OF ENTRY SIGNATURE

17 - April - 1947	Everett Devenger
19 - October - 1983	Jack Devenger

John and Alan remained silent when they looked at the signatures of their forefathers. Alan took his eyes off the page and stared at the floor for a moment before making eye contact with Heinzen. "Yes, that... appears to be accurate."

"Identification, please." John and Alan handed the banker their passports. After Heinzen jotted down some details he returned them. "Do you have the necessary account number information and passcode?"

"Wait, does this reflect the total number of visits to the vault?"

"Yes, the vault has been accessed twice since it was opened."

He turned to look at Alan. "Ready?"

Alan rubbed his forehead and nodded. "I have the details." Alan took the pen from Heinzen.

"Please fill out this form."

Alan did as he was told and jotted down in each separate box the digits that corresponded to the full account number, which he had memorized. When he was done he pushed the paperwork back towards the banker. It now contained his name, signature and the current date, beneath his grandfather and father's signature.

"Excellent. And the passcode please."

Both Alan and John leaned forward and said at the same time, "Brotherhood." Their head's turned to look at one another. John grinned and Alan nodded.

If you can sign the ledger here, both of you please." John and Alan's signature followed Everett's and their father's.

"I assume you both wish to access the vault, yes?"

John was lost in thought but turned a moment later to look at the banker. "Yes."

The phone beside the desk rang and the banker answered, "Heinzen." John and Alan watched as the banker listened to what sounded like a German man scream on the other end of the line.

The banker put the phone back in the cradle and turned his attention to the paperwork. He remained silent while Alan noticed the color in his cheeks turn a shade pale. "Everything all right?" said Alan.

"Yes... yes indeed. Please follow me." He gestured in rapid motions when he stood up and grabbed the keys. They rattled in his hands while he walked out the door.

John said under his breath, "Was that his boss?" Alan shrugged his shoulders.

"I hope you find our facilities to be professional. This way please."

When the doors of the elevator closed, Heinzen removed the keys and placed one in an elevator-panel outlet. "This will take us to the 1st chamber floor. Just a moment." He turned the key and a red light bulb illuminated from the elevator's ceiling. A buzzer beeped twice as the elevator paused in motion.

John watched the panel above the doorframe turn from '2' to 'Grnd.' A few seconds passed before a 'Z' illuminated. It continued down and another floor level was illuminated in red: 'X'. The elevator squeaked, as if it was trying to fit itself into a tight space before it came to a rest. When it stopped there was a thump in vibration, causing all three men to catch their balance.

The doors opened and they stepped out of it. Before them was a narrow hallway that extended as far as the eye could see.

"What the hell?" John turned his head. They were standing in an area no more than ten by fifteen feet wide. One single hallway stretched down a yellow-lit corridor. A slight humming sound emanated from the walls. He crossed his arms from the chill in the air. "What is that sound?"

"An air ventilation system. We keep humidity levels at extremely low levels down here. I should have warned you."

"Okay." Alan swallowed as he turned to see the brown brick walls surround him. He felt claustrophobic from the space. The hallway was no more than twelve feet tall and the sides were only eight feet apart. It felt haunted for some reason and his brother revealed the same appearance of shock that Alan felt himself.

"And where is our vault?"

"Follow me gentlemen." The sound of their steps interlaced with the buzzing sound above their heads from the vents. They started to pass dark-brown iron door frames where the entrance was imbedded one foot within the stonework. They walked fifty yards in distance, following the trail of incandescent yellow lights that illuminated the path towards the end of the hallway.

They had passed twenty doorframes when John looked closely at one of them and stopped. There was a digital locking mechanism at eye level on one of the last doors. He studied it before they came to another entryway beyond. "Do they all have these modern locks?"

"No, *monsieur*, these represent the bank's more recent facilities. One floor above is where you would find state of the art security, the best in all of Europe. The vault in both your names is down in an older part of the bank, I'm afraid."

"Afraid you say? Why so?"

"It's rather inconvenient, however it is most definitely secure. Follow me please, you will see."

Alan rubbed the sides of his arms as the temperature was no more than fifty degrees. His nose grew colder and colder as he watched Heinzen retrieve his keys once again. The door in front of them was made of black steel and it anchored the far end of the room. When he turned the key it unhinged a lock from within the wall. A loud snap of metal was heard beyond and he pushed the door open. Past the doorframe was a smaller area illuminated by a bright red light.

Alan followed Heinzen when he descended a flight of stairs. The staircase trailed away from the only source of light. He sensed the walls and angled ceiling close in around him. The red lights dimmed to provide a muted maroon glow to the dark surroundings. When they arrived at the bottom, Alan tried to take a deep breath but the enclosure prevented him from taking one. "Christ have fucking mercy," he said under his breath.

He felt some level of respite when Heinzen ushered them into an open area. The air seemed stagnant but warmer. His eyes adjusted to the dimly lit area.

They entered a small area in which to stand. "Just a moment please." John turned to see two black tunnel openings outlined in a tall curved ceiling perpendicular to one another. They were pitch black at the moment. John looked up to see a faint light bulb right before he heard Heinzen flip a switch. He was blinded a second later when additional lights illuminated every square inch of the room.

He blinked several times then focused a dusty stone floor beneath his feet.

John saw Alan squinting from the bright light. "It's a freaking dungeon down here," said Alan.

"Wait here please." They listened to Heinzen walk behind them and open a thin-metal compartment door. The black holes of arched darkness remained the same until they heard the sound of another switch. In a flash, they saw light bulbs illuminate a path down one of the tunnels. It extended thirty yards in the distance before trailing off around a corner. The tunnel on the right side of the room remained pitch black.

John turned to Alan. "I couldn't have made this shit up if I tried. Do you believe this?" Alan shook his head with what looked like a flinch. "You okay?"

"No."

"I apologize if this seems unpleasant gentlemen. Vault 21-12 is down this way, not too far from here."

"How do you get deposits down to this level?"

"We have a service elevator. We do not allow the use of them unless deposits are made or withdrawn."

"Why?"

"For security's sake, sir."

Alan followed behind John and the banker and noticed the arched ceiling sloped down to within eight feet above their heads. The walls were now six feet from one another. Alan did everything he could to hold off a full-blown panic attack. The stones beneath appeared worn. "How old is this part of the bank?"

"This was built before the bank opened, and it is the oldest area of our operation."

When they walked thirty yards, John noticed the vault-door entrances seemed more dated.

"Only a bit further." Heinzen's words reverberated off the stone walls.

John reached out to feel the coarse wall, which consisted of square and imperfect stones. He watched the doors pass by and noticed for the first time they were numbered. The doors rose in sequence with each one they passed. He saw 21-09, then 21-10, and 21-11 before he stopped himself from making contact with the banker's backside.

Heinzen turned to face him. His stare lingered as the sound of keys rattled in his hand.

"This is our destination. I will unlock it now. How much time do you require?"

"We can't say."

Heinzen nodded. "Very well then, I will wait for you down the hallway." He turned and rifled through his keys to find the one that looked the most dated. It was old, long and twisted in various extensions.

It took several twists for him to find the right fit before he opened what appeared to be an exterior door. John noticed the door was several inches thick, and when it hit the exterior stonewall, it echoed down the distance of the tunnel.

"That's it?"

"There's another door for security."

They watched the banker use his fingers to feel within the doorframe and found what he was looking for. He grabbed what turned out to be a four-inch bar and pulled down on it. A light turned on and illuminated the immediate area. Deeper within the walled area was another steel-plated door. Three feet of space separated one doorframe from another. He used another key, and when the banker used it, he opened the door and left it ajar.

"At this time I will leave you to yourselves. When you need me, I will be at the other end of the hallway. The area inside is partially lit. You'll find another switch within the vault. Simply call out when you require assistance."

They both hesitated outside the door entrance and watched Heinzen walk around the corner of the tunnel.

John noticed Alan's pale complexion. "You look like you're going to be sick."

"This place feels like a buried prison. Not... what I expected."

"You're telling me. Well, here we are. Twenty one twelve."

"Yeah." Alan took a deep breath. "After you."

John stepped forward into what felt like a rectangular stone box and pushed the door inwards.

The door creaked on four separate hinges as it turned within the room. The sound echoed from the walls behind them. They could see an open area inside the vault.

They stepped in to see the roof and walls extend above and around them. The door came to a rest when it tapped against the inside wall. Their view in front of their position was blocked and their eyes once again adjusted to a dimly lit area.

Alan turned when he entered and saw an object on the floor to his left. He furrowed his brow when he tried to make sense of it.

A cardboard box sat on the uneven stone floor beneath them. There was a small table adjacent to the far left wall. His eyes adjusted to the light and he noticed what looked like a long piece of burlap stretched from one end of the room to the other. It blocked the view beyond the area where they stood.

Alan noticed the wording on the side of the box. It read, 'Marlboro.'

"Look at this," said Alan, "a cardboard box of smokes."

"What the hell." The fabric that stretched across the room absorbed their words and sounds. John watched Alan approach the box, kneel before it, and remove the lid.

He looked inside and smiled. "Well, that's pretty cool."

"What is it?"

He watched Alan retrieve a leather bound journal from within it. It was an inch and a half thick, and he opened it to reveal yellowed and aged hand-written pages. "Looks like another journal of sorts."

"That's it?"

Alan turned to the middle of the journal and saw the date July 5th, 1945 written on one page in particular. The handwriting was familiar. "Everett." He noticed other paperwork within the box. "There's a bunch of other documents in here. They look official."

John put his hands on his hips. "This entire process, all the planning, and it turns out to be another journal." He heard himself laugh. "I guess that journal makes for one hell of a keepsake." He turned back to the table and noticed a light switch on the wall. A thin metal pipe extended above it and crossed the central part of the ceiling. His eyes followed it as it continued down the center of the room and behind the burlap. "Wait, there's another light switch."

Alan remained on one knee and leafed through the journal. "Okay. Turn it on."

John walked a few steps and hit a round green button. He heard a click and turned to see lights illuminate above and behind the burlap. The burlap material acted like a veil of sorts but the sides remained dark.

He swallowed. "Alan."

"This journal relates to the one we found in his study."

John looked up and moved towards the right side of the room. He noticed the burlap was tethered to something above their position. He gave it a slight tug before he saw the fabric drape in between two enormous rectangles that flanked the sides of the vault. He stepped to the other side of the room and pulled on the other side of the burlap. The motion left part of the fabric dangling between what appeared to be two fifteen by ten-foot blocks of equal proportions. "Alan."

"There's... something else here." John turned to see Alan removing papers from the Marlboro box. He froze a moment later.

Alan placed his hand in the box, fumbled with something, and then left it there in place. "I don't believe it."

John stepped forward and looked inside of it. In the center was the image of an embedded eagle with its wings spread to its sides. Beneath the image was a swastika. A three-digit number was below it and on the bottom left side they saw 'SS' initials of what appeared to be a solid brick of gold.

"Oh my God." Alan used both hands to lift and cradle it. "It's... Jesus! This weighs close to twenty pounds!"

He watched Alan move the brick to the table and it slammed on the surface when he placed it there.

John shook his head. "Everett, what did you do?" He proceeded to turn around and look at the burlap dangling above the area where he stood.

He walked over, yanked on the fabric and watched it fall down in sheets before him.

When it settled, a wave of dust splashed into the air. He stepped away and covered his mouth from the debris. The cloud briefly obscured the light in the room. When he was able to look, John realized the enormity of the vault. There was twenty yards of distance between his position and the far wall. Lights from above illuminated a four-foot wide path that stretched between stacks of wooden crates. Each one appeared identical to the other.

What he saw caused him to step back. His ass hit the table and his heart started to pound in his chest. Alan turned to look.

The same image, the eagle and the swastika, were stamped in black ink on 18 identical wooden boxes.

The three by four-foot crates extended side by side to the opposite end of Vault 21-12.

Chapter 22

"Heinzen... Heinzen!" Henrick put his phone away and turned to see Fritz standing beside him with his arms crossed. He turned to see Otto sitting in the van in the distance. "*Scheisse.*"

"There was no way to get them, man. No way."

"That was his brother, Alan." He paced in front of the bank. "I should have escalated the investigation. Tabs on them all."

"Who, the private eyes?"

"Of course you idiot."

"Wasn't that Karla's job? Did she fuck up?"

"Yes, but that is beside the point. I could have demanded to have all the siblings and relatives followed. We could have paid more to have their transactions traced as well."

"So you fucked up."

Henrick turned to look at Fritz. "It would have costs tens of thousands of euros. How much money did you contribute?"

"More than you from what I recall."

"We have to follow them. They eventually have to leave the bank, so we have them cornered."

"Taking on two Devengers, with a fat man and a cripple. What a fucking nightmare."

"Shut up!"

***

Neither one moved, nor did they speak. The swastikas just sat there, with the eagle atop, appearing ready to take flight.

"This is not good." John stepped between the crates and they towered over him. He kept walking and his pace stretched from five to ten to twenty steps until he saw a small open area at the far end of the room. He reached out and felt the wood crates to either side; each row was separated by one foot of space. He looked back to Alan staring at him.

"What's back there?"

John's eyes looked up to see the curved ceiling extend to either side. The top crate rested five feet from the roof. When his eyes followed each crate down to the floor, he noticed one on the ground beside him. A red crow bar rested on top of it. It was the only one accessible in the room from his position. "There's an open one back here."

"A crate?" Alan walked quickly down the opening between the two stacks. When he turned the corner, John held the crow bar and tapped the top of the three-foot high crate sitting on the stone floor. "Stop."

"Why?" He jarred the crowbar underneath the lid of the crate. Little force was required to liberate it. The wood squeaked as John revealed the contents within in it.

He dropped the crow bar and stepped forward. John used both hands to lift another identical bar of gold. "Incredible."

"Gold. Nazi gold."

John chuckled as he turned the metal over in his hands. It was rectangular in shape, with the long slides slanted further out from top to bottom. It was imperfect in appearance and muted in color. "How the hell did he get all this in here?"

"Two gold bars. Two... solid gold bars." Alan's stunned appearance broke into a smile, followed by a slow chuckle.

John cradled the gold brick in his hand and pointed to the crates. "Two? Are you joking? Look around you Alan!"

Alan turned to look at the crates. His eyes canvassed one side of the room and then the other. When his gaze returned to the open crate, it shared the same identical imagery. His face exuded the look of one trying to find words, but he remained speechless.

"There's another gold bar in here. I'm going to check the others."

John placed the gold back in the crate and it came to rest on what appeared to be flattened and worn hay. He struggled to pull the crate next to the stack of wooden containers. He grabbed the crowbar and placed a foot on one corner of the container before he raised himself to the nine-foot high stack in front of him. He heaved himself up onto the top crate where there was enough space to kneel. It wobbled slightly but only for a moment.

"What are you doing?"

John jammed the crow bar under another crate lid, and with force he removed the top lid. He looked inside. "Gold," he said. He moved to the next one and did the same. "Gold." He moved again and his foot dangled above the stack on his right. He grunted as he pried up yet another lid. He looked inside and turned to Alan. "Gold! All of them are filled with gold!"

Alan moved to the open crate on the floor and saw the bricks. There was space for four of them, which he figured out from the impressions made in the worn hay. Four gold bars in each crate. He counted and saw nine crates stacked before him. He started to walk down the pathway and counted the rows from one end of the room to the other. *One... two... three... four... five.*

He did the math. Nine crates per row, times five rows, times four gold bars in each of them. He jogged down to the end of the vault and looked at his brother who had returned to the floor. "That's forty-five crates, times four gold bars in each... 180 gold bars. Holy shit!"

John dropped the crowbar. It bounced with a loud noise when it hit the ground floor. "No it's not. It's double that amount." John's eyes did not move from what he was staring at. "You forgot the other side of the room."

Alan's head spun around. He caught himself before losing his balance. "This is unbelievable! What's gold going for now, a grand an once?"

"Maybe more. A thousand bucks an ounce. Holy... fucking... shit." John's chuckle turned into a slow and steady laugh, one that rose in volume as he lifted his hands to rub the top side of his head. He shook his head. "So Charlotte got the house in the Hamptons, Aunt Jenny got the estate in Upper Saddle River, the vineyards went to dozens of others and we got..."

"Three hundred and sixty bars of gold." Alan turned to his brother. "I think we did okay."

"What I said when I went to your condo... Fuck the grapes, I'll take the vault!" John looked down to the interior of the crate and saw two remained inside of it. "Two are missing here."

They pondered what they were looking at before Alan said, "Everett? Our dad?"

"Maybe he took one bar, and our dad took another. But it explains something."

"What?"

"How could a sheet metal worker, before the war, afford to purchase hundreds of acres in California when he returned?" He saw John nod. "It had to be the gold."

"Two gold bars. That alone could have taken a man pretty far back in the day, don't you think?"

Alan placed the lid back on the crate and fitted the nails back into their holes. "Let's go."

"What?"

"Let's finalize plans to get this home."

"Hold on a second." John picked up the crowbar, pried the lid up again and removed a gold bar.

"Taking one? Why?"

"Why the fuck not? Take the other one up front."

Alan shrugged his shoulders. "Okay. Leave that brick, take the one on the table. I'll grab the journal and documents."

John carried the gold with both hands towards the front of the vault. "We can't get all of this back in one trip."

"Maybe. We'll find out. If we can get it home all in one shot, we should."

John watched Alan rustle up the documents and journal. When he was finished, he looked to John who nodded back at him. "I'll call him."

He stepped towards the doorframe. "Mr. Heinzen! Please come here!"

"Alan. How am I going to...? I need to hide this, I don't think the Marlboro box will hold the weight of the gold."

"Figure it out." The sound of footsteps grew louder from the corridor outside the vault.

"I don't want him to see it." John's eyes searched the room for somewhere to conceal the gold. There was nothing in the vault available besides the Marlboro box. "Dammit!"

"Cover it or something."

John put the bar down, removed his sweater and wrapped it around the gold brick. He lifted and cradled it in both hands.

"Are you finished gentlemen?"

"Yes we are," said Alan. "If you can escort us upstairs please?"

"Certainly."

"Good, and we will require your assistance tomorrow as well." Alan explained their need for manpower to remove the contents of the vault. He noted a private security truck would be arriving at 9:00 the next morning.

Alan and the banker conversed and made arrangements during the long walk back to the elevator.

"We will have a service fee, depending on how many men you require."

Alan turned in the elevator to see his brother awkwardly carrying the brick. "How many men do you have available?"

"Our office can make arrangements to have anywhere from one to ten people. We are not allowed to let outside parties other than depositors—"

"Please arrange to have all ten people on hand."

Heinzen remained silent for a moment. "Will the bank be retaining your business moving forward, Herr Devenger?"

"Most likely."

When they arrived at the ground floor, Alan said, "Can you also call a car service for us this morning?"

"But of course. Where shall I tell the driver you are going?"

"Within the city, thank you." Alan watched John reposition the gold brick in his arms and he gave him an appreciative nod.

***

They waited by the elevators while the banker retrieved their jackets from his office. When he returned Alan took both from him. "Thank you. You will have your men ready tomorrow morning?"

"I will make the proper arrangements. There's a car waiting for you now outside the bank. Is there anything else I can do for you?"

"That will be all for now, thank you."

Moments later the brothers found themselves walking towards the building's main entrance. "The cab was a good idea. This weighs a ton."

"No problem." They stepped outside. "There it is." They walked towards it and entered the rear of the car. "The Bellevue Hotel please."

"Monsieur, it is only three blocks away."

"Then it's a quick ride then, isn't it?" said John.

The Driver shrugged and turned on the meter.

John looked out the window, and then lifted the hem of his sweater to show Alan the gold bullion. They chuckled before John concealed it again.

***

"There they go." Otto pointed towards the bank's entrance. Henrick and Fritz watched the Devengers exit the building.

"Let's go!" Fritz moved to open the side door of the van.

"Wait," said Otto. All three of them watched the two Americans open the back door of a black Mercedes.

"Follow them. Do it now." Henrick felt the van lurch forward. They were two car lengths behind the black vehicle.

Henrick heard his mobile phone ring. He answered with, "*Ja...* We are following them. They left the bank. I'll call you back." He ended the call and said, "Karla. She landed in Munich. She'll arrive in Bern tonight."

Fritz remained hunched over the passenger seat. "Henrick. How is that chick going to help us? She can't handle a weapon."

"It is another pair of eyes and we need them." Henrick sighed. They watched the car pull in front of a large and elegant hotel. "And now we know exactly where to find them."

Chapter 23

<u>Bellevue Hotel, Bern Switzerland</u>

"How does this work again?"

"You saw the scale, right? It read ninety kilos."

Alan looked at his computer's screen and typed 90. "Do it again."

"Fine." John stepped off the scale, put the gold bar down and returned to stand barefoot on the device. The meter turned until it came to rest on eighty-one kilograms. "Same number as before." He stepped off and returned with the gold bar. The scale indicated he now weighed 90 kilograms. "There, you see? A nine kilogram difference."

"How did you figure this out?"

"I learned it from my mom growing up. We had a cat and we had to figure out what it weighed from time to time." He stepped off the scale and put the gold down on the coffee table. "We would weigh ourselves with and without the cat. Then we could tell what he weighed. Fortunately, it works the same with a gold bar."

"A wealthy pussy, I would say."

"What, our cat?"

"No. You." Alan smiled. "You're a wealthy pussy."

"Very funny."

Alan flipped open his laptop to access the Wi-Fi in his room. "Let's see what this translates into." He opened Google and found a page that converted kilograms into ounces. He paused, then read the number out loud. "Nine kilograms translates into three hundred and seventeen ounces, approximately." He froze when he re-read the number. "Any idea what an ounce of gold is worth?"

John took a seat next to his half-brother. "A thousand bucks?"

Alan typed in "gold value" to see what turned up in the search query.

He saw the number and wrote it down next to, '317 ounces.' He switched to the computer's calculator and did the math.

"One thousand and one hundred dollars. That's the price of an ounce of gold. The value of the gold brick equates to $328,700 dollars." Alan turned the laptop to show John. "Gold has gone up a bit lately."

"I'll be God damned."

Alan wrote down the total dollar value. He multiplied the number times four, to account for the gold in each crate, and then multiplied that number against the total number of crates, which equaled 90.

He wrote down the number after double-checking the math. "We now have, in our possession, gold that is worth one hundred and twenty five million, five hundred and thirty two thousand dollars."

"Bullshit."

Alan raised an eyebrow, opened up an excel document, and translated the numbers in a column to outline the math:

$$317 \times 1100 \times 4 \times 90 =$$
$$\text{Total:} \quad \$125,532,000$$

Alan turned the laptop for his half-brother to see the screen.

"That cannot possibly be correct." He grabbed a pen and paper and did it for himself. When he was done, he dropped the pen. His hand started to shake.

"What, seeing it on paper makes it more real?"

New York, NY

"Good morning, Stephanie." Charlotte waved to her coworker she shared an office with and returned her attention to the email she was composing. She hit send, closed her email account and turned to a Word document she was preparing for management. The clock on her computer read: 9:35 a.m.

She heard her cell phone ring within her purse and moved to retrieve it.

Her brother's name appeared on the LCD screen. "Hey there."

"Charlotte, are you alone?"

She smirked. "I've got two naked men in my bed. I'm still at work."

"Yes or no?"

She picked up on the concern in his voice. "No, my coworker is here too. Why?"

"Find a private place. Please."

"Okay, hold on." She left the room, found a small conference room, and closed the door behind her. "You sound distressed, something wrong?"

"Far from it. We accessed the vault."

"And?"

"One hundred and twenty-five million dollars' worth of gold. That's what we found."

"Ha! Whatever."

He walked her through the day's events, explained the math and waited for a response.

"If this is some kind of bad joke, then you really need to see a shrink."

"I'm dead serious."

"Are you sure you did the math right?"

"I'll text you a picture for Christ's sake! I'll call you back."

"Wait—"

She groaned when the line went dead. She sat there and watched her boss pass the conference room's glass-paneled walls. He paused when he saw her and opened the door to the conference room. "Everything okay?"

"Yes, I'm waiting on my brother's call from overseas." She felt her phone vibrate. "Pardon me, I'll be back to work shortly."

"Don't sweat it, you look perplexed."

She opened the text message on her iPhone and the image of a gold bar appeared, complete with a swastika. "Holy shit!"

"Charlotte?"

"Oh, sorry Tim. I… will you excuse me please?"

"Sure." He closed the door behind him and kept his eye on her as he moved down the corridor.

She answered the call as soon as Alan's name appeared on the screen.

"Come on. How is this possible?"

"We're leaving tomorrow morning. I confirmed the airfreight

company can manage the weight of the crates. I doubled down on the security in London, we land at Heathrow Saturday evening, and then we'll check on the security facility I arranged in advance."

"Then what?"

"We fly home from London with a sample and figure out logistics on the back end. John was going to call that lawyer, Larry Goldstein. He's a bit discombobulated by the news."

"Who wouldn't be?"

"We have to figure out how to insure this, where to put it, we need your help."

"How can it possibly be worth that much?"

"Do the math, the gold bricks weigh 317 ounces each, approximately. And there are 360 gold bars total."

"Approximately is a pretty vague term."

"Get on the phone with Goldstein, okay? We signed the representation documents he sent us, he should have them."

"Jesus, this is really happening?"

"Do the math. Call me when you get home tonight, no matter what time."

"This is un-fucking believable!"

"I know, get ready to retire, Charlotte."

"What was that?" The line went dead.

Bern, Switzerland

John stared at the plate of food. The single bite he took was delicious, but he could not bring himself to take another mouthful. He pushed the plate of room-service food away and stood up from the couch. "I can't eat."

"Not hungry?"

He turned and saw his brother staring out the window. "No."

"Do you know what this means?" asked Alan.

"I have a reasonable idea, sure."

"Anything," said Alan. "We can have anything we want."

John walked over and stood beside him. "That sums it up, I guess.

The question is, what do you really want?"

His eyes scanned the city. The city was dotted with buildings, cars and people walked on the street below Alan's suite. "Do you know how much this upgrade cost, this room I mean?"

"I'd rather not ask."

"That's the point, it doesn't matter anymore."

"Of course it matters."

"No. It's a drop in the bucket now." Alan turned to face him. "The cost is meaningless."

John rubbed the top side of his head. "I don't know what to tell you, Alan. On some level it changes things, on others, it really shouldn't."

"You realize... this experience, everything here, that one-hundred dollar tray of food we ordered," he pointed to the cart, "We never have to concern ourselves about the cost of anything... ever."

John walked back to the living room and stepped towards the journal they found in the vault. "You know what Alan, this is more valuable than anything else we found." He held it up for Alan to see. "This is our family keepsake, our legacy. The gold comes second."

"Jesus Christ. Yeah, John, that's nice to have. Now you can afford to buy the company that made the journal, if you so choose."

"And what would I do with it?" He flipped through the pages before he felt his brother's hand on his shoulder.

"It's okay to feel good about this, John."

"I don't know how I feel. All I know is I'm hungry, but I can't eat."

Alan nodded. "I need some fresh air. Want to join me?"

"Nah, I want to read through this. I could use some time to myself." He pointed to the other documents they found. "Those too, might learn something new."

"That's a good idea."

"What is that supposed to mean?" John watched his brother grab his coat.

Alan opened the door. "John, you never have to work another day in your life. Ponder that. I think you'll find it's a good thing." He smiled and left the room.

He closed the door and headed to the elevator. He listened to classical music play on the speaker system but he could not identify the composer.

He shook his head before the doors opened on the ground floor. He asked himself, *I wonder how much it would cost to buy every single classical music album ever made.*

He left the elevator and walked under the domed glass ceiling in the center of the hotel. He looked up to see the amber colors and the image of two huge inlayed circular wheels. He grinned and thought, *I can hire a company to replicate this in my Hamptons home.*

He took his leave from the Bellevue and decided to stroll down *Kochergasse*. It felt good to fill his lungs with fresh air. The weather was warmer compared to the day prior and he stopped to watch several buses drive past. The exhaust fumes immediately tarnished the moment and he resumed his walk. There were fewer people in the area than he expected so he decided to look for the shopping district.

His observations took him a few blocks down the road and he saw a sign point towards *Marktgasse*. He saw more people heading towards this part of town and turned to follow the crowd.

He strolled towards the first store he came to. Alan noticed the vendor sold watches, which given he was in Switzerland, he thought rather apropos. He stopped and reviewed the timepieces on display. He paused and looked at the Rolex watch on his wrist, the one his grandfather gave to him. It kept time beautifully and it was in great condition. When he looked back to see dozens of timepieces for sale, he realized he had the means to purchase every single one of them.

The thought did not sit well with him. He could not figure out what he would do with four dozen watches of different makes and sizes.

He walked further down the street and saw a fragrance storefront. His mind thought about the clients who managed a particular cologne brand that was on display in the window. It happened to represent an active advertiser with *GQ* magazine who ran a significant number of ad pages. He now possessed the means and the freedom to tell that particular client to shove her product straight up her fat ass. He enjoyed the idea of doing so, but deep down he believed Karma would eventually catch up with the bitch. The years he spent managing difficult clients, through brutal negotiations and their high-strung demands, filled his mind with toxic memories.

He felt liberated for a moment when he thought about what he could do with his newfound wealth. He could buy the company that made the cologne and fire the advertising agency. Alan knew it was unlikely, given the brand was owned by a much larger corporation, but there were smaller companies he could buy. Twenty million? Thirty? What would it cost to execute something like that?

What city would I have to fly to in order to negotiate the sale of the company? How would I get there… a private jet perhaps? I could walk into a Lamborghini dealership, buy a car right then and there, and drive it across Europe to the company's headquarters. Then I could buy a four-bedroom condo with a terrace, perhaps an entire building, and relocate somewhere in Europe as the newly minted C.E.O. and owner.

He shook his head but stopped when he realized every idea he just formulated in his mind was truly attainable. He knew it would take time, perhaps several years to cash in the gold and manage the funds, but there was nothing to stop him. He settled on a word, one that gave him reason to pause as he made his way down the street: Limits.

He repeated the word in his head. The gold his grandfather had left for him and John would enable Alan to eliminate any financial barrier he ever encountered in the past. A three million-dollar Hamptons house was out of the question when he was in the market several years ago. He chose one that cost significantly less. Moving forward, he asked himself, was there any reason not to spend five, ten, even fifteen million dollars on a beachfront estate?

He watched a trolley pass by and he crossed the street. Every store he passed, and every product he saw, he realized that price was no longer an issue. Anything and everything he saw for sale was affordable.

He noticed there were no cars in the immediate area and realized it was closed to street traffic. Unlike New York, he felt unencumbered and safe when he moved from one side of the street to the other.

He stopped short when he saw another trolley approach and realized he had to keep an eye on large passing vehicles. He grinned before the trolley passed, and when he did, he saw a tall blond man wearing sunglasses. He appeared to be looking at Alan, but the glasses blocked the ability to make direct eye contact with him.

Alan turned and strolled down the street. He passed by a chocolatier's shop, a store selling women's undergarments and a few restaurants. He paused to see if the menu and establishment fit the bill for the dinner he wanted to share with John. He would find a four-star restaurant, pop the cork on the most expensive champagne and celebrate. Alas, the menu underwhelmed him.

He sauntered down to the next restaurant before he looked back to where he stood a moment prior. He saw the tall blond pause to look at the menu. Alan saw him turn his head, look at him, and then nonchalantly turn away in the other direction.

He stood out from the crowd with his cropped hair and six-foot-something height. Alan took several steps further down the street and then turned a moment later. The distance between he and the tall man remained the same.

He felt unnerved and decided to enter one of the stores. He turned to see himself surrounded by leather goods. A short and older man greeted him in German. Alan asked him if he spoke English.

"Of course, how may I help you sir?"

"Just browsing, thank you." Alan picked up a few items, which felt rather cheap to the touch, and placed them back down.

"Perhaps you'd like to see our wallet collection?"

"No thank you." Alan opened his phone and pretended to read an email. He chose not to look out the window and decided to take his leave. He thanked the employee and left.

He walked briskly down the street. An alcove of storefronts appeared to the side. It represented a pedestrian passageway beneath a building and between avenues. Storefronts lined the inside walkway. He casually looked over his shoulder. His stomach tightened into a knot when he saw the blond man talking on his cell phone. The distance between them shortened with each step. He passed by several couples and an Asian man with a camera. Daylight illuminated the avenue in the distance.

Cars passed from left to right in slow unison. He saw the sidewalk extend perpendicular to his position before he heard the roar of a motor engine.

A white van skidded to a stop right before him. He turned. The blond man sprinted towards him.

"Now!" He screamed.

Alan felt the man grip his jacket. He heard a door open and more yelling. He spun around to yank his arm free. The blond tightened his grip. Alan felt his opposite shoulder free itself from the jacket.

A woman screamed. The blond reached for Alan's wrist. He raised it and spun off his back heel.

The motion left Alan on the ground and his assailant holding his jacket. He dropped it. A larger man raced towards him from the van's passenger seat. He crouched his legs together, snapped them upwards and moved out of arm's reach.

He sprinted across the road. He turned to see both men in pursuit of him. Crowds stopped and watched as the van lurched forward to turn and cross the intersection.

Alan raced down the street. His thighs pumped like jackhammers as he twisted and turned to distance himself.

He saw the hotel in the distance. He sprinted towards the entrance. He threw the door open and raced inside. He continued until he came to a stop under the glass dome. He collapsed a moment later on his stomach. He gasped for air.

Several hotel employees ran over to his location. Alan flipped over to see the two inlaid circles of glass hover above him before he blacked out.

Chapter 24

<u>Bellevue Hotel, Bern</u>

John looked at his phone and the time read 1:00 p.m. on it, which meant it was 7:00 a.m. in New York. He wondered if Larry Goldstein was at work yet. He scrolled through the contacts in his cell phone and dialed Larry Goldstein's work number.

"Hello, this is Larry Goldstein."

"Good morning, Larry, this is John Devenger."

"Hello there. What can I do you for John?"

"We are in Switzerland, and it appears we will definitely require your legal services."

"Switzerland?"

"Yes. I told you we had something we inherited... Overseas? Remember?"

"Yes, of course, but Switzerland? That's interesting. What part of the country?"

"Bern, the Scheibzerische bank, we are shipping it out of the country tomorrow."

"So why all the secrecy?"

John paused and reread the numbers in front of him. "We found approximately seven thousand pounds of gold bullion in the bank vault that was in our Grandfather's name."

There was a long pause on the phone. "You have got to be shitting me."

"Nope, it's all there, 90 crates of gold."

"I... I've never heard anything like this in my life."

"Yeah, it's a bit overwhelming."

John heard the man take a deep breath and exhale slowly. "You've got quite a windfall there. What do you plan to do with it?"

"We're flying it out to London, storing it in a secure and private facility."

"Wait a minute, what's more secure or private compared to a vault in Switzerland? Why the hell are you moving it?"

John gripped the phone tightly in his hand. "We eventually have to bring it home and… Look, Larry, that's what we're doing, we didn't hire you to second guess our decision process."

"Okay, okay. Do you know the history of the gold?"

"A little. We're taking a few bricks home this trip."

"Bricks. Not coins then."

"Yes, do you have an issue with that as well?"

"Of course not. Take a breather. I have to do a little research on this. We will likely have to notify the IRS. The only legal advice I have for you is to ensure that the gold is safe and on lockdown."

"That's it?"

"For now, yes. This is a peculiar situation. I have to research this."

"Okay then, give me a shout tomorrow. We're not flying out to London until Saturday morning."

"Wait. Does anyone else know about this?"

"Our sister Charlotte. She'll be reaching out to you as well."

"Tell her to keep her mouth shut. Call me on my cell when you get to London." He provided his cell phone number to John.

"Okay Larry, talk soon." He ended the call and walked over to the coffee table. He sat on the couch and lifted the gold brick. He needed both hands to turn it over in his hands. It appeared somewhat coarse as it was an imperfect finish.

He took a moment to stare at the 'SS' initials carved into the lower portion of the object. He turned it over in his hands and saw no other markings. He lifted his eyes to see the stack of papers they brought from the vault and noticed several yellowed pages among the stack. Larry's question gnawed at him. He had no idea where the gold originally came from and it was an honest question.

The image of the initials prompted him to put the gold down and reach for the documents. He sifted through them and stopped on paperwork drafted in German. He could not decipher the communication, however it appeared to relate to shipment destinations that predated anything they reviewed in the vault itself.

Among the details outlined in the document, he identified the origin of the gold, which was dated between 1943 and 1944.

He paused on one particular location. He ceased to exhale. He felt the sensation of ice-cold venom course from one part of his mind to the next before it extended further into his soul. His hand trembled for a moment, which prompted the document to fold in front of him.

John didn't know how many times his cell phone rang, but he finally snapped out of his thought process to answer it.

"Hello?"

"Herr John Devenger?"

"Yes?"

"This is the front desk. We require your immediate presence in the lobby, your brother is here."

"Oh?"

"He is rather distressed, sir, please come down."

"Of course." He concluded the call and stood up from the coffee table and seat. His eyes fixated themselves on the document before his concern for Alan took precedence. He checked to make sure the suite's door was locked.

When the elevator doors opened, he stepped out and walked over to the front desk. The man behind the counter pointed to an office on the right side of the room. When he entered it he saw Alan sitting in a chair. Three hotel employees surrounded him.

"Step aside. Alan, what happened?" He raised his hand and John noticed he was flush in the face.

"I was chased."

"What?"

The manager put his hand on John's shoulder. "Herr Devenger, your brother ran into the hotel and collapsed under the glass dome."

"Are you okay?"

"I'm fine."

John looked at the person who seemed to be in charge. "Is there a problem?"

"Of course not, we were concerned seeing a man sprint through the hotel. We all convened on his location when we saw him collapse to the ground."

"Jesus."

"I'm fine, seriously. They helped me up."

John patted him on the shoulder. "We need a minute, please."

"Can I inquire as to why this man was... chased?"

"I was mugged," said Alan.

"Mugged you say?"

John turned when he heard what sounded like the tone of disbelief. "Are you deaf? My brother was attacked. All of you, out of the room."

"Sir, we're just—"

"Out!" John took two of the hotel workers by their shoulders and led them to the door. The man in charge followed and John slammed the door.

"Holy shit, Alan, what happened?"

Alan put the glass of water down and crossed his legs. I was walking down the street, going in and out of stores. Nothing unusual. I noticed this tall blond guy, he seemed to be looking right at me."

"Then what."

Alan went into detail about how he was followed, the tall man screamed, 'now,' and a white van pulled up in front of him. He mentioned he blacked out for a moment from hyperventilating before the hotel workers found him and that he lost his jacket.

"Could you identify them?"

"It happened so fast. The blond man, yes, maybe the fat one, I don't know. I didn't see the driver of the van. Where they came from, I have no idea."

John tapped his finger on the desk between them. "Look, let's get you upstairs. Take a shower or something. Did you lose your passport? Wallet?"

"I don't think so." Alan checked his back pocket and retrieved his wallet. From his front pocket he supplied his room key. He dropped them on the table before he noticed his wrist. The Rolex was no longer there. "Son of a bitch!" He pounded the table with his fist.

"What's missing?"

"My Rolex."

"Oh. Well, buy a new one when you get home." John watched his brother shake his head.

"That was the one Everett gave me. It must have snapped off when they grabbed my jacket."

"That sucks. I'm sorry. Look, let's get you back up to your suite."

Alan stood up. "I was trying to find us a nice restaurant. You know, to celebrate."

John put his arm around his half-brother and gave him a friendly pat. "We're not going anywhere. Not after this."

Outside the Bellevue Hotel, 10:00 p.m.

Otto and Fritz leaned against the side of the van. Fritz took a long drag on a cigarette, tossed it to the ground and stubbed it out while he exhaled.

"She will be here any minute."

"What took her so fucking long?"

"Connections, baggage... does it matter?"

Otto rubbed the sides of his temples. "We have bigger concerns."

"We do. If he gets caught, are we still going through with this?"

"Part of me hopes he does, and yes, we still have to try."

Fritz nodded and tapped Otto on the chest when they saw car pull up beside the parked van. "Is that her?"

Otto turned and saw a weary looking redhead exit from the driver's side door. She rubbed the sides of her arms from the cold evening air. She turned to look at Otto and Fritz. "There you are." She looked up at Fritz. "You're a lot taller than I expected."

"And you're a lot sexier. Didn't expect that."

Otto moved forward to shake her hand. "We have a lot to tell you, Karla. The situation is not good."

"Come again?" she said.

"Ha! Wait until she hears." Fritz lit up another cigarette and pointed towards her with his chin. "Go ahead, Otto, tell her."

Otto looked at her. "It appears Henrick is going to have a word with our friend, Heinzen. He thinks the man duped us."

"How is that going to help? I could have called him." She stepped closer. "None of you were supposed to contact Heinzen without my approval."

"Yes, but the conversation will be at the end of a barrel of a gun. He took the Beretta with him, with the silencer of course." Fritz exhaled a long plume of smoke. "Get it?"

Karla took a moment to put one and two together. When she realized what she was dealing with, her mouth went dry. "You should have stopped him. This... this is not right." Her concern grew when both men responded with indifferent gestures.

Karla felt her chest tremble. It was at that point when she realized how little control she had over the situation.

Bellevue Hotel

Alan stepped out from his suite, checked to see if anyone was in the hallway, and then placed the wheeled room-service cart outside his door. He locked it behind him.

He turned to see his half-brother on the couch. "So we're in agreement?" asked John.

"Absolutely."

"We stay put tonight. We call for our car in the morning, ask that it's parked out front and then we jump in and drive to the bank."

"After the bank opens."

"Yes, so we're not left waiting outside." John nodded. "We get in, we ensure the security truck is packed, hop back in our car and follow them to Neuchatel airport."

"Okay. What if they pursue us?"

John sat back and gave the idea some thought. "We have the security company's phone number, we call them, and then we separate and get away as fast as we can. They have to stay with the truck. That's what they want."

"Not us?"

"The only thing I come up with is this. They tried to kidnap you. Maybe they want details on the vault, I don't know. Why else would they try to grab you, and why a van?"

Alan shook his head. "How did you come up with that?"

"It reminded me of something at work. Executive ransom, it's referred to as K and R. The senior management team at Tiffany. We have security for that sort of thing in certain parts of the world."

"Really?" Alan crossed his arms.

"Sure. Not my area of expertise, but executives in Europe and South America require security. We take precautions. Kidnappings happen all the time. Then they call in a ransom for their safe return." John leaned forward. "With the vault details, they'd be able to get their hands on the gold. We obviously stay put in the hotel tonight. Lock the doors."

Alan nodded. "I'm taking an Ambien. There's no way I could possibly sleep otherwise."

John stood up. "Lock that door." He walked over to stand in front of his half-brother. "We're going to be fine. They have no idea where the gold is headed."

"If they stop the security truck?"

"It's a security truck. I'm sure they are prepared for these kinds of things. We're paying enough as it is anyway." He tapped him on the shoulder. "Get some rest."

Alan stood up before John left. "Hey, John."

"What?"

"Just... thanks." He watched his brother nod and grin.

John paused when his gaze crossed the document he reviewed earlier in the day. The origin of the gold was sitting there, in plain sight. He tapped the door handle with his hand.

"Something up?"

He knew it was the worst possible time to share what he learned. He wondered if he should ever tell Alan about the origins of the gold. After the risks they had encountered, he decided it was best for Alan to find it for himself. If he never inspected the paperwork, he asked himself if it mattered whether or not he learned the truth. He decided to let fate decide, and the answers were there for Alan to find for himself.

"Just... get some sleep, Alan."

John left the room, traveled one flight down on the elevator and entered his room. He closed the door and used the additional padlock to ensure the door was secure. When he turned he walked straight over to his suitcase.

He opened it and removed the buck knife. The blade was razor sharp. He fitted it against his calf and noticed the straps were long enough to secure it to his leg. The next item he removed was the snubnose forty-four revolver and he removed the magazine clip. He checked to see if it was fully loaded but remembered he shot a round the day prior. The ammunition box held twenty-one rounds so he took one and jammed it into the tight-fitting magazine clip. He snapped it in place and put it and the knife back in the bag.

If it came down to it, he knew he would not hesitate to do what was necessary to ensure his safety and Alan's.

Moserstrasse Avenue, Bern

He paused to catch his breath and rubbed the sides of his hips. The twenty-minute walk included a bridge crossing and the road he ascended exacerbated his arthritis.

He stood one block from the location where a taxi had picked him up two weeks prior after his last visit. He made his way down the street and turned to face the building that housed the man he was looking for.

He reached for the door handle and turned it but it was locked. Henrick turned and read Heinzen's name next to the apartment number labeled 2B. He retrieved the Beretta from his jacket pocket. He stepped back and aimed the long barrel of the silencer towards the front lock. The resulting sound was to two high-pitched "quiffs." The next sound was metalwork hitting the marble tiles in the foyer beyond. He pressed the door open. There was no resistance.

His steps echoed off the walls when he climbed the staircase. The smell of gunpowder dissipated by the time he reached the second landing.

He caught his breath and tried to ignore the pain. He walked down the hall with the gun at his side.

He came to the apartment and listened for sound. He heard nothing. He turned the door handle slowly but it too was locked. He stepped back, directed the barrel of his gun to the deadbolt above the handle and snapped off two rounds. He used his other hand to push the door open and closed the door behind him.

He heard a woman scream.

"Fraulein! Get in a bathroom or closet. Close the door. Do it now!"

"Who is that?" Her voice resonated with fear.

"Shut up! Do as he says!"

Henrick looked towards an open doorway off the living room. He assumed it was the bedroom.

"Get out here Heinzen." The couple bickered in panic. Moments later Henrick heard a door open and close. Then he saw Heinzen enter the room.

He raised his hands when he saw the weapon. "No... No wait."

"Shut up." He looked towards the bedroom. "You! In there! Do not come out!"

He fixed his sights on Heinzen's face. He stepped forward. "You idiot. Why did you not tell me there were two of them?"

"I... I did what you asked! Please, don't... I delayed them as you wished!"

"You imbecile. You should have told me there were two Devengers!"

"Look, whatever you want, I'll do it. For the love of God—"

The first bullet caught the man's index finger; it ricocheted off his cheek. He took better aim and squeezed the trigger twice. Two rounds landed in the man's chest. The momentum propelled the man against the back wall right after a dark cloud of blood silhouetted his torso. He collapsed to the floor.

He turned and stepped into the bedroom. There was a bathroom door on the right side of the room. The door was closed. He fired off a round at the top panel of the door. The blast was high enough to miss but close enough to terrify the woman inside of it.

"Get down, shut up and stay put." He heard muffled cries from beyond as he turned to leave.

He opened the door to the apartment. He ignored the body aches and ran as fast as he could down the staircase. No one witnessed him leave the building.

He concealed his weapon, lumbered down several blocks and then turned when he heard the sound of sirens wail in the distance.

Chapter 25

Gumligen, Switzerland

Karla sat on the edge of the bed and kept both eyes on the door to her bedroom. Between her arms was a musty pillow. She ignored the scent of mold in the room and shook her head. They were waiting for her.

The first knock came at 5:30 a.m. She was startled, but felt grateful her bedroom door was locked.

At one point, in the middle of the night, she had opened the window to see if she could fit through it if she needed to leave. The bedroom was on the ground floor, but the opening was not wide enough for her to fit through. She returned to bed and attempted to go back to sleep but it was no use.

She knew in her heart that the sound of the footsteps beyond the locked door belonged to a killer. The look on his face was like nothing she had ever witnessed on another human being. He appeared merciless, void of any remorse and the experience was outright disturbing to her. What concerned Karla the most was his complete and utter silence. Neither Otto nor Fritz inquired about the man's adventure, and Karla feared the gun would be used against her if she opened her mouth.

Her eyes fixed themselves on the lock beneath the door handle. She was unsure who knocked on her door five minutes prior, but she feared what would happen if she refused to go with them.

She knew from the moment they told her about Heinzen that she was way out of her element. No amount of money or gold was worth this nightmare. She put aside her dreams of world travel, property ownership and a luxurious lifestyle. She knew she would be okay, given the money she had inherited and the success she enjoyed with her career. She recalled the condescending prick she had for a boss, but one thing was for certain; he didn't terminate the lives of people who opposed him.

She heard two men bicker in the hallway before a hard knock pounded against the bedroom door. "Karla! We have to go!"

She stood up, walked over to the door and unlocked it. She opened it and saw Fritz. "I'm not going. I'm going to remain here."

"What? But you're dressed?"

"I just don't think I can help."

Fritz leaned forward, which resulted in the man leaning over her. "Listen, I think we need you."

"Not after last night. He's out of his mind. You know this, don't lie."

"Karla, I'll keep an eye on him. He doesn't have the strength—"

"I said I'm not going, now leave."

Fritz exhaled before he turned his head. "Otto! Henrick! She's not coming."

She heard footsteps come from the floor above her. They made their way downstairs. Henrick and Otto joined Fritz in the doorframe.

"You're coming. We need another pair of eyes," said Henrick.

"You guys have got this, I'll stay here."

"Get your ass in that car you rented and follow us to the hotel. We don't have time for this."

Otto stepped back to give her room to exit. "We need you there. What is wrong?"

"Come on, let's fucking go already."

"Fritz, stop. I—"

"I'll drive, give me the keys, Karla."

"They could be leaving right now for all we know. Move!" Henrick motioned with his hands to hurry up.

Karla saw the psychotic look in his eyes. She realized that if she drove herself, or if Fritz was in the car, he would eventually get out of the car and she could take her leave from the country.

"I'll drive myself. Fritz, go with either Otto or Henrick. I need a moment."

"Nah, I'm going with you." Fritz turned to Otto. "I need a gun in case I corner one of them."

"Fine."

"Move it then. Karla, hurry up." Henrick gestured for the men to step away.

Karla waited until they were out of sight. She grabbed her purse, checked to make sure her passport and wallet were within it, and then looked at her luggage.

She figured the suitcase and clothes were worth one thousand dollars altogether. Karla knew she would never see them again. It would be a small price to pay in order to secure her freedom.

She left the room.

Bellevue Hotel, Bern Switzerland

John checked his watch when he heard the hotel phone ring. It read 9:05 a.m. He answered the call.

"Hello?"

"It's me, ready?"

"Yup. I'm bringing my essentials, and the gold, in the backpack. My passport too."

"I'll have my passport as well."

"Okay then. Call the front desk and have them bring the car around. See you in a bit." John hung up and walked over to his suitcase. He retrieved what were now the two most important items in his possession. He was not concerned if the bank discovered them on his person. He knew it was worth the risk.

He retrieved the buck knife and the leather sleeve that held it and untied the straps. He lifted the legging of his pants and secured it to his calf. The leather straps rubbed against his skin and sock, but it was not uncomfortable. When he dropped his pant legging, the weapon was concealed and it did not make an impression on the fabric.

He took the snub nose forty-four and placed it at the bottom of the pocket inside his jacket. He questioned whether or not he could quickly retrieve it. He saw no other place to put it on his person and he made a mental note to wear the jacket at all times.

He picked up his backpack and the weight from the gold bar within it weighed down on his shoulder. He'd stopped by Alan's suite to pick it up earlier in the morning. The thought of a cleaning lady discovering it in Alan's suite did not sit well with him when he was awake at four a.m.

He stopped in midstride and wondered if the brick in his possession was from the destination he read in the Nazi documents. He put the thought aside when he considered the alternative: the men who killed his father and chased Alan taking the gold for themselves. He checked himself in the mirror, took a deep breath and then left the room.

He pressed the down button on the elevator and waited. A minute later it opened and Alan was standing in the back of it. Several short Asian tourists encircled him. John stepped in without saying a word.

When the doors opened, the Asians scampered off and John turned to look at Alan. "How long until the car is outside?"

"It's there." He checked his watch. "It's 9:15. Do you know what road to take?"

"It's a one-way street, right outside to the left."

Alan nodded. "I'll let you drive." The two walked side by side through the hotel without another word.

When they got to the main entrance, John could not see to either side of the building. "They have got to be out there."

"Then drive fast."

They saw the BMW parked outside and stepped out of the hotel. It took fifteen seconds to hand a Euro bill to the bellhop, get in the car and whip the vehicle around the traffic barrier to drive towards the one-way street called *Amthaugasse*.

***

"They are in a BMW, a white one." Otto put his car in drive and followed. "Henrick, you'll have to double back."

"Fritz is waiting for them outside the main entrance. Where is Karla?"

"Parked at the rear of the bank. There's a road there."

"We don't need to use the van. Knock one man down, grab the other, get him in your car or Karla's."

"I'll tell Fritz." Otto turned the car to avoid pedestrians and dialed Fritz. "They are moving. Be ready, we will use whatever car is closest."

"Got it."

Otto dialed Karla next while he trailed the BMW. They were driving with greater speed than he expected. "Karla, be ready."

"Something you should know, and it's a little disturbing."

"What?"

"A rather large security truck just pulled into the gated courtyard."

***

John saw the bank in the distance and a side road coming up to his left. "I'm going to park it down here." He turned the car.

"Here? We'll have to walk to the front?"

"Can't park it over there."

"It's not worth the risk of walking to and from."

"I'm armed. Fuck 'em."

"What?"

***

She had no choice but to remain in the car. Fritz was somewhere nearby, and armed. If she drove away, she feared they would turn on her, perhaps even try to kill her. She had to figure out how to get away, without putting herself at risk. Until then, she remained in her locked car.

Karla watched a white BMW turn down the road where she was parked. A moment later, she saw two men leave the vehicle. She recognized the bald man immediately, and when they started walking quickly towards her, she covered her face with her hand.

When she knew they had passed, she looked at them in her side view mirror. They looked up and down the street and moved quickly. She looked forward and saw Otto's car screech to a halt. She picked up the phone but saw Otto was using his.

***

"They are coming around the left entrance!" Otto turned left onto the street and watched the Devengers turn the corner. He slammed on the brakes when he arrived next to Karla's car. "Fritz! I'm right here!" Otto heard the line go dead and he stepped out of the vehicle.

He stepped forward and peered around the corner on the left side of the building. He retrieved his handgun and waited for Fritz to appear. He watched as the Devengers made their way towards the front entrance. He stepped back and turned to see Karla in the rental car. He stepped forward and saw both men were only twenty feet from the left-front corner of the building. *Fritz, where are you!*

He hit redial on his phone. After three rings, he turned and saw the Devengers exit from his view. "Dammit!" When he turned around he saw Karla's car and then Fritz at the opposite end of the building.

He checked and both men were gone. When he turned he saw Fritz jogging towards him. Otto walked quickly to close the distance. "You idiot! They were right there!"

"The left side of the building, that's what you said!"

"Left! Right fucking there!" He pointed behind him.

"You fat fucking moron, that's the right side of the building!"

***

"Gentlemen, welcome back." The manager extended his hand. John grabbed it and Alan did the same a moment later. "I regret we're losing your business."

"We plan to keep the vault open, actually."

"Very well, then. This way please." He gestured with his hand towards the elevators. "I'll be managing your affairs this morning."

"Why so?"

"Our director, Herr Heinzen, he must be running late. I have what we need to manage the process, thankfully." He grinned. "And the security detail is on hand, as you requested."

"Excellent. The truck is parked outside?"

"In our courtyard, which is secure in itself. We will have the contents you wish to withdraw placed in the vehicle. Can you tell me the size of the contents?"

"We have ninety crates, heavy ones I might add."

It was the same process as they experienced the day before. There was only one additional element: some paperwork that indicated that a withdrawal was being made from Vault 21-12. To John's surprise, they were not required to identify what the contents were, nor the scale and scope of what was being removed. Alan reminded him about Swiss banking secrecy before they entered the labyrinth of narrow tunnels.

They walked side by side and followed the manager who provided color commentary about the bank's history. When they turned the corner to Vault 21-12, ten laborers were waiting there for them.

"Ah, good. The service elevator is at the rear of the hallway."

"The tunnel you mean."

"If you want to call it that, yes. Gentlemen," the Director caught the attention of his staff, "let's expedite this. I believe you will need handcarts. They are on the second floor." He turned to Alan and John. "Let's have a look to see what we are working with, shall we?"

"Of course."

The manager unveiled his set of keys and opened the vault's door. Alan and John stepped in first. "It's all here," said Alan.

The manager walked in and his laborers followed. John turned on the light switch on the left side of the room.

When he turned back he saw the expression on each man's face turn a shade darker. The manager pursed his lips as his eyes trailed from one swastika to the next. From John's point of view, it appeared every man froze in place. The only motion he saw was that of their eyes.

The manager took a step back, and in the process, he bumped into a laborer standing behind him. He stopped and turned to look at John. "Very well then. Our men will move what is required." He used his words slowly and carefully. "I will speak to you after the process is complete."

He turned and left the vault. John folded his arms and turned to see a laborer shake his head in disgust before he moved towards the first row of crates.

***

The two of them remained silent while they finished the meal. Lunch was ordered and delivered to the conference room where they were located. Alan had recommended they stay within the building itself and John agreed without a second thought.

When Alan was finished he pushed the paper plate away and looked at his brother. "You're as pale as a ghost."

"Did you see the look on their faces?"

"Yes, I did. Frankly, I don't care."

"Why not?"

Alan finished the last bite of his sandwich. "You know the expression, better them than us. Well, this is gold our grandfather liberated from the Nazis. Better us than them." He shrugged his shoulders and took a sip on a can of soda.

"Didn't take a look at those documents, did you?"

"What, the ones from the vault in my suite? I was a bit preoccupied yesterday."

"Yeah, I know." John tapped the top of the desk. "We should, ah, get rid of the crates."

"Of course, but those swastikas are all over the gold, though."

"Yeah, but the crates make us look like Nazis ourselves."

Alan nodded. "Yeah, maybe we can do something in London." He wiped his hands and leaned back. "It will be airborne by 4:00 p.m. We will watch it take off, then drive back to the hotel."

"Please tell me the security service in London is topnotch."

"The best in the business. I did my research." Alan picked up his cell phone and made a call. "Yes, this is Alan Devenger, I'm checking on our freight shipment from Neuchatel to London?"

John listened to Alan confirm the arrangements and then he placed another call. "Yes, I have a shipment coming in tonight, and I wanted to ensure you will have people on hand for the process." He provided an affirmative nod to John. "Excellent. Thank you." He put the phone back down in the table. "Done."

John clasped his hands and gazed out the window. He stood up a moment later and looked down at the courtyard. The workers were wheeling one crate at a time to the back of the security truck. "There it is." The vehicle itself looked like an oversized security truck, complete with flat front windows, metal barriers to protect the wheels and a riveted-steel storage area. "Our pay day."

"What's the first thing you're going to do with the money?"

John turned when he saw the door to the conference room open wide.

The manager stepped in the room and provided a somber look as he stepped forward.

"Hey there. You okay?"

The Director took a seat on the opposite side of the table. "Some regrettable news, which I just received." He put his hand to his face. "Herr Heinzen has been murdered."

Alan dropped his soda can. "What did you say?"

"Murdered."

***

Henrick picked up his phone and waited for Fritz to answer. "Imbecile." Fritz answered a moment later.

"What?"

"Do you know what side of the building you are on now?"

"Fuck you, old man."

"Stay put. You move when I tell you to. I'm moving the van to the opposite side of the building." He ended the call and got out of the vehicle. He looked through the security gate and saw crates emblazoned with Nazi emblems being wheeled to the back of the truck. He then tapped on Karla's window.

"You remain here. When the truck leaves, call me."

"Henrick, it's over."

"*Nein*! We will get the truck, we have the weapons."

"You're a foolish old man. What is the point?"

"You will thank me, girl, you will thank me. Don't move until I give you the word." He stepped away and back into the van. Karla watched him drive away and turn the corner.

***

"Let's get the fuck out of here. They are blaming us!"

"You're losing it, John. It's very sad, but they know we didn't do it."

"Well let's get out of here, regardless. They are done packing the truck. He just gave us the word."

"He did?"

"You were in the bathroom. For quite awhile I might add." John watched his brother provide a perplexed expression.

"What do you want, nature called."

"Taking a shit at a moment like this. Get your things, let's get back to the car."

Alan followed John into the courtyard and saw the driver waive to catch their attention. "You two, the Devengers I presume?"

"Yes."

He sauntered over in a casual manner, which contrasted with the Swiss bank employees. "So," he smirked, "your Nazi stuff is ready to move. Did they tell you we could not fit it all?"

"No."

"There's one remaining crate inside the bank."

Alan nodded. "That's fine. John, any concerns if we leave one behind in the vault?" His half-brother shook his head. "Good, let's go, we'll grab our car out—" He looked towards the gated entrance. "John, the car should be parked on that road back there."

"Wait here, I'll check."

He heard Alan ask the security driver if he knew where Neuchatel airport was before he stepped away.

He noticed a small guardhouse and a door beside it. When he got closer, a security guard from the bank appeared. "Can I help you?"

"Our truck is leaving, and my car is parked outside the gate. We'd like to leave."

"You can exit the main entrance, then walk around the building."

"That's not going to happen, it's right there. Unlock the door and let me out please."

The guard raised his hand and stepped inside the small office. John watched him place a call and then returned outside. "Go ahead, then. Is he joining you?" He pointed towards Alan.

"Yes. Thanks."

John stepped through a doorframe and he was standing in a small holding room. Another door remained closed in front of him. A buzzer sounded and John pushed the door forward. Moments later he was standing outside the building.

***

With Fritz out of the car and somewhere on foot around the bank, Karla knew it was the best time to plan her escape. She waited for the website on her cell phone screen to provide flight options. She glanced up to see a familiar bald man standing not twenty feet away from her vehicle.

"Oh." She watched as he walked over to a parked car and opened the driver's side door. He placed a backpack on the passenger seat. Her hands froze during the process.

She was told to call Henrick if she saw anything suspicious. She looked in the side view mirror and down the length of the side road: the old man was out of sight. She hit redial and he answered on the second ring. "He's right here! Now!" The sound caught John Devenger's attention. She turned and realized her window was open a few inches to give herself fresh air.

The next thing she saw was the bald man staring at her with a look of serious concern. His eyes shot down the alley in both directions. When he turned back, he pointed at her. "You... who the fuck are you?"

She watched him walk toward her. "Holy... shit!" She locked the doors and rolled up the window.

He moved to the driver's side and pounded on the roof. "Who are you?" He tried to open the door.

"Oh my God! Henrick!"

He squinted his eyes when he heard the name.

The man staring at her furrowed his brow, knelt down out of sight and returned with a buck knife in his right hand.

Her cries for help went unheard. Devenger's eyes looked up and down the alley. He stepped forward, paused at the front left tire and slashed the knife forward. A moment later, the car lurched forward on a slight angle. She heard air hissing from the gash in the tire.

She did the only thing she could think of and slammed on the car's horn. "Leave me alone!" John moved away as the sound startled him. Within seconds he was back at the security door pounding to be let inside the bank.

When he moved out of view, Henrick was beside her vehicle a moment later. The pistol was in his right hand. "What happened?"

"He... he was right there!"

"I saw him. Did he cut you with the knife?"

"No, thank God, he—" She watched him walk over to the security gate to look inside.

She then saw him dash down the street and out of sight.

***

John crossed the courtyard with a brisk pace. He motioned to the driver and to Alan to get in the vehicle. "We're leaving."

"You cannot drive with me in the truck."

"Shut up and drive. We're going with you in the truck right now and you're going to let us."

"You don't understand, I will be fired."

"Then we'll make it worth your while."

Chapter 26

<u>Ridgewood, NJ</u>

Larry Goldberg checked his watch and shook his head. It was 8:00 p.m. on a Friday night. He hoped his partner's vacation to Anguilla was time well spent because he knew the time he was spending doing his job was not sitting well with him.

Right after he snapped his laptop shut his office phone began to ring. He believed, for a moment, that a higher power was tormenting him. "Come on." He cleared his throat and answered, "Hello, this is Larry Goldstein."

"Hi there Larry, this is Charlotte Devenger."

"Hello. Nice of you to call. Late on a Friday."

"I'm sorry for the timing. I was planning on leaving you a message."

"No problem." He smiled and remembered the walk he took with her in the house she inherited. "How's that Mattituck property?"

"It's fine. I'm still reminding myself I own it, but I haven't burned it down yet thankfully."

"Well thank goodness for that. I bet the meal my wife is making won't fare as well. She scorches everything. So what's up?"

"I believe my brothers gave you a call. I'm following up as they asked me to do so."

He nodded. "Yes, they did."

"I'm checking in, a liaison of sorts to ensure everything goes smoothly on this end."

"That's forward thinking on their part."

"So... any news?"

"About what they should do with the gold?"

"Obviously, yes."

"I told them to bring home a sample. We may have to notify the IRS, but I have not done any more research beyond that."

"Okay. Is something wrong?"

"Nope." He leaned forward and opened his laptop. "Where did it come from?"

"The vault. I thought you were aware of this."

"That's not what I'm asking. What more do you know about the gold itself?"

"Oh. Well, we know our grandfather liberated it from the Nazis. It's a rather large sum, and he deposited it in a Swiss bank."

"So... it's Nazi gold."

"Yes, that I can assure you."

"Oh, how so?"

"I spoke last night to my brothers. Let's just say when and if you see it, there's no doubt where it came from."

Larry opened his laptop, opened a search browser, typed in "Nazi Gold" and looked at the results.

"Larry?"

"Sorry, I... I'm just jotting down some notes." Larry moved the pointer on his screen to 'Images' under the search bar. The screen was filled with swastikas embedded in gold bars. "I think I have a rough idea of what you're talking about."

"What, the gold?"

He closed his laptop. "When your brothers return, I suggest they put that gold bar in a deposit box, right away."

"There's got to be more than that. Are you familiar with this kind of process, inheritance from overseas that is?"

Larry thought it best to end the call. The affinity he once felt for her subsided, given her blatant naivety. He wasn't sure if greed was blinding her or she was just a clueless gentile. "Have your brothers reach out to me when they return. I'll do some more research on my end."

"Okay, well thanks for taking the call so late on a Friday."

"Yup. Speak to you soon." He ended the call.

He shut his laptop, sat back in his chair and rubbed his temples. "What the hell did I get myself into," he said aloud.

218

He turned to see a ten-year-old picture of his family at the edge of his desk. His hair was darker then and his kids were all teenagers at the time. He laughed when he thought about those years. His three children, and their ages, extended the teenage phase for a much larger period of time: 13 years in total. He picked up the picture and looked at their smiles. He remembered why he treasured this particular photo. All three of his kids, within the picture itself, appeared to be happy at the time it was taken. He and his spouse laughed about it when they processed the film, given the rarity of such a picture when all three kids appeared content and even-tempered.

He placed it back in the exact location from whence it came and turned to see other family photographs on the wall. His smile evaporated. He stood up and walked over to the collage of ten framed pictures. He picked up one of the older black and white images and looked at the hand-written date below the image: November 11th, 1938.

The picture was the image of his grandfather and his family standing outside their home. His wife was in the picture as well. The youngest child, their daughter Nokmimi, was Larry's mother. He looked at their faces, and unlike the picture of his family on the desk, they were not smiling. He looked at the bottom of the picture and noticed each of them had a piece of luggage resting before their feet. One bag had an article of clothing dangling from it. He paused on that particular element; why it was hanging out of the suitcase? Was it ever worn again? Did it make it out of Europe during their voyage to the States?

He placed his forehead against the photograph and felt the wood hit his skin. He took a deep breath and silently thanked his grandparents for making the right decisions for themselves and their children. He thought about what he would do if he faced the same choice and felt it would be nothing short of an impossible situation.

He placed the picture frame gently back on the hook that held it and stepped back towards his desk. He opened up a filing cabinet and flipped through the tabs until the word, 'DEVENGER,' appeared. He took out the two-inch file.

He thumbed through it, found the representative agreements John and Alan signed, and tossed them on the desk.

He leaned over them and gave thought to placing the documents in his secretary's paper shredder. He could conclude his relationship with the family forever. His gut told him it was the wisest choice. He tapped the two-page stapled documents and recalled what happened when his office phone rang. He remembered thinking that he was being tormented by a higher power, given the timing of the call.

He paused on that association. Torment was the operative word, and now more than ever, he truly felt the emotion.

He placed the documents back in the folder and then filed it back in the cabinet.

There was one thing he needed more than anything else, and that was a person who possessed greater wisdom. He knew exactly where to find it and whom to speak to about matters relating to Nazi gold.

Kerzers, Switzerland

John and Alan listened to the security guard continue to do what he had been doing for the past ten minutes. Alan thought about slapping him across the face. He knew it would present a serious problem if he chose to do so.

The driver continued to whistle as he shifted from gear to gear. Sitting on a flat surface on the dashboard, below the console, was a single twenty-pound gold brick. John sat adjacent to the window and Alan was sandwiched on the bench seat between his half-brother and the driver.

"Do you mind?"

The whistling stopped. "You don't like my whistling?"

"No."

"Sorry, no radios, but I love music. Perhaps Wagner?" He started to whistle "Flight of the Valkyries."

"Better?"

"God help me." said John.

"How much further?"

"I don't know. Twenty, maybe ten minutes. How many times do you plan to ask me?" Neither man replied and the driver smiled.

"Feeling pretty good there, Tomas?"

"Quite well."

Alan looked at the gold brick. "So what do you plan to do with it?"

"Many things. It was quite generous, thank you."

Fucker, thought John. "Do you have any idea what that is worth?" The driver shook his head. "It's almost four hundred thousand dollars."

"Can you see if anyone is following us?" interrupted Alan.

"That much? Well then, that could buy me a nice flat." Tomas smiled. "No, I don't think anyone is following us."

"How do you know?"

"Well, if anyone is, I'll use the intercom to let my supervisor know." He turned to look at both of the men traveling with him to Neuchatel airport. "Why do you Americans worry all the time?"

"We ran into a few Nazi's back in Bern."

"Oh." The driver looked down at the brick for a moment and then tapped the Swastika with his finger. "I wonder why."

"Just keep an eye on the road." John shook his head. He furrowed his brow and looked at the driver. "Just out of curiosity, are you going to cash in the gold?"

"Of course!"

"How are you going to go about doing that?"

"I don't know. Go where rich people go to cash in gold I guess."

"If you come up with something, we're all ears." John watched his brother hold up his hands in confusion. "What, I'm trying to get some ideas."

"Look, there we go, ten kilometers." The driver pointed towards a road sign that highlighted the distance to Neuchatel.

***

Henrick pounded the dashboard with one hand as his other remained fixed on his chest.

"Henrick, my car!" Otto forced Henrick's fist back into his lap.

The pains Henrick felt started the moment the security truck drove past them on the one-way avenue in Bern. Several times his bony hands clutched his chest. His eyes continued to lock on the truck as it drove west on Route E-25, thirty miles outside of Bern.

He retrieved his cell phone and dialed Fritz. "Where are you?"

"I'm two cars behind you. Can't you see me?"

Henrick looked in the rear-view mirror and saw the white van sit higher on the road compared to the cars that separated them. "*Ja.*"

"What do you propose to do? Sit here and watch these assholes get away with the gold?"

"I'm trying to figure that out."

"I've got the guns in the back. I can pull over, get one, and shoot out their fucking tires."

"No. Don't do that, we can't risk the authorities and we need the truck."

"We have to do something, and do it now. This is a two-lane highway for Christ's sake!"

"It's too risky."

"Henrick, what is Fritz saying?" said Otto.

"Fritz, I'll call you when we get away from the town."

"Well if you don't do something, I will."

Fritz, wait until—"

A moment later, they watched the van accelerate past Otto's car. He sped forward towards the security truck. Road signs indicated that the two lanes were narrowing down to one and Otto merged with other cars on the road.

"What is he doing?" said Henrick.

"Trying to stop the truck and he cannot."

"Where is Karla? We need a third car."

"I'm not sure. She should have followed the truck, but obviously she did not."

"Call her."

Henrick found Karla's number and dialed.

Bern, Switzerland

The ring from the phone rattled Karla from her thought process and she slowly raised it to see Henrick was calling. She questioned whether or not she should answer it. "Yes?"

"Where are you?"

"In Bern."

"Why did you not follow the truck?"

"I was not... my tires, John Devenger slashed one."

"How could that possibly happen? Get on the road!"

"He came at me with a knife."

"Get another car then. Why in God's name would you—"

She ended the call. She tossed the phone on the passenger seat. Feeling comfortable enough to move for the first time in thirty minutes, she exited the vehicle. A cool breeze hit her sweat-soaked blouse. She folder her arms after she closed the car door.

She turned to see if there was anyone else in the immediate vicinity but saw no one. Her instinct was to walk to the nearest street corner, hail a cab, go to the airport and leave the country on the next available flight.

She decided to do just that and retrieved her jacket, purse and mobile phone from the car. She started to think about what she had with her, what she needed and thought it best not to retrieve her suitcase and clothes at the rented house. She would buy clothes if needed, given her purse contained her credit cards, identification and passport. All she needed was a ticket home.

Her steps took her towards the busier avenue in the distance but her path took her past John Devenger's car. She paused and wondered why they had not yet left the bank. Were they still inside? She stepped forward and looked through the gate the security truck passed through thirty minutes prior. No one was visible.

She walked back to the car, put her hands on her hips and took note of the backpack on the passenger-side seat. Karla turned to see if anyone was looking. She moved in proximity of the door handle. She bit her lip, lifted the handle and discovered it was unlocked. "Okay." She double-checked the perimeter; the alley was clear. She opened the door, grabbed the topside handle on the backpack and nearly fell inside the car from the weight of it. "Jesus."

She used both hands, grabbed the bag and threw it over her shoulder, which nearly capsized her.

In ten minutes' time she was eight blocks away and she moved towards a narrow alley off the main avenue. She placed the bag on the ground, slid the zipper open that enclosed within it was a large gold brick staring back at her. Her jaw dropped as her fingers touched the inlayed eagle, swastika and 'SS' initials.

She remembered the stories her father shared with her about the vault, where it was and what needed to happen in order to secure the gold. She recalled the dreams of her father, the promises he made on his deathbed his advice to stay the course. He said if the process took twenty or fifty more years, it was worth the wait in order to secure their family's portion of the treasure.

In that moment, to her satisfaction, she felt a family promise had been kept. It was one that had taken a generation to complete. The amount was only a pittance of what she was entitled to, but it was nonetheless in her possession. She was surprised at the other emotion she felt, but smiled when her mind focused on one simple fact: the men she was working with had obtained nothing.

She closed the bag and stepped back towards the avenue to find a taxi. She planned to be on the next available outbound flight to Brazil.

Neuchatel, Switzerland

"Otto, I think this is it. The road is two lanes wide again."

Otto shook his head. "Do you not see all the roads, the buildings and the cars?"

Henrick sighed. "Yes, I know. We have to wait." He rubbed the sides of his head with both hands. He adjusted the rearview mirror and saw Fritz driving the van directly behind them. He turned to look out the passenger window when his phone rang. "Hello."

"I see you looking at me. Can we end this joy ride? It's time to stop the truck."

"We cannot. We are going to attempt this away from civilization."

"We should not delay."

He ended the call. He saw a road sign that identified the distance to Geneva and various other destinations. "Otto, look. Geneva. That has to be it."

"There has to be open country between here and there."

"We will see."

"What do you propose we do Henrick?"

He tapped his finger on his thigh. "Try to stop the truck. Use weapons to threaten them, force them out of the vehicle, then we drive off. We have an automatic weapon with us."

"It works properly, that I can assure..." Otto watched the security truck decelerate from 100 to 80 to 60 kilometers per hour. The vehicle used its blinker to indicate it was going to use the upcoming exit. "Do you see this?"

"I'm not blind!"

The truck took the off ramp and slowed down at an intersection. Both men sat up in their seats. Henrick ignored his ringing cell phone. "Neuchatel?" He said. The truck drove around a traffic circle and headed back in the opposite direction from whence it came. The road however was a local one and not the highway.

The truck accelerated, and then a mile later it slowed down and used its turn signal once again.

"Do they know we're here? What the hell are they doing?"

The truck came to a complete stop at a traffic light. When it turned, Henrick looked up to see they were about to pass through a security gate. The name of the destination was written across a large blue sign:

NUECHATEL AIRPORT

Henrick watched the truck passed through the gate and a steel curtain slowly closed behind it.

***

John furrowed his brow when they passed through the gate. To his immediate right was a guardhouse, and outside he saw two nonchalant security officers smoking cigarettes. They didn't seem to have a care in the world.

"Your destination, gentlemen." said Tomas.

John smiled and wrapped his arm around Alan to squeeze him tight. "We did it."

Alan exhaled and managed to share a grin. "We did." He checked his mobile phone, given his Rolex was gone, and it read 3:00 p.m. "Let's try to find our plane." He turned to look out the passenger window and saw a white van screech to a halt outside the security fence. "I'll be God damned." Alan shook off John's arm and pointed outside the window. "Look!"

"What?"

"That's the van!"

John turned to see it but the truck had moved out of sight from the entrance. "Where?"

"Outside the gate. I swear I saw it."

The driver applied the brakes. "What is the problem?"

"They were following us." The look Alan and John shared with one another reflected a mix of relief and fear.

"Nazi's?"

"They were following us." John shook his head and then laughed. "Well, they can kiss my ass."

They turned to see a variety of single-prop planes parked in the immediate vicinity. A hundred yards across the tarmac was a larger plane that towered over the smaller aircraft.

They took their leave from the truck.

***

Otto slammed on the brakes when his car and the van were down the road from the local airport. He stepped out of the Mercedes. Henrick followed and Fritz joined them.

"This is not fucking happening!" screamed Fritz.

Otto sighed and said, "I'm afraid it is."

"You're giving up?"

"We need a plan, and now!" Henrick felt Fritz poke him square in the chest.

"We had a dozen opportunities during the drive to stop them."

"How was I to know they would fly it out?"

"Open country, a machine gun, now it's all gone."

"Well they are not gone yet," Otto said. Fritz and Henrick both turned to face him. "The Devengers and our gold, they are still on the ground."

Henrick turned to look at the security gate behind them and then the road in the distance. "He's right. We can stop the plane."

"I doubt that, Henrick. That's not what I meant." Otto shook his head. "We cannot access the airport. Maybe call in a bomb threat or something."

"But there has to be a runway. Perhaps you can access it from a nearby road."

"Then what, Henrick?"

"Shoot it! Keep the plane grounded."

"Let's go." Fritz gestured for Otto to follow. "You and me. Henrick watch the front gate."

"Wait, shoot the plane?"

"Go! See if you can stop them."

Otto paused to look at the van, and then back at Henrick. He then walked behind the van, opened the back door and retrieved a handgun. He walked back to Henrick and handed him the weapon and his car keys. "If they try to leave, shoot out their tires. I doubt you can stop them, but try."

"Stop the plane. Save the gold. Now!" Henrick took the Walther PP pistol and placed it in his pocket.

Fritz slammed the side of the van. "Move it, Otto!" He watched the fat man take the passenger seat. A cloud of dust rose from the ground when Fritz slammed his foot on the gas.

***

Alan stepped forward and shook the pilot's hand. "Is that our plane?"

"Yes sir, it's being refueled at the moment."

Alan and John turned to see a fuel truck parked beneath the plane's left wing.

It was enormous compared to the other planes on the ground. It was thirty yards long with a wingspan of twenty yards, parked at the end of the runway. The plane was white, except for a red logo on its tail and Alan thought it looked like a miniature version of a 747. He doubted if the twin turbine engine could manage the weight of the gold.

"You are aware of the weight of our cargo?"

"I have it indicated here on the paperwork. You called it in recently, yes?"

Alan nodded.

John placed his hand on Alan's shoulder. "If you can give us a minute, I need to speak to my half-brother."

"Of course. We will fuel the plane, load the cargo, and we should be airborne in an hour's time."

"Great." John pulled Alan away from the pilot.

"Yes?"

"We should go with them."

He turned to face him. "Leave on the cargo plane?"

"Yes. How else are we going to get out of here?"

Alan shook his head in confusion.

"You said you saw that white van outside the gate, yes?" Alan nodded. "So they are out there. What if they are waiting for us? What happens if they get their hands on us?"

"I see your point."

"Do you have your passport?"

Alan nodded. "You?"

"Of course, we needed it at the bank." John turned to look over his shoulder. "We will have to leave everything behind at the hotel though."

Alan sighed. "Well, everything can be replaced. I had a pricey jacket, and... shit."

"What?"

"The journal."

"What about... oh shit."

"It's back in the hotel room. Your room, come to think of it."

"Well, maybe the hotel staff can lend a hand?" said John. "We need that journal."

Alan nodded. "I can tell them we are stuck. Maybe a business conference, I'll come up with something."

"Excellent. Call them now, I'll speak to the pilot."

Alan retrieved his phone, called the hotel and fabricated a story about their car breaking down on the way back from Geneva. He went on to explain they would be staying in another city and required assistance. They agreed to manage the process for a small fee and Alan gave permission to place the charges, including the shipping costs, on his credit card. He turned around to see his brother walking towards him.

"They are taking care of it, the hotel that is."

"Really? It worked?"

Alan nodded. "That's five-star service for you. I doubted it myself. They saw no reason not to help. What about the pilot?"

"They are not allowed to fly us out, so we need to persuade him."

Alan gave his brother a puzzled look.

"Get another gold brick."

***

Fritz slammed on the brakes. The white van pulled to a stop. To their immediate right was a long grassy hill. Small homes and trees dotted the landscape to the left. Fritz pointed towards the ascending ground. "That's got to be it."

Fritz stepped out of the van and Otto followed. They froze when the roar of a plane's engine crossed directly over their heads. They turned to see one had taken flight over the hill.

Otto followed the plane with his eyes. He swallowed. "We have to stop that plane."

Fritz stepped quickly around the side of the van and the back doors flew open towards the side. He reached in and removed the compartment that held the weapons in Otto's trunk. He took out the Schmeisser machine gun and then slammed a magazine of ammunition into the base of it.

Before he stepped away, he grabbed one of the two remaining magazines. "Grab a pistol, let's go."

Otto stepped before him. "Give me the weapon."

Fritz ignored him and stepped around his large torso. "Get a fucking gun!" He took ten paces, hopped a small fence, and then stormed up the hill.

"Fritz, wait!"

The weapon weighed down his shoulder as his steps took him across the long hill. He removed the shoulder strap and held the weapon with both hands. His quick steps turned into a jog. He could hear the sound of grass being crushed beneath his feet.

Fritz turned back to see Otto stumbling on the soft earth. He was trying to keep up but the distance between them extended. Fritz noticed Otto was already out of breath. Fat bastard. When he turned he saw a plane thirty feet in the air barreling straight at him.

He dropped to his knee. When the plane passed his eyes followed it. "Son of a bitch!" When he turned back he saw he had ten yards left to climb before he reached the top of the hill.

Adrenalin and anger prompted Fritz to sprint forward. From behind he heard Otto call his name. He ignored him. His legs pumped with fury. His view changed from one of grass to a pair of landing strips and a field of sunflowers.

He saw a large plane in the distance parked at the end of the runway. A fuel truck was parked beside it. Buildings rose beyond the planes to the far left.

He squinted his eyes. Fritz did not believe what he was looking at. The security truck was parked a hundred yards behind the plane. "Shit." Several hundred yards distanced him from the area. With alarming speed he crossed the field that paralleled the airstrip to get closer. Bright yellow sunflowers snapped and fell with each step that he took.

He stopped when he came upon another fence. He was now two hundred yards from the plane. He turned to look for Otto. He was not yet over the hill. When he turned back he saw the fuel hoses being retrieved and recoiled into a circular mechanism that held them. Moments later the fuel truck pulled away. "Dammit!" He searched the ground for an area to fire the weapon but the flowers and fence were too high.

He secured the machine gun with both hands, placed the butt against his shoulder and leaned forward. He took aim at the plane's windows.

He squeezed the trigger. White flashes exploded from the barrel. Bullets sprayed out from the machine gun towards the side of the plane with violent fury.

***

The pilot concluded the cell phone call as Alan and John waited for the answer they hoped to receive. He stepped closer to the security truck.

"Gentlemen, good news to report, you can fly with us."

Alan nodded. "You were very persuasive with your supervisor. I wonder why."

The pilot and John shared a brief laugh, prompting Alan to follow suit. Not five minutes prior, a gold brick was promised to the man with a British accent.

"Do you have your passports?"

"Yes."

"Very well, then. You will need them when we arrive at London City airport."

They heard a noise that sounded like uncorked champagne bottles mix with punctures of steel. Each man turned towards the direction of the sound. They faced the plane. Sparks of white light peppered the ground in the distance. What sounded like high-pitched mosquitos crossed from left to right in front of their position. Then they heard what sounded like a loud buzz saw echo in the distance.

"What was that?"

The sound of more punctures radiated from the plane. Several black holes appeared on its tail. The pilot instinctively backed up and hit Alan in the shoulder.

"What the hell is happening?"

They heard glass shatter. Alan noticed two streams of red liquid falling from the belly of the plane. "Is that—" The buzz saw screamed in the distance.

Right before he stepped back, Alan noticed a tall blond man out of the corner of his eye. He was standing in the adjacent field. What he held in his hands rattled and flashed with brilliant white light.

When he turned back to the plane he saw a spark and then a blue flame.

His eyelids clamped down when white light exploded in front of him. He was confused why he could not feel the ground beneath his feet. Someone's elbow hit him square across the face in mid-air.

***

The last volley of bullets flew out of the weapon. Fritz paused when he noticed the blue flame trailing up towards the wing of the plane.

It was not until the echo of the explosion pounded his eardrums that he realized what happened. The left wing exploding into hundreds of flying pieces of shrapnel, engulfing the remaining part of the plane in white light. A small black cloud rose from the chaos and the mass of steel lurched to the right. A much larger explosion followed from the belly of the plane. The shock wave radiated out and rattled Fritz's chest cavity.

The remaining parts of the plane exploded from the front to the back in piecemeal fashion. The underbelly of the plane slammed into the tarmac while debris rose several stories high into the air. Blackened debris unfolded in the sky, flying outwards in random directions. What followed was a massive fireball and mushroom cloud lifting high into the air.

The flames widened and shards of metal started to fall like rain from the sky, hitting rooftops, the runway and the grassy areas around the airstrip. Loud clangs of crashing metal mixed with the rumble of flames.

Fritz dropped the weapon and surveyed the destruction. What looked like flaming meteors dropped sporadically across the landscape. He saw two small pieces of incendiary material land on the roof of the security truck. One bounced off and another lodged itself into its roof.

Fritz dropped to his knees. A moment later he saw Otto racing towards him.

"What did you do?"

"I...I was trying to shoot out the windows."

"This is a horrible!"

The two watched the fires burn, releasing massive clouds of black smoke.

***

He felt a sharp pain in his shoulder and heard the sound of metal crashing around him. Alan tried to sit up and felt two hands lift him from the ground. He looked back to see he had landed ten feet from where he once stood. He couldn't hear the voice yelling in his ear as he tried to place his feet beneath him. Someone was pulling him away from the carnage.

He saw an airport employee run over to the motionless pilot on the ground. He carried him away from the fires. The wind carried black smoke towards their position.

"What—"

"Look out!"

A chunk of flaming metal landed twelve feet away and bounced to their left.

He hit the ground behind the truck. He was staring at John's shoes. He looked up and saw John's eyes dart from one part of the sky to another and then another.

Alan shook his head from the ringing in his ears. He turned himself over, rose to his feet but his knees buckled. He bounced off the side of the truck and collapsed.

"Alan… Alan! Are you injured?"

He heard the roar of the flames grow louder. "We're going to die."

Chapter 27

Neuchatel Airport, Switzerland

Henrick did not understand why he heard the sound of loud thuds in the distance. His car was parked twenty yards from the gated entrance. When his steering wheel shuddered, he recoiled and looked out the side window to see pieces of debris flying high in the air. He gulped when he saw a black mushroom cloud rise and metal shards career down from the sky.

He rolled down his window and heard what sounded like hundreds of tin cans crashing onto concrete before he saw a security guard exit the small building besides the fence. He used a key to enter an adjacent door and closed it behind him in a mad dash.

"Dear mother of God, what has happened?"

He picked up and scrolled down to the name "OTTO" in his cell phone and dialed. After four rings, the voicemail picked up. Henrick put down the phone and listened to the low hum of flames wisp into the air. Given the location of the smoke, he surmised that the fire was enormous.

***

"How you managed to fuck this up, I'll never know."

"It was an accident!"

The two walked quickly down the hill. Smoke trails continued to leak from the barrel of the Schmeisser machine gun. Otto continued to bark out profanities at him.

Fritz slowed down to allow Otto to walk five paces in front of him. He wondered if he had any ammunition left. He used one magazine on the plane and part of another. To silence the man, he realized all he had to do was lift the barrel of the gun and drill ten rounds into the fat man's backside. He decided not to do so when Otto turned to face him.

"Did you hear me?"

"What? No, my hearing is off from the explosion."

Otto turned to see a young couple standing ten feet away from their van. "Shit."

"Witnesses."

"We have to scare them off." Otto waved to them from fifty yards away. "Get away from the van!" They looked at one another in confusion and did not move.

Otto stopped walking, retrieved his Walther pistol and fired two rounds into the air. The couple turned and ran for their lives.

"They were probably screwing in a sunflower field."

"Shut your fucking mouth! You've done enough damage."

The two picked up their pace before they opened the side door to the van, dropped their weapons in the back, and moved to the front seats.

***

John felt his cheekbone and it was tender from the slide his face took on the asphalt. He looked down to see blood on his hand. He turned to Alan, who was staring off into the distance. Dozens of burnt pieces of metal littered the area around them.

Nazis, he thought. They are outside the gate.

John coughed several times from the smoke billowing their way. His eyes could not see beyond the immediate perimeter. He heard someone scream in the distance and wondered when help would arrive.

His next thought triggered a fear he did not fully comprehend at first. If the Nazis could do this from afar, what are they going to do if they gain access the airport itself?

He recalled seeing the guards smoking cigarettes and realized the only thing separating themselves from the armed men was a thin chain-link fence. His instinct told him to run.

"Alan, we've got to get out of here." His brother appeared to be in shock and did not respond. "Alan!"

"Did you say leave?"

John lifted him to his feet by the lapels of his jacket. "Where's the driver?"

"Who?"

"The security truck driver, Tomas!" John turned and saw the man in his tan uniform staring at the black smoke rising behind the security truck. John crossed the roadway between them. "Tomas... Hey!" John grabbed his shoulder and spun him around. "We have to go."

"What are you talking about?"

"You, me, my brother Alan, let's get the hell out of here. Now!"

"I'm not going anywhere!"

John pursed his lips before he said. "Get your ass in the truck. They are going to kill us if we stay here."

"Who?"

"The Nazis! Get in the fucking truck!"

The driver looked at his vehicle. Barring the smoking piece of metal imbedded in the roof, it was intact. He looked back at the man with the bleeding welt on his face and remembered the image of swastikas on the crates. "Oh my God."

"Alan, let's go!"

Alan coughed from the smoke and covered his mouth with his forearm. He squinted his eyes to look at John. He felt his half-brother grab and pull him to the passenger door.

The three of them entered the truck.

The driver paused when he looked at the roof of the cabin. John noticed a look of shock on his face. "What are you looking at?"

He pointed. "Look."

John looked up to see a piece of metal had sliced a small portion of the roof. It looked like an arrowhead, lodged between two slits of steel.

"What the—"

"Drive!"

***

Henrick had one hand on his cell phone and the other on the grip of the pistol. He stood outside the gated fence. Waves of black smoke passed by and clouded the foreground.

He realized what must have happened. The plane... they blew up the plane. He didn't know how to feel, but part of him felt relieved. He knew the gold was somewhere behind the fence.

Henrick removed his cell phone but put it back in his pocket when he heard a truck's engine shift from one gear to the next. Far away in the distance, the sound of police sirens started to howl and grow closer. It seemed like an army of support was descending from multiple directions. The sun's rays could not pass through the curtain of smoke.

He was less concerned about the authorities after he heard the sound of the engine move toward his position. He stepped before the gate and was shocked to see the silhouette of the security truck through the black haze.

His mouth was agape. The truck turned towards the chain-link fence before Henrick. "*Scheisse!*" He fumbled to retrieve his handgun. He secured it and trained his sights on the front windshield. A second later he re-aimed his weapon at the front left tire and snapped off two rounds. One ricocheted off the chain link. Another lodged in the rubber but it did not deflate. He steadied the weapon with both hands and aimed it at the driver.

***

"Who the fuck is that?" said Tomas.

"Run him down!" John reached for his gun as the truck lurched forward.

Tomas slammed on the gas when he saw the barrel of the gun pointed at him.

The truck accelerated to twenty miles per hour before it crashed into the fence. The old man's eyes grew wide and he dove out of the way. He hit the ground the moment the chain link ripped from left to right. Two iron poles ripped out of the pavement. They smashed against the sides of the truck before it veered onto the roadway. They all heard the sound of bouncing metal pipes.

"Go! Go! Go!"

The terrified driver buried the pedal and drove away from the chaos.

He couldn't lift himself up and continued to lay on the ground. His hand gripped the side of his hip and he moaned in agony.

He turned to see the truck drive off. It left a trail of black smoke from the metal shard lodged in the top portion of the front cabin. He pulled his legs forward to get to his knees and winced from the pain. When he got to his feet his knee gave way and he tumbled to the earth.

Henrick tried again and rose from the ground. He turned to see a security guard step out from the open gate. When he called out to him, Henrick started to limp towards Otto's Mercedes. The panicked guard left a moment later.

He placed the Walther PP in his pocket when he turned to see the white van pull to the side of the road before him. Otto put the van in park and waved him over to the vehicle. "Are you okay?"

"No, did you see where they went?"

"Barely, but probably not hard to find. We have Fritz to thank for this debacle." He did not turn to look at him. "Get in, let's go after them."

Henrick turned to look at Otto's car. He considered the circumstances. *An abandoned car... near the scene of the crime.* "No, I will follow you, we can't leave the car."

"Are you sure you can manage?"

"I'll find a way."

Henrick tried to walk quickly but his injury slowed him down. He turned to see the van take off in pursuit. He turned back to see two security officials walking towards him at an alarming pace.

"You! Come with us."

Henrick shook his head but they did not stop walking. He retrieved his gun, aimed the barrel at the pavement to his right and fired off a round. They turned and ran back into the interior of the airport. Henrick assumed their absence meant they were unarmed.

He started the engine, turned the wheel and careened down the road. By the time he reached the end, a dozen police vehicles streamed past the Mercedes.

The road curved and bent before them as they traveled through the tiny village. John did not take his eye off the side view mirror. He adjusted it to provide himself a better view than the driver.

"Do you realize the trouble you've gotten me into?"

"I probably saved your life," said John. He looked at Alan, who was trembling. He placed his hand on his back. "Are you okay?" Alan did not respond.

John looked back to the driver. "You?"

"No, I'm not okay! I have to call this in, then we have to find the authorities." He picked up his cell phone and dialed. "There are procedures to follow."

Tomas spent a minute speaking to someone in German. He concluded the call and turned to John while taking a tight turn on a narrow and ascending road. "They are sending assistance."

John nodded and looked down at the gold brick on the console. "You, ah, may want to put that away."

"Shut your mouth."

He checked the side view mirror. "Where will you take us?"

"They will call me back with a location."

The road pitched and turned before they entered a tunnel beneath a hill. When they exited Alan turned to John and said, "Any sign of them?"

"No."

"Fucking Americans. Stay home next time." Tomas hit the steering wheel with his fist. "Did you see the pilot hit the ground? There's no way he survived the blast. No way!"

John did not have time to respond before a white van appeared in the side view mirror. It barreled out of the tunnel after them at an alarming pace. John sat up in the seat. "Oh no."

His mind froze for a second when he turned to his brother. "Alan, the white van. Here they come." His brother's jaw dropped and his eyes opened wide.

The driver looked in the mirror to his left. "What, those are Nazis? Fucking Nazis?"

"Oh my God." Alan watched the van grow in size within the mirror.

"Answer my question!"

"It's got to be them."

The driver slowed down to cross an intersection. He turned on a road that pointed to La Chaux de-Fonds. "I should throw you out of the truck."

"They will kill you, then they will take the gold."

The driver picked up his phone from the console. "Fucking Americans."

Alan startled both of them when he sat up in his seat. "Drive faster!"

The driver sped through a traffic intersection right after the light turned red. Buildings started to pass in rapid succession. John noticed pedestrians turning to look at the accelerating vehicle. The road narrowed a moment later and the truck scraped against the side of a parked car. The road tightened further before the truck cleared the last block of the town itself.

"They are right behind us!" The driver downshifted from the sixth to the fifth gear and hit the gas. "I don't know where this road goes."

"Okay," said Alan.

"No," Tomas shook his head, "We have to stop, or turn or something."

"Why?"

"The weight of the truck, it cannot handle sharp turns while ascending."

"Well don't stop!"

Tomas made a sharp turn on a road called Les Bulles and gained speed. It was a flat road, a country lane through farm fields. Trees lined the side of the street for the first mile.

John noticed a Mercedes tailing the van. "I think there's a second car."

Alan leaned over his lap. "Holy fuck."

"This is Tomas, we are outside Neuchatel." He waited to receive a response. "This is an emergency. I require immediate assistance."

A moment later then heard the rattle of a machine gun.

***

He leaned half his torso out the window and waited to see what the truck would do. Nothing happened. "They are not stopping!" screamed Fritz.

"Shoot the truck itself."

Fritz took aim and squeezed three bursts, which lodged themselves in the steel-plated back doors. "Shit."

"Shoot out the tires!"

Fritz gripped the upper portion of the doorframe and held it while the van turned with the road. He aimed the machine gun at the rear tires. Metal mud flaps blocked most of the exposed rubber, giving him a very small target. The gun exploded in sound. He wasn't a hundred percent sure he'd hit the tires. The truck did not lose any momentum.

He looked to see the road was going to bend to the right. He gripped the gun firmly. "Slow down." He moved from the passenger seat to the right of the van. Otto decelerated. Fritz slid open the side door and saw he had a clear shot along the entire right side of the truck. He squeezed the trigger. Silver indentations made a line from front to back. He heard a distinct click, indicating his ammunition was spent. The truck did not stop moving.

Fritz dropped the weapon and returned to the passenger seat. "We have to try something different."

"We have to get ahead of them." Otto reached for his phone. Henrick answered. "I'm going to pull ahead. Get behind them and stay put."

Otto maneuvered the van behind the truck. "Here we go." He slammed on the gas, pulled in the oncoming lane and passed the truck seconds later. He pulled ahead and saw three men in the front seat of the vehicle's cabin.

"Fritz! Open the back doors and aim the Schmeisser at them."

Fritz moved in the back of the van and pulled the crate away from the rear door. He flipped it open, rummaged through and found one last remaining magazine and loaded it. He slammed it into the base of the machine gun, loaded the first round, and kicked open the back doors of the van. The gun remained pointed at the driver when he knelt down near the opening. He put his finger on the trigger.

Otto watched Fritz from the rear view mirror. "I'm going to slow down," he yelled.

Fritz watched the three men. They appeared to be screaming at one another. They crept closer while Fritz motioned for them to slow down. He was fifteen feet away when the truck decelerated.

Fritz fumbled as the van came to a stop. He regained his balance. "Don't fucking move!" He stepped out of the van and kept his gun centered on the front windshield.

He heard Otto exit the van, cock a handgun and then move beside Fritz.

"Get out!"

"Move or I'll fire!"

"Kill the engine!"

The men inside the truck continued to scream at each other. Fritz moved alongside the driver's side door. "You better move!"

Otto gestured with his handgun as he moved to the passenger door. "Get out!" he screamed. They continued to bicker. He snapped of a round at the side-view mirror and it shattered to pieces. He then fixed his sights on John Devenger's temple.

The two brothers held their hands up in the air. The driver dropped his head, opened the door and stepped out of the truck.

They heard a car door open and close behind the truck. After a few moments of yelling the passenger's side door opened. John stepped out and Alan followed. The driver turned to dash behind the left side of the truck.

"You're not going anywhere." Henrick pointed his weapon at Tomas's chest.

"Don't shoot!"

"Step back." Henrick limped forward and kept his Walther fixed on the driver's torso. He kept his distance and came alongside Otto and Fritz. The three of them each held weapons.

Henrick noticed the side arm holstered on the driver's hip. "Can you drop the holster without removing that weapon?" Tomas nodded. "Do it now." Tomas complied.

Tomas moved beside the Devengers. "I don't want any trouble."

"Just take the truck." Alan pointed to it. "Let us be. You got what you wanted."

"It appears we did." Henrick turned to see a large field of wild flowers stretching out for hundreds of yards in the distance. "I want you to all walk into the field, and keep walking. We're taking the truck."

"Look, just take the gold, they will find the truck," said Tomas.

"Start walking."

"They are coming, they know where we are."

"Shut the fuck up," said Fritz.

Henrick pointed his weapon at the driver. "Step away from the vehicle, walk into that field or I'll kill you myself."

Henrick smiled for a moment as he watched the Americans take several steps towards the open field. He wondered if Everett Devenger had done the same, fifty years ago, to his father and the other German officers who possessed the gold. So many years, and now it's ours. The thought prompted him to chuckle. "You were fools to think you could take it all."

Tomas remained beside the truck. "They are going to kill us."

"Get moving," said Henrick.

"I'm telling you they will shoot us down in that field!"

"Get over there now!"

Otto gestured with his weapon towards the Devengers. "Keep moving."

"I'm telling you there are going to leave us for dead!"

"Shut your fucking mouth!" Fritz turned the submachine gun towards the driver and unloaded five rounds into his chest. The impact sent his body flying against the front grille. He bounced off it and landed face down before them.

"Fritz!" Otto screamed.

Tomas's body contorted twice and then went limp.

Henrick and Otto stared in disbelief at the driver. They did not see John Devenger pull the handgun out of his pocket.

Fritz heard the gunshot right before the bullet buried itself in his leg. He looked down to see the white bone of his kneecap draped in blood. His body caved in on itself.

His screams mixed with John Devenger's order for Otto and Henrick to drop their weapons. "Drop the guns, assholes, or I'll shoot!"

The barrel of the gun looked like a black pupil. It continued to stare at Otto. A moment later he dropped his weapon.

"No, Otto!"

"My knee!" screamed Fritz.

Henrick had no choice and watched John Devenger aim his gun at his face. The pistol hit the pavement a moment later.

John stepped forward. He gestured to the three men to step back. In a flash he reached down, gripped one of the handguns and handed it to Alan.

"Now the three of you. Get your asses into the field. Drag that killer with you." John watched the two older men step beside the screaming young man. "Remove his weapon... slowly."

Henrick limped and gestured towards his leg when he looked at Otto. His injury prevented him from assisting. Otto struggled to move Fritz to the side of the road. He dragged him by his left arm while John followed his every move with his handgun. A moment later the two of them were standing beside Fritz in a field of wild flowers.

John turned to Alan who was shaking from head to toe. "Alan," he whispered, "Alan, snap out of it! Get the rest of the weapons. Put them in the truck. Do you know how to drive a stick?"

"No."

"Never mind. Get the weapons."

Alan made two trips to the truck and placed the guns on the cushion between the driver and passenger seats.

John kept his gun trained on the two standing men. The wounded blond cried out for help.

"John, I'm done. Let's get out of here."

"One last thing. Alan, get a handgun, keep an eye on them." Alan went back to the truck, grabbed a gun and walked over to the edge of the road.

John walked towards the van. He turned and saw Henrick's scowl. He was shaking his head in disgust. "Just in case you try to follow us." He took aim at the left rear tire and shot at the black rubber. A gash opened and air escaped in a fury as the car tilted to the left.

He then stepped behind the truck. They heard two more shots before John walked around the near side of the truck.

"Alan, let's go."

Alan walked backwards, keeping his gun trained on the three men. He placed his foot on the security truck's step, opened the door and moved into the confines of the cabin.

John took the driver's seat a moment later. He turned the engine on, pressed down the clutch, shifted into the wrong gear but made amends. He steered the truck around the van and it lurched forward in spasms when he shifted from one gear to the next.

Within a minute the security truck was completely out of sight.

Chapter 28

<u>Fair Lawn, New Jersey</u>

Larry Goldberg removed the yarmulke from the inside pocket in his jacket. He rubbed the fabric with his thumbs and placed it on his head. The history behind the material, and the synagogue, prompted him to smile when he looked at the entrance.

He checked his watch and looked over his shoulder. Except for his car and one other, he doubted anyone else remained in the temple. It was 10:00 PM, and given services finished over an hour ago, he expected his friend of twenty years to be waiting for him inside. He'd asked for a private meeting with Rabbi Solomon earlier in the day.

He stepped through the doors and found no one else but himself in the interior of the building. It was warm and filled with light. He looked towards the altar and stepped forward beyond the pews. "Hello?"

A short bald man walked into the room and he recognized him immediately. "Larry, how are you this evening?" The rabbi stepped forward and gave him a brief hug. "*Shabbat shalom.*"

"Hello, my friend. You are well?"

"Of course, I didn't see you during the service." He gestured with his hand to the front pew.

"Work kept me away, unfortunately."

"How are the kids?"

"Excellent, thank you. Yours?"

"Doing very well. I was intrigued by your phone call, you sounded a bit distressed. What did you want to speak to me about?"

Larry took a seat. "I have two clients that are in possession of something that likely relates to our peoples' history."

Saint-Brais, Switzerland

John pulled the truck over to the side of the road, turned off the engine and switched on the cabin's interior light. He looked up to see Alan and he noticed his pale complexion. "Alan, you look like hell." He nudged him and said, "Hey."

"What?"

He turned to face him. "You okay?"

Alan shook his head and sat up in his seat. "How long was I out for?"

"About an hour."

"Where are we?"

"I don't know. We passed a town five minutes ago called Saint Brais."

His brother's head bobbled and he rubbed his eyes with his hands. "I am exhausted."

"I'm with you. This is not an easy vehicle to drive." He turned to look out the window. It was pitch black out and he could not see beyond the perimeter of the headlights. "We have to find a place to sleep."

"Like I said before, find a police station."

John tapped the steering wheel. "We would get arrested, and they would confiscate the gold."

Alan raised his hand and dropped it. "So what. It's brought us nothing but trouble. Murder, guns, the plane, the pilot." He turned to face him. "Why do you insist on going forward?"

He sat up in his seat and checked his watch. "Wait a minute." He looked back down at his phone, scrolled through the ten numbers he programmed and clicked on the name, 'Francois.' "Alan, I have an idea." A moment before he hit "send." Alan slapped the phone out of his hand. "Why did you do that?"

"You don't get it."

"What?"

"Turn around, find the police station. I'm done."

He picked up his phone. "What if we can save ourselves and the gold? We did nothing wrong."

"We can't save shit." Alan shook his head.

"Just give me a minute." He retrieved his phone and dialed Francois.

It rang four times before John ended the call and redialed. On the second ring he heard a sleepy voice answer the phone.

"It's John, we need help."

***

John stopped the truck a few hundred yards before the border crossing. In the distance, he saw Swiss flags in the foreground and French flags beyond them. He looked down and saw his watch read 1:10 a.m. He double-checked the map on his cell phone screen to confirm their location.

He turned to see Alan staring at the building to the left of the road entrance. "Well, it wasn't a bad idea. Too bad it won't work."

"Give me a minute." John leaned forward on the steering wheel. He placed his head in his arms and put his desire for food and caffeine aside. "We've got to get through."

"Or, pull over and turn ourselves in."

"No way." He looked down to the console and then to Alan. "Alan, where's that the gold bar we gave to Tomas?"

"By my feet. I noticed it before."

"Did you put it there?"

"No."

"Give it to me."

He picked it up off the floor and placed it on the flat area of the console. "There you go. Why?"

John shifted the engine into first gear and crawled towards the border pass. "John, stop the truck."

They both saw a tired official sitting in a glass booth. He was reading a book when they pulled alongside him. To Alan's surprise, he saw John take the gold, cradle it like a football under his arm, and open the driver's side door. "John!"

He stepped out, waited for the guard to approach him, and then handed him the four hundred thousand dollar gold brick.

John spoke a few words to the man, patted him on the side of his arm and then stepped back into the cabin. The guard's eyes were wide open when the truck passed him by.

Alan's turned to see the side view mirror but the guard was outside his field of vision. "Where did you come up with that idea?"

"Remember the pilot?"

"The dead one, yes."

"We don't know for certain he's dead. He just got the pilot's share. And I'm not surprised he didn't refuse the offer."

"What's to stop the guard from calling the police?"

John shook his head. "Absolutely nothing, besides the guard's own self-interest."

Temple Sinai, Fair Lawn New Jersey

"This is disturbing. Completely and totally, disturbing," said Rabbi Solomon.

Larry watched him shake his head. "Now you know my dilemma."

The Rabbi stood up and clasped his hands behind his back. He walked several paces away and turned. "Can you come back next Friday night?"

"Of course, why do you ask?"

"Let's meet again, if you don't mind, I want to invite some others to hear about this."

"I can, but I'm not sure that's wise. They will be home before then."

"With all the gold?"

"Not likely. They will bring home a sample of what they possess."

"Find out when they will return home. Get as much information about these two as you can." The Rabbi moved forward and loomed over Larry. "These Devengers have no idea how much blood is on their hands."

Chapter 29

Fribourg, Switzerland

Fritz continued to hold the tourniquet as he laid on his side in the back of the van. "Jesus, are we almost there?"

"Almost, try to stay calm." Otto looked in the rear view mirror, which he had repositioned to keep an eye on the wounded man. Behind him the trunk jostled when bumps in the road passed beneath them. The only remaining weapon inside of it was the Beretta.

He finally came upon the sign for the hospital he was looking for. It was located in a town situated between Bern and Neuchatel. A speed bump lifted the cabin and with the speed of the van, Otto noticed Fritz rise and fall, prompting the man to wince in pain. "Son of a bitch."

Otto drove down a road that led to the hospital's entrance. To his immediate right was an access road for what appeared to be employee parking. Only a handful of cars were parked, which Otto presumed belonged to late-shift workers. He steered the van into the roadway and parked in an isolated area.

He stepped in the back of the van and leaned over Fritz.

"How's your leg?"

"What do you think? Look at it, man."

"Oh you're going to see a doctor, that I can assure you."

Fritz rolled on his back to look at him. "What the hell are you talking about?"

"You sabotaged us. You ruined our chances to end this, and I've had enough of you." He reached down and lifted Fritz from the lapels of his shirt, curled his right fist into a knot and belted him square across the face. "That's for blowing up the fucking plane." He pounded him again across his cheek. "That's for killing the security guard." He raised his hand higher and swung it down from right to left. "That's for being an imbecile."

Fritz's head smacked against the floor of the van. His head wobbled and blood trickled out from the fresh wounds on his face. Otto turned to see his fist covered in blood and he dropped the man before he opened the side door of the van.

He dragged him out by his one good leg and Fritz tumbled to the ground. He tried to lift himself but could not coordinate his movements.

Otto stepped back into the van, closed the side door and then moved to the driver's seat.

He sighed when he turned back and noticed Fritz roll on the ground in agony. He pulled the van forward and then stopped. Had he let the car roll backwards, it would take seconds to crush the man to death. He wasn't a killer, so instead he put the car in drive and left Fritz on the ground a few hundred yards from the emergency room entrance.

He chose not to take Henrick's advice. He would let Fritz live.

When he pulled out of the parking area, he picked up his mobile phone, called the operator and asked to be connected to Fribourg Hospital. When someone answered, he said, "There's a wounded man out in the parking area, he requires immediate medical attention. He is bleeding and needs assistance."

"What is this all about?" the hospital receptionist asked.

"I was just driving by and saw him there. This is the hospital, yes?"

"Yes, but—"

He concluded the call and steered the van towards the highway entrance.

He dialed for Henrick and he answered a moment later. "It's taken care of."

"What is?"

"Fritz. I dropped him off at the hospital. He's out of our hair for now."

"Dear God, why didn't you—"

He concluded the call and opened the back compartment of his cell phone to retrieve the SIM card. He then snapped it in two and tossed it out the window.

Cours-La-Ville, France

John turned into the long driveway before he saw a light turn on in the two-story home. He checked his watch and it read 5:35 a.m.

He pulled to a stop and looked for an emergency brake. There were several levers to choose from so he skipped the step. He was too tired to attempt or correct a mistake. He turned and roused his half-brother to consciousness. "We're here."

Alan woke up, rose up in the passenger seat only to see an expression of complete shock emanate from the face of Francois. He watched the long-haired Frenchman step forward and eyeball the security truck from front to back. "There's your friend."

"There he is. Let me do the talking."

"I need a bed."

John exited the vehicle and when his feet hit the ground, he thought about collapsing to the earth. He did not think he had the strength to walk. "Francois."

"John, what is this truck? Where did this come from?"

John turned back to see Alan remain inside the truck. "Alan, wait there." Alan shrugged his shoulders and flopped down on the bench seat.

"John!" His head snapped around. "What the hell? A security truck? You never mentioned this."

"I know. It's a long story."

"Well you better start talking. My relatives, this is their farm house and property. They are overseas, but this?" He pointed at the truck.

"Look, I can't keep my eyes open. I promise I'll tell you everything in the morning."

"It will be daylight in an hour." Francois curled his eyebrow. It was obvious John did not understand what he was trying to tell him. "I need to know what this is all about."

"Give me a break." Francois didn't budge. "Jesus Christ. Can you at least make me a cup of coffee?"

Francois shook his head and gestured for John to take a seat on the front steps of the home.

The two sat down and John proceeded to share the story. It took twenty minutes to explain everything: His father's death, the contingency plans, the vault, the ambush Alan escaped in Bern, the exploding plane, the chase and Tomas's murder. He concluded with an explanation of how he got through the border crossing and Alan's pleas to call the authorities beforehand, but less so when they crossed into France.

When he was finished he looked at Francois. He sat in disbelief and shook his head. "All this, for the gold."

"There's a lot of it."

Francois turned and gave his friend a look that John was unfamiliar with. Gone was his affable and charming demeanor. It was replaced with one of complete shock. "John, you have to call the authorities."

"Yeah, I know."

"You are innocent." Francois stood up and stretched his back. "How is your brother?"

"He's a bit, I don't know, out of his element."

"John, please. You look like shit."

"I'm fine, we both are. Do you have beds for us?"

The Frenchman turned to look at the truck. "I want to see it."

"What, the gold?"

"Now."

He started walking towards the truck and John joined him. They walked side by side until they got to the rear of the truck. Francois froze when he saw the bullet holes. "Dear God."

"Yup. Now you know what we've been through." John opened the two rear doors. The stacked crates sat idle in front of them. "There you go."

Francois's eyes roved over the swastikas and crested eagles. He took a moment to process the repetitive images. "Straight from Hitler, I see."

"Liberated."

"And the gold. Open one of the crates. I want to see it."

John sighed in frustration before he stepped into the truck. There was no way to remove a crate easily as the truck was loaded from top to bottom. "Francois," he used his hands to express the difficulty of what was asked of him. The Frenchman folded his arms and stood in place.

"Fine." John leaned up, used both hands to grab the bottom side of a stacked crate and pulled it forward. "Step back."

"Why?"

"It's... heavy." He struggled, but a moment later a crate tumbled from the stack. It crashed on the rear fender of the truck, bounced off and shattered when it hit the ground.

Francois saw it fall before him. He leaned down, rummaged through the wood and hay, and saw another swastika. This time, it was imbedded in a gold bar.

He stood up without touching it. "I want this truck out of sight. We can hide it in the barn."

The idea made sense to John and he stepped down from the truck. He gave Francois an appreciative smile. "You're a life saver, Francois."

"What I said before, I was wrong."

"How so?"

"You're not so innocent after all."

Gumligen, Switzerland

Henrick leaned up from the bed when he heard a car pull to a stop and park outside the home. He tried to stand but when he did pain radiated up and down his leg. He remained seated on the bed. When he heard the door open, he said, "In here."

Otto stepped forward and his profile filled the doorframe. He looked at Henrick. "You can thank me for having a spare tire in the trunk of my car."

"The van had a spare as well, what's the point?"

"We'd be in jail otherwise."

"You did not kill him. Why?"

"I'm not a killer Henrick, you are. I'm going to bed."

"You will not." Otto stepped away. "Otto, get back here!"

He returned to the bedroom's entrance. "Henrick, it is already morning. I suggest you shut up, get some sleep. We will talk later."

"It's not over. Not for one minute."

Otto's brow furrowed. "Where is Karla?"

"She is not here, but her things are. They are still out there somewhere."

"Wait, where is she?"

"I have no idea and I don't care. It's just the two of us." Henrick raised two fingers in the air. "Two. You realize what happens if we can get it? All of it?"

Otto shook his head. "I'm going to sleep. If you make another sound, if you say another word, I will beat you into unconsciousness." He raised his bloody fist to emphasize the point.

Otto turned, found the bedroom he'd used the night before, removed his shoes and collapsed on the twin bed.

***

The sound of Henrick's voice woke him up. He opened his eyes and saw daylight illuminating the far side of the bedroom. He turned over, rubbed his face, and caught a whiff of gunpowder in the process. This confused him until he remembered firing his weapon in the air to scare the witnesses by the van. The smell must have lingered on his flesh.

He could only hear intermittent words from the kitchen on the second floor. "Tracking... *Ja*... Both Devengers... Authorities." Otto stood up and stretched his back. He sat back down on the bed and thought about what Henrick could be planning upstairs.

He considered the idea of washing up, packing his items and driving his car back to Germany. He doubted the authorities were aware of his involvement, except for the risk that video surveillance at the local airport had caught his car's license plate. That was the immediate threat, but he knew the other and much larger risk was whether or not the police identified Fritz. If he confessed and identified Otto, Henrick and Karla as co-conspirators, then Henrick was right; he should have killed Fritz. That thought led him to think about Henrick conniving with someone on the phone upstairs.

He stood up, left the bedroom and walked up the stairs. He wore the same clothes from the day before.

He stepped into the kitchen and Henrick turned to look at him. He continued to speak on the phone as he gestured for Otto to take a seat. He waited patiently while Henrick concluded the phone call.

"It's done, we will know where they are going."

"The Devengers?"

"Of course, who else?" Henrick leaned forward on the table. "We have fifteen thousand dollars remaining from what Karla gave us. I just placed a call to my contact in Madrid."

"The private investigator. That's who you spoke with."

"Yes. He is going to monitor their credit card transactions. Track police frequencies, check the airlines, the trains, everything." He nodded. "We will find them."

"Interesting. There's only one problem." Henrick waited for Otto to continue. "I'm out. I plan to wash up, get my things, and take my leave."

"And leave tens of millions of euros on the table?"

"Call Fritz at the hospital, maybe the authorities have not found him. The two of you can hobble around Switzerland and try to find them."

"Don't be an ass, you know you should have killed him."

Otto stood up and walked over to the cabinet. "You should have kept the fifteen thousand for yourself, Henrick." He opened several cabinets and found what he was looking for.

"They are out there. The gold is out there, all of it. How can you leave now?"

Otto lifted the heavy skillet from the shelf. He felt the weight of it in his hands and turned around to look at the back of Henrick's head. "You have to know when to call it quits."

"I thought this might happen. I have an offer to make. A request, perhaps it will change your mind."

Otto gripped the handle of the skillet tightly. "What is it?"

The man he looked at rocked back and forth in his seat. "You can have three quarters of it. The gold, you can take the lion's share. All I ask is for you to give it some time. Let's wait to see what Madrid comes back with." He turned to see Otto holding the skillet. "That's all I ask. Think about the money. They cannot stay on the run, they will turn up."

"If the authorities find them first, we get nothing."

Henrick grinned at him. "If we get nothing, then we move on with our lives. But if we get the gold, our lives will change forever, yes?"

Otto stared at Henrick for a long time. A moment later, he blinked, pursed his lips and gave a quick nod.

"Good, then." Henrick noticed he was holding the skillet. "Hungry?" He pointed towards the fridge. "Eggs, make it for two. I'm famished."

Chapter 30

Cours-La-Ville, France

Alan opened his eyes when he heard the stairs echo with creaks from someone's steps. The room he was in consisted of simple furniture and dark blue walls. He turned to see an empty twin bed next to him. He did not remember seeing John or Francois go to sleep.

For a moment, he didn't know where he was, how he got there, the town he was in or even the country. He furrowed his brow and tried to sit up in bed but his body would not allow it. His phone read 1:00 p.m. and he was confused why every square inch of his body felt haunted by exhaustion.

He heard John and Francois speaking in the downstairs kitchen. He ignored their words and thought about what had transpired the previous day.

He knew it was Saturday, the truck they drove into France was parked in a barn, and he was due back at work in roughly thirty-six hours. His concern for employment took a back seat to more pressing issues. His mind kept replaying the experience of a shock wave pushing him off the ground and throwing him backwards in the air. This memory mixed with the sight of Tomas whistling "Flight of the Valkyries," yet a few hours later, he witnessed the man receive multiple gunshots to the chest. Tomas had been murdered right before his eyes. He could not stop thinking about seeing the man's blood drip slowly off the front-end bumper of the truck.

He snapped his eyes shut but the memories seemed to play out in vivid colors on the back sides of his eyelids: Gunshots riddling Tomas' body. He thought about what could have happened if those bullets landed in his torso or John's. He said to himself, maybe the dead man was right. Maybe the Germans would have mowed them all down if they had walked out into the field.

He sat up in bed when something occurred to him about John and what they had been through. He felt a wave of energy lift him to his feet and he threw on dirty clothes to hurry downstairs to find his half-brother.

He walked into the kitchen to see fruits and breads on the table before John and Francois.

"There's Mister Sunshine, good morning," said Francois.

"John, I need to speak to... no wait." He stepped forward.

"What's the problem?"

"Nothing! I mean, I don't know how to say it." Alan heard himself laugh for a second. He could not recall a time in his life when he had used the phrase. "I realized upstairs, just now, you saved my life. You saved us."

"Okay, whatever." John sat back in the chair. "Are you okay?"

"I'm here! You're here, that's all that matters!" He smiled and placed his hands on John's shoulders. "You saved my life."

John nodded. Alan loomed over him. "Alan, take it is easy, you're over-reacting."

"Ah, what a wonderful moment." Francois grinned. "Nice to see the billionaires getting along so well." He tossed Alan an apple. "Would the two of you like to share some tea during this tender moment?"

The taste of the apple unleashed Alan's appetite, given he had not eaten anything since the previous morning. He sat down and found himself consuming everything within arm's reach. "Thanks, John, thanks, Francois."

John was about to mention his thoughts on what they should do with the gold but his half-brother just sat and smiled between mouthfuls of food. He was pretty sure Alan set a time record for inhaling a croissant. In two massive bites, he swallowed it without seeming to chew the bread.

"You two eat up, get some energy. We are going to walk into town in a few hours."

"Sounds fantastic!" said Alan.

Hoboken, NJ

She took a sip of wine and flipped through a dozen cable channels. The television was not helping to alleviate her concern about John and Alan, nor was it helping to pass the time. When her cell phone rang Charlotte jumped off the couch to grab it. She saw the LCD screen and it read, 'LARRY GOLDSTEIN.'

"Great." She shook her head and answered the call. "It's Saturday night Larry, this is unusual."

She heard him hesitate before he spoke. "Hi, Charlotte, is this a bad time?"

"Yeah, it is." She sat up. "What do you want, Larry?"

"I'm sorry if I'm disturbing you, I just wanted to check in on your brothers."

"Why?"

"They are clients of mine, is there a problem?"

"There might be. Look, can I call you later?"

"Are you okay? You sound distraught. What's wrong?"

She knew she had fifty other people she could call if she wanted to talk to anyone. Larry Goldstein was not one of them. "I have not heard from them lately. When I find out what's going on I'll call you."

"Okay, but I'm on your side, Charlotte. Are you there?"

"I'll call you later." She ended the call and stood up. She heard herself say, "Assholes."

Gumligen, Switzerland

Otto checked the thermostat and turned it up to 24 degrees Celsius before he turned to see Henrick seated on the couch. A bag of crisps was beside him, complete with tatters of crumbs on the cushions.

He put the conversation with his wife aside, one that was not worth replaying in his head, and grabbed the remote control from the table.

A black and white movie was playing on the television screen and it showed several smiling people dancing. He sat down wearing a t-shirt and boxers and the chair creaked from his weight. He turned the channel to find some news.

"I was watching that."

"Not anymore." Otto turned to see Henrick express frustration and he smirked.

It took a minute to find a local television station with news and he found what looked to be the beginning of an evening broadcast. The image provided was an aerial view of black smoke rising from an airport. He turned up the volume.

"News tonight from the Neuchatel airport disaster. It has been twenty-four hours since a cargo plane exploded, killing three people and injuring ten others. Our reporter Max Frisch is in Neuchatel."

"Developments tonight in what officials are calling an unwarranted and unusual attack on a British transport company's airplane. According to the Federal police commissioner, the cause of the plane's explosion was not mechanical. Video footage captured at the scene was shared with news outlets as families and concerned citizens demand answers from police officials."

The image of Fritz was grainy, but there was no question what he was doing. The video was taken from a hangar and showed him firing a weapon from several hundred meters away. The anchor provided commentary on the one-minute video before the video image shook violently before going black. Police transcripts were read while the station replayed the video.

"Authorities have a suspect under arrest. He was found at a hospital in Fribourg. He has been transferred to a more secure medical facility and is under armed guard for the time being. His identity is being withheld until the investigation is complete."

Otto muted the TV and turned to see Henrick staring at him. "You are a fool."

"Shut up. I have one weapon left to use. You do not."

"You should not have given him a chance. We should get out of the country."

"He will not speak."

"How do you know?"

The argument continued before they both saw the television screen provide a close up of a Nazi swastika, eagle crest and SS initial. They were embedded in a gold bar. Otto's jaw dropped and he unmuted the television.

"...No one knows where she found the gold, but it was found hidden in her luggage while in transit at the Bern International Airport."

"Nein!"

"The bar is valued at over two hundred and ninety thousand euros and authorities say she planned to return home with the gold to her native country, Brazil. Customs officials discovered the bar when it was passed through bag screening machines at Bern International airport. She remains in custody and authorities are questioning her about where and how she obtained the illegal Nazi artifact."

Otto threw the remote at the TV and turned around to grab the arms of the chair. A moment later the seat bounced across the floor and smashed into the kitchen table twenty feet away. The table, and what was resting on it, crashed to the ground.

"That dirty little whore!" screamed Henrick.

Cours-La-Ville, France

John watched Alan saunter down the road in front of him. He couldn't help but notice what seemed to be an extra bounce in his brother's step. Francois walked beside him as they made their way towards the town of Cours-La-Ville.

John found it odd that Francois remained so quiet. It was not his nature, and when he tried to start a conversation, his friend provided little to no feedback. John realized Alan was far enough away for him to speak without his half-brother being heard. "Francois, are you upset with me? With us?"

Francois walked another twenty yards before he said anything. "I don't know whether or not you've involved me, or my relative's property, in a crime."

"Criminals? You think we stole this?"

"Of course not, John, I just..." He walked a bit further before he stopped John with his hand. "This is very dangerous. I'm really worried about you. And him," he added, motioning towards Alan, "His head is in the wrong place."

"He was not himself this morning."

"But John, come on, how does one guy go from being a snob to a saint in three days?"

"Snob is kind of harsh word."

"That's your description, not mine." Francoise said.

John appeared puzzled. "You've called him that for all the time I've known you."

"Yeah, well maybe things have changed."

"I'm certain they have."

"What are you talking about?"

"Gold. Millions of dollars of it."

John waved his hand in the air. "He always had money."

"I'm not talking about him." Francois poked John with his finger. "I think the gold has put your head in the clouds. You should have gone straight to the federal police."

John nodded. "Maybe we will."

"I don't think you will." They continued to walk down the street. "Do you know where the gold came from?" John did not turn to make eye contact with Francois. "Do you know or not?"

"It's irrelevant. Our grandfather liberated this from Nazis."

"You do know, don't you?" Francois moved ahead of John and started walking backwards while he faced his friend. "Tell me, now."

"Fuck you."

"My God, you can't even say it, can you?"

"You know we plan to share some with you, right?"

Francois stopped so abruptly John almost walked into him. He put his hand on John's shoulder. "Come on, John, have you thought this through?"

"I'm sorry, are you my fucking conscience now? Would you rather have heard the Nazis got it?"

"Of course not."

"Well then cut us a break, take a crate or two, and quit your job and travel the world. How does that sound?"

"Fine, then tell me the origin of the gold John." John shook his head.

"My God, from death camps? From Auschwitz? Treblinka?" His American friend did not respond. "You have some serious issues my friend if you can't tell me."

"Why do you care so much?"

"Because this village, my family's neighbors during the war. They were Jewish." John stopped walking when he heard this. "We never saw them again. Do you understand?"

John put his hands on his hips and stared at the ground. "Let's catch up with Alan."

Francois walked behind him. He could not understand John's response to their conversation. He wondered if he had ever really known John, or if the gold had completely changed his friend's perception of the world around him.

***

They had entered the main thoroughfare of the village when Francois pointed down the street.

"You guys need some clothes. The shops here are open for the next few hours. Why don't I leave you here and I'll come and find you, then we'll grab a bite."

"Sounds good." Alan turned to see both men look at him with concerned expressions. "What?"

John shook his head. "Nothing."

"Then we'll head back."

Alan heard what sounded like a bicycle bell ring and he turned to see an older Frenchman riding down the street. Between his handlebars he noticed a bottle of red wine bounce gently within a straw basket. He nudged John again and caught Francois's eye to make sure they took notice of it. The skinny old man cruised at a steady and slow clip before he tipped his cap to them when he passed them by.

They watched him drive up and over a small hill and out of sight. "So charming." said Alan. When Alan turned Francois was already a block away. "He is angry with us, isn't he?"

"The less you know, the better."

"Why do you say that?"

"Let's call Charlotte and let her know what's up. Do you have any juice in your phone? Mine's dead, hope we can find charging chords here."

Hoboken, NJ

Charlotte realized during the sixth call she had made to relatives that the wine was starting to affect her ability to speak. She wrapped up the call to her uncle and placed the phone down beside her.

She unmuted the television and took her last sip of wine. The spent bottle, a very expensive one, was from a vineyard that Everett used to own. She thought about the uncle who now possessed it and stood up to use the bathroom and wobbled, which made her realize she wasn't just tipsy; she was wasted.

The toilet flushed and Charlotte made her way back into the living room. Her cell phone came to life, which did not surprise her. Many relatives were inquiring with her about John and Alan. When she saw the name ALAN on the LCD screen she felt like screaming.

"Dear God, where have you been?"

"Hey there."

"Did you hear me?"

"Charlotte, calm down."

"Why has you phone been off?"

"We were conserving battery power."

Charlotte sat on the couch. "I've been worried sick."

"Let me fill you in."

She listened to the story, which ended when Alan mentioned they were in a town called Cours-La-Ville. When he recapped what happened the day before, she felt her stomach tighten into one bulging knot. When Alan finished, she asked him to continue. With no mention of the police, she was ready to scream. "When will you call the cops?"

"We need to figure some things out first."

"Well, now's a good fucking time! What have you been doing all day?"

"Well, I just bought some slacks, shirts and some shoes."

"You're shopping. Just... shopping. Seriously?"

"Yeah. The only clothes we had were soiled, and they stunk. Sorry we didn't call you sooner."

"Jesus Christ, I think you've lost your mind, you both have. It's time to get out."

"We're alive and okay. I have John to thank for that."

"Whatever. I'm getting an ulcer on this end of the phone and you're gallivanting in French villages." She sighed. "Put John on the phone. Now." A moment later she heard John's voice. "What the hell are you doing? Call the cops!"

"Look, we'll call you later, I'm not in the mood for this."

"John… John!"

Chapter 31

<u>Cours-La-Ville, France</u>

Alan opened the front door and left the house. It was chilly but the sun's rays felt warm when they hit him. He heard birds chirp in the distance.

He looked back over his shoulder and shook his head. John was still arguing with Francois, and when the opportunity to leave presented itself, Alan gladly took flight. Every idea that was shared over breakfast heightened Francois's anger. It was obvious that the friendship that existed between him and his half-brother was being tested. Anything short of calling the Federal Police warranted a tongue lashing from the Frenchman.

The idea he and John came up with the night prior was not going to work and Alan knew it. Hiding the gold on the property was out of the question, given Francois's temperament. If they hid the gold at a nearby storage facility, it may prompt a response from the authorities. They both feared the crates, and their Swastika insignia, would ruin their chances. Flying it out of the country was a risk not worth taking, given the money and transportation required. Driving the security truck anywhere would likely end with highway authorities pulling them over, given that the company that owned it probably wanted their vehicle back.

Francois kept repeating himself. *Call the police... tell them what happened... you've not committed any crimes other than an illegal border crossing.* Alan thought about the border guard. Would he, who accepted a bribe, testify against them? He doubted it.

He needed to clear his head and come up with a new idea.

His steps took him towards the barn in the distance. It was a hundred yards away and down a short hill to the right of the house. Beyond the building were open fields that had yet to be plowed for the season's harvest.

The setting helped to relax him and he felt the bright sun warm on his shoulders. There was no one around in sight and he enjoyed the setting of wide-open fields, trees and the scent of fresh air. He paused and stood between the barn and the house and turned around to take in the setting. He felt safe and comforted by the fact that no one, least of all the Nazis, would likely find them out here in the country. Even if they or the police drove by on the road, there was no way to tell what was hidden in the barn. He thought it was almost too easy, given what they had been through, and he wanted to thank Francois again for helping them during the process. He was quite certain they would be in custody had it not been for the farm and barn itself.

He stepped forward to the front doors of the barn and opened one of them wide enough to enter the structure. It creaked before he stepped inside of the building.

The foundation of the building was made of stone and he noticed windows high above that were open to the elements. A bird in the back end of the room flapped its wings before rising to the rafter to take a seat on a handrail. Alan whistled to the bird but he did not respond. Beneath him was the security truck, which accounted for a large portion for the ground space inside the structure. Alan walked around the side of the vehicle. His fingers touched the indentations from the bullets. Fortunately, they had not penetrated the interior. The shattered side view mirror still contained a sliver of triangular glass.

He stepped in front of the truck and kicked a small clump of hay in front of him before his eyes turned upwards to see the bird. The two were staring at one another. The bird had tan feathers and wings but it was not a species Alan could identify. His eyes drew themselves on the contents of the rafter and he paused when he noticed several stacked wine crates.

He paused for a second, and remembered the old man riding on the bike the day prior. He recalled the man's bottle of wine and how it jostled from the road within a straw basket between the handlebars. He knew from past trips that the French drank it with the same frequency as water. He was jealous of French wine producers, and their local clientele's appetite for wine. If Americans drank wine with the same frequency as the French, his family's vineyards would be all the more valuable.

He turned when he thought about what was in the truck and what he could do with the money. He put his dreams aside when he remembered the last time he started daydreaming about his newfound wealth. The result left him sprinting down the streets of Bern.

He looked up and saw three crates, complete with French wording and logos on the sides of them. He put his hands on his hips and thought about the imagery on the gold crates, and the contrast between the two: Swastikas and French wine. "Huh," he said out loud. His eyes turned to the bird and he said, "I might have an idea. How can I get up there?" The bird tilted his head but he did not reply.

Alan saw a set of stairs at the far end of the room, located behind a wooden gate of some kind. They were diagonal and he noticed it was a sharp climb to the rafters. He was unsure if they were stable enough to hold him. He moved forward and opened the gate. The first step creaked when he put his full weight on it. He climbed upwards. Alan turned to look when his head popped above the rafter's floorboards. The bird was ten feet away and Alan said, "Hi there." A second later the bird took off in flight and flew out the open window. The air filled with dust and Alan coughed when it hit his face. He shook it off and took two more steps before he kneeled down on the rafter. He looked down to see the security truck and took notice of the metal imbedded in the top portion of the vehicle.

He shook his head and raised himself off his knees. There was more room to move about than he expected. He walked to where the wine crates were located. They were all empty, but for some reason, the crates were filled with hay. He dumped the contents out of each of them. He placed one upside down and checked the bottom. It was intact on all sides and Alan leaned down to sit on it. He let his full weight slowly press down and the wood frame creaked but it did not split. He lifted another one and felt it weighed about five pounds.

He took two of them and moved back to the opening of the staircase. He took two trips up and down to retrieve them and placed them behind the back of the security truck. "Let's see if this works." He grabbed some handfuls of hay nearby, placed them in the bottom of the wine crate, and opened the back door of the truck.

Moments later, he had two gold bricks nestled in hay within the wine crate. He lifted it with both arms and jostled the box to see if the gold bars would hold. They remained square in the crate. He tried again with greater force to break it with the weight of the gold. He considered adding a third brick but thought it would likely weigh too much.

There was room enough for six bottles of wine, or as it turned out, two bars of solid gold.

He dropped the box to see what would happen from three feet high. It remained secure. He removed the gold and saw the hay beneath it was crushed. He looked around the barn and saw a half-dozen bales of tightly wound hay and wondered if he had enough on hand.

The answer he was looking for, and the solution to their dilemma, was right there in front of him.

He repacked the gold with fresh hay, closed the wine crate's lid and took it with him when he left the barn.

He walked quickly across the field towards the house and stopped when he got to the front door. He called out to John through the screening, folded his arms and waited for him to arrive.

John stepped outside and looked at his grinning half-brother. "What are you smiling about?"

Alan pointed to the wine crate. "I've got something to show you."

"Wine? Now, of all times? I've never seen Francois this pissed off before."

"You just proved my point."

Hoboken, NJ

Charlotte picked up the phone when she heard it ring and answered without looking to see who was calling her.

"Hello?"

"Charlotte, it's Alan."

"Tell me now you've cleared things up with the cops, and you're on your way home. Anything less and I'm going to kill you."

"We're figuring things out on our end. We're going to need your help."

"I'll let you know if I'll help after you tell me you went to the police."

"Well, that's the plan."

She exhaled. "So you came to your senses."

"Of course! Hey, we have a lot to look forward to. We plan to call the authorities back in the states."

"Come again?"

"We have another shipment to plan for. Get a pen and paper."

Chapter 32

<u>**Cours-La-Ville, France**</u>

"Back it up! Right there." Alan gave the okay sign with his fingers to tell the driver to stop the truck.

Alan walked to the front cabin and asked the man to step out of the vehicle. He asked, "Parlez-vous, Anglais?"

"A little, you want them in the barn?"

"No thanks, just place them outside, along the side of it." He pointed to the open area in front of them. The barn doors remained closed. "How long will it take to unload them all?"

"I don't know." His partner opened the back of the shipping truck. "Two hours at most. Where's the wine? Vines, I do not see."

"We're shipping a rather large collection back home to the states."

"A lot of wine monsieur. A bit unusual, yes?"

"It is. My family is in the wine business."

The driver smiled and whistled out to his partner. "Jacques!"

Alan stepped back and watched the men start the process of removing 200 empty wine crates from the truck. He was thankful to find a company to supply the necessary crates, despite the fact it took four days for them to arrive. He turned when he heard John call out his name.

His half-brother stepped beside him. "Impressive… expensive, but impressive. You think this is going to work?"

"I'm one hundred percent confident. Let's check one out." He pointed to the first stack of crates.

"I spoke to Francois a moment ago. He called me from work. We've been here five days and he reminded me of that fact."

"So?"

John put his hand on Alan's shoulder and he stopped walking. "He wants us out Alan, and soon."

"What's his beef? You two were thick as thieves when you greeted one another a week ago."

John started walking towards the crates. "He said something to me during our walk to town. There were Jewish families in this village."

"Okay, and how does that relate to our predicament?"

The two started walking again towards the crates. "None of them returned after the war."

"And how does that relate to our situation? He's stretching history a bit. Offer him another crate."

John watched Alan step away. He knew for certain that Alan had not reviewed the documents they had found in the vault. Francois's history lesson, and the guilt he conveyed during their conversation were affecting him. He wished he had never read them, and hoped Alan remained blind to the truth.

Alan handed him an empty wine crate and John felt the weight of it in his hands. "Sturdy, don't you think?" said Alan.

"He mentioned his aunt and uncle will be home next Monday. Frankly, I don't believe him. He wants no trace of anything. Nothing, you understand?"

"I do." Alan smacked him on the shoulder and smiled. "I have to call Charlotte." He stepped away and retrieved his cell phone.

"I think I'm out of a job." Alan turned to look at him. "I called them this morning, I don't know if I can reconcile this."

John thought about his own circumstance. When he did, he thought about whether it mattered. His job, and Francois's concerns, seemed all the less important given the value of the gold. "Then it's all the more important we succeed. Right?"

"No shit Sherlock!"

Alan grinned and stepped away before he dialed.

New York City, NY

"This is Char—" She looked at the caller ID and saw it was John.

"Oh, hey there. Thanks for hanging up on me the other day."

"Sorry, I was a bit distressed. We've got our shit together. The wine crates just arrived."

"Good." She leaned back in her office chair. "Are you sure this is going to work?"

"No."

"Then why go through with it?"

"I can think of one hundred and twenty five million reasons. Come on, what would you do?" She had no reply. "That's what I thought. Did you find a storage facility?"

"I did." She shared all the details, including the dimensions and costs. "Sound good?"

"Nope, rent two of them, we're going to need more space."

"What's the problem?"

"The wine crates take up more room, and there will be about 180 to 190 of them."

"This is nuts. You'll be happy to know the trucking company will be onsite when you dock."

"Good. What about Goldstein? Did you call him?"

"He called last weekend, and again yesterday. I didn't take his call. Do you want me to share the new details with him?"

"Absolutely. I will call him as well before we fly home."

"Okay, I'll ring him now."

"Good. So start making plans."

"For what?"

"You think we're not going to take care of you on the back end? Come on sis, your working days are over."

She sat back in her chair and shook her head. "I'm only doing this to get your asses back to the states, and for Everett of course."

"What about him?"

"He wanted the two of you to do this together, the least I can do is do right by him."

"That's very touching."

"Just let me know the flight details. Email them to me." She tapped the top of her desk with a pen. "I hope for your sake this is all legal."

"Hence Mr. Goldstein."

He recognized the number that appeared on his office phone. "Hello there, Charlotte."

"Good afternoon Larry, how are you?"

"Excellent, glad to finally connect." He leaned forward on his desk. "So what's the latest?"

"They called me this morning. They'll be home early next week, either Monday or Tuesday. The gold will arrive a week after that."

"Interesting. How are they doing it?" She spent the next five minutes explaining all the details to him and he took copious notes.

"So just like that, straight into the storage facility. I assume it is very secure?"

"Yes, I researched their operation and went there myself last night."

"And you want me to ensure they can legally claim it as their own?"

"That's why we hired you, Larry. And I assume we're on the clock right now?"

He nodded. "Yes."

"Okay then, so what's the next step? Do John and Alan have documents to sign?"

"We'll have everything ready when your brothers return back to the states." He lied but thought he sounded credible.

"Good then, should we set an appointment now? Figure out a location?"

"Nope, I'll call you back."

She paused. "What should I tell—?"

"Does Alan's cell phone work overseas?"

"Yes, it does."

"Good, I'll call him then, and circle back with you. Thanks, Charlotte." He didn't wait for her to reply and he hung up the phone.

He took out his cell phone and placed another call. "They are moving forward and bringing it all back to the states."

The Rabbi sighed on the phone and said, "Very well then. The timing will actually work in our favor. You are coming tonight, yes?"

"I'll be there at 9:00 p.m."

"So will our friends."

"Wait, how many people did you invite?"

The line went dead.

Cours-La-Ville, France

John watched the process take place a hundred yards away in the distance. He heard the truck beep and back up towards the front entrance of the barn. A moment later it parked and Alan stepped back into view.

He saw the look on Alan's face and he didn't know what to make of it. He was light on his feet, appearing one smile short of seeming outright giddy. John thought about the past eight days they had spent together and how Alan was now almost unrecognizable. Compared to the younger brother he knew, he seemed more at ease, relaxed and approachable. When he got on the plane with him, Alan, as usual, exuded a pretentious and snobby attitude. Now he seemed affable and good hearted. He had been chased, shot at and terrified into a catatonic stupor. For the past week however, he was much more at ease with himself, and he seemed overjoyed at times for having come up with a pretty solid solution to the crisis they faced.

He recalled saying something to his sister over the phone and how Alan was not his usual self. John wondered if this Alan, the one giving him the thumbs up in the distance, was expressing his true nature for the first time. He didn't seem to care about his job or the fact they were likely wanted by the authorities. Perhaps it was seeing Alan in casual clothes that gave John a new impression of the man.

He realized something else. For the first time in his life, Alan was making an actual effort to get to know him.

He gave thought to the plan Alan came up with, his enthusiasm about it and the arrangements he made. John tilted his head and wondered if Alan's ego was simply just riding a wave of its own making. He asked himself, is this all about greed? Does he only care about the gold? He realized after he said it that perhaps he was misjudging the man. Perhaps, he thought, I'm a purebred cynic.

He started to walk towards the barn after the truck unhinged its cargo container and pulled back onto the road. It was gone a moment later. He turned back to see Alan staring at the wine crates.

He had to admit that Alan came up with a brilliant plan. The gold would be transferred and stowed into the empty wine crates, using hay to protect the bricks from the motion and themselves. Two gold bars would be placed in each wine crate and then they would be stored in the cargo container. It was longer than the security truck, which provided the room they needed to store all of them. They would nail each crate to ensure the contents within them remained hidden.

The trip they had taken back into town provided access to an Internet cafe. They got the names of supply companies who could service their needs, and an order was placed for 200 empty and unmarked wine crates. They also got the names of transportation companies as well. Alan managed the negotiations and they ordered a truck to deliver a cargo container. It was one suited for international shipment and the same universal size that was used around the world. The trucking company would come back in two days' time, hitch up with the idle trailer and they would make their way to the east coast of France. At the main docking facility in Bordeaux, a shipment was scheduled with a freight company that had a transport scheduled from the French city to New Jersey's largest port, outside of Newark.

The process was painless as Alan used his Platinum American Express credit card to pay for everything.

Alan suggested they rent a car and follow the truck to ensure it got to the Bordeaux docks safe and sound, and flights would be arranged the following day.

It was cheaper than flying the gold out and anyone who inspected the contents would assume their shipment represented unmarked crates of wine. They would note the content as such on paperwork to avoid unnecessary questions. The fact it was being shipped out of Bordeaux, one of the central wine regions in the world, provided additional cover for Alan's plan.

He stepped beside him and patted Alan on the back. "You did well. What's the risk in all of this?"

"Worst case scenario, we get arrested at the airport." He turned and smiled at his half-brother. "But then Charlotte manages things on the back end while we get out of trouble over here."

John nodded and turned to see a long row of stacked wine crates. "It's worth the risk."

"One hundred and twenty five million in gold... ya think?"

They shared a laugh that seemed to go unending. When it did, John didn't think he had ever shared such an extended laugh with another person. He gave thanks to the fact it was an experience that happened with Alan.

"Well John, I hope you're well rested."

"Why is that?"

"Because we've got a big job ahead of us." He pointed to the hammers and nails they'd purchased in town and then pointed to two hundred wine crates that needed to be packaged.

"Oh... Shit."

Fair Lawn, New Jersey

Larry pulled the front door of the synagogue open and heard men arguing in the distance. It closed behind him.

The doors to the congregation room remained closed and he heard what sounded like a dozen people arguing. When he opened them he saw seven people in total.

"There he is." The rabbi waved him over and appeared relieved to see him. "Now we'll get some answers."

"How long have you known about this!"

"Who are these Nazis?"

"How did they get it?"

A chorus of questions exploded in his ear while Larry made his way to the front of the room. Several of them rose to their feet and expressed rage and anger while they pointed to Larry.

"Hey... Hey!" Larry gestured for silence but his efforts enraged them further. The rabbi stepped beside him.

"That's enough! All of you." The small congregation of men went silent. "Don't shame this man! He came forward, he chose to confide in me and this is how you treat him?"

"We want answers."

"And you'll get them, Howard, settle down."

Larry turned to the rabbi. "I want a word with you, right now."

"Well, share it here."

He grabbed the rabbi's jacket lapel and pulled him towards the door. "Now."

Voices in the main room picked up when they took their exit. "You better have a plan, Goldstein!"

Larry nudged the rabbi through the doorframe. He slammed the door shut after they were alone. "What is the meaning of this? Why are all these people here?"

"I told you I was going to invite some friends."

"What have you done?" He stepped away and put his hand through his grey hair. "God knows how many ethics I violated telling you about this."

The Rabbi put his hand on his shoulder. "God has his own set of ethics, and your conscience got the better of you." He smiled. "That means you did the right thing."

"They are going to kill me in there."

"Then they'll have to get through me." The rabbi opened the door. "Come on, let's see if they have any ideas about how to resolve this injustice."

Cours-La-Ville, France

John tapped the second nail in place and then lifted the wine crate from the ground. It weighed 45 pounds and he carried it to the shipping container. The wine crate felt sturdy in his hands, and although it was heavy, it was manageable. He placed it beside ten other wine crates near the open door frame and realized it was time to move them towards the rear of the shipment container.

He wiped his brow and looked into the depths of the dark rectangular box. Ten wine crates of identical size and shape were stowed in the rear. He gave thought to the value of each wine crate, roughly $750,000 dollars, and multiplied it times the number of crates. By themselves, twenty of them were worth fifteen million dollars. Whatever pain John felt in his lower back seemed to evaporate when he turned to see 180 wine crates waiting to be packed.

He looked up to see Alan staring towards the house. He rubbed his hands on his new pair of jeans and continued to stare. "Alan?" said John.

John walked past the container and turned to see Francois storm down the hill. His expression was not one of a pleasant nature.

"Guys, we need to talk." He gestured with his hands, "Now."

"Sure. You okay?"

Francois stopped dead in his tracks when he was ten feet away. "No John, I am not okay! You have a cargo container parked outside my family's barn. I'll assume all the Nazi wealth is going in there?" he pointed to the wine crates, "And then they all go in there, right?"

John furrowed his brow. "We talked about this."

"You left out some details, didn't you? It looks like a factory operation here." He paced alongside the barn and rubbed his head. "Jesus Christ."

Alan stepped forward. "We'll be gone in two days."

"Well that is not good enough. I spoke to my relatives this morning. They want you out."

John stepped forward. "Francois, be reasonable."

"I'm an accessory to a crime here, and my family is as well. I want you both out in the morning."

Alan raised his hands. "What crime? We've done nothing wrong!"

"Pack it up and get it off the property." He lifted one wine crate off the ground, shook his head, and tossed it to the side. He turned to walk back into the house.

"Francois, come back." John turned to look at his brother. "Did you see him pull up?"

"Nope. I turned around and he was walking towards us."

"Well what the fuck are we going to do?"

"Let's see how much we can get done. If it's not finished in the morning, there's nothing we can do about it."

John smirked. He wanted to offer gold to Francois but he had rejected the idea with considerable vehemence. He knew offering a larger sum would only make the situation worse.

He asked himself if the gold was worth sacrificing the friendship. The answer came to him a moment later.

He grabbed another box and casually walked over to the back of the security truck. He took his time packing the next crate.

***

John placed the fortieth wine crate in place and hobbled out of the cargo container. He arched his back and saw the sun cresting over the skyline. He noticed Alan sitting on a crate and toying with a piece of hay in his hand. "Done?"

"Today, yes. God help me if there's no ibuprofen in the house."

John turned to see the lights were on in the kitchen. "I'm going to tell him we need another day."

"Want me to come?"

"Absolutely not."

Alan held out his hands in confusion. "I just—"

"No, I'm sorry, that was uncalled for. I've just known him a long time. I'll take care of this."

"And if he says no?"

John shrugged his shoulders.

It took him a few minutes to cross the ground between the barn and the house. He opened the back door and stepped in to see Francois on his cell phone.

John leaned against the kitchen sink and waited. Francois seemed in no hurry to conclude the call and ignored his presence. By the time Francois was off the phone, John had been standing there for five minutes. He turned to look at him but remained silent.

"Sunday morning. That's how much time we need. That's when the truck is coming back."

Francois leaned back and clasped his hands together.

***

John was certain that by the time the ten-minute conversation was over, their ten-year friendship was as well.

He opened the back door and found his brother standing against the side of the house. He pursed his lips and followed John across the grassy field.

"What did you hear?"

"Everything." Alan waved off the shameful look his brother gave him.

John sighed. "Well, at least I convinced him not to turn us over to the police. For a moment there, I thought we were screwed."

"You handled that really well, and you bought us a day."

"One day. Just one."

Chapter 33

Gumligen, Switzerland

The phone call roused Henrick from a deep sleep. He saw the time on his cell phone read 2:05 a.m. He recognized the private eye's name and took the call.

"What say you… and why so late?"

"We got some hits on Alan Devenger's credit card. Several unusual charges."

"Tell me."

"I don't know what to make of it. He placed a three thousand dollar order with a manufacturer that apparently supplies wine crates. There's a charge from a trucking company, but more importantly his card was charged by a company called Darwiche International."

Henrick sat up in bed. "What do they do?"

"Overseas cargo transportation."

"Very interesting."

"We also have an idea where they are located. We noticed some minor transactions in a town called, Cours La-Ville, France."

"Excellent." Henrick grinned. "You have served us well, my friend."

"I'm not your friend. Unless there's anything else, our business with one another has run its course."

"Wait, tell me more about Darwiche International. Where are they going, what is their plan?"

"I can dig around, make some inquiries. It's going to cost you though."

"Name your price, Falkner."

"Three thousand euros."

Henrick knew he had enough to cover the expense, but not by much. "I want it by noon today."

"I'll see what I can do."

Cours-La-Ville, France

Alan moaned when he lifted the wine crate to the rear of the shipping container. He rested his head on his arms after he did so and John rose to his feet. A faint butane gas lantern illuminated the area between the barn doors and the storage container. The metal beneath John's feet echoed with his footsteps as he lumbered with the crate in his hands.

He placed it next to the others. He reviewed the setting of the container itself. Although it was dark, it was packed from side to side, two crates high, and the cargo covered all but seven feet of floor space.

John turned back to Alan. "Please tell me we are done."

"That's it."

"Thank God." He lumbered over to the doorframe and took a seat next to Alan. His legs dangled beneath him. "What time is it?"

"7:00 o'clock. I can't feel my lower back."

John nodded and exhaled slowly. He turned and saw 10 empty wine crates on the side of the barn. To the right of their position were the stacks of empty crates that originally held the gold. He could clearly see the Nazi insignia and eagle crest on the sides of them. "We have to repack the security truck with those."

Alan turned to look at them. "Shit. I thought we were done."

"Come on, let's bang it out." John wobbled when his feet touched the ground. He tried to figure out how much time they had spent packing the gold. He subtracted the time it took to walk into town to rent a car in the morning, to eat breakfast and to finish their afternoon lunch break. He figured it took them nine hours to pack the remaining crates with gold.

He walked around the shipping container and saw the rental car parked next to Francois's car in the driveway. He turned back to see Alan rubbing his chin and staring at the security truck parked in the barn. "What's up?" He walked over to him.

"We should ditch the truck somewhere after nightfall. When it's dark."

"No argument here."

"I'm worried about the Nazi crates, and when they find them."

"Who cares?"

"The authorities. Look at the swastikas."

John stepped forward to look at the Nazi crate closest to him. "Well, they are not staying here. What do you propose?"

Alan crossed his arms. "Do you think Francois would let us burn them?"

John nodded. "I doubt it, but I'll ask."

Gumligen, Switzerland

Otto sat in the chair across from Henrick. He was speaking to the private eye in Madrid and the conversation was a brief one.

"Bordeaux. They are shipping it out, overseas."

"When?"

"Tomorrow night."

Henrick thanked him and ended the call. "We bought ourselves another chance, Otto." Henrick leaned forward with his elbows on the kitchen table. It wobbled from his weight. Otto saw him clasp his hands and lean his head against them, seeming to be in prayer.

Otto knew the wait was worth it, despite his concerns. He repeated John and Alan Devenger's names in his head several times. Their family's treasure was not yet out of reach.

"We will be there first thing in the morning. Pack up," said Henrick.

Otto promised himself that if he were ever within arm's length of Alan or John Devenger, he would snap every bone in their body.

Hoboken, NJ

Charlotte knew her friends were already waiting for her beside the ferry dock outside her Hoboken condo building. They had a fun night planned, which included several stops at Upper West Side bars. She grabbed her purse and started towards her front door when her home phone rang.

She looked down and saw it was Larry Goldstein calling. "Again?" She took the call. "Hi, Larry, I'm just on my way out, can this wait?"

"Charlotte dear, a quick word. When is the shipment coming into dock?"

"A week from Monday."

"Okay, at Newark? Is that still the plan?"

"Yes. I have to run, please give me a shout tomorrow. Cool?"

"No problem, I'll speak to you then."

Cours-La-Ville, France

Alan slammed the sledgehammer against the bottom side of the last Nazi crate. Lights from the side of the barn illuminated the operation. He picked up the pieces and walked over to the five-foot high stack of broken timber and tossed them onto the massive pile. It stretched fifteen feet across and six feet high. He could not believe the time and the enormity of the project. The ninety crates, and the task of breaking them down, resulted in several hours of hard labor and a massive pile of old wood.

He dropped his ass to the ground and checked his cell phone. It read 11:33 PM. His body temperature started to plummet from the sweat on his shirt and the chill in the air. He turned when he heard John call out to him.

"Time to light the fire," he held up a gas can. "Francois gave us some fuel."

Alan leaned back on his arms and placed his legs out in front of him. "Really? Now he's helping us?"

"I explained how it's in his own best interest, and his family's. The less associated they are with Nazi gold, the better. He agreed."

"I'm surprised he's allowing us to light this up here, on his property."

John nodded. "Well, he was not pleased when I gave him two options. Let us burn it, or let us store them in the barn."

"That was ballsy."

"Whatever. He's turning down millions, and I want to get the fuck home. He stopped and looked at the tin gas can. "He gave us something called white gasoline."

"Got a match?"

"Yeah." John looked at the hand-written lettering on the side of the can. "He said it's extremely flammable, they use it to clean machinery or something."

Alan was ten feet away from the woodpile. He sat up and watched John dump fuel on the shattered wood. He circled the perimeter and when he got around to Alan, he stood up from the ground.

"Francois demanded we clean it up, as best we can, in the morning."

"So we ditch the security truck somewhere, drive back, wait for the shipping company to hitch up the cargo and we follow them to Bordeaux."

"We have to fit in the cleanup process."

"Should we dump the truck tonight?"

"Fuck that. I'm spent."

"What if the wood's still burning or hot?"

"He said he wanted us gone." John turned and shrugged his shoulders, to imply the cleanup would never happen.

Alan furrowed his brow. "There's nothing there, between you and him anymore, is there."

"Nope." He lit the match and used it to light the top side of the matchbook. "Ready?"

"Light her up."

John flipped the matchbook and it had enough weight to cover the distance between them and the wood.

The light blinded them. Alan gasped and stepped back. A moment later he and John fumbled backwards.

They hit the ground and squinted to see a massive maelstrom of flames rise before them. "What the fuck!" The heat pushed them back further. The sound of the raging fire consumed the enormous woodpile.

They felt the heat and stepped back further. A smoke cloud formed above the flames and it reminded Alan of the airplane disaster.

"Jesus! The fuel!"

John nodded. "He was not kidding, that was dangerous."

"White gas?"

"That's what he told me."

They rested their hands on their knees and leaned over. "You feel that? Back up some more." They heard the sound of air escaping from the wood and smoke filled their eyes. "Move. It's the wind."

The scent reminded John of camping trips with the Boy Scouts. He turned and watched the side of a nearby crate, and the Nazi emblem, turn black from the flames that enveloped it.

Alan pulled John back further until they were thirty feet away. "That is one hell of a fire. Look at it."

The fire raged with intensity. They could see small clusters of shrubs two hundred yards away in the distance across the open field.

John started to giggle. "He got even with me."

"Who?"

"Francois. Think about it." His laughs grew louder. "I think he wanted to scare the shit out of us."

"Ha! Well, we escaped the Nazis. A French pyromaniac is not going to get in our way." Alan joined with his brother in laughter.

"Now if you see another Nazi with a machine gun, we're getting the fuck out of here."

The chuckles from one brother sparked another and before long they were howling in laughter. Twenty-foot high flames continued to fill the area with light, smoke and the incessant hiss of burning wood.

The two brothers heard the kitchen door open behind them and they turned to look. "Francois!" yelled John. "Come over here!"

"Join us!"

Francois put his hands on his hips. He did not move.

Alan waved to him. "Hey! You got any marshmallows?"

They kept laughing. Francois turned to move back towards the kitchen. This prompted an even louder howl of laughter and it brought tears to John's eyes. The bonfire of flames was bright enough to cast Francois's shadow against the side of the house.

Geneva, Switzerland

Karla remained locked inside the windowless room. The door opened a moment later and the security official closed it once he entered. His steps echoed against the walls and he stopped two feet short from the desk between the two of them.

He tossed Karla her passport. "You will catch the next flight out of the country, and you are never to return again to Switzerland. If you do, you will be arrested and face penalties, which would include jail time. A guard outside will escort you onto the plane."

He turned to leave. He left the door ajar and Karla nearly leapt out of her seat. All she could think about was getting back home to Brazil.

Chapter 34

Les Trembles, France

John pulled the security truck to the side of the road. He turned off the engine and jumped out of the cabin. He walked back and saw Alan step out of the rental car.

The sunrise took place ten minutes prior, which was roughly the last time he passed another car on the road.

He pointed towards the row of short pine trees to his immediate left. "This is it."

Alan nodded. "Looks like as good a place as any. How are you going to do it?"

John searched the perimeter. "The angle of the road is too steep to be in the truck itself. I think we aim the truck towards the woods, hit the gas and I'll hop out before it plows into the trees."

"I'll back up to give you room. Want me in the cabin with you?"

"No. Let's do this."

John backed up the truck so it crossed the intersection on an angle. He checked for traffic. Given the hour of the day, he was not surprised they were alone. When the rear tires of the security truck rolled off the road behind him, he put the truck into first gear and opened the driver's side door.

He released the clutch and hit the gas. It hit ten miles per hour when it bounced off the road. He positioned himself on the driver's side step, kept it in gear and ten feet before he hit the first tree he jumped out of the truck.

He hit the ground and flopped on his side before he rolled. When he turned to look the truck plowed into several short pine trees. He heard the truck snap tree limbs and collide into what sounded like rocks before one last thunderous crash echo beyond the immediate perimeter.

He stood up and walked over towards Alan. There was a clear path where the truck had driven and the engine started to grind on the first gear and choke out in bursts. It seemed to cough and wheeze before it died.

"You did it. Nice work."

John nodded. "Let's get going."

***

Alan pulled the rental car he drove in front of the house and they saw Francois standing there in his bathrobe. Alan noticed two large plastic bags were beside his feet. "He's waiting for us."

John pointed to another man walking near the barn. There was an unhitched truck parked ten feet away from the cargo container. Between the home and the barn smoke continued to rise from the black ash heap where the crates burned the night prior. "Let's make this quick."

They stepped out of the car and Francois walked over towards their vehicle. "The trucker is here."

"It is, thank you for everything you did for us Francois." Alan extended his hand but Francois refused the gesture and waved him away.

John turned to Alan and said, "Deal with the driver, okay?"

"Sure." He stepped away.

John looked back and grinned at Francois. He pointed at the plastic bags. "Those are our things?"

"They are."

"I took the liberty of stashing the weapons in the truck. I assumed you wanted nothing to do with them."

"Of course not. What about the weapons I lent you, the buck knife and what not?"

John stepped back into the car and retrieved the handgun and buck knife. Both were stowed in the glove compartment, a decision John made the night prior in case they ran into trouble. He stepped forward, checked to make sure the driver was occupied, and handed them to Francois. "These saved our lives. I lost the rifle."

"What about the burnt wood?"

"We do not have time to clean it up. You asked us to leave, so we're leaving."

Francois shook his head. "Leaving a mess for others to clean up, so American in nature."

"The result of your decision, Francois. I'm sorry you will not accept a gift from us, would your aunt and uncle accept a gold bar as a token of our appreciation?"

"I don't think so, John," He folded his arms. "I'm sorry to see you didn't make the right decision."

"And what would that have been?"

"The authorities. When they find the truck, they'll find you. When they find you, they'll assume something other than your innocence."

"We'll take our chances." He grinned and turned to see Alan directing the driver towards the cargo container. "I'll compensate your family for any costs involved with the cleanup of course."

"I think we're done. There's no need for that. Goodbye, John." He turned and started to walk away.

"Wait. Francois." John trotted over to him and extended his hand. "We've been friends for ten years, can we at least wish ourselves well?"

He used his free hand to point towards the bags besides the front door. "Take your leave."

John remained there and watched Francois open the front door to enter the house.

***

The driver throttled up and turned onto the road. Alan and John followed in the rental car. John caught sight of white smoke rising from behind the home and realized that the fire had been burning for nearly nine hours.

A few minutes later they turned on route D504, which headed west towards Bordeaux. The truck, and its cargo, rolled forward on the road at a slow and steady pace.

Fair Lawn, New Jersey

"So it is agreed then. All of us. The ship docks on Monday the 13th, is that correct, Larry?"

The group turned to look at him. He nodded. "It does indeed. I spoke to Charlotte Devenger this morning. The brothers will be home before then of course."

"That could present a problem. This has to be a surprise."

"When will we get the word out?" Asked the oldest member of the group.

"We think the Friday prior makes sense. We have a name for it of course, to solicit empathy."

Larry crossed his legs. "I can't wait to hear this. What do you come up with?"

"Schindler's Gold."

"That's outrageous!"

"Do you have a better idea?"

Larry shook his head. "Come on. No one's going to believe that."

"But the media will, that's the most important part. They'll buy into it and then spread the word. Our contacts in the press will lend a hand. We're also planting stories on sites like Wikipedia to make it easy for reporters to find and confirm the authenticity of the news story."

"So deceit, on top of ethics violations." He turned to the rabbi. "I should have kept my mouth shut."

The rabbi nodded. "Yes, you could have. But if you did nothing, and people found out you let this happen, how would you feel then?" He rose to his feet. "Your relatives who did not make it out of the Holocaust, what about their memories?"

"Take your guilt trip and shove it," snapped Larry

"You will not speak to him that way!"

"Coward!"

The chorus of voices dimmed a moment later when the rabbi shushed them to silence.

The tall man who remained silent during the escapade rose to his feet. The foreigner stepped around the table and looked each person in the eye. "Is everyone clear on what they need to do?" His thick accent carried across the room. He leaned on the table and Larry took notice of the size of his muscles and imposing demeanor. "Are there any concerns?"

"What happens afterwards?"

"Leave that to me, it will be a joyous moment in our people's history when we bring the gold home." He turned to Larry. "You will be a hero for this, is that any conciliation?"

"No."

He walked over to where the lawyer was seated. "Are you that naïve?"

"Of course not." He swallowed and leaned back when the forty-something retired soldier loomed over him. "Look, I'm in this with you. I just don't like the way it's coming together."

"It serves a purpose. There are other ways of doing this, you know."

Larry looked at the man but he did not see one shred of human empathy in the man's eyes.

"Our people will be there at the docks." He turned to the rabbi. "Get your people there as well." He turned back and gave Larry an imposing stare.

Chapter 35

<u>**Bordeaux, France**</u>

Henrick tossed the spent candy bar wrapper out of the window. "I'm still hungry."

"We have nothing more." Otto watched Henrick open the passenger door and step out of the parked car. "Where are you going?"

"To smoke." He slammed the door shut.

He lit up and purveyed the landscape. Otto's Mercedes was parked across from the gated docking facility. A security guardhouse was there as well, which only complicated matters. They had remained parked across the road on a perpendicular street for seven hours, checking to see whether or not the Devengers showed up with the gold.

There were numerous storage facilities in the immediate area, which made their presence seem all the more small. The setting seemed to define their chances as well. Henrick knew the opportunity to capture the gold was slipping away, given the lapse in time. Waiting to see if the Devengers showed up was the only reasonable option. If they did not travel with the shipment itself, there was no way to tell which truck entering the gated facility belonged to them. They had watched dozens enter the facility but there was no clue what it looked like, or what each container held.

Henrick and Otto discussed calling the private eye, but they could neither afford nor ensure details about the shipping container itself. Henrick took a long drag on his cigarette, and hoped the Devengers' greed would play itself out: they assumed they would not let the gold out of their sight until it was safely stowed in a transatlantic ship.

Henrick extinguished his cigarette and got back in the car.

"Still trying to kill yourself?"

"What, the tobacco? Shut up."

Otto tapped the steering wheel and watched another truck enter the docking station. The gate remained closed before the guard opened it after checking paperwork. "There it goes, another one."

"They have to show up. How could they not?"

"We can't wait here forever."

"They ship tonight. We have to stay."

"Yes, we will. But—" Otto turned to see Henrick chewing the side of his thumb. "I need a break. I'll be back."

"What now?"

Otto closed the driver's side door and was relieved to smell something other than Henrick's body odor and cigarette stench.

His eyes looked across the road towards the guardhouse. He furrowed his brow for a moment before he opened the car's door and retrieved a map. "I'll be back." He sauntered across the street.

The guard watched him approach and he opened a sliding-glass window. Otto leaned forward. "Good day, I was hoping you could help me find my way to…" He searched the map and chose a random town. "Tresses?"

The short guard stood up from his seat. "Well it is nowhere near here, there's a gas station down the road, ask them."

"I see." Otto turned and saw the mechanism that opened the security gate. "Can you tell me—?"

"I can't help you sir. Please step away from the security gate."

Otto nodded and checked the size of the window frame. "Very well then." He stepped away and moved back to his car.

***

Henrick rubbed his temples and noticed the car's clock read 6:00 PM. "Dammit, where are they?"

Otto watched another truck drive by. "This is asinine." He leaned forward on the steering wheel. "Are we sure there are no other docks in the area?"

"I checked the map again and again. Nothing."

"This is not going to work."

"Then what do we do, go back home? Forget everything? I'm not going back to that shithole, Otto."

"No argument here."

"Thank you, let's wait."

"No, I mean you live in a shithole. You should have saved your money."

Henrick looked down and saw the pistol was placed beside Otto in the driver's side door. He wished at that moment he had access to it.

They remained silent for another moment before they saw what Henrick assumed was the one-hundredth truck pass their location. A car followed behind it.

The vehicles passed forty feet in front of them and Henrick noticed the distinct profile of John Devenger's shaved head.

"Look!"

Otto looked up just in time to see John in the passenger seat. "Son of a bitch." He turned on the car engine.

The car both Devengers occupied followed the truck and they made their way around the traffic circle to the security gate. A moment later it opened. Both vehicles passed through it and gate closed behind them.

"Here we go."

"What do you suggest we do?"

"Leave that to me." Otto cruised around the traffic circle and parked the car ten feet from the guardhouse. He grabbed the map and left the car.

He stepped out and smiled at the security officer. He slid the guardhouse window to the left. "Hello again."

"I told you I cannot help, your car is blocking the entrance."

"*Ja*, I know." Otto stepped closer with the map. "It's these damn roads." He put the map on the rim of the window.

"You have to move!"

Otto pointed to the map. "Do you know where…?" his eyes looked up to see the guard was within arm's reach.

"Get back in—"

Otto used both hands to grab the man's lapels. He yanked the fabric. The guard's body hit the window frame. Otto arched his back quickly and picked the guard off from the ground.

The guard tumbled through the security window. Both men crashed

296

to the earth. Otto jumped up on one knee, cocked his arm and pummeled the guard in the face.

One hand held the man's jacket while the other delivered three crushing jabs to the side of the man's skull. He paused and noticed he was still conscious. He drove his fist square into the center of his face. He remained motionless thereafter.

He let go of the lapels and grabbed the fabric around his upper chest. The other hand grabbed his belt buckle. He lifted his body off the ground, walked a few feet to his right and tossed him to the side of the guardhouse. He flopped and rolled over on his side.

Otto reached his head and arm into the window, identified the green button to open the gate and pressed it.

He got back in the car and slammed on the gas to drive into the complex.

***

The truck stopped before them. John looked up to see the name of the ship they were looking for. "*The Dahlia.* There it is."

Alan leaned across John but he could not see the name outlined along the top rim of the ship. "Huh?" He stepped out of the car and John followed.

The two men saw the enormous name of the ship spelled out thirty feet above their heads. The ship was over seventy-five yards long and remained motionless in the water.

They left the car and stepped beside one another. "Well, there she is." Alan grinned from ear to ear and put his arm around John. "Thank you."

"For what? This was your idea. I should be thanking you."

Alan pointed to the driver and beyond him they noticed a man with a clipboard walking towards them. He pointed towards Alan and John.

"*Vous devez déplacer la voiture!*"

Alan asked John, "What did he say?"

"I'm not sure." John stepped closer and asked the truck driver, "What did he say?"

"Move zee car."

John turned back and noticed their rental car was parked next to the truck. There were no other cars in the immediate area and directly in front of him was a massive storage facility. Another similar building paralleled it a few hundred yards to his left. He turned to see dozens of cargo containers to the right beyond the dock official who was walking towards them. The entire area was paved with asphalt from one side to the next. Behind them, the boat rested in what looked like a wide river or sea inlet.

"Alan, check out the cranes." He pointed to a three-story yellow crane to their left and a blue one behind them. He nodded. "This is more industrial than I expected."

"It's massive." Alan stepped towards the truck and asked the driver to open the rear doors.

"What's up?" said John.

"I want to see how the boxes held up during the drive."

The driver unlocked the back doors and opened them.

What Alan saw brought a smile to his face. "There it is." Except for several out of place wine crates, the boxes remained intact, upright and undamaged.

"I'm surprised they didn't get jostled around."

They motioned to the driver to close the doors and saw the shipping official step towards them.

"Eplacer cette voiture! Il n'a pas ca place ici. Quels sont vos noms?"

John understood the last part of the sentence. "We are the Devengers."

"Vous êtes en retard, le bateau part dans une heure."

Alan looked to John for answers. "I think he's telling us the boat leaves in a few hours."

The four of them heard what sounded like tires screeching in the distance. The dock official furrowed his brow and took a few steps to his immediate right. John, Alan and the truck driver stepped beside him.

Alan noticed a car two hundred yards away to their left barrel through the road between the two warehouses. Tire smoke rose behind it. It completed its turn to the right, leveled off and faced the four men from afar.

Alan squinted his eyes and saw a Mercedes logo. He could not see the men driving it. The brown color of the vehicle matched the one they encountered outside of Neuchatel Switzerland.

They all heard the engine growl and its tires erupt in smoke. The Mercedes raced towards them.

"John."

"It can't be."

The car accelerated at an alarming speed.

"Shit!"

"You know them?" Asked the truck driver.

Alan's head snapped around. "Get in the car! Guys!" he turned to the others, "get the fuck out of here!" The two Frenchmen remained motionless and appeared confused. "Now!"

John ran behind the car and Alan followed. The car's engine growled as it approached their position. They ducked behind it and looked through the windows.

Alan turned to see the passenger window in the Mercedes was down. He noticed the barrel of a gun extend outside the window. He screamed to the Frenchmen, "Get down!"

He turned back to see the car pass from left to right. The gun flashed several times. The driver's side window of the rental car smashed into a thousand glass fragments. They tumbled into the car.

Alan turned to see the clipboard hit the ground. The Frenchman landed a moment later.

The Mercedes passed. They heard tires screech against the asphalt. John jumped to his feet. He grabbed Alan's collar. He pointed to the building in front of them. "The warehouse! Run!"

Alan did not hesitate. They sprinted in unison across the roadway. The engine throttled up behind them. John snapped his head to the right. The car sped up and angled towards them. "Faster!"

John's legs jackhammered like pistons. He gained speed. Alan kept pace. They were twenty feet from an open door frame.

Two bullets imbedded in the steel wall. Alan turned to look. The car was thirty yards away. The old man fired the weapon but there was no sound.

"Hurry!"

They lunged through the door and tumbled onto the ground. They heard the car slam on its brakes.

John got to his feet before Alan. Air raced in and out of his lungs.

They heard German voices yelling at one another. John surveyed the area. Hundreds of cargo containers sat in rows next to one another. He looked up to see a massive white roof with glass skylights.

"We have to hide."

"Did the others get shot?"

"I have no idea." He pointed towards a stack of containers across the way. "Over there. Move!"

***

Otto kept the engine running and stepped out of the Mercedes.

Henrick removed the empty magazine from the bottom side of the pistol and replaced it with another. He checked the glove compartment. There was no more ammunition. He slid the top side of the barrel to cock the hammer and got out of the car.

Otto pointed to the truck. "It's right there."

"Good, let's kill them and then leave with it."

"Don't shoot to kill." Otto stepped towards the doorway. "A beating, and a good one. Both of them."

They entered the warehouse and turned to see hundreds of containers, but no sign of either man. "Do not leave my side. Understood?" Otto turned to find something to use as a weapon. He saw nothing of use. When he turned back Henrick had stepped away.

Otto caught up with him. "Henrick, stop." His cohort continued to walk forward. "This will not work."

"Find them!"

"It's too big. The gold. Let's take it and leave."

Henrick peered across the open floor. He heard a sound in the far right corner of the building. "Over there!" He pressed the trigger. The silencer quipped in sound. The bullet made impact with the steel wall. They both heard a scuffle. "Trap them like rats."

Otto walked forward but stopped when he saw a desk in the corner of his eye against the wall. Next to it was a rectangular box. "Henrick, look." Otto jogged over to the desk. He saw the box held a red fire extinguisher. He grabbed it, removed the metal pin and returned to where Henrick stood. "Let's make this quick."

"*Ja.*" Henrick stepped forward.

They stepped into the middle of the building. A massive corridor thirty feet wide ran from one end of the warehouse to the other. Idle cargo containers were placed perpendicular to the sides of the building. Several feet of space separated one from the other.

Henrick directed Otto to look towards the right side of the building. Henrick eyeballed the opposite side. There was a doorway entrance behind them and a wider one adjacent to accommodate the containers. The gate was down. He knew they were trapped.

"Let's go."

They walked slowly down the corridor. Henrick kept the gun pointed forward. Otto held the fire extinguisher. They were halfway down the corridor. Henrick motioned with his hand to stop. "Anything?"

"No. Let's rattle their cage." He checked to make sure the extinguisher worked. It screeched and hissed when a white plume of fire retardant escaped from the nozzle.

Otto saw a contraption that allowed for the handgrip to remain depressed. It weighed fifteen pounds. He depressed the extinguisher's nozzle, locked it in place and threw it high in the air towards the far left corner of the building.

The white plume circulated and howled in mid-air. It came down on a container in the far left corner. They listened and saw white plumes envelope the area surrounding it.

The sound of the extinguisher screeched and echoed off the steel walls. They moved diagonally across the corridor. The extinguisher spent itself within a minute. They heard footsteps echo against the right side of the building. They turned and saw Alan running in the distance. He crossed from left to right against the far wall.

"Fire!" Otto screamed.

Henrick aimed and fired five shots. Bullet holes penetrated the steel wall. Sunlight peaked through the metal gashes. Alan jumped behind a container.

"Get him!"

***

Alan sprinted to the far right corner of the building. He tried to slow the air racing in and out of his lungs. He waited and hoped the Nazis would not see him.

A moment later he heard John smack the side of a container. He smacked another and another. The sound moved away from his position and footsteps followed. When he stepped around the container he saw a fat German sprinting towards him. He was alone.

It worked, he said to himself. He noticed the sprinting German did not have a weapon. He was fifteen feet away. "Hey there, fucker!" He turned and ran around the back of the container and sprinted down the pathway from whence he came.

He stopped short before he entered the wide corridor. He turned his head and saw John approach the other German. He came up behind him and raised the fire extinguisher above his head.

He turned a bit further to his left and saw a man's fist. It flew straight at his eye and buried itself in Alan's face. He heard a metallic thump across the way a moment later.

He tumbled back and hit the side of the warehouse. His head wobbled before he felt himself being lifted off the ground. He could see the roof out of his one good eye. He was airborne for a moment before his body hit the floor. He bounced and rolled across the cement before crashing against a container.

He looked up to see the fat German walk over, grab his shirt and cock his right hand behind him.

***

John saw the remnants of the gun in pieces on the floor. He tossed the extinguisher. The old German appeared shocked when he turned to face him. John did not wait for him to raise his hands.

He jabbed his left fist forward and hit him square in the face. He stumbled back, found his balance, and charged forward. John stepped aside, grabbed his right shoulder, and used his free left hand to apply an upper cut to his kidneys. The old man turned back and contorted from the impact. John let go of the shoulder. He knotted his right fist and pivoted on his left foot. He landed a devastating right hook. The old man's head snapped back before he collapsed to the ground. His body went limp.

John was surprised what he did next. He laughed.

When he looked up he noticed the fat man pounding Alan's face into a bloody pulp.

"Hey asshole!" He stepped over Henrick's body. His steps turned into a sprint to cover the distance. At one point he thought he could body tackle the kneeling German.

He skidded to a stop. His adversary stood up and turned to face him. John realized then how tall the German was. He appeared to weigh more than two hundred and fifty pounds.

"A fat fucker, aren't you."

Otto wiped the backside of his bloody hand on his pants. "Your turn." He said.

The fat man came straight at him. John took two steps back. The German charged with his arms to the sides. When he was close enough John cocked him with a right and left jab. His fat neck did not move. His arms enveloped John and squeezed his sides. John had no angle from which to punch.

The German raised him above his head and threw him against a container. John bounced like a deflated basketball towards the fat man. He rolled on his side and got to his knees. The German was in firing range. He stood up and applied a body shot. His hand embedded itself in fat but then recoiled outwards. The side of his head took a blow that left him dizzy.

He felt himself being lifted off the ground. His arms and legs waved around before his torso hit the concrete floor.

He grabbed his rib cage. "Son of a bitch!"

Ten feet of ground separated the two. John wobbled before he got to his feet. Blood dripped from cheekbone. He wiped it off and saw the German charge at him. He ducked and rolled toward him. The German tripped and tumbled. "You little shit!" he yelled.

He looked for the fire extinguisher. It was nowhere in sight. He turned back but Alan wasn't there.

He looked back at the German. Blood trickled out of his nose. He turned to face John. "Now I'm going to kill you."

His arms came up and reached for John. With all his might John landed body blow after body blow. His right and left fists swung with speed but stopped when an upper cut sent him backwards. He landed on his back and stared at the ceiling. The German knelt over him and started pounding his face. His head snapped to either side a half-dozen times. He felt a tooth loosen, his cheekbones radiated with pain and his left eye went dark.

In the corner of his right eye he caught sight of Alan. He wobbled forward. He held the fire extinguished above his head. Alan swung the extinguisher over his left shoulder before the German's last blow came crashing down on John.

The loud thud of metal echoed in the warehouse when it landed on Otto's head. Otto wavered for a moment. Alan took no chances. He lifted the extinguisher again and swung it from right to left. The German collapsed to his side and hit the floor.

Alan dropped it, stepped back, hit the side of a container and slid down to the ground. His face was excessively bruised and bleeding. "That was one tough son of a bitch."

John flopped on his belly. He got to his knees and felt his contorted face. "Well, Alan, that makes us even."

Alan tried to catch his breath before he spoke. "What do you mean?"

"You just saved my life." He grinned and felt a loose tooth wiggle in the back of his mouth.

***

Police lights continued to illuminate the area. John moved the icepack to the other side of his face. He turned and looked at Alan sitting on the chair provided to him. His face looked like a bright red and bruised tomato.

He saw two ambulances sitting near the entrance to the warehouse where the fight took place. Alan tapped John on the shoulder when the fat German was wheeled outside. "There he goes."

"Good riddance."

"What happened to the old guy? Did you kill him?"

John shook his head. "Nah. He was foolish. Why he charged me, I'll never know."

The police escorted the other stretcher. They stood up to see if he was conscious. John felt relieved for a moment when he saw the old man turn to look at them. An oxygen mask covered half his face. "Thank God."

"What?"

"Well, if he had died of a heart attack or something… I don't know, maybe we'd go to jail."

"No way. Hey, John, watch this. Hey!" He caught the old man's attention. "Hey Nazi! I got something for you!" Alan put his hand in his pocket, pretended to fumble around, and removed it with his middle finger extended and upright. He grinned. "Suck on that, asshole!" John laughed.

They watched the old man turn to look the other away.

"*Monsieur*, if you don't mind, we'd like a word."

The brothers turned to see a short man in a police uniform.

For the next ten minutes John and Alan explained what happened. They mentioned how they were fired upon, defended themselves and then received assistance by the French driver and the shipping official.

The statements made by the dock official and cargo driver cleared the air in regards to any wrong doing by John and Alan. The investigator believed, on some level, that their actions saved lives and at one point he expressed his appreciation for taking action. He mentioned, however, that they would need their testimony to process the charges made against Henrick and Otto.

Alan thanked him and said they did not need additional medical attention. They expressed gratitude for the ice packs, which both of them needed. Before he left, he told the brothers to stay put. Another officer would take them to police headquarters.

The next person they spoke to was the dock official. "You two, I hope never to see again," he said in broken English.

"Same here. Were you injured?"

"No. We dropped to the ground. No shot."

"That's good."

"The captain of the *Dahlia*. He asks, do you want the container shipped? We can load it onboard. Police say it's okay." Alan nodded. "I'll tell him yes?"

"Please do."

"Excellent."

John put his hand up for a moment. "Wait, before you do so, can you give us a moment to discuss the matter?"

"But of course."

When the official stepped away, John turned to Alan. "Do you want to stick around?"

"Hell no."

"What about the ship?" Alan shook his head in confusion. "Why don't we travel back to the states on it, and stay with the gold."

Alan provided his brother with a puzzling look. "Come on, seriously?"

"Why not, do you really want to go with them?" He pointed to the police officers. "And wouldn't it be wise to keep an eye on the gold itself?"

Alan removed the ice pack from his face. He nodded a moment later. "Screw it, I'm likely out of a job anyway."

"I'm going to bribe the captain."

"How?"

"With a gold bar of course, what the hell else do we have to offer?"

Alan watched John walk across the docking area to their cargo container. He followed him a moment later and trotted over towards their shipping container. "Isn't this kind of obvious?"

"Get the bags out of the car."

Alan did so and heard John open the unlocked container doors. Alan returned with the bags they bought in the French town. "Open your bag Alan." John placed a gold bar amongst the new clothes his brother purchased. They were all soiled and some items reeked of body odor.

John used his hand to wave the stench away. "We have to get home, we're starting to smell like Europeans."

He shut the back doors, checked to make sure they were secure and locked and walked over to the boat's entrance ramp. He double-timed it up the steps and Alan kept pace. They both turned but did not see any police officers take notice of their leave.

When they got to the doorway a man dropped the magazine he was reading. "No! No! No! No allow on boat!"

"Get me your captain."

He stood up and raised his hands. John and Alan brushed past him. "El Cap-I-Tan! Hello!"

Several other men came forward and stopped John and Alan. A melee of voices rose in volume and temper.

**

A young and dark skinned man pointed to the chairs in the room they were directed towards. "Sit." He slammed the door behind him.

"Well, we're on the boat. That's a start."

A few minutes passed before the door opened. They turned to see a man with receding grey hair walk into the room. He wore glasses, had dark eyes and his broad shoulders stretched beyond the frame of his body.

"I am the Captain, Ziad Charine. What is the meaning of this?"

"I am John Devenger, and this is my brother Alan."

"Yes, I know who you are. Everyone at the dock knows who you are. Everyone can see you had the crap beaten out of you." He pointed towards their faces. "Your cargo is stowed onboard." He raised and lowered his hands. "Now what the hell do you want?"

"We have a small request to make. We are shipping wine back home."

He sat down. "Really? Is that why you wanted to see me?" He smiled and raised his hands out in front of him. "Thank goodness you are telling me this. I had no idea whether to ship your container to New York, or dump it in the ocean."

John shot a glance towards Alan, who raised his eyebrows. "Look, we have an offer to make."

"We leave in ten minutes." He stood up from the table. "You are wasting my time. Get off my boat."

"That's why we are here. We'd like to come with you."

He opened the door. "What do you think this is, Carnival Cruise lines? Get off!"

John nodded before he motioned for Alan to retrieve the gold bar. Alan did so and he dropped the brick on the table. The structure shook from the impact.

"Will that cover the expense? Do you have two extra beds?" said Alan.

Ziad shut the door. He stepped back and took a seat. The Captain stared at it before he tried to lift the gold.

John smirked. "And when we get home, you'll get another one."

A full minute passed before he spoke. He cleared his throat and extended his hand. "Gentlemen, welcome aboard the *Dahlia*."

***

The boat pulled away from the dock and Alan and John watched from the topside deck. They noticed the police officer that questioned them. Alan pointed towards him. When he looked up and noticed the brothers on the boat, his jaw dropped. John and Alan waved.

Alan noticed the anger on his face. The officer spoke into his intercom and a moment later every cop, a dozen in total, looked towards them.

"Uh oh."

"That's going to put a damper on the investigation," John said.

"Like I give a shit." They laughed together and waved goodbye.

Alan turned and could clearly see inside the pilothouse of the boat. Ziad smiled and gave him the thumbs up before he turned and appeared to bark out orders to a nearby deck-hand.

"We're golden."

"Literally."

"He's not going to turn the ship around," said John. "And he's got incentive on the back end. Nearly eight hundred grand in total." John shook his head. "Do you think the French will send a boat after us?"

"We should be in international waters in the next hour. We didn't commit a crime, and unless they call in the navy, they can't stop the ship."

"Ha! The French navy. Whatever. Hey, we have to call Charlotte, tell her the details."

"You're right, we'll be out of contact. Our cell phones won't work at sea."

He took out his mobile phone, but before he dialed, he put his arm around Alan. "I could not have done this without you. Everett was right."

Alan felt the warmth of his brother's arm. For the first time in his life, he felt truly comforted by it.

Chapter 36

Nyack, New York

He put the can of valve oil down and checked the long cylinder in front of him. He tested the knobs and then the clarity of the barrel to see if any obstructions or debris remained. The instrument he held was ready for assembly, however Doron Mossik chose not to do so.

He was confident about the training he had and his experience. He did not doubt his ability to perform as expected. His main concern was the size of the crowd, if he would be heard and what would happen if he forgot the sequence.

He closed the hard case, checked his watch, and realized he had less than two hours to get to the docks at Newark Bay.

New York City, New York

Charlotte turned on her computer and went to *The New York Times* homepage.

She checked her watch and cursed herself for having to come into the office. Her brothers were scheduled to arrive later in the morning and she wanted to be there. Her boss the day prior mentioned an important deadline for a project that was fast approaching. She needed her there for the entire day, and then some.

When she scrolled halfway down the homepage of the *New York Times*, she paused when she saw the words, Schindler's Gold, appear in a headline.

Whatever comfort she felt about her brother's newfound wealth was gone by the time she finished the second paragraph.

"Oh my God!"

She jumped out of her seat, grabbed her coat and purse before she flew out her office. She raced down the hall and gave thought about how to get to the docks in Newark Bay as quickly as possible.

Hudson River, New York

"Thanks, Ziad."

"No problem my friend." The Captain waved goodbye.

John stood up from left the galley table with a roll of bread in his hand. He opened the galley door and walked down the hallway. Sunbeams greeted him as he walked down the corridor towards the main deck. He opened the door and felt the sun's rays and cool-river breezes greet him. He squinted and covered his eyes with his hand to block the sun.

What he saw astounded him. Not two hundred yards away was the Statue of Liberty. At the far end of the bow he saw Alan standing with his hands in his pockets. He seemed to be relaxed and simply enjoying the view. John approached him.

"Hey there." He turned and saw Alan's face was healing well. Besides a few remaining bruises, he was almost one hundred percent healed. "You look good."

"You too, but wait," Alan looked at the side of John's face, "Nah, you're still ugly."

"Shut up pretty boy."

They stepped forward and leaned against the deck rail in front of them. They were five feet from the bow of the boat. "She's beautiful, isn't she?" Alan asked.

"That's quite a sight." John admired the size and scope of Lady Liberty, which from the water was all the more impressive. "I was there for the one hundredth anniversary."

"Really? With your mom?"

"Yup, we made it up from Pennsylvania."

"Was it awesome? I think Reagan was there too."

"It sucked."

"What?"

"We ended up at what turned out to be a raging keg party. Thousands of cars, drunken buffoons everywhere."

Alan laughed. "How old were you?"

"Ten, maybe eleven. We could barely see the statue. Spending a day with your mom, in the hot sun, surrounded by drunken idiots. It was a nightmare."

"Ha! Well, now you could probably buy the statue itself."

"I know. Do you have cell reception yet?"

"Yeah, just got it." He checked to see the number of unread emails. His smartphone was actively downloading them. The number surpassed five hundred and Alan placed the phone back in his pocket. "Ugh. I don't know if I want to go back. Or for that matter, if they will take me."

"Why would you?"

"I'm still ambitious. I still want to make a name for myself." Alan turned to see John grin and shake his head. "Go ahead, let me have it."

"Nah." He put his arm around his brother. "I get you now Alan. It only took thirty years."

They turned to look at the Manhattan skyline. A steady and warm breeze caressed the brothers as they enjoyed the view together.

Newark Bay, New Jersey

Doron parked the car, grabbed his hard case and followed the trail of people towards the dock. He swallowed when he saw the large crowd congregating in front of him. This will not be easy, he said to himself.

He turned to see a cohort of his whistle and wave for him to come over to his position. When Doron stood beside him, he said, "The crowd is much larger than we expected, are you okay with this?"

"I have no choice. I made a promise. Same as you."

"I know, let's get into position, the others are waiting for us." He motioned with his head. "By the rafters, over there."

"I see them."

"Let's go."

***

Charlotte paid the cab driver and left the vehicle. She stepped forward and surveyed the landscape.

She could not understand what she was looking at. A hundred yards away, and near the dock, she noticed a raised platform made from stacked crates and plywood. It seemed like a haphazard structure, made on a whim. It was parallel to the dock, and between her vantage point and the water were several hundred people. She turned to look at a dozen buses pull up behind her. They were school buses, which further confused her. After the doors opened, she saw dozens of Hasidic men step towards the dock. They wore black robes, beards and hats. Men poured out in unison before other women of Jewish descent, followed. She noticed what looked like a fabric screen stretched between rows of seats.

"What the hell is going on here?"

She turned to her left and saw a half dozen news vans. Their long antennas stretched towards the sky and camera crews sat on the rear and side bumpers. She was appalled to see a well-coiffed reporter getting her hair checked by an associate near the CNN van. She couldn't tell if the person was a reporter or a runway model.

She moved towards the crowd. Beside her was a tall man wearing glasses and a yarmulke. "Excuse me, why are all these people here?"

"Same as you, to see Schindler's gold." He furrowed his brow. "Didn't you read about it in the papers?"

"I saw the story online today. Why do they call it Schindler's Gold?"

"I don't know, but it's a big deal. Are you Jewish?"

"Me, no, I... ah... I know the guys on the boat."

"The Devengers? Everyone will know them pretty soon, did you see the news vans?"

"How did... who came up with... oh never mind."

She weaved herself through the crowd and found someone who looked to be in charge. He was holding a clipboard, chewed gum and barked out orders to the dock laborers.

"Sir, can you help me?"

"Not now lady, I'm busy."

"Are you in charge?"

"Hey! Get Johnny out here!"

"I'm Charlotte Devenger, I'm John and Alan's sister."

"Yeah. So?"

"Who are all these people?"

"Look, I told you lady, I'm busy, speak to that guy over there, he put this thing together." He pointed towards a man in a suit on the other side of the makeshift podium.

She froze when she recognized Larry Goldstein. He was chuckling and shaking hands with people who stepped forward to greet him.

She did not take her eyes off the man and approached him.

"Larry."

He turned and gave Charlotte a big smile. "Hello, Charlotte! I'm so glad you're here!"

"What the hell is this about?"

"Well, isn't it obvious?" He raised his hands and gestured to the crowd. "We're here to welcome home your brothers. And the gold of course, isn't this amazing?"

She felt like slapping him across the face. "You put this together?" Memories of the conversations she had with him came to the forefront of her mind. She had disclosed everything to him, from the size of the cache to the airport disaster to the confrontation at the dock in Bordeaux. "You son of a bitch. Who are these people?"

"Oh you'll find out soon enough, trust me."

She turned to see a ship called the *Dahlia* coming towards the dock.

***

Alan watched his brother put his cell phone in his pocket. He looked down and said, "Well, it looks like I'm out of a job."

"They fired you with an email?"

"Yup. They sent the notice to my Gmail address. It came from the head of human resources. It appears they cleaned out my desk last week. Plus, no severance."

"I'm sorry John. Did you really expect a severance?"

"Well I—" John looked up and stared straight forward. "What's that?"

Alan turned to look. He noticed a large congregation of people a few hundred yards away by the side of the dock. "What the…?"

They stepped forward to the tip of the bow. Two boats were docked a few hundred yards apart from one another. Between the two vessels, they saw the crowd.

They covered their eyes from the sun with their hands and gazed forward. "Who are those people? Why are they at the dock?"

"I have no idea. Did Charlotte tell people about this?" asked Alan.

"She wouldn't. No way."

The boat pulled closer and soon they were able to make out the faces of the people. "Can you recognize anyone?"

"No." John pointed to a crowd on the right side of the dock. "Why are those people waving Israeli flags?"

Alan leaned forward and noticed one flag in particular. He saw the Jewish star in the center of it. He turned and saw a small cargo vessel docked on the right side of the pier. It flew the same flag.

***

"Now is the time. Let's get ready."

Doron opened up his hard case and checked his instrument. He took a deep breath and exhaled. The crowd in the distance was larger than he expected. He didn't know if his nerves would subside long enough to complete the task at hand.

He reached down and retrieved the longest portion of the barrel. He removed the second portion, the end piece, and placed it at the bottom of it.

When it was pieced together, he held a clarinet, complete with a mouthpiece and numerous touch points. He checked to make sure it was assembled properly and then turned to look at the other musicians. There were fifteen in total and he stood in the second row of the rafters.

The leader of the band waved to catch the attention of his fellow musicians. "When I give the word, let's start with *Hail to the Chief*. Then we'll throw a little *Hava Nagila* their way. Sound good everyone?"

The group nodded and smiled as they started to tune their instruments.

314

"Oh my God. There must a thousand people over there."

"Is that a news van?"

"I have to see if Ziad can... can dock somewhere else."

John jogged down the length of the boat and saw Ziad in the pilothouse. He waved to him and caught his attention. He sat one deck higher from where John stood. He was talking to a deckhand and pointing to the crowd. "Hey!" yelled John. He jumped and waved to catch his attention. "Turn away! Now!" He gestured with both of his hands to turn to the port side and away from the dock.

Ziad looked down, smiled, and gave him the thumbs up sign.

"No! Not good!"

A second later the ship horn blew at an excessively loud and deep volume. He hit it multiple times and when he stopped, John heard the sound of yells, hollers and cheers coming from the dock. He ran back.

Alan smiled at what appeared to be an ecstatic and joyful crowd of people. "John, look!" He waved and the crowd grew louder. He pointed to several camera crews racing towards the front end of the dock.

"This is not good! Put your God damn hands down Alan." John stepped behind him and pulled his brother's arms down to his sides.

Alan turned to face him. "What's the problem? They are welcoming us home."

"Does any of this sense?" Alan did not answer. "Does it?"

"I don't know."

"Is it good the world knows about the gold?"

He froze as the boat drew closer to the dock. "No... no I guess it isn't. Do you think they know we have it with us?"

"Why the fuck else are they here?" yelled John.

John stepped back and rubbed his head. He turned when he heard the sound of *Hail to the Chief* being played somewhere out in the crowd. "You've got to be fucking kidding me." He turned, stepped forward and saw a small band standing atop several rooftops. His arms and head collapsed on the deck rail.

They looked down and saw a raised platform. To the side they saw several amplifiers and a man he could not identify holding a microphone.

"Look!" Alan pointed to the side of the platform. "There's Charlotte!" He waved to her. The crowd must have seen him wave as the volume of their hollers and cheers grew louder.

"I'm going to kill her if she arranged this."

"I'm so glad to see her. She... wait, she doesn't look happy."

"I wonder fucking why!"

***

Larry Goldstein looked up and saw the Devengers. He motioned with his hands for the music to stop.

He tapped the microphone and the speakers emitted a loud screech of feedback. "Hello... hello?" He heard his voice amplified. "Ladies and gentlemen, friends and family, please give a warm welcome to the liberators of Schindler's gold," He directed their attention to the two men standing on the bow of the boat. "John and Alan Devenger!"

The crowd erupted in enthusiastic cheers. Larry smiled when he saw several young men jump up and down at the back of the crowd. He started to speak before the band started to play *Hava Nagila*. The crowd clapped in rhythm to the music and several people began singing along.

The boat came to a rest alongside the dock and a diagonal ladder was placed before the boat's doorway. Deckhands ushered John and Alan away from the bow. Dock workers coordinated their movements and secured ropes in order to fasten the ship to the dock.

Larry turned and pointed when he saw the cameras train their lenses on the doorframe that lead to the staircase. Larry caught Charlotte's stare and watched her shake her head. He raised his microphone.

"I am Larry Goldstein, John and Alan Devenger's attorney, and when you hear their story, I think you'll realize the sacrifices they made for this moment warrants our respect and appreciation. And now they are home, safe and sound." The band played *Hava Nagila* again as everyone waited to see the Devengers exit the boat.

The first person to appear in the doorframe was Captain Ziad. When he stepped onto the stairs, he turned, removed his captain's hat, and gave the crowd a bright smile and a big wave. The crowd cheered and he stepped aside.

Larry said into the microphone, "I guess that's the Captain there. Ah, yeah, a big welcome then." When he cleared his throat the microphone picked up the sound. "Bring out our heroes, the Devengers!"

Ziad continued to wave. One of the deckhands stuck his head out and smiled. The Captain barked at him and shoved him back inside the boat. Alan peered out a moment later.

He hesitated as the crowd began to clap. Ziad stepped behind him and nudged him in the ass. When he was standing on the staircase the crowd exploded with applause.

"There's Alan Devenger everybody!"

It didn't take long for Alan to enjoy the attention given to him. He waved to everyone and walked down the staircase and smiled.

Larry Goldstein looked up and saw John Devenger. He was standing with his hands on his hips with a look of disgust on his face. "And there's his brother, our other hero, John Devenger!"

A moment later the brothers were standing on the raised platform with Larry, several Rabbis and a very tall and stern looking man wearing a suit.

John grabbed Larry, bear-hugged and squeezed him with as much force as he could administer. "You did this, didn't you?"

"I did."

"You won't get one single gold bar."

"Do you really want to be known as a grave robber?"

John released him and Larry saw a look of shock on his face. The lawyer patted him on the shoulder and grinned for the cameras.

Larry stepped away and returned the microphone to his mouth. "And now a word from Rabbi Solomon, one of the organizers here today. Many of you know him."

The rabbi took the microphone from Larry. "Ladies and gentlemen, member of the press, and those of the Jewish faith. I want you to always remember their names, John and Alan Devenger. These two men have done a great service to our people, to the entire worldwide Jewish community. Words alone cannot thank them for returning the single largest cache of gold that was stolen and taken from our ancestors during the Holocaust."

He turned and gestured to the Devengers. "Your actions, the risks you took, the dangers you encountered. I have heard what you've been through. When the world hears more about your experience, they will understand the significance of this moment." The crowd shared their appreciation with a long and steady applause. "We know where the gold came from. Your grandfather, Everett Devenger, a World War Two hero, liberated it from Nazis. But beforehand, everyone knows where Schindler's gold came from. It came from places like Auschwitz," The Rabbi paused to let the crowd feel the weight of the word itself. "The gold came from death camps like Treblinka. It came from Dachau, it came from Chelmo," the rabbi turned to face the Devengers, "Majdanek, Mathausen, Sobibor. Dozens upon dozens of places that represent the final resting place for millions of our people. We will never forget what happened."

John dropped his chin the moment the Rabbi said the word Treblinka. It was the death camp cited in the German documents he reviewed back in the hotel room before Alan's chase. What perplexed him more than the crowd, the speech or the circumstances, was the emotion he felt. On some level, he felt relieved: He didn't have to hide from the truth.

Rabbi Solomon stopped speaking and turned to face the now-silent crowd. "This gold, as you saw in the papers, it was named after another great man, Oskar Schindler. He was a man who saved thousands of lives. This is not his gold, and we know for certain he was not involved in this massive Nazi heist of wealth. The two men here before you today, John and Alan Devenger, these two men have closed one small wound from that horrible time in our history. These two men, perhaps they have brought all of us a bit closer, perhaps their decisions have reminded us of where we came from. But most of all, they have connected the generation here today to the ancestors whom we lost years ago. And for that, the Devenger name is one the next generation should pass along to the next."

The crowd started to applaud. "Remember what our people went through, but also where we are today." The applause grew louder. "Remember the sacrifices our forefathers made, but also their children's success." People started to cheer. "And never forget how we, as a people, will always move forward together. We will honor our loved ones, and always respect men like John and Alan Devenger who honor our people's history." The crowd let forward a thunderous volley of applause and cheers.

John and Alan shared a look that lingered for a long time.

"And now, please welcome the Senior Director of the Jerusalem Simon Holocaust Center, Efraim Zukoff, who will speak to the future of Schindler's gold."

The tall dark man walked past John and Alan. He turned to look at them but he did not smile. He took the microphone from the Rabbi and stepped forward. "Shalom." Many in the audience replied with the same word. "On behalf of the entire Simon Holocaust organization, a group that is dedicated to hunting down Nazi war criminals, stolen wealth and artifacts, we wholeheartedly thank John and Alan Devenger for choosing to return this gold to our people. Their story, and their names will be enshrined forever so that we never forget those who lost their lives to the most evil entity that ever walked the earth, the Nazis."

He turned to look at the Devengers. "The gold will be transferred to the boat, the *Tzedek*. It is docked here and it will transport the contents back to Israel. The Yad Vashem Holocaust Museum will take possession of it and provide the opportunity for the public to see it for themselves." He turned back to the crowd. "Would all of you like to see it? To see the gold we speak of?"

Chants of 'yes,' 'now,' and 'show us!' were hollered across the crowd. Efraim turned again to look at the Devengers. "Would one of you like to say something before we see a sample of this gold?"

Alan and John declined to speak.

"Very well, let's see for ourselves what you have accomplished." The microphone whistled when he handed it back to the Rabbi. Efraim directed the Devengers to walk up the staircase and reenter the boat. Ziad joined them.

Several minutes later Efraim exited the boat. John and Alan were not with him when he returned to the stage. He used both hands to hold the gold bar and lifted it for everyone to see. The camera lenses zoomed in to get a closer look.

The rabbi pointed to the gold brick. "For those who cannot see, the inscription features an eagle crest and swastika. Three numbers, nine nine nine appear below the Nazi logo. And two initials, SS, are in the bottom left corner."

He paused and turned back to the crowd. "Please, let us join together in prayer, and once again thank the Devengers."

***

Alan stood on the top deck of the *Dahlia* and watched the crane lift their cargo container slowly from the depths of the ship. It felt like the perfect analogy. As the crane removed his grandfather's treasure, it felt like his heart was being ripped out of his chest as well.

Sixty something million dollars. Sixty... fucking... million dollars.

It dangled in the air for a moment before cables moved the cache down onto the bed of a truck. It landed with a thud, and when it did, Alan had to turn away.

He was ruined. One of the top publisher posts in the publishing world: gone. Everything his grandfather left them: gone. The money he spent on all the contingency plans: gone. The beatings he endured, the kidnapping attempt, Tomas's murder, the near-death experience at the airport: witnessing the handover of the gold into rightful hands seemed like a fitting end.

He slowly turned to look at John. "I have no idea what to say."

"Maybe it's better we don't say anything."

They watched from above as the truck drove down the dock. It parked next to another crane and the ship named the Tzedek. Cables lifted the container and placed it on the deck of the Israeli ship. He noticed several men appear on the top deck of the freighter brandishing Uzis shortly after the gold was stowed within the belly of the boat.

"It's over. After I sue him for every penny he owns, I'm going to beat the living shit out of that conniving fucker Goldstein."

John nodded. "I can't wait to introduce him to my Glock nine millimeter." Alan nodded and tilted his head, seeming to seriously consider the use of a handgun. John nudged him in the shoulder. "Snap out of it, I'm only kidding. Besides, it could be worse."

"How could this possibly get any worse?"

"Well, we've got one crate remaining back in the vault. Remember?" Alan rubbed his temples. "That's, what, a little over one point five million?" John nodded. "Whatever. A pittance compared—"

They heard their names being called from across the boat. They turned to see Ziad directing Charlotte to their location on the boat. She walked forward and extended her arms. "Thank God." The three of them embraced in a hug that seemed to have no end. "You're finally home."

"We missed you."

"You're the best, Charlotte."

"I love you guys."

When they let go she was crying. "You made it, both of you, together."

They spent several minutes speaking to her before Alan asked to have a moment with John. Charlotte walked down the length of the boat.

"What's next for you, Alan?"

"I think it's a good time to take a break. I have a favorite little town in Italy, called La Villa Strangiato."

"Sounds nice."

Alan put his arm on his brother's shoulder. "Want to come?" He smiled. "God knows, we'll have plenty of time on our hands."

John silently nodded and thought about Everett, and what he told him in the video recording. He remembered the advice he gave about being cautious, but more importantly, he remembered his last dying wish.

He thought about his half-brother and the emotion Everett expressed when he spoke about the two of them. He looked at Alan and knew in his heart there was no 'half' between them anymore. The emotion he felt rose within him and his eyes creased to a close when he turned to embrace his brother.

"I love you, buddy."

Alan paused before he returned the hug. "Same here, John. Same here."

When John let go he wasn't looking at a distant relative or someone that was just a friend. He was looking at the full-fledged brother he loved.

Epilogue

September 12ᵗʰ, 1945

Left the docks of Tilbury six hours ago. Now I'm sitting on the deck with two thousand other guys enjoying a cool ocean breeze. No one's talking. No one, but its kind of nice.

I'm finally leaving Europe, but I'm leaving behind a dozen friends who didn't make it. I write this with a heavy heart. Every time I feel lucky about going home, I think about the guys that never will. But there's nothing I can do about it…. Nothing. If someone calls me a hero when I get stateside, I'm just going to ignore them. They don't have a clue, not a Goddamn clue.

The sun is going down now, about half an hour before sunset. They say the boat will take eleven days to make the journey. Eleven sunsets to go before we pull into New York, then I'm home. Maybe we'll be lucky with the weather and I'll get eleven straight sunsets before we hit the docks. That would be the cat's pajamas.

This is my last entry in this particular journal, because there's no reason to go on. I have written three, shipped one home and have the other two with me. Who knows, maybe I'll write a book one day. Maybe I'll never open the pages again and pass them down to my kids.

And I also have to account for what's back in Europe, in writing, just in case I pass away between now and when I get home. Someone will get this journal, probably my Mom. If so, I love you Mom, but I'm not going to get all sappy when I'm this close to seeing you. Besides, I'm not seeing any icebergs, so I think we'll be okay.

Whoever reads this, If I die, I've left something behind in a Swiss bank. This last page is to note what you'll need to access the vault. It's in my name, however maybe there's someway to use the account number and passcode to access the vault itself. I'm not going to write what's in it. Let's just say… go to Switzerland! The details…

The Scheibzerische Bank
Bern, Switzerland
Account Number: 5501 445549 1002 062112
Passcode: Rosebud

Like that passcode? Thought it was clever.

I'll tell you how I got it and what's inside when I get home. Seven men died, it's a long story. I lost three close friends.

After what I went through, and found, I did some digging around. I have something else to share in case I die. Let's just say, I took an active interest in hunting down Nazis after the war, which included a few AWOL incidents, which probably cost me a promotion and a week's worth of KP duty in the mess hall. But the risk was worth it.

While the army was going ape shit to find the Nazi, Ernst Kaltenbrunner, at the end of the war, everyone converged on Lake Toplitz. The idiots never thought to stop transportation routes leading towards the lake, given all the hubbub. So, a buddy and I high-tailed it to Wienern and caught a convoy heading straight to the lake. But this time, we cut a deal. Tommy got a 1/3rd, so did I, and we left the rest to five German Wehrmacht guys. Not a single shot, thank God, I wished my other run-in had gone that way. The war was over, no one wanted to die and we all got what we wanted.

So the stash is in Wienern. I don't know if you'll ever find it, but we took our time hiding it… Two days of effort, the fucking water was FREEZING! From the center of town, head west on Lake Gundlsee's southern shore. When you pass the town, find the first stream that runs into the lake, and then follow it a mile inland. We made two crucifixes on both sides of the stream, about forty feet from the water's edge. They are both the size of a breadbox, dark stones. Trace it back to the stream, head up fifty yards and you'll find a side of the stream that opens a bit on the right. A huge evergreen is just beyond it. Right in the center of the stream, dig… three feet down. We covered it with a shitload of rocks, heavier ones on top. The stash should hold up to the elements – what we hid, it's definitely waterproof.

The army never got wind of this.

And it's worth the trip. It's God's country up in the Austrian mountains. I'll go back a few years from now. Maybe sooner, but first I'll go to the vault.

When I do, I'm set for life. I have to keep telling myself that, no matter what, the road ahead has taken a very interesting turn. Where it will lead, I don't know, but I'll never be hurtin' for money. Ever.

They just rang the chow bell, we eat at different times. Shit on a shingle, round two, coming up – God, get me the fuck out of the army. I'd kill for a sirloin steak, a six pack and a soft bed right now. But then again, why am I bitching and moaning.

I lived.

- Everett Devenger

PERCUSSION PUBLISHING

Percussion Publishing Is proud to present the next great Armageddon Thriller:

The Second Coming
by Presley Acuna

<u>Available now on Amazon and Kindle.</u>

Synopsis: The Second Coming

The year 2020 is a year of crisis. In the midst of the Times Square New Year's celebrations, an act of domestic terrorism suddenly kills hundreds. A political leader is assassinated soon thereafter. Tel Aviv is destroyed by an Islamic radical group.

The world stands poised for nuclear Armageddon.

YORDON ANTROPOS, a monk of the Mount Athos monasteries, appears on the scene and begins to manifesting Godly powers, performing miracles and inspiring a unification movement across all of Islam, which that quickly grows to the point of threatening control of Middle Eastern oil and creates a shift in the global balance of power.

A revisionist priest of the Chicago Archdiocese, THOMAS PRISCIOTTI, is recruited by the Vatican to join a task force of military, political and religious leaders with the mission of thwarting Yordon's plans. As the Christ-like madman grows in power and influence, Thomas' faith and fealty are increasingly challenged. Only by reconciling his doubts and convictions, will he be able to use a weapon, long kept secret by the Vatican – a weapon that could save the world from this the all-powerful, self-professed Messiah.

Review a sample of Percussion Publishing's forthcoming novel on the following pages.

The Second Coming
By Presley Acuna

Preview

The congregation extended out in all directions; each face basked in a wash of neon, every breath a vapor in the cold, December night.

It was noisy. A dissonance of automobiles, sirens, helicopters, music, corks, fireworks and breaking glass wove through the jangle of the crowd.

It was New Year's Eve 2019, Times Square, New York City, and the Babel metropolis of brick, concrete, metal, glass, neon and soot, and the swell of humanity. Thanks to satellite technology, a worldwide audience estimated at over one billion people was also tuned in, watching the ceremony from afar.

Times Square was a riot on happy gas. Policemen astride horses and wearing crowd control gear moved in formation -- multicolored lights reflecting off their helmets and shields, like technological Roman centurions. They sifted through the crowd, breaking up fights, urging people to keep moving. They were expectant, as if intuiting something bad was going to happen, and the crowd was volatile, as was the world.

The planet was a dynamite stick primed by the tumultuous events of 2019. The Middle East was in meltdown, poised for Armageddon. Terrorism was on the rise domestically, fueled by events abroad. Survival gear and weapons sales were at record highs.

The thickening crowd was making it harder to move. Spotlights blazed white at the foot of the One Times Square, from the roof of which the New Year's Eve Ball was traditionally dropped. The huge TV screen bolted onto the side of the building depicted fifteen-foot high images of the evening's hosts, with the very same Times Square scene behind them, ad infinitum. On the stage, a band stormed through its rhythms and beats as a hip-hop duo took turns shouting out to the crowd, while a gaggle of celebrities, media notables and local leaders stood waiting for their cues from the wings.

Just then, an Elvis like figure, clad in a white leather suit, stepped forth and swayed his arms above his head in time to the orchestral fanfare.

The digital display read, "11:45."

Elvis in White Leather was about to speak into the microphone. The band quieted.

"Thank you, thank you, ladies and gentlemen! It's grand to see you all out here in this downright righteous cold weather!"

Laughter and catcalls from the crowd. He knew how to tap the mood.

All of a sudden, there was a commotion in the midst of the audience standing before the stage. Flashes of fists and angry faces. Shoving and shouting. Immediately, policemen began to cut their way to the source of the conflict, tasers and riot gear held high above the crowd as they converged from all corners. Then, from the epicenter itself, a flame erupted from a gnarled wooden club held high by an unshaven, desperate looking figure. His head pivoted left and right frantically. His jaw clenched nervously, flickering lights reflecting off his widened eyeballs. He waved the club, the flame roaring and growling as it was whipped by the winter wind, creating the space around him. On his lapel could be discerned a yellow cross.

The flame was formidable -- far larger than the club warranted. The ring of policemen closed in on the demonstrator. Someone yelled for help. Sirens could be heard in the distance.

The lunatic figure pointed the burning club at the stage and yelled, "Blaspheming bastards! Charlatans! You will all burn in hell!"

With that, the madman conjured a 3D printed firearm and began firing at the stage. Instantly, the crowd panicked. Elvis in White Leather, until then, frozen in shock, disappeared -- ushered away by a phalanx of serious, corpulent men in suits. The camera shook and lost its balance up on the giant screen.

The Tower clock read, "11:52."

A helicopter abruptly appeared above the heads of the crowd, startling everyone and whipping wind at people's faces and clothing. Hot lights shown down from above.

"You'll never get me! I'm already gone, you pigs, and tonight you'll die too!" bellowed the torch bearer. He touched himself with the burning club and set himself ablaze. His clothing ignited at once.

At the same time, other burning torches appeared throughout the throng. The torch-bearers proceeded to touch those around them with the burning pyres, before setting themselves on fire. The reaction was instant and violent. Those who found themselves in the uncomfortable vicinity of the firebrands tried to climb over each other, screaming, in an effort to get away. The first burning demonstrator lurched heavily to and fro, unabated in his hurling of slurs and diatribes of doom. He swung his torch again infecting more people with the flames. In moments dozens of people were shouting for help as the flames enveloped them. The police closed in.

A megaphone barked, "Stay where you are. Help is on the way. Throw yourselves on the ground and roll! For God's sake he's setting them all on fire..."

The megaphone was snatched away.

The lunatic, crumpling under the demands of his burning body, spat out his final words. "Repent or you will burn in hell!" With that, he let out a blood curdling scream and hurled the club into the crowd before collapsing to the ground.

The Tower clock patiently changed its display to: "11:56."

The club arced through the air, creating another epicenter of fire as it landed on an unsuspecting fur-clad woman, immolating her and those around her as she spun and grabbed anyone within reach in a blind clutch for help. The chorus of screams grew louder. People tried to run but found themselves crashing into each other. The crowd was simply too thick, the flames too hot. Anything the fires touched immediately caught fire.

The clock read "11:58."

The ball began its inexorable descent.

The police waded through the chaos of burning victims, but there was nothing they could do. The heat of the flames and the pure panic of the people around them deterred their progress. The stink of seared flesh, singed hair, scorched fur, and melted synthetic fibers clotted the cold air.

The clock, indifferent to the danger, changed its display to "11:59." The ball was halfway down its predetermined path.

Times Square was now a chaos of flames, sirens, spotlights, policemen, ambulances, set against the incongruous laughter, noise makers, fireworks and strains of "Auld Lang Sine", emanating from the First Night tents, where the revellers were as yet unsuspecting. Despite the magnitude of the disaster, the crowd was so big in New York City, that for many, the calamity went unnoticed.

And above it all, the clock read, "12:00."

The New Year had begun.

The Second Coming
By Presley Acuna

Available now on Amazon, Kindle and other online book retailers.

Pick up a copy today!

And to find other fantastic novels across genres, come visit us at:

www.PercussionPublishing.Com

**PERCUSSION
PUBLISHING**

Kendall Smith lives in Ridgewood, New Jersey with his wife
Allison and giant baby boy, Connor. He is employed in the ad
tech business in New York City and makes time to write before
going to work and during the commute itself.

Author Contact Information

First and foremost, thank you for buying Vault 21-12. An author's appreciation for their readers and fans is rarely noted in the written form – I thought it wise to do so.

Given the age we live in, a writer and his audience should have the opportunity to connect. So, don't be a stranger. Feel free to reach out to me on Facebook, Twitter or email:

Email: AuthorKendall@gmail.com

Twitter: @AuthorKendall

Facebook: Facebook.com/percussionpublishing

Keep in mind, I have a day job, so if I don't respond right away give me some time to get back to you. Thanks again and stay touch. I promise to cook up something to publish in 2016. And... depending on how this novel sells, perhaps John and Alan will find their way to that other stash Everett hid deep in the forests of Austria.